Praise for Betsy Dornbusch and *Exile*

Betsy Dornbusch's *Exile* launches an epic fantasy series that promises a rich, brooding atmosphere.

—*Library Journal*

Necromantic magic, deadly political intrigue, and a reluctant hero torn between his duty to a foreign queen and his desire for revenge... Betsy Dornbusch's *Exile* kept me reading into the wee hours of the night, breathless to find out how Draken's story would end.

—Courtney Schafer, author of the Shattered Sigil series

Betsy Dornbusch's *Exile* is a non-stop adventure with a fascinating world and some terrific magic.

—Carol Berg, author of Novels of the Collegia Magica

...it's a good, exciting and entertaining fantasy novel for adults, because it's something a bit different. I think that readers who get caught up in this novel's world will be thrilled to read what happens to Draken, because the story is a nice combination of familiar elements and a touch of originality and freshness. It's an excellent summer read.

—*Rising Shadow*

From the first line ("Cut her throat. His own wife."), readers of Betsy Dornbusch's *Exile* know they are in for a dramatic and exciting tale. ... Any reader who joins her for the ride will be glad they did.

—Lesley Smith, author of *The Changing of the Sun*

EMISSARY

EMISSARY

THE SECOND BOOK OF THE SEVEN EYES

BETSY DORNBUSCH

NIGHT SHADE BOOKS
NEW YORK

Night Shade books may be purchased in bulk at special discounts for sales
promotion, corporate gifts, fund-raising, or educational purposes. Special edi-
tions can also be created to specifications. For details, contact the Special Sales
Department, Night Shade Books, 307 West 36th Street, 11th Floor, New York,
NY 10018 or info@skyhorsepublishing.com.

Night Shade Books™ is a trademark of Skyhorse Publishing, Inc. ®, a Delaware
corporation.

Visit our website at www.nightshadebooks.com.

10 9 8 7 6 5 4 3 2 1

Library of Congress Cataloging-in-Publication Data is available on file.

Cover art by John Stanko
Cover design by Claudia Noble
Interior layout and design by Amy Popovich

Paperback ISBN: 978-1-59780-832-3

Printed in the United States of America

For Grace

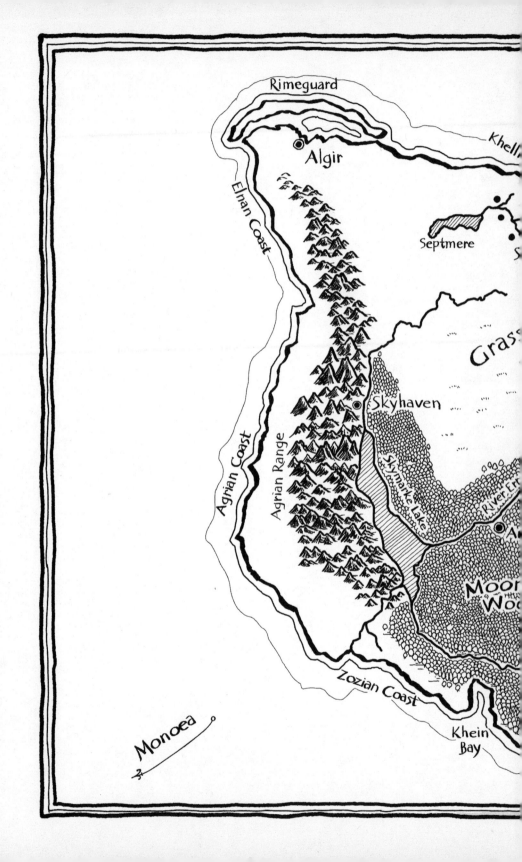

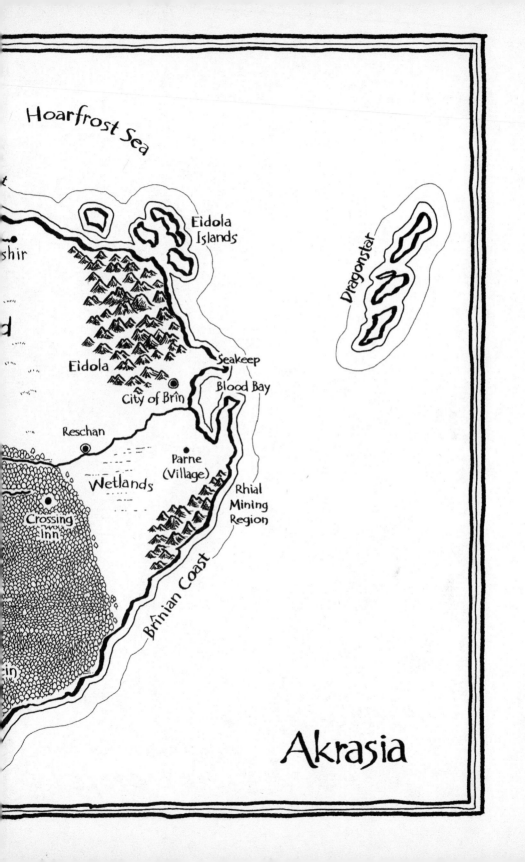

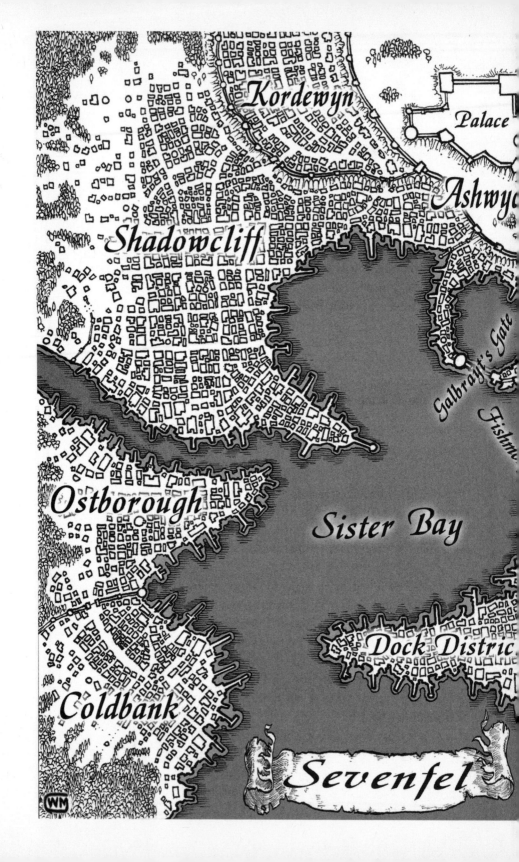

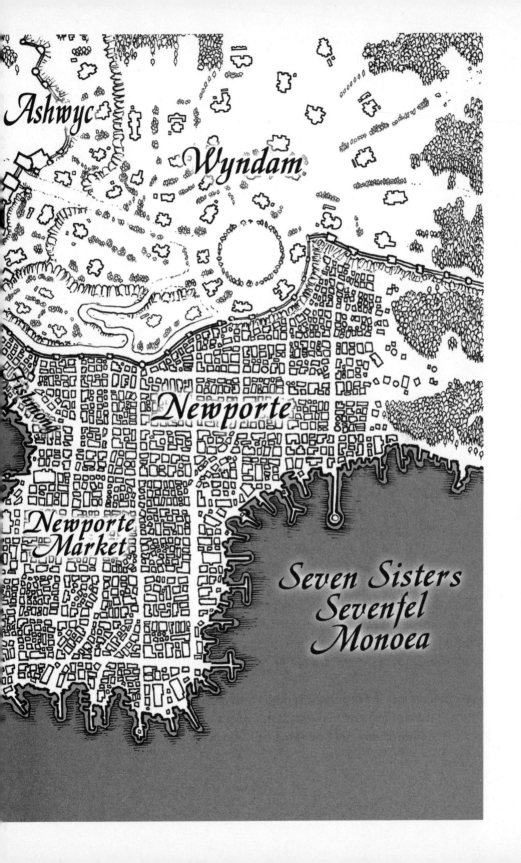

It is honorable to kill in the light, not from the shadows.

—Akrasian Proverb

CHAPTER ONE

Morning dawned early and violently in the Brînian Citadel. No one, slave nor noble, could sleep through the clatter of swords, much less the shouts ringing through the torchlight. The Khel Szi himself had sword in hand. A foreign soldier had called Prince Draken's card in the brutal dance of death in the courtyard of his own palace.

Muscles screaming to yield, Draken lifted his sword and met the oncoming high-line strike, allowing it to clang against his hilt. He grimaced at his shoddy defense. His opponent's blade skittered off his sword and across the bracer and upper arm protection of his armor harness. He was glad he'd taken a moment in the chilly pre-dawn darkness to strap them on. Still, the shock of it drove him a step back. He cursed. When that blade struck his bare chest, it *would* draw blood.

"No, Drae, protect your high line. Again!" Captain Tyrolean attacked as before, same form, same balance, same strike.

There was no honorific in the practice lists, no "Night Lord" or "Khel Szi" or "Your Highness." Here, Draken and Tyrolean were not Prince and honor-liege but student and teacher.

Draken gritted his teeth against his sore muscles and lifted his sword again. Every day they rose well before the last of the Seven Eyes had slipped beyond the horizon and each of those days, Tyrolean never allowed Draken to stop a moment before full daylight crested the dome of Brîn's Citadel.

As Tyrolean's sword went up, it caught the glare of sun against its dulled blade. It flashed against his brawny shoulders, turning him into a hard, pale godling of war. Only neat lines of scarred hashmarks marred the perfection of his muscled chest. Faint steam rose from the crown of his dark head.

Tyrolean's narrowed eyes were his only tell, but Draken didn't recognize it quickly enough. Tyrolean's blade flashed, slipped across Draken's chest. Blood stung him as it welled from the cut.

Tyrolean shook his head. "Don't ever let your guard down."

"That was cheating. You turned to stone, Ty."

Tyrolean finally lowered his blade, his black-lined eyes crinkling in a rare smile. "Cradle tales again, Your Highness?"

"Aye, I've got to learn them, haven't I? Children like stories." Draken wiped the sweat from his eyes. He was hot despite the cool ocean winds slipping through the gates of the protected palace courtyard.

"Your royal get is still in the Queen's belly and for many moon-turns after it's born all it'll want is a dry nappie," Tyrolean said.

"Aye, and you're the expert, are you? Having no children of your own." He backed off toward the table. The cut already had that tightening tingle that told him it was closing. Damn, damn.

"That I know of."

A rare joke, so Draken forced a chuckle. He kept his back to Ty and stripped off his bracers, made a show of pressing a cloth to the wound. "A shirt," he told Kai, his body slave. The lad scooted off to find him one.

"Not too bad, I hope. Does it need sewing?"

"No. It's just a scratch." Kai returned. Draken pulled on the shirt and turned to Tyrolean. "It's already stopped bleeding." And stung like nettles as it closed. He tensed as a slight tremor tickled his bare feet. He looked down. Odd, that.

Tyrolean didn't seem to notice as he walked to a nearby table tended by a slave and took the two goblets she offered with a polite thanks. He sipped from both, even though they'd been poured from the same jug. Poison could coat the inside of one or the other goblets. Draken had given up trying to talk Tyrolean and his szi nêre out of tasting for him. The sweet morning wine was cold and good.

"Rumors claim Lord Ilumat sent Queen Elena gifts of late," Tyrolean said.

The Queen had many suitors before Draken had arrived at the Akrasian court. Though they doubtless had infinitely more husband potential, Draken tried not to worry. After all, she was spending her pregnancy in Brîn in order to stay close to him.

He rubbed the back of his sweaty neck. He needed a good scrubbing if he were to meet the Akrasian lords today. "Rumors you've confirmed, I assume."

"Via your Ghost," Tyrolean said.

Draken's brows climbed and he glanced around before he answered. His sister Aarinnaie, Szirin of Brîn, wasn't someone they discussed in public. "You spoke with her?"

Tyrolean shook his head. "A message only, script in chalk on the floor of the temple by my kneeling mat."

Sounded like her. "It'd be convenient if she would appear in public sometimes. Even if he hasn't said as much to me, Rodkhim Vannis wants to ask me for her hand." He cocked his head at Tyrolean's expression. "What? He's not a bad man, Rodkhim."

"Rodkhim can't manage her."

"It's not as if she listens to me either." It was a fair match. Rodkhim's father was City Comhanar of Brîn, an old, respected family—as close to nobility as Brînians got. "Perhaps marriage would suit her better than playing the vigilante." As well as his secret royal assassin.

"Scouring Brîn of your father's corruption is a noble endeavor."

Draken grunted. "A dangerous one, you mean."

Tyrolean's lips tightened. Draken had noticed a distinct tension around the subject of Aarinnaie recently. It vaguely worried him that Tyrolean, who had ever been a close confidante of the Queen, knew something he didn't. But Tyrolean changed the subject before he could question him.

"You still treat your sword as something you're holding rather than part of you."

Draken lifted the practice sword with its blunt edges in acknowledgment and handed it off to one of the armory slaves. Muscle memory developed from training on the bow left him feeling he was carrying the wrong weapon. "I didn't learn much from Bruche."

"He wasn't there to teach you. He was there to protect you."

Draken's spirit sword-hand was in his well-deserved rest, no matter how Draken missed his council. For now, Draken was just glad he'd been able to conceal how quickly his cuts healed.

"I think you should spar with Seaborn," Tyrolean added. "It'll come quicker that way. She's the blade you fight with."

Draken opened his mouth to argue he wasn't about to bring the greatest treasure of the Brînian Principality into the practice lists, but the city gate bells pealed through the early morning quiet. Both men fell still and listened. Four palace szi nêre stationed at the Citadel gates drew their swords and archers on the wall nocked arrows, though Draken had no real worry the bells meant something needing his attention. With the days of Newseason lengthening into Tradeseason and the moonroutes at their most expansive, it might be confusion over shift changes.

The echoes of the bells against the crowded buildings and the faint reverberation off the Eidola Mountains towering over the city of Brîn kept Draken from making a proper count of rings. He frowned at Tyrolean, unable to determine if it was a warning of attack or some other announcement.

Tyrolean's eyes narrowed. "I hope it's not another scuffle between the servii and the gate guards."

It was a point. The Akrasian servii stationed at nearby Seakeep liked to drink, fight, and whore in Brîn, which had myriad opportunity for all three. But the servii weren't so happy when tossed out of the city at daybreak, and Brînian soldiers tolerated their presence grudgingly at best.

The immense carved doors to the Great Hall opened to frame Draken's chamberlain Thom. An impassive moonwrought mask concealed half his face from cheekbone to hairline, and the hazel eye painted on it was a neat match for the other, real one. The flesh of his face was strained and reddened against the silvery moonwrought, probably because the Head Seneschal followed Thom closely, scrolls clutched in his hands. Gods, it was an administrative day. Of course, when wasn't it, for a Prince?

"Why the bells, Khel Szi? Too early for guard change, isn't it?" Thom asked in broken Brînish. He shoved his many thin braids back from his face and his real eye locked on Draken's.

"We were just wondering the same thing."

The Seneschal, Hina Shaim, surnamed for the patron god of peace and truth, cleared his throat. "Khel Szi, several matters require your attention. The Lords' Council convenes at Seakeep this morning. Lord Va Khlar would speak with you prior. As well, the city mason's guild representatives have been asking for an audience for two sevennight now. I've put them off, but they're most insistent and—"

Draken shot him a glare for interrupting his conversation with Thom, but a clatter of hooves on the cobbles at the palace gate cut off his reprimand. They all turned. The szi nêre swung the gates back as a royal messenger in Akrasian Greens galloped straight for them, slowing his horse only when he saw Draken. He brought with him the acrid scents of blood, fear, and the sea. The horse snorted, its belly heaving as it panted.

Halmar, Comhanar of the szi nêre, pushed past Hina Shaim and Thom to stand at Draken's side. Muscles strapped his broad frame and he was newly inked with even more sigils of war and honor. Jewelry glowed against his dark skin: earrings, rings, and armbands.

The rider threw himself to the ground barely a stride from Draken's feet and fell to his knees. "Your Highness, Seakeep is under attack!"

Elena. She'd ridden for Seakeep the night before to prepare for the High House Council. Besides the Queen, four of the highest nobles in the land were there. The keep, a a battered stone fort with a high tower, rested on the point of high land where the River Eros met the sea, across from the Brîn city gates over a flat, windswept field. A fair errand's ride by horse; a good hike on foot.

Draken swallowed hard to clear his voice. It still came out guttural and rough. *"Who?"*

"Monoeans, Your Highness. Three ships bearing their banners."

Cold seized Draken, despite the warming sun. His old countrymen had come to call. If Monoea was here with any show of force, she would destroy Seakeep in a day and turn her attention to the City of Brîn. Seven damn them all, what was this about?

"Are they anchored yet?" he asked.

"No. Sailing back out of Blood Bay. Came in by skiff overnight, we think. There's a sizeable force surrounding Seakeep."

"Or another ship. One that grounded troops downcoast," Tyrolean said. "There's a small port at Rhial, abandoned from the mining trade."

"Damn, damn, damn, there could be other Monoeans attacking elsewhere, then." If Draken knew Monoean tactics, some of which he had helped devise during his officership in the Monoean Black Guard, there were most certainly more. "Sound the alarm again, raise the duty troops, and those at rest. Any who are able must come. We must stop them at Seakeep."

He ordered horses and strode inside to pull on the rest of his armor and fetch the sword Seaborn. The lad Kai helped him silently, though his hands shook and he dropped a few pieces of armor. Mail, his leather breast and back plates, hinged arm bracers, greaves, thigh protection in the way of a metal-strapped loose kilt, and extra knives soon weighed Draken down. He remained silent as Kai armed him, suffering the free reign of his curiosity. Had his cousin-King learned he was Khel Szi? Would the Brinians learn of his sundry heritage from his former countrymen? Exiled from Monoea after false accusal of murdering his wife, pulled unwitting into a war with the gods, and risen to a Prince's throne he didn't want, he'd been left with little of himself but bloodstained hands.

The only good, uncalculating thing that had come from his exile to Akrasia was Elena. He had already endured the loss of his wife, a wound so deep no amount of happiness could more than scar over. He'd be damned if he'd let Monoeans, the gods, or anyone else take Elena from him.

Kai dropped his hands when he finished, his braided head bowed. Draken laid a hand on the boy's shoulder before striding down the hall. As he walked, he drew Seaborn from its scuffed scabbard, but the gods had left no message for him in the white depths this day.

The city bells rang again in a quicker, unceasing cadence. By the time he snatched up his bow from a waiting armorer and entered the courtyard, Tyrolean was mounted, ashes from the Citadel temple smeared on his forehead. A groom held Draken's saddled horse and his shield, fielded in black and painted with the same crimson snake Draken had tattooed around his bicep. His helm hung off the saddle. He went around the horse to strap his bow to the other side, using a pull-knot he'd learned aboard ship as a Monoean bowman.

The Citadel priest limped closer, clutching a bowl of blood, his greyed head bowed. Draken started to wave him off, but under Tyrolean's stern gaze, he submitted to letting the priest bless and anoint his brow with Khellian's horns. The priest's fingertips were smooth as the flat of a honed blade as they caressed his forehead. A tingle, like glamour magicks, coursed through him.

He stared hard at the priest, who bowed his head and murmured prayers for Khellian's aid. *No. Must be my imagination.*

Had the old priest ever done service to Khellian on a battlefield altar? Likely not. Draken couldn't imagine his dead father dragging along a priest and wasting time on prayers before killing someone. *In that we might be alike, Father and I.* His stomach didn't sit well with the thought, nor with the delay. He pulled from the priest before the words were done and nodded to his szi nêre. They led him through the city at a quick pace, clearing the way through curious passersby headed for market and business. Despite the ringing bells and the appearance of their Khel Szi on the streets the Brînians maintained their tenacious hold on their business at hand.

The city gates were barred. He had to wait for another scouting report anyway. He circled his horse, which skittered at the squeal of the gates rolling open. He was young and had yet to be blooded in battle, though he was purportedly the best-trained horse in Brîn. "Be easy, Tempest."

Though every instinct urged Draken to race across the dirt road spanning the several-thousand-stride run to Seakeep, he dismounted, tossed his reins to a waiting stablegirl, and climbed the steps against the wall.

Slowly the rigid formations of the grey-armored Monoean attackers came into focus under the rising morning light. He asked for his glass and cursed when he put it to his eye. Rows of Monoeans, protected by three lines of shield-men, made a rigid barricade between his soldiers and Seakeep. He eyed their formations, calculating. Four septinaries . . . no, five. A clear tactical mark of Commander Zyann—a legitimate cousin to the King, unlike Draken—and suggested how many soldiers they faced behind those rows. Oddly enough, though, he didn't recognize their tabards. Some sort of red symbol that he couldn't make out through the glass.

"I'll put their ranks at fair to three hundred," he said grimly. "Seakeep won't hold for long under that."

"Seakeep is not defenseless, Your Highness," Tyrolean said. "The High Houses brought companies of servii and their best guards."

Draken handed the glass to him. At the moment the Monoeans were preparing to burn down Seakeep's gates by hurling bags of fire oil against them. They exploded into flame as they hit. Armor, helms, and upraised shields deflected most of the arrows raining down on them from the battlements. Monoean archers stood behind lines of armored and shielded attackers, shooting flaming arrows over the keep walls.

Every line of Tyrolean's body tensed as he peered through the glass.

A hundred battle-ready Brînians and twenty-five Akrasian servii commanded by a horsemarshal stationed in the city awaited Draken's orders just outside Brîn's walls. A few more Brînians were straggling in. Despite their calm, orderly assembly, Draken shook his head, his jaw set. It wasn't enough. Even with the servii inside Seakeep it might not be enough.

His fingers itched for his bow, though his arrowheads couldn't penetrate Monoean armor. He had charged Brînian blacksmiths with developing a harder alloy and wood stock for arrows some turns of the moons ago, but he'd not pressed them. Akrasian longbows were in short supply, as well as the servii trained to shoot them, and mines were nearly spent of weapons-grade metals. Truth, he hadn't anticipated attack from the Monoeans or any other trade partner. Until today.

Blast it, he thought. *Outnumbered, and we don't even have decent arrows.*

"Hie, a rider from the cliffs, Khel Szi!"

Bows creaked.

Draken squinted through the glass. "Hold! He's one of ours." He went down to ground level as a Brînian sailor barreled up, his bare, inked chest slicked with sweat, his snorting horse flecked with foam from outracing the arrows of enemy. A fletched shaft stuck from the back of his arm. Blood poured down his side. Draken bid him to speak with an impatient wave of his gauntleted hand.

The rider's dark face was pinched with pain. He more fell than threw himself from his saddle and knelt. "Enemy attacking the seaside wall with hurling balls. Three ships are dropping anchor in the Bay."

Draken stared at him, incredulous the rumors had proved true. "Fools all! No one is fighting back?"

The runner flinched but his unblinking gaze met Draken's. "Not from ships, Khel Szi. I heard Seakeep is firing on them from the clifftop, though I did not see it."

Elena must be cursing Draken roundly. The delay in defensive maneuvers was his fault. He'd taken the Brînian navy under tight control amid efforts to eradicate rampant corruption; the navy had practically become a merchant marine operation, rife with piracy and extortion. Not to mention their blatant disregard for the Akrasian crown. Each fleet comhanar and ship captain had standing orders not to act without direct command from the Citadel. He hadn't had time to meet and vett each one. Now he was wishing he'd enacted an innocent-until-proved-otherwise policy, though it was damned difficult when so *many* of them were corrupt. Besides, how was he to know they would actually follow their new Khel Szi's policy under duress?

He almost heard Bruche's dry chuckle and could imagine what he'd say: *A Prince knows such things.* "Did they use the boatcaves to get here?"

"No, Khel Szi. The caves are secure. No Monoean came through there. I was inside all night."

Gods, he was probably a fishnetter or salt boiler. Draken had only just come to realize the inked sigils and jewelry on his adopted people indicated caste and position; he had no idea what they all meant yet. "You have my gratitude. See to him." He gestured to two healers waiting inside the city gates to help the bleeding messenger, shoved down the thought of their macabre presence, and turned to Tyrolean.

The Escort Captain met his gaze and then turned his head to look downcoast, though all that lay within view were the cliffs and the edges of a few bridges spanning the River Eros. Constant haze and mists, especially on this hot, humid morning, concealed most of the other side of the river.

Draken mounted Tempest, thinking hard. According to maps, Brînian downcoast was more hospitable to landings than the well-defended Blood Bay. It had plentiful small bays and shallows for dropping skiffs and rowing ashore. The better for trade . . . and smuggling. "The nearest cove is a day's hard ride, maybe three to march."

Tyrolean shrugged his brawny, fishscale-clad shoulders. "It's been in the works then."

Aye, for a sevennight at least, *and* the attack could be more widespread than Draken first thought. If the Monoeans brought five septenaries to Seakeep—three hundred and fifty soldiers—how many other septenaries were roaming the countryside? Countless villages and holdings were in danger. He slammed his fist against his saddle. Tempest skittered again, forcing Draken to haul on the reins. The charger chewed his bit and snorted. How in Khellian's name had Monoea marched so many soldiers through Old Brînish farmland and mines without his receiving a warning? And why? What had inspired this attack? That it was happening now, with Elena and the High Houses in residence at Seakeep, raised his ire and suspicion. Had a traitor betrayed them? Or had some magicks informed the Monoeans? Surely not . . .

"We can outnumber them, given time to gather troops," Tyrolean said, keeping close.

"We don't have time." Not against the nimble, brutish Monoean army. Draken watched another three of their soldiers scale the gates. It took a hailstorm of arrows from the gate tower to bring down just one. The other two Monoeans continued doggedly up, using their wide-brimmed helms to shield their backs.

A flock of Monoean arrows soared up to cover them. The Akrasian Escorts inside Seakeep braved the arrows to roll hurling balls down the gates. That did the trick. He wondered if the winds actually carried the screams of the falling men to his ears or if the sound was imprinted upon his memory from countless battles.

He started thinking out loud, giving his people a short course in Monoean battle tactics. Horses crowded round him as he spoke. "They'll keep on the gate. It's their only way in since they've no large artillery. When we attack, they'll form a phalanx with shields and spears. We're enough to break through." He hoped.

"Spears are Moonling weapons," the Akrasian horsemarshal said. He spat on the ground.

Draken marshaled his patience. "They don't usually throw them. They stake the butts in the ground and make a wall with them."

Tyrolean's brows drew down. "You seem to have made a study of Monoean tactics, Your Highness."

A study, indeed. Draken schooled his expression to betray nothing.

The Brîn City Comhanar urged his horse closer. A chain looped his torso diagonally from one shoulder, marking his rank. Vannis was his name. Grey laced his woolly locks and battle scars etched his dark skin. "Shields and spears make a damned prickly wall, I remember from the Decade War."

Draken nodded. "Aye, Comhanar. Behind the phalanx, they will have seaxes and metal-strapped gauntlets for close work if . . . *when* we break the line. Few if any longswords. If you see one, it's on a commander or a lord."

"Seax . . ." Tyrolean's dark brows fell, shadowing his lined eyes. "So they stab?"

"Aye, Captain." Comhanar Vannis said. "Monoeans block and hit with their bracers and stab with their long knives for a killing blow."

Draken eased a breath from his tight chest as Vannis unwittingly helped protect his secret past. "Their whole strategy is to fight close and dirty. It cuts the leverage of swinging a longer weapon." He paused. "As I understand it."

"So what do you suggest, Khel Szi?" Vannis asked. "We've only bows and our longswords."

"They've got field position, too," Tyrolean said. The land separating the city gates from Seakeep was a rock-strewn, treeless expanse with no cover from arrows; the enemy could see them coming.

"The best we can do is trap them and divert their attention from Seakeep," Draken said.

Draken wished futilely for Mance magic. King Osias's arrows landed precisely where he wanted and his magic could block them as well. For that matter, he wouldn't turn down the Moonling Abeyance, valuable magic which stopped time. But he was on his own in this, and there was only one way to crush the Monoean attackers. It would fair cost him men, horses, and weapons, but he had no choice, not with Elena and the High Houses inside. He outlined his plan to the dubious Akrasian horsemarshal, the war-painted Brînian Comhanar, and Tyrolean.

"We'll lose horses," the horsemarshal said.

"We'll lose more than horses, but we are out of time." Draken raised his voice to be heard over the chatter of his troops. "Comhanar, order the men accordingly. Shields up as soon as we're in bow range."

"Aye, Khel Szi." The Comhanar dipped his chin. He put on his helmet, covering the Khellian's horns painted on his brow, wheeled his horse, and shouted orders to his men.

Tyrolean drew near enough for a private talk. "You cannot fight, Draken. You're Prince."

At least Tyrolean wasn't asking him how he knew so much about Monoean battle tactics. "We need every man." Draken's attention remained riveted on the gate. He tightened as arrows flew toward it like a swarm of riverbugs. Flames licked across the oiled wood like ginger ripples on a black pond.

"You're not just any man, Highness."

"No. I'm not. Elena is at Seakeep and I am sworn to protect her." He touched the chain around his neck. Elena's pendant bound him to his position as Night Lord and his vow to protect her, by honor if not by some magic he hadn't run across yet.

"Not by your own person. Not in this. If we lose you and Elena in the same day, what will happen to Akrasia? This is madness."

Madness? Tyrolean didn't know the half of it. "Odd, I thought being Prince would save me from fruitless arguing."

A muscle twitched in Tyrolean's cheek. "Apologies, Your Highness."

Draken sighed. "It's the only way to get through the gate and protect Elena. See there. It's aflame already. They'll be through in little time if they aren't already."

"The gate wood is still quite green. It won't burn so easily," Tyrolean said.

"It won't stand long to the heat of Monoean oil." He'd seen it burn ship wreckage on calm seas for the better part of a sevennight. "Come. Opportunity wanes."

He alone knew how to fight Monoeans, and he must lead by example, without faltering in his resolve, or his strategy would fail. If the gods saw fit to let him die this day; so be it. It might be their sword in his hand, but it was his Queen and child at risk in Seakeep.

They had a third as many soldiers as the Monoeans. He took a moment to examine a few of their faces, his heart clenching. Many of them likely wouldn't make it through the opening assault. But it wasn't the first time he'd led men to their deaths and wouldn't be the last. He spurred his horse, and his szi nêre fell in to flank him. Tyrolean let him ride without further protest, though Draken could feel his disapproving glare drilling a hole through the back of his armor. Five quarters of conscript Brînians spread into three rows behind twenty-five Akrasian mounted Escorts.

Peculiar, undulating battle cries drifted across the field from the enemy. Draken had never heard it before—it sounded like a mourning wail, the sort professionals sang before kings' funereal processionals. *Lesle . . . I never heard the lament of your passing.* Did she even have an altar—

Tempest yanked hard on the reins, trying to break into a gallop. Draken blinked. Around him horses were falling back or leaping ahead with no thought to formation. *Godsdamn it, men. Focus!* With a hoarse shout he yanked Akhen Khel from its scabbard. Sunlight flashed in the blade.

One breath, then another. His heart thudded in his throat. All around him battle cries rose up. The men reined and spurred their horses back into thundering formation.

Arrows soared overhead, forcing him to sheathe his sword and yank his shield up. Men screamed, drowning out the Monoean war cries. The acidic stench of the burning oil roiled through them as he held Tempest to a controlled canter for the attack. As they reached range, arrows hammered his sheild. Draken rode by feel rather than sight, forced to throw himself forward as his horse leaped over a screaming mount rolling in agony from the arrow sticking in its chest. Its rider lay stunned, face in the churned dirt.

He wanted to use his bow for return fire, but the Akrasian servii behind him were fair deadly enough with bows for the broad target of Monoeans swarming the gates, and his own hands were tied up with reins and shield. Their arrows scored the sky and fell into the smoke clogging the air in front of Seakeep.

His stomach clenched tighter yet. Had the Monoeans broken through the gate? Were they bursting through with blade and bow to spill the blood of his countrymen? Had they found Elena?

Men shouted. Hooves pounded. Draken's blood roared. The world tilted up at him and sprang back to right as Tempest stumbled over a fallen Brînian and his gait went lopsided. Lame, but Draken kicked him on. Tempest was as good as dead anyway. He only needed to carry Draken to battle. To Elena.

CHAPTER TWO

Oily smoke choked his lungs and stung his eyes, filling him with a strangeness he recognized but couldn't put a name to. For a brief moment all fell silent as if an ocean had closed over his head. Sharp heat seared his back, radiating from his sword harness, and the urge to draw the blade tingled cold in his hands.

Bruche?

Silence.

Phantom sensation, like in a lost limb. Draken gritted his teeth and drew the sword. It glowed white and cut a swath through the smoke. The hollow ring of hooves thrashing against steel shields sang out ahead. Voices clogged his ears from all sides. High pitched shrieks and thundering shouts. Bodies and flailing limbs. Blood on his tongue. Smoke clogging every breath. He swung blindly at a dull grey figure emerging from the smoke. His sword skipped off it with a jaw-clenching clang.

His horse kept moving, snorting and screaming, ears pinned, gait lurching. Every stride threatened to jerk Draken from the saddle. He dug his heels into Tempest's sides. Then abruptly they leapt, climbing, hooves pounding over their own horses and screaming men and flailing bodies and the collapsing wall of Monoean shields. Stone walls and narrow guard towers whirred by him as he passed through the ash and kindling that had been the new gates to Seakeep. He had the distant sensation of terror. Or the sensation that he *should* be terrified. He wasn't certain which.

The world twitched sideways. The pavestones of Seakeep's courtyard grabbed him and slammed him down. Helm and sword clattered away. He lay unmoving, stunned as the tang of blood thickened the reek of smoke. Someone screamed their death, an undercurrent to the clash of steel and grunts of soldiers. His armor felt like a seacleaver's suckered grip closing around his chest.

His lungs sucked in a harsh, stinging breath, balking at the thick air. It leaked back out in a whine. Curse the Seven, this was like drowning all over again. Whoever was dying carried on screaming behind him.

He turned his head before his body could refuse to move and shoved feebly at the ground with his hands. Sharp pain in his neck made him wince. He wiggled his toes in his boots to make sure he could. Seaborn lay dull and clean-edged, well out of reach. His horse thrashed, trying to regain its feet, mouth yawning wide with the effort. Draken started to shove up but a boot thudded against the middle of his back. It didn't hurt much; armor was good for something. He caught the flash of sun on a sword in his peripheral, blinding as gods' lighting. He shoved to one side, trying to anticipate the blow. Steel rang against the flagstones near his head. Whoever swung at him snarled and then the weight fell away from his back—

Draken pushed to his hands and knees, scrambling for his blade. A boot kicked it further away. Something bludgeoned his back, knocking him down again, though his knees were under him and he managed a crouch. His lower back seized and his bad knee bent too far. He grunted, desperation warring with pain. *Elena—*

A dead man makes no echo when he falls. Three such dull thuds surrounded him. He shoved up again and met no resistance. Tyrolean stood to one side, both narrow blades crimson to the hilt. Halmar panted just behind him, gore-splattered from the tip of his longsword to his shoulder. Behind them, all around them, soldiers fought and ran.

The screaming was from Tempest, bones jutting from both forelegs.

Instead of helping Draken up, Tyrolean strode a few steps to grant mercy to the charger. His blade cut him off mid-scream. The smell of fresh blood and acrid horse urine competed with human waste expelled by those who had died around them. Draken cinched off rising bile with a hard swallow.

A muscle in Draken's back protested every twist of his body and his knee felt like someone had flayed the inside with a fish knife. He nodded as Halmar offered him a hand up, and limped to retrieve his sword. His shadow was sharp at his feet. Odd to realize the warm sun was beating down while the dead surrounding them made such a quiet, cold space. All around the courtyard Brinians, Akrasian Escorts, and servii beat the Monoeans back, confining the fighting to walls and corners. His soldiers were armed with longswords and the Monoean seaxes couldn't hold up against them.

His back seized as he bent to pick up Seaborn. "Tow-er?" His voice broke over the word, caught on the pain. Halmar gave him a worried look, which he ignored as he eased upright, teeth gritted.

"Enemy made it inside. I was headed there when I saw you fall." Tyrolean led the way to the tower steps amid strewn dead and injured. None threatened them; everyone was too involved in their own close fights.

An Escort sprawled in front of the tower entrance, dead from a nasty gash that left his head dangling off his shoulders at a very wrong angle. Another moaned, eyes wild, clutching the stump of his sword arm, his greens stained with crimson. Draken swallowed and looked away. He was like to bleed to death before a healer could reach him through this melee. The arched wooden door hung from its thick hinges, wrenched from its bolts by a pry bar.

Fury and fear roiled through Draken. If anything happened to Elena he would hunt down every last man responsible and—

Halmar stepped aside from the tower entrance, bloodsplattered and stinking and calm.

"Let no one pass, Halmar."

"Aye, Khel Szi."

Draken ducked under the sunken lintel and strode up the steep, winding steps. Doors had been forced open; more quick work with the prybar. A few rooms held collections of dead Akrasians, gory from deep slashes, ghastly in their fine clothing.

"The Monoeans inside have swords," Draken said shortly. They'd be officers—prized, highly trained warriors. Landed and minors raised to the fight.

His thighs burned from the steep climb but thuds and shouts echoing down the spiral stairs urged him to keep on. He had to slow to step over another body; someone had killed an Escort and shoved her down the stairs head first. She'd left a bloody smear on the steps and crumpled into a sharp curve with a landing beneath an arrow slit. The reek of salt and bowels made the stone walls close in as he climbed past her. His fingers tightened on his sword hilt. One of Elena's favorite guards, she would have been close to the Queen, or running to her aid.

He fought the urge to shout Elena's name. It would only warn her attackers she was there and he was coming. Two more turns and he'd be at her quarters. He slowed just enough to quiet his bootfalls, though his roaring blood and a muffled scream urged him to rush in. Four grey-armored men clogged the narrow steps ahead, talking in hard, excited voices. The crack of wood echoed back to him against the stone and in a heartbeat two of them pressed through an entrance. Someone screamed beyond.

Draken snarled. His legs pumped and he rushed the nearest Monoean, stabbing his blade under the man's back plate into his kidney. The soldier twisted with a grunt, nearly wrenching his blade from Draken's hand but mostly serving to injure himself irreparably. Draken grabbed him by the shoulder armor and shoved him out of the way. Tyrolean cursed and pressed against the curved stone wall in order to keep from getting dragged down with him. Armor clanged as he tumbled down the steps.

The next soldier turned, seax raised in one hand, an axe in the other. He swung the axe at Draken, forcing him to lean back hard on his back leg, which was down a step. Draken swung but the seax's small crossguard caught on Draken's. The soldier pushed hard, trying to unlock them, shove Draken back, anything. Seaborn was angled up, out of reach of doing much damage, but the tip of the seax was close to Draken's chest—one good shove from the Monoean and it'd pierce his leather armor—and Draken had to use brute force, uphill, to push him off. Fools all, he didn't like being downstairs from his opponent, but there was nothing for it, no room to slip through and grab the high ground. He swung with his double-bladed sword but the Monoean used his steel arm bracer to block it. It was too short a swing to do much more than bruise the bastard anyway. Draken grunted a curse as his blade skipped over the bracer. The Monoean stabbed with his seax toward Draken's face, forcing him to tip his head and shift down another step. The Monoean's blade caught his forehead. Blood poured from the wound into his eye and it stung like a viper bite. He lost his balance, tilting dangerously.

Tyrolean caught Draken, gauntleted fists thudding into the back of his armor, and shoved him back upright. The Monoean's axe crashed into Draken's mailclad arm, breaking links and ripping through flesh. Gods spare him, the angle was too awkward to break the bone. Still, agony pierced his battle-rage.

Draken snarled in frustration. The Moneoan raised his axe again; Draken thrust out with an awkward twist to his blade, caught the metal strapping on his vambrace with the tip of Seaborn. The Monoean's axe crashed to the floor. Using the wall and his bleeding arm to brace himself, Draken struck the less protected seax arm from beneath the wrist, grunting with exhertion. The Monoean cried out, thick and guttural. The seax skipped against the wall and clattered away, the better part of a hand and forearm with it.

The tower seemed to rock back and forth as Draken tried to catch his breath.

Someone screamed again from the room beyond, pleading, terrified. Draken grabbed the soldier by the collar of his armor and spun around, shoving him back toward Tyrolean to finish the job with his dual swords. His aching legs pumped up the last few steps and he burst through the broken door of the room.

One of the Monoeans had Elena's maid cornered. She panted screams, lined eyes wide with terror. She threw a cup at her attacker, who raised his seax with a snarl. Tyrolean shouted as he rushed in, drawing his attention.

Another had Elena locked in battle, nightgown swirling around her feet as she lifted a sword for a strike with two hands. The Monoean darted in to try to stab at her. Draken's heart skipped, but Elena yanked back just in time and swung, the blade missing her belly swollen with their child. The Monoean blocked her awkward swing with his metal-banded bracer and snarled a laugh.

Draken rushed toward Elena, sword upraised, gripped too hard. He crashed the edge down on the shoulder plate of grey armor. Pain ratcheted up his arm as he struck but he kept his grip on Seaborn. The Monoean staggered and tried to turn. Elena took the opportunity to try to stab into the apparent weakness on the armor, but the long sword ruined her leverage. It also put her dangerously close to the Monoean again. He reached out with his free hand and grabbed the front of her nightgown, trapping her within stabbing range.

In that moment, all noise and reek and fear fell away. Draken's arm swung up as if Seaborn led it. The blade caught the Monoean under the arm. Blood spurted and a rough scream penetrated Draken's clarity. He drew back and stabbed at the break between the backplate and curving shoulder protection, angling to hit the heart. The tip of his blade stalled inside the body—stopped by the inside of the Monoean's armor.

The Monoean reeled into Elena and she cried out as his weight fell into her, toppling them both. They fell in a heap, Elena writhing beneath a mass of heavy grey armor. Draken leapt forward, grabbed the Monoean by his arm and hauled him off. He moaned and swung his seax feebly. It clattered to the floor. Draken slammed his boot into the join between the Monoean's head and neck armor. An audible crack and he didn't move again.

Tyrolean was just finishing his man off. The maid slumped against the wall, blood blanketing her nightgown. Damn. Draken dropped to a crouch by Elena, wincing as his knee protested. Her sword lay to one side. Her fingers crept for its hilt and then froze as her eyes met Draken's.

He set his blade aside and reached for her, gathering her into his arms. He knew his armor must not be comfortable for her to rest against, but he couldn't resist holding her tightly. "Are you all right? Elena?"

She moaned softly and pressed her face against his chest.

"Elena? Talk to me."

She just clung to him tighter, her fingers curled around his arms, one of them digging into the healing wound in his bicep. Her whole body shook and her breath hitched. He kissed her hair and stroked her back. "Be easy, my love. I have you."

A strange tremor ran through him, from his boots. Elena startled in his arms. He blinked down at the floor. A spiderweb of cracks spread through the wood under his boots. Earthquake? Or some ethereal horror? Crises seemed to come in groups.

Tyrolean's tall frame caught his eye. He'd removed his helm and held it under his arm, his head cocked to listen out the doorway. "I think we're secure for now. I don't hear anyone coming up the steps. Halmar must have it guarded as you said. I'll check and be back."

Draken turned his attention back to Elena. "I'll take you out of here." He started to lift her, but she pushed back on him and slipped a hand between them to wrap her arm around her swollen belly.

"No! It hurts."

He bent his face to her hair. She smelled of floral bathwater, her hair still damp. "We cannot stay here."

"I mustn't move. I need a healer . . ." Tears streamed from her black-lined eyes. "Please, Draken."

"Just until Tyrolean comes back." He settled down onto his knees, ignoring the sore one, and held her close. She tried to ease against him but her back stiffened and she moaned softly. The baby? Draken couldn't will himself to ask. He just held her, his throat tight.

"It's clear," came Tyrolean's voice again. "The enemy are all dead or captured."

"I'll carry you," Draken said. He released her to rise and swipe at his blurred eye; his hand came away smeared with red. The sting was gone. He ignored it and wiped his sword on the nearest cloth he could find, a blanket from her bed, and slipped it into its scabbard. Then he knelt again and lifted her as gently as he could.

She gazed up into his face. "You're bleeding."

How would he explain all his unnaturally healing cuts? "A scratch. I'm fine."

She twisted her neck to look back at the room as he carried her out. Her breath caught. "Melie . . ."

Her maid sprawled in the corner in her bloodstained nightgown. The Monoean who had attacked her lay nearby, his head nearly severed by Tyrolean, but too late. It would take buckets of salt water to scrub the floors clean.

Tyrolean stood in the doorway still brandishing his two bloody swords. "I will see your maid is handled with care, Your Majesty. Do you have orders for the prisoners?"

Elena closed her eyes and leaned her cheek against Draken's shoulder. "Kill them." Her words were soft, muffled against his chest. "Kill them all."

CHAPTER THREE

Draken leaned over the stone wall of the tower at Seakeep and pressed his eye to the viewing glass. Elena's carriage and a large host of Escorts made their way across the field to Brîn and his healers. They were almost to the gates. He longed to be with her, but there were things to tend here. He sighed and turned round to study Blood Bay again. The many trade ships had given the Monoean ships space, mooring on the far side of the Bay or moving out beyond the breakers to drop anchor.

His armor felt too tight on his sweaty skin. Blood had dried in the creases of his fingers. The side of his face was stiff with it, mostly his own. He'd waved off the healers in order to examine the three Monoean warships on Blood Bay. Doubtless healed skin lay beneath the crusted stains.

Tyrolean, Halmar, and another szi nêre, Konnon, who had survived the morning gathered behind him. All were gore-splattered and warming themselves by the great flaming fire lighting the top of the tower. There wasn't much room left for the two barefoot boys who kept the flames of Seakeep going night and day. They were quiet as cats. Below on the seawall, Brinians and Escorts worked side by side, stripping Monoean dead of their valuable weapons and dumping the bodies unceremoniously into the sea.

Three damn ships, just as reported. A drizzly fog rolled in, ready to close over the land. Ahead of it ran a chill wind that cut through the warm sun still shining overhead. The Monoean ships were deadly shadows, their sails fading to mist as they retreated. The ships were nearly to the partially constructed twin towers guarding the entrance to Blood Bay.

Draken cursed under his breath. A retreat, but he'd wager his throne it wasn't permanent. This was the Monoean Navy come to call, the most powerful waterborne force in the world. It always dragged death in its wake. It simply *didn't* retreat. Plus, they'd left prisoners here, even officers. Also unheard of.

He lowered the glass but still stared out to sea. Trade ships were armed against pirates, and plenty of foreign war galleons had been refitted for transporting goods. The heavy weaponry wouldn't have drawn more than a cursory glance. And this was *supposed* to be peacetime. Still. The Monoeans flew war banners any Brînian fleetman would recognize.

Tyrolean spoke. "From downcoast as we thought. The baywatch thought them trade ships. From Felspirn or further."

Draken shook his head. The White City sailed ships to match its legendary ghoststone walls, with sails like snow. He remembered their elegance contrasting with the practical grey Monoean battleships in Sister Bay in Monoea. "Felspirn traders wouldn't come past the Hoarfrost straights, not with the Eidola Islands to navigate. And our bay watch patrol should have recorded their passing the Bay. So why didn't they?"

Brînian coastal defenses had been laid well before his time and the Eidolas were difficult to navigate anyway, but Draken's father had let the fleet and bay watch age shamefully during his reign. Doubtless he'd thought falling in league with the Mance King and launching a war against the gods negated the need for a properly maintained navy and coastal guard. With all Draken had to learn and do while taking the reins of the Brînian city-state, improving the defense of Blood Bay and the coast was one of many duties fallen by the wayside.

Besides, a Sohalia ago he'd been a part of the Monoean Royal court and there'd been not a whisper of plans for invasion then. He would have known . . . nay, as the court's resident adept on Akrasia he would have been intimately involved. What had changed? Why now?

Except *now* left little time to examine the question and do something about the possible answers.

"I sent word to ready two ships to prepare, Khel Szi," Halmar said.

The shifting winds tugged Draken's locks forward. He shoved them back. "Only two?"

"The better part of the fleet is out on trade patrol." As part of their surrender terms to Monoea after the Decade war, Brîn had agreed to policing the trade routes against piracy. Or rather, the Akrasian crown had promised Brînian patrols to the Monoeans. "The *Bounty* and the *Reavan* are still in dry dock."

"Sail the *Bane*, then, to take the request to parley."

"May I speak freely, Your Highness?" Tyrolean sounded sharp.

Draken waved a hand of assent, though he didn't turn around.

"The heads of three High Houses lay dead. Va Khlar is already retreating to Reschan to bolster its defenses. The Queen was nearly killed. There is small chance at parley from our end."

How Draken loathed his birthright that set him ahead of his friend. And yet, others were listening. This was wartime and he could ill afford questioning. Besides hindering his ability to lead, some questions might lead to uncomfortable answers about his past.

"Thank you for your advice, but we must try. Monoea is too valuable an ally and too dangerous an enemy. Send the galleon to follow. We must make some show of force." Ideally they'd have matched them ship for ship, but he had fair faith in the *Crossing*, a heavy battle galleon. "And have fresh scouts ride downcoast. I've a bad feeling this isn't their only attack."

"What of the prisoners?"

They still huddled, disarmed and bound, in the courtyard.

Kill them. Kill them all. Elena's last words to him still resonated.

Such an act could lock-step them to war, even more so than the Monoean attack. They couldn't win a war Monoea chose to wage. He felt certain this had been a warning, especially now with this retreat. But how to relay that to Elena without betraying his intimate knowledge of Monoean armed forces eluded him. He started down the tower steps. When the curving stone walls had cut the wind and cloaked them in darkness punctuated only by arrow slits, he spoke.

"Keep the prisoners chained for now. Bring them into the great hall, out of sight." Elena wouldn't see them from the Citadel, but Escorts might relay to her they were still alive. "I want only Brînian guards on them. I'll see to them later."

"Your Highness, I thought the Queen—"

"Captain." Draken backed up to the wall and paused on the steps.

"Aye, Your Highness?"

"Didn't you ever put off unpleasant chores as a child? Snatch fruit from market stalls? Borrow a horse for a ride or run away from home or steal kisses or skip temple to fish?"

Tyrolean's eyes narrowed. "My father would have whipped me."

Draken sighed. "Mine, too. Good fortune they are dead. Do as I bid. It is mine to answer to the Queen, not yours."

"Aye, Your Highness." Tyrolean passed him, trotting with all the nimble energy of a man fresh from rest and half Draken's age.

Draken snorted softly and paused to peer through an arrow slit. He couldn't be certain but he thought the Monoean ships dropped anchor outside the breakers protecting Blood Bay. He watched his own ships get halfway across the Bay before he sighed and went down, avoiding looking into the room where the Queen had defended herself. He and his szi nêre had to step around the maids and soldiers carrying bodies and scrubbing blood stains.

Thom met him at the bottom step. His brow above the mask was furrowed. Draken bit back a curse. "What now?"

"Khel Szi, Moonlings await your audience at the Citadel."

Moonlings? He stared at Thom a couple of breaths before it came back to him. Lady Oklai was due this sevennight and had seen fit to travel quicker than he expected. Perhaps the Abeyance aided their speed. "Of all the bloody days . . . Send word I will come. In the meantime make certain she is welcomed and cared for. See to it yourself, Thom."

"May I mention another thing?"

Draken resisted bouncing on the balls of his feet. He was in a mood, he knew, and if Thom had the stones to hold him up when he could see that so clearly, it must be important. "Aye?"

"It's odd, and I'm not certain it's important . . ."

"Thom. I am pressed for time." He leveled narrowed eyes at the Gadye.

Thom cleared his throat. "Right, Khel Szi. It's just . . . the Monoeans. They're touched."

Touched? Not possible. "What are you trying to say, Thom?"

"They've no fear of us. No fear of our threats. They aren't resisting, but they aren't frightened at all. One mentioned he was glad to die and hoped he could die by your hand."

"Mine?" Clearly he'd have to see for himself. "It doesn't matter. They're still condemned, by order of the Queen. Keep the Moonlings happy for me until I return."

Before the Gadye could answer, he turned to Comhanar Vannis, who strode toward him. He was as bloody as Draken and ignoring a couple of shallow slashes on his arms and chest. Trails of blood had crusted on his skin. None of the Brînians seemed to mind that Draken wore armor after the style of the Akrasians, but he wondered what sort of blessing the Brînians had to fight without such protection.

Draken lifted his chin in greeting. "What news, Comhanar?"

Vannis' fingers wrapped his sword grip like he might draw again at any moment. The guards on the battlements and on the ground kept arrows to the string. The attack had everyone's back up and well it should. "Fair rough, Khel Szi. Apparently the Monoeans put in another galleon downcoast and divided into big guerilla bands. We've had a couple of runners from outlying villages this morning, during the battle."

"Seven bloodied gods. Are they killing or just putting people out of their homes and looting them?"

Vannis' voice dropped and he glanced around them before answering. "Killing, Khel Szi."

The Comhanor stood politely, his wizened face an absent mask, while Draken cursed more. Draken stumbled to a stop when he realized he was waiting for orders. They needed help. More soldiers. Servii—Draken's servii at Khein. But that was several days' march and he only had fifty of his own in the city to augment the three hundred or so Escorts accompanying Elena. Half of them had died in the battle. With the attack still fresh on his mind, he wasn't willing to send Akrasian Escorts away from their Queen. She came first.

"How many troops can you spare to send out from Brîn City proper?"

Comhanar Vannis blinked. "Just the on-leave. A hundred or fewer. And it's a risk."

Aye, a bad one. "Khellian's stones, there's nothing for it. Call them to duty. And Comhanar? They should stalk the Monoeans. Stealth. Break them into squads of no more than a dozen each."

"One runner reported groups as large as thirty, maybe fifty."

"Like I said. Stalking. This is strike-and-retreat action. Gods willing it won't all turn to war."

How he wished he could lead a band himself, tell Vannis all he knew of Monoean tactics. He wondered how many people would die to inadvertently keep his past secret. "They should—no. No further detailed orders. I just know if fifty or a hundred Brînian troops go tramping about, the Monoeans will find a way to massacre them. They are superb, if the morning was any indication, at head-on battles. Our men need to be agile and quiet enough to strike and escape, but they'll have to work out details on the march."

◆ ◆ ◆

The Brînian Citadel couldn't be more different from Elena's spare, light-sucking Bastion at Auwaer or the sprawling grey palace straddling the Sevenfel Cliffs over Sister Bay in Monoea. He wondered if he'd ever get used to striding directly into the circular Great Hall right from the brightly planted courtyard. The Brînian throne sat at one end on a dais, gaudy even amid the splash of bright tiles and gold-leafed pillars. Artists had been touching up the murals inside the dome, but they'd obviously been shuffled out for Khel Szi's esteemed guests. What people did remain: some of the Seneschal's staff, szi nêre posted at the three doors, and slaves seeing to the refreshments table, shot wary looks at the Moonlings waiting to see him.

Draken had ridden as quickly as he could back to the Citadel, but no one in the Moonling war party—impossible to think of them any other way—smiled when he strode into the Great Hall. For a breath he considered sitting on his throne, but he was filthy and a deep frown already creased Lady Oklai's dappled face. Instead he approached and knelt as a courtesy, to be on level with her. His szi nêre took up position on either side of the dais.

"My lady. It is my great honor to greet you."

She held off answering for a long moment, and when she did, her tone was acerbic. "Indeed, it is mine for your taking the time."

A beat. "It's been rather a busy morning."

"Too busy to bathe after battle, I see." Her wide nostrils flared and her lip curled.

Were the Moonlings that fastidious they could not stand the presence of battle grime? Truth, he knew few of them. Oklai was clean, the pale leather strips that formed her long skirt were spotless even at her heels. The ribbons on her spear, though, were stiff with old, brown blood. The blade at its tip looked to have a keen edge.

He suppressed an annoyed sigh, rose, and slung himself in his throne anyway, an arm hooked over the back. Hang the mess it would cause, and hang Oklai's offense. "I was already late for the audience, my lady," he said with pointed irritation. "How may I help you?"

Her contingent, a group of a dozen small warriors better suited to the Norvern Wildes of Monoea than the bustling city of Brîn, stepped into formation. The ribboned butts of their spears made a sharp *crack* against the floor. Every ribbon was also stained dark and stiff with old blood.

Draken blinked and rose his brows a heartbeat too late for wry regard.

"Once my people did you a good turn." The fur Oklai wore over her shoulder rippled like a live thing as she eased closer on silent feet clad in woven sandals.

He dipped his chin, trying to hide his silent, deep breath. "As I once did yours."

"You spared one of my people from slavery."

Or a more sinister purpose, to judge by the Mance who took her. Draken let his free hand run along the armrest of the throne, examining the smooth wood, blackened from the touch of his ancestors. The great halls of the great nations seemed to share the habit of excrutiatingly slow conversation.

"I had considered the debts between us settled," he said, because she surely was here to ask for something. "Perhaps you think differently."

"Debts? No. Not between us. Between you and the gods."

Draken couldn't hold back a snort but did manage to not say something very rude.

Oklai glided closer. "Your actions are a portent."

He narrowed his eyes, striving for the brashness of his father. But his throat was too dry. "Actions."

"Sparing a Moonling of a life of slavery."

He let that sink in, catching a glimmer of her purpose. His tone was careful, noncommittal, though the topic rankled. He'd perfected his smooth speech in the previous few moonturns dealing with powerful merchants looking for tariff exemptions. "I've made no secret that I abhor slavery."

"And yet you keep them." Her gaze followed a pretty house slave as she brought another pitcher of wine for their guests.

"I've reduced the duties of every slave in the Citadel. They are each given proper meals and enough sleep time." The slave was sundry, curved in all the right places, meek as a sleepy kitten, and a favorite of the szi nêre. "They've also protection from those outside the Citadel, as well as those within." The nêre and House free staff hadn't been best pleased with him, and he knew he couldn't fight the leanings of a whole culture. But inside *his* house no one gave of themselves what they didn't freely offer.

"But you still call them slaves. Some of them with Moonling blood?"

"Sundry, only." Damn her, that was Akrasian prejudice against mixed-bloods, not his. He was no hypocrite, being sundry himself.

Her lips tightened and her spear moved in her hand as she adjusted her grip. His szi nêre tensed on either side of him.

It was a thin victory. She might hate sundry better than most Akrasians but she still expected . . . whatever it was she bloody well expected. Fools all. He didn't have time for this.

He lowered his arm from the back of the throne and leaned forward, settling his forearms on his knees. His tired muscles strained against his armor. He had to beat down the frantic urge to escape the suffocating mail and plates and straps. "As you see, I've many duties to attend. How may I be of assistance to you, Lady Oklai?"

The Moonling drew herself up. "In my blood runs the direct lineage of Queens, as yours does kings."

Draken's eyes narrowed. "There is only one person in Akrasia I call Queen."

"We are in Brîn, are we not?"

"Which is a principality of Akrasia. This you know."

"And Elena is a newcomer here, compared to my people."

"I have neither time nor inclination to debate—"

"This is no debate. It's simple fact. Elena is not the only Queen in Akrasia, nor the rightful one."

He sighed. Weariness prickled the insides of his eyelids. It had been a long day yet and the sun had just passed its zenith. "Lady Oklai, that is treasonous talk. Do not force me to arrest you. We are friends, or at least I thought we were. I don't—"

"Are we? Friends? And yet your Queen enslaves my people. You keep slaves in this very house."

"Slavery was established long before I sat the throne of Brîn."

"But you *do* sit the throne. Your actions condone slavery, Khel Szi."

His jaw tensed. A hard silence, broken by his soft voice. "You know I do not."

"And yet you've done nothing to free them since you arrived."

Arrived? Did she mean to Brîn or on the continent of Akrasia? She had intimated she knew something of his personal history when they'd first met. He couldn't take the risk of his guards and others overhearing if she made a point of using it against him. He rose and stepped off the dais. He made no pretense of hiding his height advantage, drawing himself up. "Have you seen the gardens, my lady?"

She frowned but accompanied him out to the courtyard and the grounds inside the walled Citadel. City noises filtering through the gates faded as they walked among the trees. They had grown stout and tall, protected by the Citadel from the sea. Great ribbons of moss draped the limbs and the everpresent sea breezes rustled the leaves. The skies overhead were still mostly blue but grey edged it—the thick ocean mists drifting in. They probably entirely concealed the Monoean ships by now. He tried to let the fresh scents and cooling breeze settle him. Difficult while still crusted in the blood of his old countrymen.

"You were a slave once in Monoea," she said at last. "You know what you must do."

He walked quietly for long moments until he could be certain the alarm singing in his veins wouldn't reach his voice. "Here, I am a slave to politics and economics. I have duties beyond your people."

"You have a duty to the gods' will."

Again and again, someone tripped him up with the gods. "Those same gods who gave me this sword and told me kill my Queen with it. Who are you to claim to know their will?"

"You killed a Queen and averted war."

"I killed the woman who loves me, who now carries my child. The gods wanted me to leave her dead, but I could not. Since then, ruddy silence from the lot of them. So don't harp on me about the gods. They already proved they will force me when they wish my service. Until then, *I* decide." Eidola claim his soul, he would decide anyway.

"I see you will take more persuasion." The last was more hiss than word.

He bit down on a retort, refusing to rise to her bait. "I want to help. I would see all the slaves freed. But I can't, not right now."

"When, then, Khel Szi? Time does go on. Princes always have pressing duties. So when will freeing the Moonlings become yours?"

He stopped walking, fists clenched, shoulders painfully tight under his armor. Again, it felt as if his breath was constricted. "Fools all! Do you see I am still bloody from battle and preparing to drown my dead? Queen Elena barely escaped the attack with her life, much less that of our child. There are more lives at stake right now than a few slaves. I'm trying to stave off a war we cannot win."

"I fear it is much too late for that, Draken." Her words fell flat against the live sounds all around them and she turned away.

He stood a long time, watching her tiny body walk back to the great domed Citadel, the palace of his people, until the wind turned the whispers of leaves to menacing jeers and damp, sticky mist closed in all around.

CHAPTER FOUR

Elena was still within her chambers with her healers. The maids in the outer sitting chamber eyed Draken with open shock and dismay at his soiled appearance.

"You'll not want to upset Her Majesty, Khel Szi," one of them gathered the courage to say.

She was paler than some slaves in the household, and delicate-featured. Dozens of tiny braids crossed her head and dangled over her shoulders. She must be from Septonshir, the Seven Lakes region over the grasslands. Born a sundry slave, and her mother stoned to death for the crime of mixing blood, likely. He'd heard 'Meres were fanatically intolerant of sundry. She dropped her gaze demurely when his attention settled on her.

"Inform my Queen and the healers I'll be back when I'm more presentable."

"Aye, Khel Szi."

Light shining through the sheer drapes in his chambers cast jagged, sword-like shadows from the balcony railing across the tiled floors. Incense burned, filling the rooms with its familiar sultry scent. Draken felt as if he sullied the clean space as he stripped his blood-encrusted armor and clothing. Kai put it in a basket for cleaning.

Draken frowned. Someone had sheared the boy's locks this morning. Since Kai had helped him arm for the battle.

"What happened, Kai?"

Kai kept his head down as he knelt to remove Draken's leg armor and unbind the sandal straps. "Hina Shain caught me with Lunae, Khel Szi."

Another slave. But it was odd he found trouble with it—especially from the Seneschal. Brînians were free enough with sex and affection, in marriage and out. Slaves weren't allowed to marry, but coupling was encouraged among them to keep stock up. "If she pleases you, and you please her, then carry on."

Kai's gaze flicked up to his face in surprise, then he ducked his head again. "Master Hina sold her to an island bloodlord. Delivery next sevennight."

"Hmm. Shall I buy her back?"

A silence. Then, low: "The bloodlord fancies her, Khel Szi."

"Does she fancy you?"

Kai looked up again, then set his armor aside carefully. Blood flaked off it. A bare whisper: "Aye."

"Carry a message to the bloodlord that he should rethink his purchase."

Kai gaped at him. "The bloodlord—"

"Answers to me, does he not?"

The boy blinked rapidly. "Aye, Khel Szi."

"Thom?"

The Gadye looked up.

"See to this business, will you?"

"Aye, Khel Szi." His mask made him stoic. Gadye were firm believers that sundry were a blight and slavery was too good for them. Draken decided to not give a hang whether Thom approved or not.

◆ ◆ ◆

Draken had given Elena the nicest rooms in the private apartments. They had been his father's and security was better since they were deep within the Citadel. Draken preferred his smaller chambers with the balconies and view over the courtyard, though it was still odd to sleep alone most nights. The way of royals, but he didn't much like it.

"She is resting quietly, but there was some bleeding." The healer looked grim, standing in the dim antechamber of Elena's apartments. Dark circles underscored her lined eyes. "I fear the battle proved too much for the child."

Draken stared at her, stunned. "It is lost, then?"

"No, Khel Szi. Not yet. But she must be kept quiet and calm."

"She is very far gone on. Seven moonturns at least. The baby might survive."

"I don't like the chances. The baby would be better born in two more moonturns." A slight, weary smile. "If anyone can get her to stay quiet, it would be you."

Right, then. He eased a breath into his tight chest, his hand on the door, before pushing inside. Elena lay on her side on the bed. A great headboard inlaid with an iridescent shell mosaic shadowed her and gauzy hangings shifted in the light breeze. She smiled when she saw him. It looked stiff. His smile felt the same.

"You look well enough." He sat on the side of the bed and laid his hand on her swollen belly. Her dark hair was damp and braided.

She tugged him down for a kiss. His lips lingered on hers for a long moment. They'd bathed her. She smelled of nightsong and sweetmilk. He wanted to feel her all over her skin, to reassure himself she was all right. He settled for running his fingers down her long, black braid and laying it over her shoulder.

"I felt the baby move a little ago."

"That's good," he said. "Very good."

She took his hand and examined his broad fingers, his palm, the brand marring his knuckles. The slaves were right. He was glad he'd scrubbed away the blood. She lifted her fingers to his brow. "I think I remember a cut on your forehead. It was streaming blood."

"It must have been from someone else, from the battle." Lies came easier every day. One day the gods surely would make him atone with the truth.

She nodded and shifted to sit up against the cushions. He adjusted the covers over her lap as she reached for the bedside candle and lighted it with a flick of her fingers. Remenant magic from his exchanging a Mance King's life for hers. "You saved my life. Again."

"I am your Night Lord."

She gave him a tentative smile and fingered her pendant hanging about his neck. "I didn't expect to require your direct aid quite so often."

"I wish you didn't. But I doubt the Monoeans thought they'd find my lady Queen with a sword. You held them off well."

"Not well enough. Melie . . ." Her fingers tightened on his, then loosened.

"You are safe, Elena. That's all that matters."

She shook her head. "You don't care about her loss?"

He stroked her arm and gazed at her face. Too pale, even her lips. The shadowing beneath her black-lined eyes betrayed her exhaustion. This close he could see every deeply toned facet of her dark irises. "I don't mean to sound cold, but you mean everything to me and to Akrasia. This doesn't mean I don't understand what the attack cost you."

"I wanted to be brave, to be a Queen. If I hadn't fought they might have just taken me hostage, but I couldn't think . . ." Her words choked to a stop. "I was terrified."

His throat tightened. He pulled her up into his arms. "You were fair brave, Elena. You defended yourself and our child, and that is the same as defending Akrasia herself."

She stayed quiet, resting against him. "I sometimes wish I didn't have to put the country before you." She made a soft, amused noise. "No. If I'm honest, I wish you didn't have to put the country before me."

"Is that why you wanted me? Because you knew I would be Prince and you knew we would have that in common?" He was only joking. Mostly.

"No. I wanted you because you are handsome and strong and honorable. Someone different, and yet the same." Her voice was soft.

"The same as what?"

"As me. At the center of things, and yet alone as well."

"You aren't alone. You won't be alone again, I swear it." He would drive every last Monoean from their shores if it came to it. He shifted to kiss her. Her arms slid around his neck and he felt his muscles relax into the familiar cadence of holding her, of her breath against his neck, her hands on his back. Desire rose, but now wasn't the time. They stayed that way for a time and then he gently helped her to sit up against the cushions.

"How many did we lose?" she asked.

"Fifty-two Brînians dead, no count on Escorts yet. I expected no less taking on a Monoean phalanx."

"You crushed it."

"At great cost, aye. We lost most of the horses."

"And how many Monoeans died?"

"We estimate three hundred with some twenty in chains at Seakeep."

"And their ships?"

"Retreated to just outside the Bay. I sent a request to parley."

"*Parley?* I thought I told you to kill them all. Kill the prisoners and sink those ships."

Her sharp tone finally warned him off blurting something else without thinking. He took a breath, preferring to discuss the baby, her health, ways to keep her quiet, anything but the possible ramifications of this attack.

"First, most of our ships are under repair, patrolling, or at trade. Second, the whole of Monoea's army outnumbers ours easily ten-to-one. Its navy outnumbers our ships three-to-one. If we go on the offensive and destroy those ships, King Aissyth may send a fleet of ten next time. Or thirty."

"You've thought this through, war with them."

Irritation bit at him. Was it not his duty as Prince to consider risks to his country? And as Night Lord, risks to her. "We cannot fight Monoea in a real war and win, Elena."

"Such talk is treason."

He pulled his hand from hers. "The truth is not treason, my Queen. Lying to you would be."

Her dark eyes drank in the light, vanishing it into their depths. In these abrupt moments, when she was more Queen than woman, peril shadowed her. Draken felt a sharp pang beneath his breast bone. Where had the mother of his child gone? The Elena he loved? He longed to touch her hair, to soothe her, but he didn't dare try to break through that armor.

Damned Monoeans, stealing her from him when they had so little time together. Common sense told him that the King Aissyth had no overt foul intent. He knew his cousin-King. Something, a reason that made sense, had driven him to attack Seakeep. But then, Draken bore the gods' sword and hard lessons had taught him to ignore logic for instinct.

"As you say." Aye, her armor was strapped on tight, now. He wondered sometimes if he ever managed to really pry it off her. "Why would the Monoean King attack us?"

He rose and crossed to a table to pour them both wine, not really wanting a drink but needing to buy time to shift to thinking like a Prince rather than a lover.

King Aissyth was far from weak. But still . . . "This attack doesn't strike me as King Aissyth's way. There's nothing in Father's scrolls, nothing in recent history to anticipate this animosity. This season and last, trade has gone on as ever." There, that must sound distant enough.

"You think his lords masterminded the attack, then?"

"I don't know. That would indicate outright rebellion. The Landed are not autonomous as your High Houses are with their troops in Akrasia. The King controls all."

"An example I should perhaps follow."

Draken didn't answer. That was her right, if she willed it. He would happily hand over command of his own Akrasian troops at Khein. Others of the nobility, perhaps not, especially now that most of her Council were dead, leaving a collection of young, unproved heirs.

She smoothed her narrow hand over the coverlet and took the cup of wine he offered. "And what would you do to eliminate this threat, since we cannot fight them and win?"

"As I said, offer terms. Find out what the King is about before we rush into battle again." He wondered if she thought him craven as she studied him. She could order his ships to attack and there would be nothing he could do.

"Fine. Greet their ships, then. Meet them and talk," she said. "But commit to nothing. See to it personally."

He blinked and his mouth went dry. *"Me?"*

"You are my Night Lord. In my absence, you are my voice. They must know you as such. They will abide by you. But heed me now. If they will not make terms, or if they attack again, then we must strike back with our full might. I would rather our people die free than live enslaved."

He bit down on mentioning the hundreds of slaves already in Akrasia and Brîn, though he was certain Oklai would have. "And the prisoners? They would make a pretty offer for terms."

"No. Kill them and offer their bodies to Khellian on a pyre. We need the gods' favor far more than we need Monoea's."

He'd heard of it, invoking old magic with barbaric, superstitious sacrifices. But he reckoned it pacified the people more than the gods. He swallowed the news of the guerrilla strikes he'd ordered that morning on the grounded Monoeans, and that their own ships were outnumbered in the Bay. He simply bowed his head and strode away, frustrated and knowing she was right.

This attack needed a sharp retort, but he was still loathe to kill the prisoners straightaway. He could learn things about why they attacked if there was a commander among them. His feet carried him to the courtyard. The day was stretching longer, nearing evening, though still warm. All this fighting and talking and bathing . . . he should crave a meal and sleep but what he craved more was escape.

After bidding a slave to ready horses, he found Tyrolean in the temple. The captain knelt before Zozia's altar, a sheer white cowl obscuring his features. When Draken had stood for a few breaths and the captain didn't acknowledge him, he walked closer, silent on his bare feet, and dipped his fingers in Khellian's bowl of blood. He kissed them, tasting metallic salt as if he'd licked his sword blade, and sketched a rough Eye on the bare skin over his heart. It couldn't hurt.

Tyrolean pushed back his white cowl and got to his feet. "Your Highness."

"I want to question the prisoners. Will you come?"

"I thought you were meant to kill them."

He sighed. "We had this conversation before, Captain."

"Aye. We did."

Draken glanced around at the temple, avoiding Tyrolean's gaze. It was peaceful, made of the purest white stone quaried in Felspirn. Water ran over Ma'Vanni's icon, softening the bright paint and trickling over stones and shells at her feet. Tyrolean spent a lot of time in here. Mostly alone. There was the priest also, but he was old and creased, with his tender hands and worn voice.

"She didn't say when," Draken said. "She didn't say immediately. Come."

He turned and led Tyrolean back to the horses. His szi nêre waited with horses of their own. "Are you bloody mind-readers?" Draken asked Halmar.

"The stableboy informed Seneschal Thom of your request for horses."

He mounted Sky, who snorted and tossed her reins. "There are dozens of orchestrations that go on inside the Citadel without my knowing, isn't there, Halmar?"

A slight smile tugged at the szi nêre comhanar's pierced lips. "Hundreds, Khel Szi."

The door to the great hall of Seakeep had been pried open like the tower door, hanging off great black hinges like a broken tooth. Inside, the Monoeans sat chained to each other. Draken had been wrong in his count. Two dozen faces tipped up as he stopped inside the door to let his gaze adjust. Bruising mottled their skin. Blood and grime dirtied their grey under-padding. Armor, glittering a little where the dull grey paint had been scratched away to reveal bare shiny metal, made an untidy pile in a corner. The seaxes and other weapons were stacked more neatly. Draken's eyes narrowed. He'd ordered Brînians guard them and wondered what had happened to that. Elena?

One Escort was testing the weight of a seax, whipping it through the air. Another grinned as he watched. "I wouldn't give that to my girl for a Sohalia trinket," he said.

Draken cleared his throat. "She could do fair worse for a weapon. Many of my soldiers died by them this day."

The Escorts snapped to, fists to chests. "Night Lord!"

Next to him, Tyrolean drew breath as if to speak. Draken held up a hand to stop him from admonishing the Escorts to call him Highness. He liked them calling him Lord. Made him feel closer to the action.

"Sixty-four, to be precise," one of the Monoeans said. His pale hair was grey with dust and clipped tight to his head as Draken's used to be. An altogether practical custom most Akrasians and Brinians eschewed. And now Draken, as well, though his locks were tied back from his face.

The accuracy caught Draken off guard. He'd known, of course. He reported to the Queen after all. Either someone had been talking in front of the prisoners or this Monoean had eluded capture long enough to make his own count. The latter, by the looks of him. Older than the others and sharp-eyed. He had a thick black smudge on his forehead. All the prisoners did.

Draken acknowledged him with a slight dip of his chin. The Escorts' eyes widened. But thirty years of Monoean military protocol was a tough habit to break, and courtesy cost little when spent on a dead man.

"Your name, Comhanar?"

The Monoean didn't balk at the Brinish. "Laran Kupsyr, Your Highness. For that is who you are, yes? The magical Brinian Prince?" Not a trace of disdain tinged his voice. By the gods, he was really asking.

And Draken knew him—or rather, the name. He was part of a Landed family, not a minor one. But the son of an important Landed lord should be attending his King at court and fussing at politics, not killing Akrasians and Brinians on a tradeseason morning. Aching tension settled deep in his bones. The man was military; the crispness of his tone, the capable hands laced with caluses. Zozia's Name, what had driven him to take up the sword here? Certainly nothing good. And how was Draken to find out without betraying all he knew and how he knew it? He could think of one way, but it left a foul taste on the tongue.

"May I see it? The gods' sword?" Kupsyr asked.

For long thudding heartbeats Draken didn't breathe.

"Reckon it'll be the last thing you see," the mouthy Escort said.

Draken cleared his throat again, felt annoyed with its spindly sound. "Halmar. Unchain Commander Kupsyr and bring him."

His szi nêre moved to act, though the order was outside their duties. Tyrolean moved to follow.

Draken lowered his voice. "No, Ty. See to a proper place to execute them— outside somewhere, and private. No point in more mess. The slaves are overwhelmed as it is. I'll be back shortly."

He made Kupsyr climb the many steps to the wall overlooking the sea. The Monoean stumbled once, his chains still binding his arms behind his back. Halmar hauled him to his feet, twisting his arms awkwardly. The man gasped in pain. At the top, the siz nêre released him and stepped back.

The two men stood together at the sea wall, for all purposes alone. Mists chilled Draken despite his armor and cloak and must have dampened Kupsyr to the skin through his sweaty, quilted armor padding. It was a long time before either spoke.

"Are these your slaves?" Kupsyr gestured behind them.

"My guards. Szi nêre. Landless warriors, blooded all. Sworn, not enslaved." This he said with no little pride. His guards were arguably the finest soldiers in Brîn and Akrasia.

Kupsyr grunted. "You're going to kill us."

"Those are my orders."

"Fair enough. Ma'Vanni knows the kings have held us separate from the gods' will long enough. May Ma'Vanni keep us."

His little speech sounded just as Thom had said. "You disagree with the King's Decree." Not King Aissyth's decree, Aissyth's father's. Though it had been Aissyth who eradicated slavery.

"That law calls magic heresy," Kupsyr said. "And yet, here you stand with a magic sword and orders to execute your prisoners."

Draken raised his brows. "You're a rebel, then?"

"Disagreement does not make rebellion."

But it was the first stone on the damned road. Draken just looked at him.

Kupsyr shook his head, impatient. "Magic is the gods' will, manifest. You're proof of that. You and that sword."

Draken's hand strayed to the hilt, fingers playing with the loose bit of leather wrap. "How did you hear of Seaborn?" *Let's see how much you know.*

He didn't disappoint. "It's all over Sevenfel. The new Prince with the magic sword Ahken Khel. The Prince who stopped a civil war between Brîn and Akrasia and won the heart of the Queen."

Draken turned and leaned on the seawall, staring out into the mists. "Why did you attack us this morning?"

Kupsyr remained silent, but a deep frown creased his face. Out here in the light, such as it was, dirt and blood splatters shone in stark relief against his pale skin and hair.

Draken sighed and gave up on the Brînish. He lowered his voice and switched to Monoean. "You are the commander of these troops, sir?"

"What's left of them," Kupsyr said with a wry twist of his lips before his expression cleared. Draken guessed he'd been coached in case of capture.

"I have heard the Monoean nobility is granted some provision for disagreeing with orders, if the reasoning behind them is suspect." But did that hold true with taking orders from a rebel lord? And which Landed dared go against the King?

"I never said I disagreed with the orders to attack, nor the reasoning," Kupsyr said.

Unease swelled in Draken's belly like grain-bread soaked in wine. "Who is your liege, since it is clearly not King Aissyth?"

A tightlipped frown was Kupsyr's only answer.

"I know something of your culture, as you obviously know something of mine. You wear nothing to show you're someone important." *And yet, I know by your name you are.* "If you cooperate, I might be able to strike a deal."

"For?" Rough, grudging.

"The manner of your death. I think we can do better than cutting some minor veins and stringing you on this cliffwall to bleed out down the stones for half a sevennight, eh?" He was irked and impatient enough to follow through with it, too. Questioning this man was a gamble, and Draken was losing.

"Speak to Captain Yramantha. She's got more information and more to gain from your cooperation than I."

Yramantha. The same who had dumped Draken unceremoniously into Khein Bay, carrying out his sentence of exile.

"What does *my* cooperation have to do with it?" Draken asked.

"Important people want to meet you, to know how you come by this sword and by the magic. How you turned a godless country into a righteous one."

Righteous? Brîn? His gaze flicked to Halmar's impassive form, cloaked by shadow. "Meet me? You could fool wise Zozia with your actions, and you certainly fooled me. It seemed your troops fair meant to kill me."

"And yet you did not die for all our trying."

Draken snorted. "And how will they use the information, these important people?"

"To overthrow the King and reinstate holy law."

The King—his cousin. Even though he'd been disowned, they were still family. Draken didn't disdain the gods enough to taunt their anger by going against his own blood. This was all much, much worse than he thought. And he still didn't quite understand how he and Brîn played into it. But at least Kupsyr had given him a taste of what he was up against.

"Is that all you've to say, then?"

Kupsyr gave a tight nod.

"I do not condone much of the gods' actions, but I dare not tempt their anger by going back on a parley. We have made terms. I will abide. How will you die?"

A brief hesitation, his chin lifted. "On the edge of your sword."

"Do you need time to pray?"

"My actions are my prayers. I have done what I came to do."

"Which was to kill my people? To start a war?"

"To bring you back to Monoea. For where you go, Your Highness, the gods surely follow."

. . . *back* to Monoea. There it was. Kupsyr knew Draken's past, knew who he was. He had to put a stop to this before it went a breath further. But before he could draw his sword, a breathless Brînian runner appeared on the stairs and dropped to a knee.

Gods, what now? What was so imperative it couldn't wait until he finished executing this man? "Speak."

"A visitor at the Citadel, Khel Szi. The message said 'ghost'."

Imperative, indeed. He waved the messenger away, and when his footsteps faded, he nodded to Halmar, who came forward and pushed Kupsyr to his knees. Draken detected a tremble running through the Monoean at the whispered hiss Seaborn made as it emerged from its scabbard. The faint glow of godslight shone in the depths of the blade. Or a reflection of sunlight peering through the misty clouds. Draken didn't look up to check.

"May the will of the Seven become the will of all," Kupsyr said.

Halmar held Kupsyr upright with his big hands as Draken slid the blade into the Monoean's shoulder at an angle, just behind Kupsyr's collarbone, sheathing Seaborn within flesh and bone and heart. Kupsyr's eyes widened and his head lolled back. Bloody spittle bubbled over his lips. He gasped and sprayed a fine mist with his last breath. His slumping body put his full weight on the sword, twisting Draken's arm awkwardly. Fools all, he should have withdrawn it straightaway.

But he hadn't, and the blade didn't come free as easily as it had slid in. He had to twist it and wrench it free of the slumped, limp body. A slick coat of crimson heartblood concealed its godslight and spread in a gleaming pool over the flagstones on the battlement.

"String him up on the wall so the Monoeans can have a look at him." His voice was rough. He cleared his throat. "Then we'll start on the rest."

CHAPTER FIVE

Draken strode into his private quarters, stripping his blood-stained cloak from his bare back and tossing it to Kai. "Go."

The slave boy bowed his way out. Draken waited for the outer doors to close. All remained silent. A gentle sea-stained breeze drifted in through the balcony doors and the place smelled fresh with flowers, though not enough to cover his own stink of death. He must remember to have some flowers sent to Elena's room.

"We're alone," he said to the empty room. His voice echoed off the bright tiled surfaces. "Show yourself, Ghost."

The slightest of rustlings and Aarinnaie Szirin of Brîn, royal assassin and Draken's half-sister emerged from the thick waxy leaves of an Oscher tree outside the open shutters leading to his sitting room balcony. She lowered the hood of her long-sleeved tunic, brushed the excess bark from her palms, and gave him a veiled smile before executing a slow, perfect curtsy worthy of any High Court in the world.

Mud caked her worn leather boots. Grey bark and white riverbank dust streaked her dark clothes. Her nails were ragged and black with dirt. A Gadye must have braided her long black curls into a hundred thin plaits—a curious affectation, that—but several curly strands had escaped around her face. She reeked of sweat and horse.

Draken poured her wine. He tore a few fragrant herbs from the brightly painted cache pot on the sideboard to drop into her flagon and gave it to her. "What's gone wrong now?"

She took the drink and said with faint amusement, "Politics suits you, brother. You're as abrupt and cynical as any lord I've ever met."

"It's not every night you track dirt on my rug, Aarinnaie." He waited, arms crossed, while she drained the cup.

She lowered it to reveal a grim line to her mouth. Her tone flattened. "Bad rumors in the city. There's an inland herding village on the other side of the

39

Eros. It's called Parne. I heard tell that the village has been massacred. Dead to the last babe."

He stood silent and stiff a long moment. "Where did you hear this?"

"At enough taverns I thought it worth bringing to you." She set her flagon down on the nearest stone-top table with a careful clink.

"Do they think it's Monoeans who did it?"

"No one knows, not yet. But it's the logical leap, aye? What with the Monoean warships still on Blood Bay."

He cursed, low. His hand fell to toy with the loose strapping on Seaborn.

She added, "May I ask why are they still here after the attack this morning, apparently un-sunk and free?"

"We're hoping to make terms." He watched her face. Though its militant neutrality and the stiff line of her shoulders revealed little, foul curses had to be leaving a sour taste in her mouth. She knew Draken's past, all of it. His mixed bloodlines. His exile. The truth and lies behind his wife's murder.

"I've had enough killing for one day," he said.

"I haven't."

"If you were here at the Citadel, you could have fought."

Her lips twitched. "I serve you better on the streets. Was making terms your idea?"

"Aye. I meant for First Marshal to handle it, or maybe Tyrolean. Elena is insisting I attend it myself," he said, and went on before she could interrupt. "Before you rant about us dying of peace, know that she wants me to kill them all. It was only by a hair I convinced her of the folly in underestimating the Monoeans' capability for retaliation."

She hissed a breath. "You'll be recognized."

He shook his head. "I don't think so. I saw the prisoners this morning. None were familiar."

No point in worrying her, but even so, he wondered. Kupsyr had recognized him and played him with a gambler's face . . . . Fools all, the man was dead. No one on Akrasian soil knew anything, yet. Draken shoved his mind to the problem at hand. A whole village, slaughtered. It didn't seem possible. But with Monoeans wandering the countryside, he expected it. And he alone would know Monoean carnage if he saw it. He was fair acquainted with the chaotic savagery of wounds left from their seaxes. He needed to see it for himself to make a judgment. And truth, he wanted to know what the Monoeans were capable of. He thought he knew, but this somehow sounded outside that. What purpose would massacring a village serve?

"How far away is the village?"

"You can be back by dawn." She had the uncanny ability to know what he was thinking from only the vaguest of clues. A Gadye trait.

His gaze flicked up to her braids again, struck with sudden curiosity about her heritage. Her skin was darker than his, though they shared their father's blue eyes. Their father certainly hadn't made any efforts to withhold his seed from any willing, and perhaps unwilling, women, but by all accounts his Princess-bride had been fullblooded Brînian. Could Aarinnaie be part Gadye? From their father's side? That would mean they both carried Gadye blood. Perhaps he was more mongrel than he thought, though plenty of Brinians had blue eyes.

"What?" she asked.

"Wait here. I must send word to Elena and collect Tyrolean and Halmar." He rubbed her shoulder gently. "Be easy and have another drink and a meal. I imagine you could fair use one."

He stepped out to find Halmar guarding his door with a slave waiting attendance. Her wrapped trousers and tunic looked in good repair and she was clean. Good. His instructions were being carried out, then. He might have to keep slaves for the economy's sake, but he would treat them like people rather than banespawn.

"Aarinnaie Szirin is within and wishes a meal and wine," he told her. "Halmar, walk with me." He explained about the village Parne as they went down the corridor.

Halmar frowned. "It is unseemly for someone of your prominence to attend the scene of an attack, and dangerous as well. Enemy might linger in the area. I suggest you send Captain Tyrolean or a contingent of the Queen's Escorts to investigate."

Risk Escorts rather than Brînians, of course. "Do you recall I was just at the scene of an attack this morning? Even unseemly and dangerous, this is something I must see for myself. If we go to war against Monoea I would have all the proof of their wrongdoing."

At Draken's decisive tone, Halmar pressed his pierced lips together and said no more.

Draken sent a footman after Tyrolean and another to ready the horses and four Szi Nere. To steady his nerves, he saddled Sky himself. He wished he had time to speak to Elena but it would be better to have facts in hand, after they knew what they were dealing with. Instead he sent a message that there had been a "suspect incident" and he felt he must examine the scene himself. It would alert Elena to stay in the Citadel and perhaps keep any spies busy pondering in his absence.

◆ ◆ ◆

As they rode inland to Parne, out of the reach of the damp trade fog common to Blood Bay, the great moons Ma'Vanni and Khellian and also little Zozia rose, lighting the night. Pickbirds circled the town in eerie silence, a swarm of jagged shadows against the dark sky. It was a plain place; three rows of serviceable, wooden two-story structures in town and some cottages spread out on farms beyond. There was a market square that wouldn't hold more than fifteen stalls, which was enough for this village and its surrounding farmers.

The small party's seasoned chargers shied at the metallic scent of blood before they even breached the gates. Inside, bodies slumped in aimless piles, some in groups, some alone. Vermin scattered at their approach. Blood beetles swarmed over the dead in droning clouds.

Draken pulled his sword out so that it reflected the risen moons, shedding a pure, white godslight on the scene. He blinked and realized he could see rather better than usual for night. An effect of the Seven Eyes? He might ask a priest later. Now his stomach soured at the dark stains spread around each body. He swallowed and schooled his expression, unwilling to show weakness even to his closest guard and advisors.

No one saw him hesitate. They were too busy staring at the death arrayed before them.

"Korde had a busy day here." Draken's voice sounded weak to his own ears and he sketched a gesture of respect over his hollow chest to honor the dead's escort to Ma'Vanni's watery realm. No one answered as he walked amid the carnage. They trailed loosely behind him.

Every body had a stab wound to the jugular. Blood splayed like crimson Sohalia fans. They all lay where they had died, including the children, some gripping toys in soft hands. It looked to have happened in the middle of an ordinary morning. Packages and foodstuffs scattered the roads.

"Something about this isn't right," Aarinnaie said.

"Besides that they're all dead?" Tyrolean said.

Aarinnaie made an impatient noise. "No. It's just . . . odd. Wrong. There's something off. I don't know. I don't like it."

Nearby, the typical Brînian array of jewelry glittered under the light of Draken's blade. Most of the bodies were younger than he was, and strong. This had been a vibrant village. These were his people. Fury surged, obliterating reason and thought. *No. Time for that later.*

Aarinnaie was right. Something was off about the whole scene. He'd never seen this village before but he had the sense it was all wrong somehow . . . wrong even beyond the butchery.

He knelt by the body of a mother, his arm resting on his upraised knee, his armor tight over his chest and stomach. No sign of rape or abuse beyond the vicious stab wound in her throat. Her skirts still wrapped around her legs as if she'd simply dropped dead where she stood. Her two children lay a few paces away. The boys shared their mother's ginger hair. It shone bright against her dark skin.

"Sundry," he said. Maybe that was why they'd been killed.

"No," Aarinnaie said, her tone sharp. "It's dye. A local practice to honor Zozia's Bright Eye."

Draken nodded and glanced up. Zozia burned particularly bright during Trade, even appearing at the edges of daylight sometimes. He had a funny tingly feeling on the back of his neck, spreading down his spine. The gods were watching.

"They are still stiff, Khel Szi," Halmar said, walking toward him from another slumped body. "We are not so long behind the killers."

Aarinnaie added quietly, "There must have been many Monoeans to attack so quickly and ferociously. They don't appear to have had time to fight."

"They don't appear to have had time to scream," Tyrolean said, his tone arid.

Still holding his sword up, Draken reached out with his other hand and fingered the beaded chain belted around the woman's middle. An unused dagger hung from it. He closed his eyes against the sun-dried blanket of blood staining the front of her gown, the ethereal chill rising from her lifeless body. Fury made his blood rise again. "Fools all. What a cruel, pointless waste. They didn't even loot the bodies, just killed them . . ."

His voice faltered as he realized the significance of that. A pack of Monoeans wandering enemy countryside, Brînian countryside no less, and they weren't looting? Impossible. Brînians had murdered and pillaged their way across lower Monoea during the Decade War. Vengeful Monoeans wouldn't let an opportunity like this sit.

"Khel Szi. Will you come?"

Draken turned to Halmar, who led him through the market. It smelled of decay and blood with the sickening tinge of sugary fruit. He longed to sail into Ma'Vanni's cleansing sea winds. Instead he followed his szi nêre.

A young girl's curls shifted over her still face. The light from his sword gleamed on the delicate bloodied necklaces around her throat. He shifted his gaze and put his sword away, not wishing to see more. Ahead, reassuringly bulky muscle strapped Halmar's body, shifting under his dark skin like snakes under sand. He led Draken through more pools of blood and past random bodies to a long low house. There was more wrong here yet. He just couldn't put his finger on it. But it didn't have the feel of Monoean battlefields, and he'd seen enough of them to judge.

"The commonhouse, Khel Szi. A gaol with a prisoner."

There were no dead inside the low-slung structure. He flashed his sword around the corners. All were empty but one. Wooden slats blocked out a cage. Inside a man stood, his fingers clutching the bars of his prison. His gaze widened at Draken's approach, and he lowered himself stiffly to a knee, his head bowed low between thin shoulders.

"Khel Szi," he said, his voice rough with disuse or disease.

"Rise," Draken said.

The man got to his feet, moving as if in pain. He kept his gaze down.

"Are you slave or free?" Draken asked. He had no brand or collar, but neither did Draken's house slaves.

"Free, Khel Szi."

"What is your name?"

"Carock, Khel Szi."

"Carock. Why are you in the cage? Did the attackers lock you in?"

"Attackers? No . . . Khel . . . Szi." Still with the rough voice. It broke over each word.

"Bring the torch." Halmar lifted it closer and he examined the man's eyes. Broken veins bruised the whites.

Draken glanced at Aarinnaie for advice or explanation, but she offered none, keeping to the shadows with her hood up, well behind Tyrolean, Halmar, and the other three szi nêre. Ever the Ghost. No one but Tyrolean paid her much mind, as was Brînian way with females, even those of skill and rank.

"What is your crime?" Draken asked.

"Blasphemy. I was . . ." His voice failed him and he coughed.

Draken gestured and Halmar fetched him a ladle of water.

Carock drank, nodded his thanks. "I was outside, chained in the square, awaiting my muting. I blinked, it seemed, and I was here."

A witness who was insane, or not clever enough to know what he'd seen. Or perhaps he yet suffered the shock of the attack. Draken strode forward, reached through the bars, and grasped Carock's hand to look at it. Calluses lined the palm under each finger. Nothing between the thumb and the forefinger or heel of the hand, as on a swordsman. No deep creases in the fingers marking a bowman. Next he examined the man's face. No bruises. Not a mark on him but his eyes.

His szi nêre edged closer, hands on hilts. The man trembled in his grasp. Draken released him with a low snort of derision. He'd forgotten himself. As Khel Szi, chosen by the gods through the sword on his back, he was untouchable by all but those closest to him and his body slaves. Draken usually ignored that; he had enough trouble keeping his crown on straight without worrying over every cultural nuance. He strode off, speaking to Thom. "This is his lucky day. Free him and send him away."

Aarinnaie hurried to follow. She spoke in a low tone, meant only for his ears. "You're letting him go? His crime must be serious indeed if they meant to cut his tongue out. Must have spoken against you, Khel Szi, or the gods, or Elena."

"What's wrong with his eyes?"

Her lip curled. "Eventide. A potion that makes people not care. They say once you've had it a few times, you can't go without it. He's surely that far gone. It's the tongue that'll blacken next, the nose, the co—" She gave a delicate shrug. "Other places."

All of which made Carock useless as a witness.

Tyrolean approached him, thumb hooked in his sword belt. "My lord Prince, what shall we do with the dead?"

Draken turned and looked back at the massacre, fixing the image in his mind, trying to remain keen to important details. Dread churned in his gut and weariness dragged at his shoulders. This meant war for certain. How could he stop it when there was no evidence the Monoeans did not do this? "The Citadel will pay the bodymongers to carry them to the sea."

The dead had told them all they would.

He rose and stared out, back the way they'd come, toward the sea. Beyond, further than fifty horses could run in relay, the sea met the sky and formed the cloud-bridge Ma'Vanni used to ascend the heavens every night. Beyond the white city of Felspirn on the Lahplon Continent and beyond even their Island Seas.

Divine Mother, what happened here? His fingers gripped his sword hilt tighter. The blade held its ghostly white gleam steady. No answers from above. But this he knew for certain: the massacre at Parne was no Monoean cutwork.

CHAPTER SIX

Word came from Blood Bay of the intention to meet, if not to make terms, at least to speak. Ghotze, Akhanar of the *Bane,* came himself to inform Draken, hauling the Monoean messenger along with him. The unfamiliar, pale lad, skinny under his minimal armor, stared at him closely. A black ash spot on his forehead the size of a thumbprint showed beneath a helm that looked too big for him.

"You spoke with them, Akhanar."

"Alone, as you bid me, Khel Szi." Ghotze hadn't questioned that order. "But they sent this lad back to confirm their intent."

The way the messenger lad looked at Draken, he felt as if a bane breathed down the back of his neck. "How eager to parley are your superiors?"

"With you? Eager, Prince."

A trickle of sweat ran down his back under his light cloak. Draken looked to Ghotze. "And what is your opinion of their eagerness, Akhanar?"

Ghotze snorted and wrinkled his brow. He had spent his life and career on the sea, first as a trader and a merchant, and then taking his place in the Akrasian Navy, though no self-respecting Brînian called it anything but the *Brînian* Navy out of earshot of the Queen. Elena's father's Sword War should have been called the Navy War. Akrasia hadn't attacked Brîn only to get Seaborn but to attain Brîn's fleet and control Blood Bay, for security and trade. That same Navy had been sent to attack the Monoeans and it had taken many Sohalias to recover even a shadow of its former glory.

Ghotze had been in the Decade War. He hated Akrasians, but he hated Monoeans better. Draken expected to endure a series of insults. Instead, Ghotze said, "I couldn't hope to judge, Khel Szi."

Draken waved a hand. "Come. You must have some idea. Speak freely."

"They are difficult to read, Khel Szi."

Draken resisted rolling his eyes. Ghotze apparently had a stubborn streak. He could respect caution in the presence of the enemy though. He gave up, told the Monoean messenger he'd come on the morrow, and waved him back to his skiff.

"I understood you are ordered to meet them as Night Lord," Tyrolean said when Draken appeared at the docks the next day in traditional Brînian attire of loose black trousers tightened with his sword belt, his upper body bare but for Elena's pendant, the Szi moonwrought band on his brow, and white war sigils swirling over the brown skin of his shoulders, throat, and face.

"Khel Szi outranks the Night Lord and we are on Brînian seas," Draken said. "They might as well know how closely Elena and I are aligned. Two countries are better than one, eh?"

Tyrolean returned a bland nod.

Draken grunted and wondered what Tyrolean really thought of him in his native attire. What was the Akrasian too courteous to say? Fair much, he suspected. But the ink was the only disguise he could think of to augment his thick locks, earrings, and tattoos.

The *Bane* was the smaller of his two new ships, a sleek three-masted schooner designed to lead a nimble squadron. She had three harpaxes to use for boarding enemy ships, ballistae, and her small crew doubled as skilled longbow archers. Dressed in dark sails and indigo paint, in the right light she blended with sea and sky until she was within bow range. Today she wasn't sailing in secret, though. Two of her topsails were the banners of Akrasia: the royal Seven Moons on a field of green and Brîn's crimson sea-snake on black. She was technically Draken's ship, the official Brînian Royal ship, and therefore should be named after him. But he'd insisted on calling her the *Bane*. After all, a bane attack had led him to Elena and his new life in Brîn. It was a reminder of all that could go wrong in life, and how it could go right, as well.

The sea rolling under his feet again felt soothing, but his stomach tightened as she drew close to the anchored Monoean ships.

"Khel Szi, what do you know of the Monoean navy?" Akhanar Ghotze asked.

Rather more than he could admit, having served it for the better part of his military career. "I've studied under my father's lectors and strategists."

He had endured tiresome lectures. Should it ever come to war between his old and new countries, he had to know what misinformation and prejudice he faced in leading Akrasia against his old homeland.

"Aye, Khel Szi. That is well, then." Ghotze didn't sound too certain. Most seamen counted live experience as the more worthy.

Good fortune for me I've got both. If he told himself he had good fortune enough times, perhaps might one day it might overcome the duplicity that ruled him now. Nevertheless, he managed to strip the dryness from his tone.

"Maintain a steady course, and keep to their broadside as a precaution." The wind off Blood Bay came mostly from behind the Monoean ships during Tradeseason, an advantage in attacking from the Monoean's position. He glanced up at Thom, who hung unmoving in the rigging watching the enemy ships for any sign of pulling anchor or attack. Captain Ghotze had grudgingly admitted only a Gadye mask could see at that distance.

Draken grabbed the rail and leapt down the steps from the quarterdeck to the main deck where a few of the crew were fine-tuning their speed to the shouted orders of Ghotze, who knew his business well enough to keep to the broadside of Monoean warships and was courteous enough not to say it to the Khel Szi.

Draken focused on the whitecaps beyond the breakers instead of the nearing enemy ships, and he fought back the dread of being found out for a sundry fraud. Though bastards could inherit in Brîn, mixed-race bastards certainly could not.

"Hie, Khel Szi! Parley flag!" Thom called down.

Draken narrowed his eyes. A flag had climbed the rigging of the nearest Monoean ship. "That is well, then."

"Aye, Khel Szi," Ghotze said. "And they do not fire upon us though we are within fair range."

"Perhaps their captain has shifted to caution since the battle and the executions."

Ghotze shook his head. "I think something else stays their arrows, Khel Szi."

"Magic." Or the threat of it. Draken sighed and glanced back at the white peaks of Eidola poking through its interminable mists, wishing again for the Mance King's council. But pressing duties had kept Osias in his mountain fortress for many sevennight.

The vague thought passed that Osias might be magicking peace for the moment. No. Foolish—

Not so foolish, that.

Draken stilled. *Bruche?*

No answer. Obviously. Gods, here was proof that wishes were madness . . .

Akhanar Ghotze snorted, and it took Draken a breath to realize he was responding to his comment about the magic. Ghotze was too pragmatic to hold with such nonsense as magic, even a magical sword, as a weapon of war—they'd had this conversation before. But then, he hadn't seen all Draken had.

"Let them fear your magic, Khel Szi," Ghotze said, "if it will spare Brîn."

"And Akrasia."

"Aye, Khel Szi."

Draken strode to the forecastle, nodding absently at the sailors' respectful greetings. Four archers held arrows on the string at the rail. He peered over their shoulders. They were gaining enough sea on the Monoean ships to no longer need the glass. He recognized the lead ship fair well, the *King's Folly*. Paint fresh, sails mended, the crew moved with precision. Yramantha had apparently done well for herself: a woman whose skin had seen too much salt air and rough wind, a woman who knew the sea and kept tight command. She'd last been running patrols and exile drops in the small schooner that had brought Draken to Akrasia, but no longer. The *King's Folly* was a proper warship, if an aged one.

Draken cast a sullen glare to the moonless morning sky. Curse the bloody gods. He hoped nightmares plagued them all during their daytime rest. If gods even got nightmares.

He stood firm as Monoean bowmen trained their arrows on him. Each had that odd ash mark on their forehead. "What are the markings for?"

Gotze shrugged. "A new sect? Who knows?"

The Monoean warship outmatched them man-to-man, but the Brînian galleon *Reavan* was on tack, set to close in with a few gusts of wind, and her forecastle and aft bristled with archers. Fires to light the arrows burned in metal trenchers behind them.

Waves buffeted the ship hulls. Breezes luffed the sails. Banners snapped. Draken's heart pounded hard in his chest. He cleared his throat and shouted in Brînian, "I am Prince of Brîn and Her Majesty Queen Elena's Night Lord. Who among you is authorized to make terms?"

Muttering rose up on the other ship and then the duty bell rang a single, clear peal. Everyone around Draken stiffened.

"Hold!" he shouted before an arrow could be loosed. Every bowstring on the *Bane* eased a finger-length with an anticipatory creak.

On the *King's Folly*, the hatch to the aft castle opened and the captain strode into view. They'd kept her safely tucked away until they'd determined the Brînians' frame of mind, until he'd announced himself and held his fire. Draken relaxed a little more and gave the order to loose the sails and lash the ships together. Of course they couldn't touch side by side, but bars were set between the rails for the purpose. In the easy seas of the Bay, they should be fine.

Yramantha walked to the rail and gripped it with both hands. She looked the same: reddish hair frosted with grey, narrow-hipped, and broad-shouldered, but for the large black spot of ash. Intertwined crescent moons were embroidered onto the shoulder of her uniform. He lifted his chin and let her have a good look at his tattoos, war ink on his face and chest, his jewelry, his hand resting on Seaborn's plain hilt, and the battered scabbard.

He told himself she would see what she thought she was going to see. He told himself she thought she was seeing a Brînian Prince, a stranger.

Still. They knew each other. They'd socialized and spoken, the last being right before he'd leapt into the sea at the point of her sword. His voice was more difficult to disguise. He did his best to let his carefully cultivated Brînian accent obscure it.

"I come to inquire about a Brînian attack on Quunin in my country," Yramantha said in passable Akrasian.

Draken hand clenched into a fist. He knew the town Quunin. His mother resided there, cast from court in shame over having birthed the child of a Brînian slave. Had she died in the attack? He forced a breath into his tight chest. Or had she long gone to rest under her shrine? At least two Sohalias had passed since he'd had word of her, well before his wife's death and his exile to Akrasia.

He switched to Akrasian and let his voice drop to an ugly growl. "And it has aught to do with us?"

"The attacking ships bore crimson snake banners," she replied, her tone haughty. "*Brînian* banners, Your Highness."

The dried ink tugged on his skin as his brows lowered. Who had ordered ships marked with the Brînian standard to attack? And why hadn't Kupsyr mentioned it amid all his talk of magic? He muttered a curse. Thanks to Elena's orders, Kupsyr was too dead to ask.

And then he cursed himself seven times a fool. Brînian mercenaries would do anything for enough Akrasian rare, or even Monoean gold. Maybe Kupsyr wasn't privy to the attack. Maybe Yramantha wasn't part of the rebel faction. Maybe they were just using her. Or the rebel faction had just used Kupsyr. Or there was some other mischief afoot.

He had to restrain himself from rubbing his temples as the first threads of a headache wound through him.

Yramantha leaned out a little further over the rail. "Curiously, the very next day after the attack on my country, Brînian trade ships arrived at Sister Bay."

"As I would expect, since the Akrasian Minister of Trade approved their route." Though Draken did not know that for a fact.

Yramantha glanced at Tyrolean, who stood close enough Draken could hear his breath. "Think, Your Highness, how it all looks from our side."

"Fair odd," Draken admitted.

"We questioned the incoming trade ship captains closely, but they'd received no word of attack," she said.

He knew well what such "close" questioning entailed. He frowned at the thought of Brînian tradeship captains on Grym's torture racks. "I know nothing of this, but I will seek out the truth of it. My Queen has no wish to war with your country."

"I find that difficult to believe. Your people invaded my country once."

"That was in another King's time. Another Khel Szi. Not this Queen. Not me."

Her tone tightened. "Quunin burned to the ground, including their vessels, destroying the fishing industry and taking hundreds of lives."

He'd already borne punishment for one crime he hadn't committed. He'd be damned if he'd do it again. "As I said, I will personally investigate—"

"Forgive my bluntness, Your Highness. The new royals on the Akrasian continent are unproved. King Aissyth has no reason to trust you."

Tyrolean stood still as stone next to him. A bow creaked. Wind exhaled from loose sails. Rigging rattled against a boom. Draken filled his lungs with clean salt air, willing patience.

She went on. "Indeed, we've heard astoundingly little from your Queen since she ascended two Sohalias ago. My King is not certain if she is rude or frightened, or both."

Draken might be a new Prince, but he was not some pup to draw blade and fight over an insult or insinuation. He carried on looking at her, holding his peace.

Yramantha raised her voice. "Will you come aboard the *King's Folly* and speak terms with me in private? I swear you will be safe from harm and returned in good time."

The deckboards creaked behind him. His szi nêre, no doubt. He sighed. Fighting their guardship over him would just drag things out. But he had to know what she would say, if it matched Kupsyr's talk.

Sorting their positions once they arrived on the other ship seemed designed to drive him mad—who would stand where and such, mild corrections of bravado, and convincing Yramantha's first mate that Draken was not trying to get her apart from the others in order to slit her throat, nor have his way with her in a violent manner. They wanted to hold his sword for him, as well, and argued the point extensively.

"Fools all! She bloody well asked me to come, didn't she?"

At last he handed his sword over to Tyrolean. "Don't cut yourself."

"This is a bad idea, you're going in there alone."

"Everything I do is a bad idea. I'll be fine." He was getting as good at lying as a Reschanian fur trader passing off reedy stag pelts as fine horsehide.

In the captain's cabin they sat at the table, an elaborately carved thing more suited to a Wyndam city estate than a warship. Maps and battle plans scattered the top. From what Draken could see upside-down, one of them was the plan for the attack on Seakeep. He touched it. "You can toss that one in the rubbish."

Yramantha leaned back in her chair, her arms crossed under her breasts. Her bloodstone uniform was embroidered with a design of three inter-twined crescent moons—a sigil that had nothing to do with the Royal House of Moneoa. "I assume you did not spare the prisoners."

Draken bit down on the defensive bile welling up in the back of his throat. "We executed them as humanely as possible. Their bodies burn yet in the tower bowl. A tithe for Khellian and an honor for them. Ma'Vanni will accept them as esteemed warriors."

"That is disappointing. But it is my King's dearest wish this matter be resolved diplomatically and that our countries maintain friendly terms." Yramantha spoke in a rote way, as if rehearsed.

Odd way of showing it, attacking Seakeep. But diplomacy was more about what went unsaid and undone. "It is my wish, as well. I see no need for further bloodshed."

"And yet we have the devastation of Quunin to think of."

So much for diplomacy. "And the attack on Seakeep. Three of our High Houses are dead. I think we have paid our debt—one we likely did not owe."

She considered him for a long breath.

He lifted his chin. "What would King Aissyth have me do in reparation, should we find this is not some ruse by outsiders or rebels to implicate my people and start a war?"

She waited a few breaths to speak, long enough to make Draken wonder if he'd hit upon something neatly. Her answer made him abandon the thought, though. "Perhaps the rebels are yours. Rumors of a great battle between Akrasia and her principality Brîn fly on the trade winds, Your Highness."

"That's why you attacked us . . . because you considered us weakened by civil war?"

"Am I to assume those rumors are baseless?"

His lips tightened into a frown before he could stop his reaction from reaching his face. "The unrest is resolved."

Triumph tugged at the corners of her mouth. "Since those rumors are true, so too may be the recovery of certain magicks linking you to the gods."

Torn between a surge of curiosity and wariness of the truth, he spoke cautiously. "That notion likely raises many questions."

"I rather think there is just the one: *why you?*"

He was still sore from the beating he took during the battle, from fighting, from hard riding, from tension. Her words wound his aching muscles tighter. "Monoeans call magic heresy. In some quarters of Sevenfel you could be beaten just for saying the word."

"In some quarters of Sevenfel they used to hang people for murder." She held his gaze. "Now we *exile* them."

Fine. She knew who he was. "State yourself plainly, Yramantha."

"You recall my name?"

"We shared a dance at the Ascension Day Ball last Sohalia. Lesle was mildly jealous. I am a busy man, Captain. What do you want from me?"

"I didn't believe it when I heard," she said, leaning back.

"That I am Khel Szi? It is my blood."

"The Monoean royal family is also your blood."

"They do not claim me."

"Your mother would, given a chance."

He stilled.

"I thought you'd like to know. She lives. She would beg clemency from the King on your behalf."

"The Monoean kings leave the law to the will of the gods and have done for two generations. Aissyth won't protest the tradition of eschewing my mother, nor her bastard son."

"The kings severed us from the gods," she hissed. "You, Prince, are a conduit to them."

He leaned back from her vehemence, staring at her, puzzling together what she said with what Krupsyr had said. The truth dawned with a chill. "You attacked Seakeep *because* of me."

"It worked, yes? Here you are."

The bloodshed . . . he could barely gather coherent thoughts to argue his point. "A diplomatic visit . . . an audience . . . you only need ask . . ."

A caustic laugh burst from Yramantha. "Who in Akrasia knows who you are, Draken vae Khellian? If I spoke to you thus at the Citadel you'd be dead before nightfall."

His jaw tightened. "My name is *Khel Szi*."

"Indeed." She flicked her gaze over his face, up to the band on his brow. "As your many names combine to make the whole of you, so too does the blood of enemies mingle in your veins. You are supposed to be wrong. Heathen. Sundry, aye? And yet the gods gift you with their own magicks. Perhaps not in spite of your heritage, but because of it."

"I have a duty to Brîn. To my Queen."

"No, you have a duty to the gods. We cannot let you die at the hands of prejudiced heathens. You must come to Monoea. You must take your rightful place."

Rightful place? He was already here, in it. "Your King is sworn to kill me if I seek your shores. My Queen will never let me go, and you should not want me. I am not the godsworn you think I am."

She shook her head. "Nor are the kings."

His heart lurched and stilled. "Monoea will fall if you touch the royal family."

"We've faith to take their place."

"What *faith*?"

She lowered her gaze. "Things could go very badly for your Queen. But she needn't know who you are. She needn't know anything until things are settled at home. She can bear her child in peace."

"Our child. *My* child."

"There won't be a child unless you do as we ask."

"Tread lightly." His voice shook with anger. "Those who threaten my Queen tend to die."

"You had a King first."

"Who banished me!" Draken couldn't make sense of all she was saying, pieces of a cutwork toy with no schematic to put them together. A rebellion? Faith— as if they did not all pray to the same gods? How did he play in? He was no longer Monoean. All he understood was why they'd insisted he come in here unarmed. If he had Seaborn, she'd be dead.

He snorted, a burst of forced bravado. "Elena will not listen to you, no matter what you say, no matter what you threaten. And I will never come to Monoea. Even if I were able, I would never aid you in rebellion against my cousin-King."

Yramantha rose off the bench, opened a hinged box on the lipped shelf along the curving wall, and pulled out a beribboned lock of black hair. It was longer than his arm, sliding on the maps between them like a thin snake. Next to it she placed a delicate moonwrought necklace with a small blue jewel. A child's piece. Draken recognized it well enough. The pendant had been a gift from her mother, dead since Elena was young.

Draken couldn't tear his gaze away from that lock of hair. Another lie, it had to be. Anyone could have cut a lock of black hair and pass it off as hers . . . but for the little curl next to the straight pieces.

He reached out and closed his fist around them both. The lock of hair was silky, sickeningly familiar, against his palm.

"May the will of the Seven become the will of all."

Draken twitched his gaze to her face.

"Come home, Draken. Where you and your magic belong."

CHAPTER SEVEN

Draken sat in the captain's cabin as they sailed back, elbows on his knees, watching Tyrolean think. The familiar feel of the boat cresting over the gentle waves did little to soothe him. He told Tyrolean of the attack on Quunin, and that Yramantha had asked Draken to come to Monoea.

"She seemed overly interested in my magic." His fingers toyed with the loose wrapping on Seaborn's hilt. "They're rebelling against Aissyth. They think the kings have kept the people from the gods' magic."

Tyrolean gave him a sharp look, lined eyes narrowed. "At the moment, I'm more concerned with this Brînian attack on Quunin."

Draken waved a hand, hoping he appeared impatient rather than anxious. "Come Ty, there's not so much to ponder. It was obviously a rogue pirate crew paid by some Monoean rebel lord to attack Quunin. Rile things up, launch a rebellion."

"Your Highness, there is nothing simple about 'a rebel lord.' The last one started a war with the gods."

"Truls was a King and a Mance. And a rotted fool." Draken rose to pace restlessly around the tight confines of the cabin. He didn't want to think about Truls, but Tyrolean had a point. The Mance King had gone to great lengths to secure control of Draken's magic and turn it against the gods. How far would the Monoeans go? Or were they even after the same thing? Frustrating not to know.

He had his own quarters under the aftcastle, but this cabin was closer to the deck. Easier to keep an eye on things. He thought the Monoeans wouldn't harass them after offering terms. Obviously they thought him of some importance . . . and he was ruddy godsworn, no matter how he protested it. But he hadn't exactly agreed to their terms so he certainly wasn't about to turn his back on the Monoeans entirely. He knew his former countrymen too well.

Draken's bare back chilled from the salty wind blowing into the room. He latched the shutters. "King Aissyth maintains an advisory council. Old families, powerful Landed, they're called. Like our High Houses. But the High Houses would never dare come after the Queen."

Tyrolean grunted. "Don't be so certain. Rebellions usually center on power."

Things clicked into place. "And religion is most useful in securing power."

"It's been a valuable enough tool for you, Your Highness."

Maybe that was a joke? Or had Tyrolean taken insult? Draken scrubbed his hand over the back of his stiff neck. Before he could offer amends, Tyrolean went on.

"Do you understand the significance of their using a Brînian ship to attack?" No. Not a joke then. "The entire Brînian fleet, trade ships and all, answers to the Khel Szi and the Night Lord. To you. Whoever did this meant to implicate *you*."

"But I didn't order it!"

"Proving innocence has always been a harder road than proving guilt. I assume that's the same in Monoea."

Tyrolean had a way of unpeeling layers of subterfuge to get at the truth. Dangerous habit, that. Draken quit playing with the loose leather and drew his sword. He sighed at his dull, wavering reflection in the flat of the blade. No ethereal light banished the gloomy chill of the cabin.

Godsworn, indeed. Perhaps the Seven meant for him to die this morning and were having another go. Times like this he missed Bruche's commiseration on such thoughts. "No Prince is without enemies, and it wouldn't take much to light a fire under mine."

"An enemy here at home, you mean?"

"Aye." Reluctance tinged his voice. It wasn't really what he was thinking.

"No one disputes your claim to the throne. You are the legitimate heir, your father's son. He admitted as much in front of dozens of witnesses on that ship."

The ship where he'd been tortured into accepting the magic from the gods. It rested at the bottom of Blood Bay, sunk during Truls' battle and the holy storm that had resulted. Perhaps they were passing over the ship just now.

Draken shrugged off a chill. "Aye. Perhaps that's the problem. My father was not a good man."

Tyrolean gentled his tone. "You've always viewed your magic as a curse, Draken, but it's a gift. I wish you could see that. Doubtless the gods do."

"And this might a way for the gods to prove how deserving I am, is that what you're saying?"

"Precisely."

Draken grunted. "Aye, that's what I'm afraid of."

◆ ◆ ◆

The day stretched into evening as the crew rowed the *Bane* back to its mooring, the first of the moons glistening on the waves and in the darkening sky. Little Zozia brightened the far horizon, flickering from over the sea as Khellian edged past her. A small ferry carried Tyrolean, Draken, and his szi nêre ashore from the anchored *Bane* as darkness fell, two brawny sailors rowing hard against the river current swirling into the bay. The river and sea combined, sluicing though the gate via underwater locks, which split the river in two directions before the water hit the mouth. The massive, rusted contraption let a barge captain easily choose the Bay or a smaller drogher driver choose the caves without fighting the massive drag at the mouth of the river.

To avoid the river, the sailors took a small gate and narrow tunnel cut into the bayside cliff to reach the boat caves. For a time quiet encased them, but for the condensation dripping from the tunnel walls and the oars slicing the water. The shadowy, torchlit boatcave opened up before them. Flowing from the rivergate, water chimed constantly against the ancient, petrified docks, black from ages of exposure to grimy water. A train of six passenger droghers slid through the gates as he climbed from his boat. He heard a string of surprised Akrasian containing his title, but no one tried to attract his attention or pay respects.

Draken nodded to barefoot dock slaves slinging heavy, wet ropes and seeing to passengers and boat repairs. He fairly felt Halmar's disapproving frown from behind him, but he would see the slaves freed one day and in the meantime the least he could do was treat them as people, not wares.

Halmar stepped past him to lead the way up the damp, twisting stairwell from the boatcave to the clifftop. It opened up outside Seakeep onto a large, flat stone platform designed for receiving ceremonies. Pillars surrounded it, supporting an arbor overhead. Brînian banners luffed and flapped in the breeze. The platform provided a grand view of Blood Bay and the waters of River Eros spilling into the sea at the cliff's feet, though full darkness had fallen so he more heard than saw the barges and droghers cluttering the river. Faint shouts carried up from the steep cavern protecting the Eros. Seakeep looked as stark and solid as usual, the black maw of its broken gates the only indication soldiers had fought and died there. Draken gave the Bay a cursory glance, noting the Monoean ships were still anchored. Halmar and three szi nêre clinked softly behind him, his constant shadows.

Sky waited for him, tail swishing, and she nickered as he patted her neck and mounted. He felt a pang of regret at losing Tempest in the battle. The royal breeder had already started the journey to the grasslands to search out his replacement.

Draken crossed the expansive field at a canter, eager to get back. Twenty-five of Elena's Royal Escorts met Draken at the Brîn city gates, standing in two lines, ordered by rank. Their horsemarshal, a woman whose name escaped him, dipped her chin to him. "Your Highness, the city is . . . uneasy. Her Majesty thought it best we escort you."

He blew a breath between his lips, hissing his distaste for the need. But he could hear the pervasive shout of the throngs of people topped by a distant chant. "The Queen remains at the Citadel?"

"Aye, Your Highness, awaiting news."

His message had frightened her enough to keep refuge at his palace then, as he'd hoped. He added dryly, "I take it news of Parne has filled the ears of Brîn."

She inclined her head. "Just so, Your Highness. And your errand this night."

Khellian's stones. No wonder they were thronging the streets. They must be frightened witless. He had to speak with Elena straightaway. "Lead on then. But blades away. I will not have bloodshed this night."

His szi nêre drew in close, and the Akrasian guards surrounded them all. Swords were kept loose in scabbards, backs tensed, dark faces hardened.

Stern, alert city guards opened the gates, bowing their heads to him as he passed. Archers lined the wall and a fresh shift of guards waited inside the guard house, sharpening weapons, tending armor, making a meal. Comhanar Vannis had seen to security. Inside, storied buildings loomed, all soulful, faded colors softened by the sea air and moonlight. In contrast, railings cast jagged moonshadows around balconies and rooftop terraces. The buildings reminded him of aged men and women, worn by a life of work, tattered around the edges but still prepared to get up and do it again the next sunrise.

Or maybe that was just how *he* felt. It had been a long day and all he wanted was his Queen and his bed.

The short inner wall held back the crowd, loud but peaceful, thronging the streets like it was an endseason feastnight. When they were stuck the third time for several heart-racing breaths, shouting crowds pressing from all sides, Tyrolean gave him a sharp look.

"Either you give the order to draw, or I must, Your Highness." He shouted to be heard over the din. "We must get through, even if it means cutting our way."

The Escorts shoved on, shouting in broken Brînian at the people to move aside for the Prince. They moved a few more paces. Sky snorted, tossing her mane and rolling her eyes. She nudged Tyrolean's bay gelding with her haunches; he pinned his black-tipped ears. The crowd swelled and pressed them to a standstill again.

One of the Escorts glanced at Draken and shouted, "We should go back!"

Draken twisted in his saddle. They weren't far from the gates but a mass of Brînians had filled in the space. What in Khellian's name did they want?

The acrid scent of terror rose from the crowd and it pushed two men against one of the Escorts. He growled at them and kicked them away. From Draken's other side, Halmar drew his blade a handspan and looked at Draken, his brows raised. A chant, dull but rising in pitch: *"Khel Szi. Khel Szi. Khel Szi!"* until woman's scream broke it. The sea of heads dipped and rose as a fight broke out nearby. Men rushed into the fight, scrabbling and punching. The crowd tried to back away but couldn't.

Before he thought about it, Draken drew his sword and thrust it into the air. It caught the light of the risen moons—Zozia, the moonwrought jewel glimmering against the expanse of black sky, and glowering Khellian, rising quick as a snarl. Their light sparked along his blade and Akhen Khel reflected it back to the gods. The gods were speaking to the blade, and to him, and even if it wasn't in so many words, the message thrummed through his arm into his clenched heart. And he knew, damn them. He knew. The Brînians were again at war.

The crowd hushed at the holy light. Every face tipped upward and a few of the more pious managed to sink to their knees. The Escorts and his szi nêre stilled. Only Tyrolean seemed at ease, gazing with calm eyes at Draken.

"People of Brîn. We have been twice attacked, this you know."

The crowd answered with an angry roar. The fierce light heated until it seared his palm through the leather wrap on his grip. He tightened his grip and straightened his shoulders, bearing the pain. The gods had once tried their worst and he had survived them. He would survive this too, damn them. Draken twisted his arm to reflect the gods' light around at them. It caught on faces and in eyes. Heads bowed and bodies flinched.

"Parne! Parne is dead. Destroyed!" someone shouted. A few tried to take up the chant of "Kill the Monoeans!" It couldn't get much weight behind it though. Someone shouted something about murdered Akrasian High Lords. Draken waited, gritting his teeth against the burning sword in his hand. When they hushed, he went on. He felt as if he had to force his words past the urge to say something else, as if strong drink muddled his mind.

"The Monoeans attacked, aye, but have agreed to diplomacy in future. They have suffered their own attack . . ." The symmetry of the assaults struck him. His voice faltered. What if the gods drove this conflict? And that was the last thought of his own. His throat swallowed, cleared. Words flowed from his tongue. He was helpless to stop them. A chill filled him, aching in his bones worse than Bruche ever had. *Do you see Akhen Khel? The gods have blessed us with their light and guidance. With their aid, I will solve this. Brîn and Akrasia will be safe again.*

Sky snorted and tried to move forward since she was free of Draken's hand on the reins. The sharp motion brought Draken back to the forefront of his own mind. He strained for control, sweat trickling down his back, reached for the reins, steadied her.

"Go home. Feed your families. Trade your wares. Hold your children close. I . . ." He gritted his teeth but it was no use. He could not master his tongue. Other words burst forth. *I will bear these difficulties for you. I am your Khel Szi, sworn to protect you. I swear myself to you again this night.*

His head bowed and his arm brought the flat of his sword to his brow, the gesture of loyal military service. He trembled, sick inside from trying to resist. The ethereal chill closed in tight, enclosing his heart in ice. It squeezed. He gasped in pain, but no one heard. No one noticed. A cheer reverberated against the buildings and for several breaths, it seemed the crowd would never part. He stared straight ahead, still gripping his sword, body locked in point on the gods' light.

You've proved yourselves, he thought viciously. *You own me. So give your slave a path, give me some aid, damn you . . .*

The icy grip shattered as if a mallet had struck a block of ice, shards of cold flooding from him, scouring his muscles and veins, draining back into the heat of the sword's glow. The godslight shifted and narrowed from Seaborn into a hot, white line that cut through the crowd. Those who it touched shied away, creating a narrow passage wide enough for one horse. As Draken pushed forward, his guards following closely, it seemed a thousand hands touched him, sliding over his thighs and feet, tugging at the loose fabric of his trousers, reaching up to touch the ink on his arms, to rub across his metal armbands and bracelets. But rather than sapping his strength, it seemed to bolster him. By the time they reached the main road leading to the the Citadel his ache and trembles had ceased. He was able to sheathe his sword. His szi nêre were able to once again ride abreast with him. The people did not follow.

"They're doing as you said. They're going home," Konnan said, twisting in his saddle to look back.

"Who are they to refuse the command of the gods?" Draken retorted.

Konnan just stared at him, then blinked and looked away.

"The command of the gods, eh? To the temple then, my Prince?" Tyrolean asked him in a low tone as they dismounted in the courtyard of the Citadel and handed their horses off to the grooms.

"You saw what they did, Ty?"

Tyrolean nodded. "And I saw you fight their favor."

Before Draken could fashion an inoffensive reply, Thom met him at the door to the Grand Hall. Two fresh szi nêre waited behind him, and Kai in case he wished to shed any clothes. He kept his cloak but shed his boots, as was custom. The hall was drafty from the breezes blowing in through the open eaves of the dome. "I need to see the Queen straightaway."

"She is with visitors, Khel Szi, in her lounge," Hina answered.

He frowned. "What visitors?"

"Moonlings. The Lady Oklai and—Khel Szi? Is everything all right?"

Draken was already striding away toward Elena's apartments.

CHAPTER EIGHT

He heard Hina calling after him but it was all he could do not to run. As far as he knew Elena had never met Lady Oklai. What would possess her to receive the Moonling leader *now*? A slave made to intercept him at Elena's door; it was customary to wash one's feet before stepping into private quarters, but he pushed by and thrust the louvered door open.

The place with thick with floral incense. Tiny figures surrounded a low, casual dining table, lounging on cushions. A few Moonling guards stood by, holding their ubiquitous spears. Opposite the table, four royal Escorts waited behind their Queen, hands resting on sword hilts. Elena sat Brînian style, her legs crossed beneath the swell of her belly, a cup of something hot in her hand. It steamed up in the cool air of the room, the fog muting her features. The cup stilled on its route to her lips and her brows raised. A smile broke through her mask of diplomacy.

"Your Highness," she said.

Fools all, Draken could actually believe she was glad to see him.

"I came as soon as I heard we had guests." He strode into the room, letting his big body impose on the space inhabited by smaller people. Halmar followed. Draken didn't stop him. "I am sorry. I was unavoidably detained."

Elena sipped and put the cup down. "We were just chatting about your mission."

"I see. This is all very cozy, then."

"You are among friends. What did the Monoeans say?" Lady Oklai asked.

Draken forced himself to take his time. He crossed to the bowl and washed his hands, let a slave dry them. There was a cushion next to Elena. He settled and ran his hand over her back. Oklai watched the gesture, a smile playing on her lips. It might be misconstrued as fond regard by someone who didn't know better. The lantern light picked out each dapple on her forehead and cheeks. He didn't want to lie and have to explain to Elena later.

"They want me to come to Monoea. A diplomatic mission."

"Out of the question," Elena said. "We'll send someone else."

"Prince Draken has his charms and can be very persuasive," Oklai said. "If my saying so doesn't overstep."

Draken reached for his wine. Better to drink than to correct her. He preferred Khel Szi; the title and name was an effective diversion from his past. He had the distinct impression that Oklai used his given name to remind him of said past—and her knowledge of it.

"Persuasive, aye," Elena said. "But he has his duties here. And our child will come soon."

"I have heard the Monoean people are quite stubborn once they fixate on a notion," Oklai said.

Draken wished for a bitter ale rather than wine; better to complement the conversation. "I wasn't aware anyone in Akrasia knew much about them."

Oklai tipped her head. "It's a well-known trait, one I have witnessed myself."

Draken clenched his fist under the table. "By all accounts Monoeans are intelligent and well-educated."

"And cruel," Elena said. "The world over knows the cliffs of Sevenfel are filled with the skulls of our people."

Mostly Brînian skulls. "That was a long time ago, my Queen."

"You sound as if you are defending them," Elena said.

There. Oklai's smirk again.

"I am a military man. I've got a healthy respect for their capability. That is all."

"Prince Draken thinks we could not face Monoea in war and win," Elena said. "I'm curious about your thoughts, Lady Oklai?"

Oklai's bark-colored eyes locked on Draken. "I think he is correct. A war with such a formidable enemy would surely devastate Akrasia. We should do all we can to prevent it. And as you say, Your Majesty, he has matters of concern at home."

"What possible reason could they have for invading? They don't need anything from us that they haven't achieved with trade treaties," Elena said. Not a question she sounded as if she wanted an answer to.

"There is something we have that they don't." Draken held Oklai's gaze.

"Which is?" Elena said. She looked reached out and selected a piece of fruit so she missed the tightening around Oklai's mouth, the subtle stiffening of her back.

"Slaves?" Oklai said, her eyes narrowing. Draken's jaw clenched.

"That makes no sense," Elena said, impatient. "Why would they want our slaves?"

"They wouldn't. I'm speaking of magic." Draken leaned forward, his forearm on the table, feigning relaxation. Two could play the threat game, damn her. Times like these he missed Bruche. He'd have an idea how to get the better of the Moonling. "I wonder how much they really know about our magic. It might be intriguing to find out."

"Your enemies can learn much from the questions you ask," Elena said. "Something my father repeated often."

"Just as we learn from the suggestions enemies make," Draken said.

"The races keep to themselves overmuch," Elena said. "I've little doubt they all have magic which could be put to good use to benefit Akrasia."

"Or to benefit themselves," Draken said. "Which seems to be the way of it."

Oklai rose. "Moonlings have only simple elemental magic. I wouldn't know much about others' magic nor Monoean reasons for wanting it. I will leave such things to Prince Draken to discover. Your Majesty, thank you for seeing me."

Draken watched their farewells, thinking the Abeyance was anything but simple. When she and her guards were gone, he reached for his cup. The wine tasted sour on his tongue. Were there fresher bloodstains on their spears? Difficult to say in lantern-light.

"Odd little creature, isn't she?" Elena said.

"Not so odd. Dangerous," Draken muttered.

"Draken. She is just thinking of her people. We don't have to suspect everyone has any more of an agenda than that, not without proof."

"'Every agenda wears a mask of courtesy.' That's from a Monoean King."

She raised her brows at him, but smiled. His heart, taxed from the icy grip of the gods and anxiety from Oklai's presence, lurched. He lowered his voice so the slaves and guards at the perimeter of the room would not overhear. "I think I offended you before. I am sorry, Elena. I would have things be easy between us."

White teeth emerged to catch her bottom lip. "My frustration is not your fault."

He lifted her hand and kissed it.

She ran her thumb over his knuckles and lowered her hand, still holding his, to her lap. "Things seem tense between you and Lady Oklai."

"Aye, they are. Oklai came to me asking for help freeing her people from slavery. I could have handled it better."

"What did you tell her?"

"I said Va Khlar advised against it for economic reasons. That it was too soon. And that I would speak to you when the time was right."

"Which is now?"

"The timing's been bad all round. I was fresh from the battle when she asked for an audience. And . . . you asked."

"I was merely curious."

"I realize I have little more than a hunch to go on, but please, Elena. Do not trust the Moonlings. Do not allow them near you. Stay within the locked gates of the Citadel."

She lowered her gaze for long breaths. "Oklai offered me protection at Skyhaven in case the Monoeans attacked Akrasia again."

He hated frightening her. He hated leaving her worse. "We don't need it. I have some ideas on your protection." He explained about the meeting with Yramantha, about the attack on Monoea perpetrated by someone under Brînian guise, and the request for him personally to attend diplomatic talks with the King. Before he could launch into the delicate topics of their fascination with his magic and his suspicions of rebellion, Elena cut him off.

"No, Draken, you cannot go. We'll send someone else."

"The timing is poor, I grant you. It seems to be a problem of late."

Elena ran her hand over her belly. Draken wondered if the baby moved. "No. This isn't just about poor timing, though it is suspect. They attacked us without provocation. We cannot let the Monoeans dictate further terms."

"This is the kingdom of Monoea we're talking about, not some Dragon Isle pirate. They are allies, we value their trade, and they—"

"Outnumber us ten-to-one." She sighed. "I'll remind you, we won the battle and the odds were more like two-to-one."

Excellent. Now she doubted his word and he had no way to prove how he knew Monoean military numbers without betraying his past. "Elena. That wasn't the bulk of their army—it didn't begin to touch it. We lost valuable lords and soldiers. And you—" His throat felt dry. "If I had reached you a breath later things would have gone very badly."

"And yet I held him off with the sword, aye?"

"Aye, my love. It was well done. But there are things you don't know."

"Such as?"

Good question. Which path could he take that wouldn't lead to the whole truth?

"About Parne." Fairly safe, if gruesome, ground. Maybe it would convince her the Monoeans were not to be considered lightly, even though he knew in his bones it wasn't their doing. He told her about the massacre, some details of the dead. Silence. She stared at the remains of supper spread over the table.

He reached for her hand. "I know it's difficult to take in—"

She shook him off. "Did you find any Monoeans? Their trail? Anything at all?"

He bristled under her accusatory tone. "No. We've had reports of roving bands and the wounds looked like they could've been done by their seaxes. Except . . ."

"*Except?*"

Damn. "None of the victims fought back."

"How do you know?"

"They looked as if they fell dead where they stood. No wounds on arms or anywhere but clean stab wounds to the throat." He paused, wondering if he should give voice to vague suspicion. He had no proof, no real evidence of Moonling involvement. But he couldn't ignore how well their spears worked in the Abeyance when other weapons did not. And then there was Oklai's gloating attitude.

Elena pushed up from the table, graceful despite the weight of his child growing within her, and carried her wine to the window. The night cast quiet shadows over her softened body. An altogether appealing sight. She seemed to mostly take the pregnancy in stride, and his role as a father and her highest lord. But should he tread on the hem of her gown as Queen, she stiffened like a sail at storm.

She didn't reach out to him for help nor gesture that he should join her, so he clenched his jaw and didn't move, just rested his fist on his knee. "If it was the Monoeans, I wonder if they had help. Magical help. Something that kept them from fighting back."

She frowned. "What do you mean? Like a Gadye potion in the wells?"

He spoke slowly. Would that it were so simple. "Perhaps. The one witness left alive was on eventide. Aarinnaie pointed it out to me. Which makes him not much of a witness, of course. But he got me thinking." It hadn't, actually, but he didn't want to argue.

"Eventide? That isn't so potent. A whole village potioned into not fighting back? I don't know of a brew that does that."

She shook her head derisively. "Parne is a farming village, aye? It's of no value."

"No value except that they are our people, yours and mine."

"You mistake my point." Her voice was a whip, cutting through the last of his confidence. "I merely mean Parne was in the Monoeans' path so they cut them down. Out of spite, or hatred, or whatever is driving these attacks. They wouldn't loot Parne because there was nothing to take."

He got to his feet. His voice was harder than he meant, but he was frustrated. Never mind they were talking about two different things. "The Monoeans attacked because they think we attacked first."

"They acted without proof."

"They thought they had proof. Elena! A whole town was destroyed by ships flying Brînian banners. Of course they thought they must retaliate. Just as you are angry over Parne and Seakeep, so are they over Quunin."

She stared at him, lips and cheeks pale against the shadows surrounding her. "You *are* defending them."

That chilled him. Was he? "No. But I understand them. If I'm to go as emissary—"

"You aren't going anywhere."

"I must start with a clear head and be cognizant of both sides. Otherwise Monoea will take us to war and they will win."

"Paranoia does not become you, Your Highness. You are Prince of Brîn, a warlord, not some craven diplomat." She spat the last as an insult.

"Was it paranoia, then, when I suspected Reavan of foul intentions?"

"How dare you?" A hot snarl of warning. One he should heed. But his blood was up.

"You didn't believe me then and look how that turned out. Reavan murdered. Countless others dead. Truls dragging us into war with the bloody gods. He very nearly convinced you to execute me."

"Perhaps I should have done!"

"Perhaps," he growled, "if only to spare me from delusions that will get us all killed."

Her cup flew from her fingers like a stone from a sling. Red wine splashed at his feet and spilled over the tile. He stepped aside easily, fists clenched. Her dark eyes were unfathomably feral, lips pulled back in a snarl. Peril squeezed every sense, narrowed his attention on her.

"Apologize at once." Her voice shook with fury.

A small voice retorted to his anger that she was his Queen. He had sworn himself to her. He *loved* her. He squashed it. "I refuse to apologize for trying to make you see reason."

He strode out, slamming the louvered door open. The szi nêre in the antechamber jumped to attention but wouldn't meet his eyes. He wished for boots. Damn these Brînians and their customs. Bare feet didn't make the same satisfying thud against the floor, even with two szi nêre stalking behind him.

Tyrolean ambushed him in the corridor. His tone was one of perfect courtesy as joined Draken in stride. "Your Highness, a scout from the border wardens is waiting to speak with you. I've a sense it's urgent."

"Gods, what now?"

Tyrolean only shook his head mildly. "He wishes to speak to you alone."

Brînian and Akrasian aides hovered around separate tables set up near an interior door leading to the more private areas of the palace. Beyond, candles and lanterns flickered against the bright mosaics and murals on the curving walls of the Hall. Eyes lifted at Draken's arrival. His face must have looked stormy because every conversation hushed into silence.

The scout waited among the aides, not taking the seat that had probably been offered. He paced instead, dusty from the road and still armored, but saluted Draken when he appeared. "My Lord Prince. I am Escort Loir Poregar."

Poregar . . . he knew that name. But from where? More curious, why was an Escort serving in the border wardens?

"Speak freely, Poregar." Draken reached for the cup a slave handed him and gave it to the scout, then nodded to the slave to pour another.

Poregar sipped and swept a glance over the others present. "Thank you. Perhaps more privacy, if it pleases Your Highness?"

Draken nodded and led him down a few steps off the hall to a room he'd claimed as his own, his father's scroll chamber. It suited the purpose for private conversation well enough. The szi nêre took position outside the room, knowing he only let them into his library by invitation.

"Sit, Warden. Have a drink. You look exhausted. Have we met?" An indirect way to find out why Poregar was tramping borders rather than guarding one of the palaces or forts.

Poregar obeyed, though it wasn't protocol for him to sit while Draken kept his feet. Draken couldn't sit still, nor stand still, too agitated from his fight with Elena. Poregar's clothes were damp with sweat and fog, and he shed horsehair onto the chair and floor as his legs shifted; all sure signs of a long, hard ride. "We have not, my Prince, though I was with your troops from Khein at the battle on Sohalia."

Draken raised his brows. "You transferred to the border wardens?"

Poregar dipped his chin. "A short loan only, Your Highness. My brother is Commander of the Wardens."

Ah, that's where he'd heard the name. "I suppose you have some expertise to offer them?"

"Aye. There is a developing situation along the border."

A situation. Draken stalked the room and eyed various things on shelves. They lined every wall to the ceiling, scrolls arranged in some order he'd yet to fathom, treasures tucked amid them: inscribed gifts of state, mementos from generations past, loose jewels of which he'd never seen the like, even seemingly worthless trinkets like shells. He'd left it all in place, half-believing that he might inherit some wisdom from the Princes and Kings who came before him. He wondered if any of them had to deal with stubborn Queens.

Poregar made a slight noise and Draken realized he was waiting for Draken's attention. "Apologies. It's been rather a long day. Which border?"

"The old border between Brîn and Akrasia." Poregar took a moment to continue, gulping down more wine. "Attacks, Your Highness. Whoever does it comes in and kills all the animals."

That got his attention. "All the animals . . . you mean, like on family farms?"

Poregar swallowed and blinked up at Draken, then rose with an apologetic dip of his chin. His fingers were white around his cup. "I mean whether it's an old man on a farm with one goat or a livetrader's fowlpens or a horse breeder, every animal dies. Only four so far but they're moving upland along the border, from the Brînian coast. At this rate they will cross into the grasslands within a sevennight or two."

Poregar stopped. Breathed noisily. Gulped a little wine.

Draken replaced a loose, uncut jewel on the shelf and turned to face him fully. "What aren't you telling me?"

"Sometimes it happens in daylight. One farmer went in for a midday meal, and by the time he came out the animals bled out in the paddock. The worst lost nearly four hundred goats and the latest crop of newborns as well."

That would take some doing. Draken released a slow breath. "Let me guess. Dead of stab wounds to the throat."

Poregar blinked. "Every last one, Your Highness. Have you had a prior report? If you don't mind my saying, we've been trying to keep this quiet. Can't have Brînians blaming Akrasians and so on. Being on the old border, as it were."

"Just an unlucky guess. Were the farms Brînian or Akrasian?"

"Aye, both. And a small Gadye plot that grows the pipeweed so popular in Reschan."

And with a certain Mance King. "Do you know the Monoeans attacked Seakeep?"

Poregar gave an uncertain nod. "I'd heard."

"Do the attacks on the animals predate that?"

Poregar considered, lips pursed. "Started the day after, I reckon."

Draken was impressed. "How did you get here so fast?"

"I was running my regular patrol, which my brother knows, when he sent for me. My route leaves me half a day from the border. So I got there fair quick, Your Highness. A day after the first two attacks. Then I rode hard for the Citadel."

Draken nodded. "What you might not have heard is there was an attack on an inland village two days ago. The villagers were all killed . . . all but one. All died of stab wounds to the throat."

"The one who didn't die . . . a witness?"

He shook his head. "No. Burnt on eventide. But . . ." He had no idea why he was about to admit his suspicions to this stranger, except that Poregar seemed competent and the coincidence grated. "I'm not convinced it's Monoeans that did it, especially after what you just told me."

Poregar grunted and shook his head. "It can't be the same as on the border. No possibility of their traveling so far and quickly. Which means there must be more than one band of attackers roving about."

"Four hundred goats? A small army, more like," Draken said. "If it's Monoeans, they must have put in at the Zozian Coast."

"All respect, Your Highness, it's all rocky shallows along Zozia. No one can navigate it; even the fishers don't. And Agrian is all cliffs on that side, besides that they'd have to cross the mountains. They'd put in at Khein, have to."

"Which wasn't guarded when I . . ." Draken silently cursed his near-slip. Few people knew he'd ever been at Khein, much less dumped into the water by Yramantha to start his exile. "Well. Last I heard."

Poregar's back stiffened. "No longer, Prince. There's been some trouble with piracy down from the Hoarfrost so we keep regular patrols running through there. If they came ashore at Khein they would know. You'd have had a runner by now."

"Right, then. Thank you for coming." He bid him to rest before riding back to Khein.

When he was gone, Draken picked up a small figurine of Khellian and pressed his fingertip against the needle-sharp horns. They drew blood and he watched his skin close over the pinprick wounds. The warrior god's visage seemed no less stern in miniature.

The bottoms of his bare feet itched as if something had brushed them. "A warrior god craves war. Without it, you have no purpose, eh, old man?"

He set it down and sank down into his worn, cushioned chair to rub his stiff feet, scrolls blurring before him. Four hundred animals dead in the blink of an eye. A village of people the same. Nothing solved, only more questions, only more tangled problems. The attacks were related, had to be.

Were the Monoeans so eager for blood? Not the ones he knew. Not the King he had once followed and loved. Things might have changed, but enough to send roving bands killing across Akrasia? If so, rebellion in Monoea must be sizeable and well-funded. He mulled over what Yramantha had told him, what Kupsyr had said. *"May the will of the Seven become the will of all."* A blessing or prayer he'd never heard before. And they'd mentioned magic, both of them had done. He chilled. It was done, then. Monoean rebellion had spread to their shores, out of reach of the King, in search of a willing weapon—

Draken and his bloody, godsworn, magic sword.

Feeling bone-weary, he hauled himself to his feet and walked up the passage to his private quarters without speaking to anyone else. Deep in thought, he bent over a large bowl of scented water to splash the dust from his face and hands. He scrubbed his chest and arms.

A soft knock interrupted his ablutions. He dried his skin with a soft towel and tossed it aside. "Come."

The louvered door opened at his touch on silent hinges. Cut-work lanterns and flickering candles cast shimmering low light within. Tyrolean eased in the door, looking odd with his tight trousers ending at the ankle and his bare feet sticking out below.

"Fools all, you can wear your boots, Ty."

Tyrolean shrugged. "When in Brîn, Your Highness."

"What?"

"It's an Akrasian expression."

"Not a very nice one, I assume."

"Not particularly, no." Tyrolean walked to a low table, poured out cups of wine, and offered one to Draken.

Draken took it with a sigh. "I'm useless at being Prince."

"I seem to recall two seasons ago you were trussed like a skinned stag headed for the spit, a blade at your throat for crimes against Akrasia. And yet you managed to save us all."

All? Hardly. Enough blood had soaked the fields in Brîn that the Akrasians had a tough time finding clean ground to pitch tents afterward. "I had a fair amount of help."

"Help that wouldn't have come without you and the gods to rally it."

The Oscher wine burned a path down to his stomach and bloomed into warmth. The tension in his shoulders eased.

"Are you going to share what the scout reported?" Tyrolean asked.

"Several farms have suffered attacks, similar in nature to Parne."

Mildly. "You spoke to the Queen about Parne and your theories?"

Draken went to the table and poured out a stronger measure. "Heard our row, did you?"

"The Queen has never taken difficult news well."

"She threw a cup at me."

Tyrolean shrugged. "At least it wasn't a knife."

"I'm under a bit of a time constraint. I have to go to Monoea and I can't work out who did it from there." Well, from the Monoean King's gaol, to be more specific.

"I understand she refused your request to go." An apologetic shrug at Draken's sharp look. "Her Majesty summoned me and we spoke briefly."

"I must go, Ty. They asked for me."

Tyrolean shook his head. "Why? Surely there is someone else who can serve."

"No. It has to be me. I told you. They only want me." He debated, then went to a shell-inlaid box, opened it, and drew out the trinkets: the lock of hair and the necklace. "But there's something I didn't tell you. They threatened Elena."

Tyrolean stared, reached out.

Draken placed the items on his palm. "And no, she does not know."

Tyrolean lifted his brows.

Draken rubbed the back of his neck. "She nearly lost the child the other day. I can't frighten her like that."

"She's more likely to be angry."

Draken shrugged. "Close cousins, anger and fear. Both make a person do stupid things, like start wars we can't possibly win."

A soft snort from behind him. "You avoid war more than any soldier I know."

Draken spun toward the balcony. Aarinnaie sat balanced on the railing, legs twined through the metal rods, arms crossed, still as shadows.

"How long have you been listening in on this private conversation?" Draken said.

"Long enough." She pushed off her perch and strode toward them, her hand out for Tyrolean's wine. He handed it over without hesitation. Draken's brows dropped.

"You're right, by the way. The massacre is all the talk. The bodymonger are back from Parne. A few souvenir seaxes have already made their way into the back alleys. Won't be long before they realize those weapons didn't make those wounds." She drank down the burning stuff without a flinch. "Most people are accusing the Gadye at the moment. The brasher ones are focused on the Mance."

"I haven't the time nor means to quell rumors, Aarin."

She shrugged. "You're the one who wants to avoid war. I'm all for it. We got the sword back from the Akrasians. Now it's time we got our crown back, the real one, not that flimsy band you wear—"

"Enough. It's your job to be diplomatic with the Queen and keep us from war while I'm away, so I'd suggest—"

Her tone sharpened. "What's this? Away *where*?"

"To Monoea," Tyrolean said.

"It's a diplomatic mission. The King has requested my presence." It simplified a complicated story overmuch, but he wasn't prepared to get into all of it just now.

Her expression drew in on itself. "When?"

"Within a sevennight." He had to get off this topic. "Why are you here? Surely not to rehash Parne."

"No. I wanted to tell you I'm tracking an island bloodlord nurturing a vendetta against you. And don't feed me that 'All Princes have enemies' line again. I don't like it when your name comes up in connection with such a man."

He grunted. "Carry on, then. And come back before I'm off, aye? Brîn needs you."

"Aye, I shall see you before you're off. But will you see me?" A smile flickered before she melted back into the shadows. Stare as he might, he still couldn't work out how she moved so silently.

Tyrolean stared after her too. "I only hope she can avoid trouble."

Draken snorted. "Finding it seems to run in the bloody family."

"Your sister is a resourceful person, Your Highness."

So resourceful she had once kohled her eyes and posed as a sundry camp slave just to keep tabs on what the Akrasian army thought of her brother, their new Night Lord. Who knew what she got up to in the alleys and taverns of Brîn?

He rubbed his hands over his face. "It's all stacking up. The Moonlings, this business with the Monoeans. The Queen is furious with me—far too furious to listen to me recite the ways she's under threat even if she wasn't in danger of losing the baby. I can't even corral my own little sister."

"I wish I could be of more help, Your Highness. You apparently need more than I can give."

Draken stared out into the shadows of the courtyard and let his eye travel up to the sky. Rising moons glinted off the mists of the Eidola Mountains. Tyrolean was right. He did need more help. And he thought he knew how he could get it.

CHAPTER NINE

Mists and shadows always cloaked the craggy heights of Eidola no matter how hard the sun pounded the backs of toiling Brînians on the flatlands. The base of the mountains were a half day's ride from the Brîn City back gates, though they looked deceptively closer because a gently sloping valley filled with a few farmers and herders separated the city from the mountains. The next day had turned off fair, but with Trade winds came rain, and the ground was muddy from recent storms and made for slow going. It was well into afternoon before Draken started climbing. The mountainside, despite the fog at the top and mud at the foot, was oddly dry.

Convincing his szi nêre not to come was the easiest thing he did all day. They knew of his friendship with the Mance King, and no one in their right minds attempted the path up Eidola without good cause. Besides it being a treacherous climb, people didn't willingly go any nearer to banes than they had to. Draken had been a victim of one of the evil spirits once, and that was quite enough. But he had great need, and he trusted King Osias.

As much as anyone could trust an enigmatic, spirit-filled necromancer.

The trail to the gatehouse high on the mountainside steepened rapidly as Draken climbed. Much too soon he had to use jutting stones and petrified tree stumps as handholds, his boots scrabbling for purchase on lichens and loose rock scree. His scratches healed as he got them, little stings as the flesh knitted. It seemed every handhold made bits of mountain tumble down. His muscles soon settled into permanent protest. His knee worked itself into a dull scream of pain. Again he wondered why the damned magic hadn't healed his old hurts, only his new ones. But he decided to be glad he'd come alone; he'd just end up cursing Tyrolean's younger, fitter body.

Sorcorie Aerie, as the Brînians called the gatehouse at Eidola, clung to a grassy ledge. It amounted to a narrow three story stone structure with petrified tree roots for balcony railings, a grey stone turret with arrow slits, and steep, rusted roof. The whole structure leaned precariously over the trail. Silvery-green vines seemed to anchor the structure against the craggy mountainside. High above it, a magic-infused wall of storm clouds penned in the unsettled dead who had been unwelcome in Ma'Vanni ocean depths. Draken would have called the cloud wall a myth, but he'd seen the Mance-made Palisade around Auwaer, a wall that convinced even those who knew better that it was a void of black nothingness.

Draken paused to rest under the guise of watching a fluffy rundit explore off-trail, its long nose snuffling among the groundcover and scrubby grasses. A voice startled him. He slipped down a few handspans, scraping his palms.

"The trail and gatehouse has been here far longer than the Mance have been. Legend claims it was built by Korde himself for his first servant, before the mountains were gated. He was a sorcerer of some renown, separate from the Mance. It was he who found the way to harness the banes for his own use."

The mountain seemed to shudder slightly, as if to shake him off. Between the climb, the pain, and the mists, he really was losing it. But Draken knew that voice. He forced a smile, but it became easier as a face with dappled skin and silver-streaked dark curls appeared from behind a mist-cloaked boulder.

"Was that before or after the banes attacked the races and mixed them?" he asked.

Setia, Osias's companion, smiled back. "After. To draw attention away from his other crimes."

"Which were?"

"Binding the gods' physical forms to the moons."

Draken raised his brows. "No small crime, that."

"I'd lay down a purse of rare you didn't climb all the way up here for a history lesson."

Draken sighed. "No. I assume Osias let you know I was on my way."

Setia nodded. "One of his spirit-eyes did so."

Draken suppressed a flinch as he climbed up to her, feeling the attention of the dead prickling along his spine. Just as well the ghost was bound to Osias's will. He suspected Seaborn would kill a bane; he'd just as soon not test the theory on the side of this steep mountain, though.

"It's good to see you, Setia."

"It has been too long, Khel Szi. King Osias is most anxious for your company." She turned, missing his polite nod, and scrambled up the rocky trail like a cling beetle. He came along behind, not even trying to match her pace.

The higher they climbed the thicker the mist got, until it sluiced over his chest like an icy breath. He shivered and concentrated on the physical effort, trying to erase the feeling and warm up his limbs. It reminded him of miserable patrols along the Monoean coast, hillsides glossy with snow and ocean spray dampening the sailors to the bone, leaving them with an inescapable chill in the marrow only the heat of Newseason seemed to thaw.

Near the gate house, the trail started switchbacks, which made for easier, if longer, going. A large boulder rested at each turn and someone had graveled the trail recently, since it had yet to be worn away by winds. Setia perched on top of a boulder, waiting for him.

Draken stopped a moment and looked around. "Why does the trail change? It goes straight up the bloody mountain only to turn fair easy up here."

"For bowmen. These boulders are frontline guard positions. It's not to make it easy to climb up, it's to make it easy to get down within shooting range." Setia gestured to the trail they'd just climbed. Indeed, two Mance with bows hid where she indicated. They nodded to him, not a trace of superiority in their expressions. Draken realized what an easy target he'd made. Good fortune Brîn and Eidola were allies.

At last they broached the great stone ledge and gatehouse. No one emerged to greet them. For all the decrepit nature of the structure, the door looked sturdy enough, banded with iron shot through with thick black bolts. Setia reached for the latch, did something vague to Draken's vision, and the door swung open. It was as thick as Draken's hand was wide and rode on quiet, oiled hinges.

An unfamiliar Mance stood just inside, glowing faintly as they sometimes did in dim light. His silvery hair hung in plaits, his eyes were calm, and his silver-edged white robes were spotless. His every feature was pleasing, but for the black crescent moon that appeared like a black wound on his forehead. By comparison Draken felt dusty and rough, less Prince and more ruffian, sword and bow slung on his back like a common mercenary.

"Khel Szi." Mance made a habit of speaking the languages of others and this time it was Brînian. Draken had heard true Mance tongue used to call down the dead only a few times, most unpleasant. The Mance bowed deep in greeting, all formality and no surprise. "You are expected."

"Of course I am. Thank you, Lord Mance."

The Mance either ignored or failed to notice the dryness in Draken's tone. "And you are most welcome. Please, come in."

Setia and Draken entered the gatehouse at his gesture, brushing the sand and dust from their boots on a woven hardroot mat. It seemed odd not to bend to remove them, so quickly he'd become accustomed to Brînian custom of going without. "Is King Osias about? I need to speak to him. It's rather urgent."

"His Majesty is aware of your arrival and will come shortly, Khel Szi. Please, sit, be at ease. I shall bring you refreshments."

Utilitarian benches surrounded a few wooden tables, polished smooth from ages of use. Graffiti marred a few corners, but not in any alphabet Draken knew. Stairs in one corner of the room disappeared to a second story, Draken assumed it led to equally ascetic cot-rooms.

The aerie reminded him of the fashion among female nobles in Monoea to retreat to monastery. Elna's devotees were particularly popular with women trying to conceive and the monks liked the sizeable donations the nobility granted them. It was an effective enough practice Draken had assumed there was more going on between the monks and their female visitors than prayers and fasting. Needless to say, he'd never agreed to let Lesle go.

"Draken. Why have you come? Is it bad news?" Setia asked when the Mance had gone.

He turned to her with a resigned smile. "It's rarely good."

The sun shining through the open shutters brought the dappling in her skin into sharper relief than usual—evidence of her Moonling heritage. He gave her a quick hug. She always felt different in his arms than anyone else he knew, solid in the way of a woodland beast, strong despite her small stature, a touch of skittishness as if she might bolt at any moment. Her little body was warm as sunlight against his chest.

"I see you brought an old friend home on your wanderings, Setia."

"Old?" Draken said, relaxing at the Mance King's familiar voice. He turned to him with a grin. "Our friendship isn't so old, so it must be me you're referring to."

Osias returned the smile as he strode in, his long tunic and leggings as clean as ocean whitecaps. He reached out and clasped Draken's outstretched forearm with both hands. "You're not so old, now that Bruche is no longer with you. What news?"

"Fair much, and little good," Draken replied. He dipped his chin to his friend. "I come to beg your council."

Osias led him to one of the rough tables and gave a distracted smile to the other Mance as he brought out refreshments. "The Queen is well, I pray?"

"Well enough. We had a recent scare and the healers wish her abed. But you know Elena. She is determined to do it all." He sighed, thinking of her holding the Monoean at bay with the longsword.

"Aye, as is her way."

Draken took a swallow of wine, fruity and sweet. Osias waved off taking any wine and the other Mance retreated. "Tell me your concerns, my friend."

"First, I'm off in a short while to Monoea," Draken said. The Mance's silvery brows raised but he pushed on. "Mercenary ships flying Brînian banners attacked their coast. They apparently went intent on making war, or whoever hired them is." He explained about the retaliation on Seakeep. "When I denied ordering the assault, their captain and I came to . . . terms."

The Mance King got out his double-bowled pipe, packed it from two pouches, and lighted it with his fingertips. The familiar twined scents filled Draken's lungs. Osias drew in the smoke and arched a finely drawn brow at Draken.

"No, of course that's not all of it. It's part of a rebel plot against the King. They know who I am, Osias. They know I'm in the royal family, and they know I have magic. I think they want me to use it against the King." His jaw tightened. "They threatened to kill Elena if I don't come, and they showed me they could reach her."

Smoke veiled the Mance's features. His face was set, unreadable. "It sounds as if the King doesn't know who you are. What will he do if you come back?"

"Kill me where I stand, most like." Draken drank more and gestured with his cup. The very thought of striding into his cousin's throne room made the wine sour in his gut.

"Hmm. It makes a pretty dilemma," Osias said thoughtfully. "The Monoean King must know Elena would make war on any who would attack your person. And if he doesn't, he must be told straightaway."

Draken grunted. "She might send troops. Or she might abandon me if she finds out I'm sundry."

Osias gave one of his enigmatic smiles. "You believe your people put more stock in prejudice than your person? I do not think so. You have their faith. You've earned it."

Aye. That. Which could be at the root of Elena's anger with him. But he let it go for the moment. "I appreciate the swords at my back, but we've also pressing local concerns." He told Osias and Setia of the village Parne and about his visit from Escort Poregar. "It just doesn't have the feel of Monoean attack. Any ideas?"

Osias huffed on his pipe and stared past Draken, thinking. "I have never heard the like."

"Nor I." All he'd witnessed at Parne was laid bare by his rough voice.

"Has it occurred to you it might have been done in the Abeyance?"

Draken shook his head. "Of course. But . . ."

"But what?"

Draken's fingers curled into a fist. "Oklai and her war band came to me to ask to free the enslaved Moonlings."

"All of them?" Setia blinked.

He nodded. "But it makes no sense. I think Oklai would have threatened to attack, aye, if I didn't cooperate. And they would have made certain I knew it was them. Anonymous threats and action don't help their cause. But she only threatened to expose my past and identity."

She shook her head. "I don't know, but I can't think of another way the killing could have happened thus. I've never heard of Moonlings on the offensive, though they can be vicious in need."

"Perhaps someone of another race enslaved a Moonling to work the Abeyance," Osias said.

"Or bribed one," Setia added.

Draken played with a table knife, his food untouched. He hadn't thought of that. "Enough of them are slaves. There for the taking."

"Aye. Freedom and returning a spear would be an effective offer," Osias agreed.

"A spear . . . you mean *that's* where their magic comes from?"

Osias chuckled. "You sound surprised, even with Akhen Khel strapped to your back."

Draken scowled. "The gods enslaved me with that sword."

A tarnish seemed to creep over Osias's skin and his eyes swirled a dangerous storm grey. He stared past them all into whatever wonders and horrors a Mance could see. "You still have the gods' favor. See you keep it."

A chill crawled over Draken. He suppressed a shudder. "I admit I was hoping for more pragmatic advice. I've no idea what to do about the Moonlings, nor the killings. Elena is convinced the Moonlings will wait and the killings are Monoeans. She's right in one thing; Monoea is the bigger threat. I don't see how I can avoid going."

"And die there?"

"Perhaps the gods' favor will follow me."

"Perhaps. But I shall, for certain."

Draken shook his head. "Are you not required here at Eidola? And the souls inside you . . . You told me I couldn't cross the ocean with Bruche . . . aren't you the same?"

"A problem easily solved." Osias rolled up his sleeve, revealing the dull thick fetter around his forearm. "Akhen Khel broke a fetter once. It can do so again."

Setia's nostrils flared as she drew a sharp breath.

Draken shook his head. "Osias, no. I can't repeat what Truls did. I won't." The old Mance King breaking his fetter had started a war with the gods that nearly destroyed Brîn.

"I am not him."

"No, you're many people. Who knows if one of those spirits inside of you doesn't have ideas about the advantages of being unfettered?"

Osias arched an eyebrow. "I would know."

Draken sighed. He couldn't argue with that. When Draken had joined souls with Bruche, there were few secrets between them.

Osias laid his arm on the table. "You need me and things are in hand here. Setia will also need more of my magic to do as she must. I can't give her more without being loose of my fetter."

"You mean you want her to work the Abeyance."

"It aided you once," Setia said.

"In a war an unfettered Mance started," he retorted.

"Do you trust me?" Osias asked.

"Funny, I was just asking myself that question on the way up."

"Do you?"

Draken let air fill his lungs. He wanted to refuse but the words wouldn't come.

He started to shake his head but somehow it turned to a nod. And truth, he was desperate for his friend's help. His hand reached back to draw his sword. It shone faintly in the stony light. "Damn you. What will your brothers do?"

"They won't harm me, if that's what you're asking. I am still Mance. I am still one of them. You're breaking my bond to the land, and my will to Korde's. That is all."

Breaking the dead god's dominion over Osias. That was all, with every threat of retribution lying in wait for him. But then, Draken had never let that sort of threat stop him before. Would it anger the gods? Let it. Draken might as well not be the only angry one.

The fetter looked dead, colorless against the silvery hue of Osias' skin. Setia rose from her bench and backed away.

He raised Seaborn over his head and met Osias' stormy eyes. "You're certain about this?"

"Do it."

Draken gritted his teeth, released a stinging breath, and put all his weight behind the blow. The fetter was god-made and even though Seaborn was a remarkable sword, he doubted the strike would cut it.

The sword struck, ringing hard through his arms and chest with an unholy, deafening clang. Shuddering agony rippled up his arms to his shoulders and made Draken fall to his knees. Even so, even gasping in pain, his gaze locked on the fetter.

For a moment nothing. The blow had struck him deaf. The air closed around him like wet sand.

And then the fetter shattered into a fine, icy mist, the sort that gets into the bones and aches for days.

CHAPTER TEN

Osias fell back, shaken and pale. Setia rushed to his side with a low, animal cry. The spare Mance who had served them strode in, eyes narrowed and turbulent. "Your Majesty—"

Draken backed a step, his hands shaking.

"No longer," Osias said. His voice shuddered. "Convene our brothers and select another."

The Mance stared, then lifted his stormy gaze to Draken. His eyes and whole skin burnished dark, obscuring his handsome features and turning him into something feral and ugly—something otherborn. His breath still heavy in his chest, Draken shifted his attention to the sword. Not a notch on it. What else could the bloody thing do? He had a bad feeling he would find out. "You cannot harm him. He is under my protection."

"He is in no danger from his own kind, Khel Szi. But Korde may not be so forgiving." Draken narrowed his eyes at the Mance. They looked quite alike, all the Mance. And yet, something in the way this one moved . . . "What is your name? Have we met?"

"Jaim, Khel Szi." He didn't bow his head. "We met in the Moonling woods the night you arrived in Akrasia."

Draken stared. "You were with Reaven . . . Truls. You were the one I fought."

The first night of his exile, Draken had captured Truls when he'd been disguised as Lord Marshal Reavan. The other officer with him had attacked Draken and died in the fight. The body had disappeared, and it wasn't long after that he'd learned that Mance couldn't really die. Mortal blows just swept them back to Eidola.

A blast of thunder interrupted him. They all looked up, but Setia shied. The thunder sounded like a great hammer pounding the mountain, trembling through the stone house. It went on for a long time—long enough Draken became certain it wasn't thunder at all. When silence fell again, no one seemed too eager to fill it. Draken didn't ask if Brîn and Eidola would remain allies under the new regime. He wasn't sure he wanted to know. He had enough to deal with at the moment.

◆ ◆ ◆

Storm clouds crowded the edges of the sky, obscuring the horizon. By the time they finished the descent off Eidola, the wind had switched direction and held a wet chill. Draken's szi nêre, waiting at the bottom of the moun-tain as instructed, were too well-trained to show surprise that the Mance King had chosen to attend Draken. They inclined their heads to him and murmured words of respect, not realizing that his sleeve concealed only bare skin.

Beyond Halmar, Draken didn't know his men that well. He watched their reaction to the Mance carefully, but none recoiled from him as if they found him repulsively ugly. Solid men, then, with no menacing darkness in their souls. He nodded, satisfied, and turned to Setia. "Care to ride with me?"

She gave him a strained smile. Halmar helped her up onto Draken's mare, then allowed Osias to ride behind him. Setia slipped her arms around Draken's waist and pressed her cheek to his back. She was warm against his stiff spine.

He said little else on the way back, though he was unable to shake the worry that Korde, greediest and least forgiving of the gods, would demand blood pay-ment for Draken removing the fetter. Despite Osias's reassurances, he couldn't help feel he'd stolen a loyal servant from Korde. Thunderheads churned over the sea, crackling with lightning. Setia's arms tightened around his middle.

"It's just a storm, Setia. It's monsoon, aye?" Bit early for it, actually.

"Aye, Khel Szi." She didn't sound convinced.

He lowered his voice. "You think it has something to do with the fetter?"

"You've stolen Osias from Korde. An offense he is not likely to forget."

He glanced up at the churning sky. "What will he do?"

"Try to kill you. Someday, I think Korde will try to kill you."

◆ ◆ ◆

It was full on evening when they rode into the city and the first drops of rain stung their cheeks. Few people paused to dip their chins to their Khel Szi. The hour had grown late and most were hurrying to beat the storm home.

At the Citadel, the Akrasian Lord Ilumat met them, pushing ahead of Thom, who obviously had something urgent to share with Draken if his tapping a scroll against his other palm meant anything. He was a high lord, landed military gentry, a distant cousin to Elena, and recently come of age.

Draken extended his hand to Ilumat. They exchanged grips.

"Your Highness. I came as soon as I heard of the difficulties."

"Difficulties?"

"The battle at Seakeep."

Ilumat's lands nestled in the fertile foothills of the Agrian Range. "You must have ridden like Khellian's horns were in your arse."

Illumat's lip curled. "Indeed. Word spread quickly."

Draken sighed. "I've had a few bad days with more to come, so lets dispense with false courtesy. Why are you here, Ilumat?"

"I'm seeing to the defenses of Akrasia."

He glanced at Tyrolean, who stood, impassive as a blank wall. Next to him, Thom's scroll-tapping sped up. "Lord Marshal Oroli isn't sufficient?"

"I have a vested interest in seeing the Monoeans undone. They murdered my father and our men."

He suppressed a sigh. "That was a wartime execution."

"The war was fair ended. It was murder. They hunted him down like a dog."

Draken blinked. The Black Guard. Had he been the one . . . ? He recalled a few Akrasians among the Brînians he'd hunted after the Decade War. "That was a long time ago."

"Men who forget their grievances tend to die from them."

"Something your father used to say?" Truth, it sounded like something Draken's father would have said.

"My *dead* father." He glanced at Osias and his lip curled again.

Draken would have missed it if he hadn't been watching people closely for their reactions to the Mance. Setia met his eyes; she'd seen it too. All he needed on top of everything else was an unproved soldier-lord with a grudge.

"Be easy, my lord," Draken said. "You'll have your chance at the Monoeans. Thom, you've been waiting to say something."

"The Queen would see you, Khel Szi. She is waiting in your rooms."

He marshaled his sudden surge of nerves, doing his best to keep it from his face. "Thom, see our guests to their quarters so they can wash off the road. Lord Ilumat, we'll receive you when we're able."

The young lord snapped a haughty salute, but Thom gave Osias and especially Setia an easy grin and led all three to their rooms.

Draken turned toward his private quarters, ignoring Ilumat's imperious scowl. He sat on the bench in the alcove to remove his boots. A slave washed his feet for him while Kai undid the straps of his scabbard and quiver to clean the weapons and lay them aside. He stayed on the bench for a moment after they retreated. His hands trembled slightly. They should be laced with scratches from his climb. He clenched them into fists, drew a breath, and opened the slatted inner doors to his chambers.

Elena waited on her feet, alone. He noted her hands were empty. Her dark gaze flicked over him, unreadable. Maybe disapproving. "Your majesty." He dipped his chin.

"What is this business with Osias? Is he just visiting?"

She never missed much. She either had servants reporting to her in the Citadel or some magic he didn't know. He shouldn't sit while she stood, but truth, the ache in his bad knee radiated up his thigh, tightening the muscles up through his hip. He sank onto a carved, brightly painted bench with patterned cushions.

"He insists on coming to Monoea with me," Draken said.

"Did you tell him I had refused that request?"

Draken was too tired for that battle at the moment. "He insisted I cut his fetter anyway." She was silent long enough he added: "I didn't ask it of him, if that's what you're wondering. I just went to him for advice."

"Why would you agree to do such a thing?"

Truth, he wasn't quite certain now that it was done. "He said he couldn't accompany me without it. I don't believe myself in a position to refuse his help." He looked up. "He thinks aiding me is important enough to give up his rule."

She turned to fix a drink. Her fingers tore the fragrant leaves. "It's a simple diplomatic mission. Anyone can go."

"They want me, Elena."

She turned, cup in hand.

He almost ducked.

Instead she carried the cup to him. He looked at his rough fingers curled around the smooth metal and then up at her.

"Draken. Do not worry overmuch. We will choose someone suitable to smooth King Aissyth's ruffled feathers."

It was the many other ruffled Monoean feathers that worried him. "Were you briefed on the border attacks?"

She took his hand. Her fingers were cool to the touch, and smooth. "Aye. Another reason why you're needed here. You shall sort it all, no doubt."

In time to do a damned thing about any of it? That he doubted. His own impotence rode hard on his mind. The truth teetered on his lips. "I do hate the idea of leaving you just now." He could give her that much, before he made it clear he had to go.

He dared to lay a hand over the swelling of her belly. If he went to Monoea, he likely would never see the child within. If he stayed, neither of them would. His throat closed and his words came out tight, choked. "It's been difficult. I want to care for you." Another time, another conversation, he might make a joke about feeling responsible for her discomfort.

"The gods shall see me through."

He slowly shook his head. The gods cared naught.

She smiled tolerantly. She didn't always accept his gruff resentment of the gods so well, but she seemed in a soft mood. Odd, that, after her tantrum earlier. "The gods brought you to me, didn't they?"

And took you from me a breath later. Only by denying their will did he still have her. Was it why Elena felt so much pain? Why their child was at risk? Gods be damned, if they were punishing his family for his bringing her back to life, then they could stuff their bloody magical sword up their arses. He already had one wife who had died in a war with them. Now he had to go against Elena's wishes, return to Monoea to defend his people in the most ineffectual way possible, and likely die for the effort. Would that even be enough? How much more will you demand of me? My bloody afterlife?

"Draken." Elena sounded urgent. She tugged her hand free. His had tightened painfully around her fingers. He took it gently again and brought her palm to his lips. She smiled and stroked her soft fingers across his chin, rough with two days' growth.

"It's not just the child," he said. "We've spent more time apart than together since we met. I'd hoped to have some peace with you."

She sat next to him and pulled him close for a thorough kiss. "I am ever at peace in your presence, my Prince."

The tension in his shoulders gave way. He drew her close and held her, stroking his hand down her back, kissing her, speaking softly, and eventually taking her to bed. But he lay awake thinking as she slept in his arms: this business with the Monoeans, villages in opposite countries destroyed, the magicks involved, animals died and bled out, and their unborn child teetering on the rift between life and death even as Draken faced his own mortality from the other half of his blood.

The slaves did well to leave him with his Queen that night as he moodily guarded her slumber. Elena slept restlessly but seemed to be soothed by his touch. At last, breakfast arrived and their body slaves waited by the door to dress them. He watched them through heavy eyes and his bed hangings woven through with bright beads, wondering if they would remain with him if he saw fit to free them. He sighed. It didn't matter. He wouldn't live to free them.

Elena stirred and rolled over, her cheeks flushed from sleep.

"You look exhausted," she observed, and winced as she stretched. She shifted her gaze from his and laid her hand over her stomach.

"And you look in pain. Shall I fetch the healer?" He swung his legs over the side of the bed, scrubbed his palms over his face, and turned to look at her.

"No, this is normal." She eased up to a sit and leaned back against the brightly painted headboard. "So the healer says."

He wondered what chances the healer gave her for delivering a healthy child. "There's breakfast. Shall I bring you some?"

"That's very kind, but I shall come to table. I'd hoped Osias would council us this morning, actually. And Ilumat is here."

"Aye, we met when I returned from Eidola."

She ignored his dry tone.

Draken signaled the slaves to come. Two carried bowls of water and fresh towels, and others came with clothes. He stood patiently while one washed his face and arms and chest, and Kai helped him bind the loose trousers around his middle with a sash. He settled Elena's Night Lord pendant against his chest. Another slave offered face ink; he waved her off.

He kissed Elena's forehead and seated her on a cushion at the low table before opening the door and speaking to the young slave girl left there as a runner. "Fetch Lord Mance Osias and his companion, aye?"

She dipped her chin to him and scampered off with a skip to her step. Before he could close the door, a footman strode up. "Khel Szi, Lord Ilumat begs audience with you and Her Majesty this morning." His tongue rolled awkwardly over the Akrasian. There was no equivalent for *Her Majesty* in Brînish.

Damn Ilumat to Eidola. He'd hoped to postpone the young lord's company, maybe until after he left. "We'll receive him here." Draken's personal surroundings would both soothe the lord's ego and keep Draken on his own turf. "And tell him to come unarmed. I'm wary of weaponry in my Queen's presence."

The footman bowed low. "As you wish, Khel Szi."

Elena picked at her bowl of fruit. "I've known Ilumat my whole life, Draken. We were tutored together and are cousins. There is no need to insult him."

"Would Reavan have done the same, my Queen, on the heels of battle?"

She flinched and stared at him, her brows drawn and her lined eyes narrowed. The door opened and the child did her best to admit the Mance King—the *former* Mance King, Draken reminded himself—with the pomp and circumstance due. Even Elena smiled tolerantly at her shy diction. Draken rose and allowed Osias to kiss him on both cheeks, and the Mance bowed to the Queen. "Your Majesty, you look well this morning."

She laughed. "I feel mostly horrible; this you know. Please sit."

He slid onto a cushion with all the grace of his kind. Setia dipped a knee to both the Queen and Draken and sat silently at his side.

"I can't help thinking you should still be at Eidola," Draken said.

Osias nodded and lifted his cup of sweet watered wine and held Draken's gaze with his silvery one. "I am no stranger to banishment, Khel Szi."

Draken said nothing as the slaves served them, refilling goblets with wine and blue glazed mugs with honeyed tea. His gaze followed them again as they went about their quiet duties. He thought back to his previous life of servile drudgery punctuated with the occasional beating. They seemed mostly well, here.

"I had hoped to see Aarinnaie Szirin," Osias said.

"Wouldn't we all?" Draken said dryly.

Elena shook her head. "She is such a wild thing, Aarinnaie."

Draken thought of when he'd caught his sister trying to murder Elena. She served him well as his royal assassin and spy. "She needs a long leash and comes to me in her own time. It was she who heard of the massacre at Parne and brought me there."

"You'll have to corral her soon, Draken," Elena said. "You should be thinking of who will best serve you as a husband to her."

Marrying her off? Truth, he'd thought of it but he didn't know who he trusted to handle her with a light enough hand. But Draken had no chance to reply because the shuttered doors swung open to admit Lord Ilumat. He bowed low as the footman announced him, his hair in a thick, smooth braid down his back, his glossy mustache perfectly trimmed.

"My dear Queen, Your Highness, thank you for inviting me."

Never mind he'd invited himself. At least his scabbard was empty as ordered.

"You are most welcome, my lord," Elena said. "I was distraught to hear of your loss last Sohalia."

Ilumat's face creased, enough to make Draken nearly believe he actually mourned his plain little wife whose blood had run thick with High House nobility. "My beloved bride, Your Majesty. And our baby daughter, too. But I must salve my wounded heart with duty to my Queen."

Elena patted the cushion on the other side of her. "Very well. Come. You're among friends."

"And a relief it is, my Queen." He sat by her, took her hand, and bent his head to touch his forehead to her fingers.

"Please, my lord, tell me what news from the shadows of the Agrian Range? And Auwaer. Did you visit?"

Ilumat's grief hardened to indignant rage. "I never made it into the royal city. There was a slaughter on my own lands, Your Majesty. An entire youngling herd, cut down. The carcasses were destroyed, pelts were so slashed and blood-stained I could salvage neither wool nor leather. We had to burn the lot and I spent my entire time home soothing my servants before rushing here. Their worries are not unfounded. It will be all I can do to feed them over Frost now."

"Have you caught the perpetrators?" Draken's skin prickled, guessing the answer.

"No. They left no mark of themselves. My herdsmen were killed with them."

"How long had it been between the deaths and your discovery?" Osias asked.

Ilumat shook his head. "Some nights, Lord Mance. Perhaps a sevennight."

"Seems a long while," Draken observed.

"They weren't due back for another two sevennight. Still fattening them and letting the wools grow. Market is after the fifth fullrise." The last he added with a condescending glance to Draken, as if he wouldn't possibly know when market took place nor understand how managing lands went.

Which of course he didn't. Draken swallowed the snarl clawing at the back of his throat. "Perhaps Lord Va Khlar can help solve your financial woes. He knows finance and the markets better than us all."

"Indeed." Ilumat maintained careful control over his expression, but he surely nurtured the full-blooded disdain against sundry commoners rising above their station. "Tell me of the attack on Seakeep. Members of the High Houses are dead, my man told me this morning."

Draken doubted that. He'd seemed well-informed yesterday on his arrival. But he explained in short terms what had happened, and that the Monoeans had requested a diplomatic visit.

"Who shall go?" Ilumat asked.

As if Draken wanted this arrogant upstart permanently damaging relations between Monoea and Akrasia. "They requested me, actually."

Ilumat's sculpted brows rose. Draken wondered if they'd been shaved that way with a blade. "The Brînian Khel Szi, handling relations for Akrasia," he said. "I hadn't thought of it."

"I am also Night Lord," Draken said.

"Of course. It's just . . ." His gaze flicked over Draken and his upturned lip tightened. "I rather assumed we had a proper ambassador in Monoea already."

"Not since the Decade War," Draken answered before Elena could.

She shook her head and stabbed a piece of fruit. "It doesn't matter. Draken is needed here."

"Aye, it seems we all are. A shame the High Houses Elders were killed. They've the leisure and means to make such a journey." Ilumat shrugged. "I'd volunteer, but it's a particularly bad time for me."

Draken's lip twitched at Ilumat's audacity. The elders had been valued members of rank in Akrasia, not feedstock dead from gasping sickness. He opened his mouth to retort; Osias shook his head very slightly.

He reconsidered and spoke slowly, as if conceit hindered Ilumat's speed of thought, which he suspected it did. "Very generous of you to offer but we must send someone of high rank. To do else is to insult the King, as well as risk losing the ambassador to an execution. Having just killed prisoners to prove a point, I'd hate to see the same happen to one of our inexperienced, low-rank nobles." He fixed Ilumat with a mild gaze. "As well, such important diplomacy takes some care."

Ilumat's lips whitened. It took a drink of wine to stain them back to regular color. "I'd suggest Va Khlar but I am certain he is loathe to leave Reschan. Protection fees run high during Trade. I daresay he survives off the coin earned in these few sevennight."

Draken set his jaw against challenging the insult. Va Khlar was capable of defending himself. He was Baron of Reschan now, even if they called him the Baron of Extortion behind his back. "You're right. There is no one else. It's why I think we should accept their request to host me."

"Draken. We've been all through this," Elena said.

"Except we haven't," Draken said. "We've barely discussed it." He abruptly made his mind up. He would go, regardless of her permission. There was no other course. Gods willing, maybe someday she would understand.

"If I may, my Queen," Ilumat said.

Draken hissed a breath. If Ilumat didn't curb his tongue, he couldn't be held responsible—

"I agree with the Prince," Ilumat said.

Draken twitched. "Sorry?"

"I agree with you. It's extraordinarily poor timing, but Monoea is a valuable ally and a perilous foe. If they have requested Prince Draken to attend talks, I think we've no choice but to agree, Your Majesty, no matter our personal concerns."

Elena set her table knife down with a soft tap of metal against wood. She was quiet for several breaths, or would have been several breaths if Draken had remembered to draw air into his lungs.

"If he leaves now," Ilumat added, "he can be back well before the baby arrives."

A sigh. She turned her head to look at Draken. He opted to say nothing. He was going, with or without her blessing, and he would likely die for his trouble. He wondered abruptly if it would be better if she refused him, if only to assuage her guilt later. Better she hate him, perhaps, than feel responsible for his death. He knew what it was to live with another's blood on one's hands.

"I see reason now, though I am loathe to let you go," she said softly.

He wished they were alone. "Ilumat speaks true. If I leave within a few days I can be back for the child."

She bit her lip and blinked, met his gaze. He closed his hand around hers under the table.

"You mustn't worry, Your Highness." Ilumat's free hand traveled down to stroke his empty scabbard. "Queen Elena is my dearest friend. I swear to keep close to her."

◆ ◆ ◆

Tyrolean was sent aboard the *Bane* to inform the Monoeans of Draken's impending diplomatic journey, and Draken ordered him privately to beg them to stop killing his people and their animals. He wondered what they'd say to that, or if the Monoeans aboard ship even had the means to stop any Monoean marauders. But not knowing precisely who was at fault, and the curious sigil that unrelated groups wore, made him feel as if he must tighten every knot.

All through a long day of enduring tailors measuring him for a diplomacy wardrobe, leaving instructions for Thom, fending off diplomatic advice—some well-meaning and some not so much—and a grueling formal dinner with local lords and families, Elena was never far from his thoughts. Besides having been away from her capital city for too long, she would be safer within the dual protection of the magical Palisade and her own Royal Bastion surrounded by hundreds of Escorts. Draken told her as much once they were alone.

Her back stiffened and she crossed away from him. "I realize you think it's your duty—"

"Truth, it's entirely *duty* on my part for wanting to keep you safe." Sarcasm nipped on the heels of courtesy. He realized his mistake too late. "Pardon, my Queen. I am too familiar." Though he could hardly become *more* familiar as her lover.

He tore his gaze from her exquisite face, strained in anger, and let his back straighten to attention. "Will you at least keep Tyrolean close?"

"I have Marshal Oroli and Lord Ilumat."

"Ilumat." The word was sharp as a dagger.

"You aren't jealous?" She shook her head. "I told you, he is a dear friend and my cousin—"

"And in the market for a new wife since he lost his last one."

Her tone tightened. "That was very unkind."

But truth. And Ilumat was of a rank to marry Elena where Draken could not. He gritted his teeth. She wouldn't understand anyway. She didn't want to understand. Ilumat's flattery probably reminded her of her mistakes with Reavan.

"You must take Tyrolean," she said. "His loyalty is with you now."

Stubborn resentment overcame good sense. "Only because my loyalty lies with *you*. I am your Night Lord and sworn above all else to protect you. I must go away, so the least I can do is find a suitable replacement to guard you. You will be safest with Tyrolean."

"I saw to my own security quite effectively before I knew you."

Even with his blood running high he didn't dare bring up Reavan again. "Do you know what *Szi* means?"

Her bottom lip twitched. "Serve."

"Aye. And that is all I'm trying to do. Serve Brîn. Serve Akrasia. But I cannot serve them without serving you first. It is my duty to keep you safe."

Her jaw clenched, forming hard lines around her mouth. She reached out and curled her fingers around the pendant bearing her image. Her knuckles whitened. For a moment Draken wondered if she would take it back, sever the ties that bound them. Instead she gave it a sharp tug, released it, and swept away with a rustle of skirts.

He started to follow. But Elena snapped a few words to the szi nêre and her own guards in the corridor outside and strode on. Her guards stared after her, nonplussed.

Tyrolean filled the doorway. He met Draken's gaze with all the affability of a stone wall. "Your Highness."

"I need a drink."

"Your Highness—"

"Out." Draken spat the word. The idea of the sea rolling a ship beneath his feet was appealing. "Away from here."

He retreated to change into plain clothes and slung his sword onto his back in Brînian bloodlord style, glad for its unraveling leather grip, battered scabbard, and dulled hilt. Despite its magical properties and keen edge, few would recognize it for what it was.

A hard stare kept his szi nêre from accompanying him close as shadows, but they followed with bows by rooftop and with blades by street. There were taverns plenty off the market, but he worried about being recognized, so he led them off-market to a scratchy-looking place with muddy hay on the dirt floor and patrons who didn't study each other too closely.

Tyrolean leaned over his flagon of ale at a sticky table. The dual curving pointed sword grips stuck up over his shoulders like half-grown horns of Khellian. He spoke over the raucous voices of trades going poorly, the crooning of whores plying their wares, and the drunk taleteller in the corner. "Care to talk about it?"

"No. What did the Monoeans say?"

Tyrolean pursed his lips before drinking again. "The Captain didn't sound surprised."

"And the killings? Parne? Did you mention it?"

"Aye, as ordered." Tyrolean was unruffled by his terse tone. "She denied it, of course."

"Of course." He wondered if Yramantha would wait for him, if they would accompany the *Bane* to Monoea. He bloody well hoped not.

The serving lass appeared. She studied Draken a moment before snatching up some money and pouring. For a moment, he feared she recognized him and would say something. But Draken's face was on no coin, and without his szi nêre and fine clothing, it was easy enough for him to pass as the bloodlord of his fabricated history. Even Tyrolean drew little but a cursory glance; Akrasians and other races filled Brîn for Tradeseason. Merchant meetings were happening all over the city. The server trotted off and Draken's shoulders relaxed a little as he glanced around at the patrons of the crowded tavern.

A rousing company in the corner drew his eye; a few brawny ruffians of the sort who found employ guarding wealthy merchants flirting shamelessly with a slight Gadye woman. A multitude of long braids sprouted off her head like bent stalks of blackgrass. She turned her head to talk to one of them and Draken sucked in a breath.

"Khellian damn me, that's Aarin."

Tyrolean twisted to look and then turned back to Draken. His top lip twitched and his nostrils flared. "Shall I fetch her?"

Her companions seemed to be playing a game of sorts, something involving flipping a knife so that it landed point down in the middle of the table. Aarinnaie took a turn, clumsily, and the men roared in raucous laughter, jostling each other. One of them didn't laugh as hard as the others, though. His eyes were deepset, shadowed by thick brows and a lined forehead. Maybe it was just the look of him, but his attention seemed drawn outside their little group.

Draken narrowed his eyes. Aarinnaie was sitting with her back to the room. Odd, that. "No. I want to see what she's up to. Who is that she's with, reckon?"

"No idea. We can ask." Tyrolean nodded and drained his flagon and lifted it to the serving girl. She bustled over and took a coin from the stack while simultaneously pouring. "Those men by the back door. Are they regulars? No, do not look just now." Shadow-eyes was perusing the room past his companions.

She aborted her glance over her shoulder and nodded. Even so, the shadow-eyed man turned his face in their direction. "Most nights, 'less they're working, my lord."

Draken was dressed as no lord, but her gaze had flicked downward. The chain to Elena's pendant must be showing from under his collar. "Working at what?"

"Tradeguarding."

Draken had no idea what that was. He dismissed her with a wave of his hand. "Thanks, lass."

"Profiteering." Tyrolean said when she was out of earshot. "They take bribes for 'protection.' Ships, taverns, merchants. Whoever they can intimidate."

Draken shrugged. Such activity might not mean they were so dangerous— though they might work for someone who was. But his curiosity about why Aarinnaie had singled them out was piqued. Maybe it had to do with her last report. "Is such activity legal?"

"Your father did not persecute such, if that's what you're asking."

"And Elena's father? Did he?"

Tyrolean drank and considered the foam slicking the inside of his rough clay mug before answering. "The King had more to worry about than Tradeseason crime in Brîn."

Another round of laughing jeers. A couple of them tossed coins toward Aarinnaie and she scooped them up as they bounced and rolled.

"She does well to hide her ability," Tyrolean said.

"No one thinks she can fight at any rate," Draken said. "She's so slight." He'd made that mistake himself.

They sat a good while, drinking another round and talking. He couldn't watch as carefully as he liked, but Draken deduced the men treated Aarinnaie as one of them. She didn't wear the wide-legged trousers favored by so many men and women in Brîn, but a long, loose tunic over tight trousers and boots, drogher driver apparel for cooler weather. Rolled up sleeves bared blades at her wrists. With her many braids, maybe they took her as Gadye-Brînian sundry.

Only purebloods like Thom got the moonwrought mask embedded into half their faces, enabling their healing and sight magic.

At last the group all got up and walked out, Aarinnaie with them. Draken downed his drink and started to rise; Tyrolean reached over and grasped his forearm. "Not yet."

"We should go after her," Draken said.

"She can handle herself. If she's spying on these men, our presence won't help."

They looked rough. Draken knew on some level she managed men like this all the time. On the other hand . . . "She's my sister."

"She's also your assassin," Tyrolean said.

Shadow-eyes lingered near the door. Surely not for another drink; custom demanded they only serve those seated with coins to hand. After several breaths Draken realized the man wasn't moving. Aarin would soon gain too much distance to follow.

"I don't like it. Why has he stayed if not to keep someone from following. And why would he keep someone from following if it were on the level?" Draken pushed back from the table. "Best get it over with."

Tyrolean released an uncustomary, noisy sigh and rose.

Shadow-eyes slid between them and the door, right on schedule. The man moved like a fighter: contained, solid, calm. Typical Brînian, loose trousers with a sea-faded pattern, rough feet bare, as was his chest. Spiraling tattooes centered on pierced nipples. Dull metal rings punctured each earlobe and his nasal septum. Up close Draken could see why his eyes were so dark; bruising stained the whites brackish grey. Eventide, then; a longtime user.

Draken paused and drew himself up, ignoring the catch of tight muscle in his lower back. "Problem?"

"You're paying a little too much attention to the lady. She's taken."

"Oh?" Draken asked mildly. "By who?"

"Me."

Draken made a show of glancing about. "She's not actually *with* you at the moment."

"So you don't deny your interest in her."

Draken just held his gaze.

"Blue eyes," the man hissed. "Like hers. Sundry. Who are you?"

His blue eyes had come from his father. Had *he* been sundry? Perhaps Draken was more of a mongrel than he'd realized.

He reached down and grasped the man's arm, lifted it to the light. Brands peaked from beneath leather bracers. "Bloodlord."

"An islander, aye. Like yourself."

Draken was fair certain he didn't mistake the man's dry tone. He locked eyes with the man. They were of a height and matched in breadth.

"They're noticing." Tyrolean.

Draken's lip curled. Fine. He'd give them something to look at then. He slammed against the man, shoving him out into the little walled courtyard that on fine days would be filled with patrons. The man reached for his sword, but Draken pressed him back against the shoulder-high wall, trapping his blade between his back and the stone. The man grunted but Draken had leverage to hold him.

"You're going to take me to her," Draken said.

The man spat at his face, momentarily blinding him. Draken blinked and the man shoved, making Draken back a step. The man went for a dagger at his belt, jabbed it toward Draken. It sliced through his shirt and into the skin under his ribs, forcing Draken back again. He winced at the cut and went for his sword, but the motion left him open. The man snarled and slashed out again, but one of Tyrolean's narrow sword blades nicked the man under the chin, slicing through the tender skin there. Blood welled from the narrow cut and dripped down his throat. The man froze, forced to lift his chin lest Tyrolean's blade cut him again. Draken shrugged out from between them.

"You would dare defy your Khel Szi?" Tyrolean murmured.

The man blinked his muddied eyes and flicked his gaze to Draken's face. "No. That's impossible."

Draken tipped his head and shrugged. "The lady is my sister. Aarinnaie Szirin. Obviously I'm most interested in her destination."

The man stared, swallowed. "They'll kill me if I take you."

Or withhold his drugs, more likely. No matter what he said before or his brands, the man was obligated to whoever Aarinnaie was investigating.

Tyrolean released him but kept the swordpoint wavering near him. "Take us or it will be my pleasure to cut your rotten heart from your worthless body. Give us your weapons."

His gaze flicked between them again. His lips in a thin line, he slowly drew his sword and handed it to Draken, and then his dagger. Tyrolean put his blade away and searched the man, coming up with two more daggers. He gestured with one of them. "After you."

"This way," the man said, and strode past them.

Draken's nerves ran hot and high. The ordinary population on the street parted for them; bloodlords with determination in their strides made paths best avoided.

The man strode without talking, quickly splitting off into a nearby alleyway and along the backs of the buildings. Tall craggy walls closed in tight on either side. Insects swarmed, trapped amid the waste smells and piles of rubbish. Draken wiped them away but they tormented his eyes and ears. He cursed and ducked his head, waving his arm again. They walked for blocks, darted between horses and carts across a street, and into another alley. Shadows closed in ahead; the buildings made a dead end. It was partially blocked by an abandoned cart. Shadow-eyes shoved it aside. A small group crowded behind it, standing amidst the rubbish, centered on Aarinnaie. Her hands were fisted. No knives out. Yet.

One man was so black in clothing and skin Draken had a tough time making out detail in the dim light, like weapons. Another bald man had a long-sword strapped across his back and was tall enough to wield it with ease. The third seemed younger and more skittish; he bounced on the balls of his feet and had some rudimentary bits of armor, thin, cheap leather. No weapons to hand; he must think he wouldn't need them against this mere slip of a young woman.

Her gaze flicked from the three men surrounding her to the newcomers. Her eyes narrowed. Draken pushed ahead of Shadow-eyes. Tyrolean grunted and strode closer. Too late, Draken realized it could be a trap for him. Gods curse him, he was so eager to get to Aarinnaie he had forgotten to *think*.

He drew a breath so he would sound off-hand rather than alarmed. "Bite off rather more than you could chew?"

The men looked back at him; eyes narrowing in quick assessment. He knew what they saw. Whatever weight Draken had lost in Monoean gaol and the abuses he'd suffered at the hands of the Mance King last Sohalia had been more than replenished by hard training with Tyrolean and a rich Prince's diet.

Aarinnaie snarled and her body tightened. "I'm fine, nêrel baak." *Warrior-brother.*

He forced back his annoyance and gentled his tone. "I was talking to *them*, sishah."

She frowned at his use of the affectionate form of sister.

"Sisk?" *Sister.* The big one frowned, a flash of silver at his teeth. His eyes were bloodshot, though not bruised like Shadow-eyes's.

Draken could not read minds as the Mance did nor how the Gadye seemed to. Maybe because he knew Aarinnaie and because she knew him so well, he guessed her torn thoughts and dilemma in that moment: should she shelter her ability or shelter her position? This dilemma he could solve for her, if not in a particularly pretty manner. But he had Tyrolean at his back. She was trapped alone against the wall, three hulking bloodlords between her and him.

He wished for an ambiguous bow. He wished for anonymity. But he only ever carried one sword. *Feel free to keep quiet*, he thought at it. But as he drew, Seaborn glowed in the dim light filtering between the clothing strung overhead to dry and reflected off the worn stone of the buildings.

"Ahken Khel," the darkest breathed. His eyes were very white in his face, his teeth yellow between his lips.

Draken held his gaze. "Aye, so lay down your arms and no one has to—"

The darkest leapt toward Aarinnaie, curses hissing from his lips even as blades hissed from their sheathes. She moved soundlessly to meet him, knives flashing in her hands. Draken didn't give her good odds; the man was immense compared to her. He moved toward her, but the big swordsman engaged with him. He didn't attack outright, but more put himself in Draken's way with perfect form and expert slashes of the longsword to hold him at bay. Draken heard scuffling and grunts behind him; Tyrolean must have engaged Shadow-eyes. The third, younger man closed in on Aarinnaie's other side in tandem with the dark one.

Draken grunted and slashed, knocking the swordsman's longer blade out of the way. The blow resonated up his arm, still sore from the fighting he'd done the day before. But it made an opportunity for him to slip through. Aarinnaie dashed at the darkest fighter, using her diminutive size to her advantage. Draken had always wondered how she managed to kill warriors twice her weight; now he saw she used her opponent's own chauvinism against him. Quick and agile, she darted inside her opponent's guard, stabbed her blade up into his chin, and shoved him away almost before blood spouted from the wound, bright crimson against his black clothing. This flashed in the corner of Draken's eye; he was too busy striking Seaborn across his opponent's back. The ready blade sliced through the thin leather armor as if cutting hot oil. The dark man fell with a ragged scream, hands scrabbling at the dirty stone floor of the alley, trying to twist onto his stomach, but not moving from the middle down. His eyes glowed in his dark face. Draken kicked his sword away and finished him off with a messy swing at his throat. More thick blood fouled the air.

Behind Draken: footsteps, a rough slamming noise and a violent grunt. Draken spun. The bald man lay dead at Tyrolean's feet, blood draining from two neat puncture wounds, eye and jugular. Shadow-eyes was gone. Tyrolean leaned against the wall, chest heaving. His dual blades hung loosely at his sides. His arm bled in a thick stream down his hand; a nasty slash had torn through his tunic. He didn't curse, but his alabaster skin had taken on a grey cast in Seaborn's bloodstained glow

"Tyrolean!" Aarinnaie jumped over the big man she'd killed and pushed by Draken. She gently pried the weapons from Tyrolean's hands, laid them carefully on the ground, and examined the flooding wound. She reached to lift his tunic.

"I'm all right, Princess." Tyrolean drew back.

She growled, pulled her other wrist blade, and sliced off the hem of her long tunic to bind the wound. "The arm wound is fair deep, Captain."

"And your middle?" Draken asked.

"Shallow. Ribs stopped it. We should get back."

Tyrolean was right. They needed to move on. Shadow-eyes could return with friends. He knelt and wiped his sword clean on the dead swordsman's thigh. His wounds had done the job but lacked the efficient finesse of an expert. Doubtless his performance would be a topic for his next training session with Tyrolean.

"Who are they?" Tyrolean asked.

Aarinnaie scowled at his arm as she wrapped it tightly. "Your attackers on Monoea—or related to them, at any rate. You two ruined my cover."

"Some cover, given they were holding knives on you," Draken said.

"It was just a fight to prove my worth. An initiation." Irritation clipped every word.

Draken shook his head. "Aarin, I know you feature yourself my spy—"

"Who else have you got?"

He ignored that. "They're just a few ruddy mercs."

"No." The word sounded like an arrow hitting stone. She drew in a breath and straightened her shoulders. "That one," she nudged the giant dark man with the toe of her boot, "is the son of the most powerful islander family. Father shamed them once. Khisson is a bad enemy, and he wants revenge on our house. He also still harbors great resentment for the Akrasians. He thinks we should enslave everyone who isn't Brînian. That you've taken up with the Queen and are fathering a bastard sundry destined for the 'Wrought Throne only fuels his ire."

He squatted by the dead man. On his hands were brands of three intertwined crescent moons. He narrowed his eyes. The same as had been embroidered on Yramantha's uniform. "So you believe they accepted a commission to attack Monoea?"

"I don't believe it. I know it."

"This might be best discussed back at the Citadel," Tyrolean said, voice tight.

"You know all I do, now." Aarinnaie glanced at Tyrolean. "I need to keep my ear to the ground and I can't do that locked away in the Citadel. The other Khisson got away to tell the tale. I need to stop him talking."

Draken frowned. Khisson was a proper Brînian name, old and respectable. He knew he'd heard it somewhere before. "Aarinnaie—"

She narrowed her eyes. "You aren't going to try to order me home, are you?"

"He *is* your Prince," Tyrolean said gently.

She looked impossibly young to be splashed in blood. Once they had been at odds. Draken had gone to great lengths since to keep that from happening again, granting her the freedom she craved. She built too many walls around herself, but he didn't dare tear them down. She might need them. She would need them, when she no longer had him to protect her. "No. I'm not ordering. I'm glad I saw you, actually. I leave for Monoea in the morning."

She stared at him. "You mean you're really going? I thought Elena would stop you. By the Seven, I think you want to die."

He stared at her, willing her to say no more. Tyrolean was watching too carefully. He spoke slowly, so she would understand. "I am ordered by Queen Elena."

"Why? She wasn't going to let you before. What happened?"

Ilumat happened. "I need you here. Home, I mean. Elena needs your help with Brîn."

Aarinnaie frowned, opened her mouth, then shut it. "I cannot. I just . . ." She swallowed. "Please. You must understand." She bolted past them fleet and silent into the shadows and alleyways lacing Brîn's underbelly.

Draken eased a breath from his chest, too weary to chase her down. Fools all, she'd only run again after he left. "Elena suggested I marry her off. Not a bad idea. She could be someone else's problem, if I can keep her in one place long enough for a ceremony."

Tyrolean stared after her. "Are you looking for advice or sympathy?"

"Both." He grunted. "Neither."

He studied the dead men, trying to memorize them but be quick about it because as stoic as Tyrolean was, his breath was labored and blood already blackened the binding Aarinnaie had fashioned.

The dead were already cooling. He shoved down the sick feeling in his gut as he straightened. He learned nothing but the brands on their hands, which he would check against the House Scrolls later. Maybe there was some history there. He had little doubt they did answer to House Khisson, as Aarinnaie said, but the design and evidence suggested curious connections and politics at work. "Come. I must send someone to clean up this mess we've made. "

He had a bad feeling the city couldn't be scrubbed free of rebellion as easily as it could be scrubbed free of blood, which reminded him of the previous attacks. As they walked back to the Citadel, he explained to Tyrolean about the Escort Poregar coming to speak to him about the slaughter of animals, and about Ilumat's similar issue on his lands. "Osias suggested the Moonlings are at fault."

Blood stained the front of Tyrolean's tunic as he held his injured arm against his chest. "The Moonlings? Why would they attack like this?"

"Oklai asked me to free the slaves. She considers herself a Queen among her people."

"There is only one Queen. She knows that."

Draken stared at him. Akrasian privilege was like battlements inside the mind. He decided not to try to broach them. "I have spoken against slavery. She considered me an ally, but her timing was poor. Of course she doesn't see it that way."

"So you agree with Osias? It's the Moonlings doing these killings?"

He bowed his head in thought. "No," he said at last. "I don't. I think Oklai would have threatened me with more if she could. I think it is Monoeans, or something else at work."

"Banes? They could possess all of them and allow themselves to be killed."

"It doesn't seem their way, unless someone is suicidal." As he had been . . . Gods, that was all he needed. Another influx of Banes. But Osias and the other Mance would know.

Draken thought of his boots slipping in the fresh-spilled blood of the villagers. Moonling slaves. Ilumat's complaints. The strains of rebellion in Brîn, from an island House conveniently available for mercenary action right when the Monoeans, too, seemed restless for war. The shared sigil.

"Something you said to me once, Ty. It is honorable to kill from the light . . ."

"Not from the shadows. I remember. An old Akrasian saying." He paused. "The Moonlings strike me as shadow people."

Draken glanced up. Clouds were closing in over what small bit of sky he could see. "Aye, well, the Moonlings aren't the only ones with blades in the dark."

CHAPTER ELEVEN

The send-off party was a small, miserable, bedraggled group, huddled under a dripping tent on the riverside platform: Draken, Tyrolean, Osias and Setia, and Akhanar Ghotze, captain and commander of the *Bane*; on the other side, the Queen, Lady Marshal Oroli, and Lord Ilumat. Banners dragged down from the constant rain. At least the platform was stone to keep them out of the muck. The fields between Brîn and Seakeep had become a churned, muddy mess. Draken thought when he got back he ought to see into putting in proper stone roadways . . . until he remembered he wasn't coming back.

His back stiffened as he listened to Ilumat and Elena wish them good fortune on their journey. It was all very proper and chilly and he found himself wishing they could just board the bloody boat, even if the journey was leading him to his death.

He dared a glance at Elena when they were about to depart for their skiff in the boatcaves. She stood in a tight knot with Ilumat and her guards and had no expression as he thanked her for her good wishes. The words sounded flat to him, insufficient and mundane.

His throat tightened and his heart twisted. Still angry, then. Ever the Queen. He turned to go, stepping out into the rain to head for the passageway down and striding away.

Soft, slippered footsteps across the wet stone. "Draken."

He turned.

Elena had broken from the others. Pelting rain dripped off her black hood and ran down her cheeks. She blinked up at him. He could read nothing in her dark eyes or pale face.

"My Queen?"

She stepped closer and threw her arms around him, her face pressed against his neck.

A long sigh escaped him and he folded his arms about her, pulling her close though her belly made the embrace a little awkward. *"Elena."*

A shudder ran through her and her arms tightened. "Don't be away long."

There were no words. He kissed her cheek and then her mouth, set her back, and strode away while he still could.

◆ ◆ ◆

If Draken considered the weather an ill omen he might have had Ghotze turn the ship round before they left Blood Bay. Rain lashed down late in the night and into the next morning, and so on for three days, whipping the sails and dripping off the booms, soaking lines, clothes, sails, and everything else not under cover. The Monoean ships were not in sight, so they must've gone on ahead.

Traveling in a cabin was a novel experience, and boring. He was used to working at the myriad of duties on board and sleeping in the hull with other off-duty crew. Whenever the shift bell rang, he had to resist the urge to go topside and report. After enduring days and nights of endlessly roiling sea with nothing to do, pulling lines for hours in the stinging spray seemed preferable to his cabin and the damp stink permeating the tightly shuttered space. Once a day he pulled on his heavy oiled cloak, toggled it tight over his chest, and climbed to the deck to keep Brimlud, the helmsman, company. As the storm persisted, the crew got progressively snappish.

On the fourth morning, Draken held onto the rails and lines on deck as the ocean swelled beneath the ship and harsh crosswinds tormented the sails overhead. Their progress stalled as they rode over a white-tipped wave and his stomach flipped as they slid down the other side and shot forward again with the shifting winds. It was a familiar sensation, and not entirely unpleasant, though it forced him to keep a tight grip. Brîn and her islands had long since disappeared from sight. He doubted he'd ever see her again.

The helmsman dipped his chin as Draken climbed the steps to the quarter-deck, though his dark squinting eyes never left the sea ahead. Grey laced his hair, soaked and hanging limp and thinning over his head. Deep crevices lined his brown face.

"Keeping course in this, Brimlud?" Draken asked. He had to raise his voice over the creak of riggings, snap of sails, and the waves slapping the hull.

"Fair holding, Khel Szi. Just slow. Be a day off, maybe two, weathering this storm. If it don't worsen."

"And will it?" In his experience, no one could predict the weather like a craggy old helmsman.

Brimlud lifted an eye to the steely sky and blinked. "Reckon so, aye. Island with a cove two nights hence if we see real trouble."

"That'd be Newfar, aye?"

Surprise creased the skin around Brimlud's eyes deeper. "Your father wasn't none for maps, pardon my saying, Khel Szi."

"No pardon necessary, helmsman. Truth, he wasn't." *And I'm little like him, thank the gods for small favors.*

"Don't much like being out of sight of the Seven for so long," Brimlud went on. "But I reckon with you aboard, Khel Szi, we're safe enough."

Draken snorted. He'd be less surprised if the gods dragged him into the sea and shredded him to bits. He made his way to the rail, shuffling from handhold to handhold as the ship listed and creaked. Rain slipped under his cloak and soaked his shoulders. The sailors ignored him; they were too busy fighting the wind and lashing rain for pleasantries. He caught a few wry looks though. Only a bloody fool would be out in this. Or a desperate one. At least his appearance in Monoea would give King Aissyth something else to think on than making war with Brîn and Akrasia.

He stayed until rain ran in rivulets down his spine and chest under his cloak. Nothing ahead but a blur of grey seas and skies, and silvery, stinging rain bridging the two. At last it even drove Draken back into cover. Tyrolean was sharpening well-honed weapons and Osias sat wrapped in his cloak, staring at nothing.

Draken remembered the Mance had once manipulated the currents on the Eros. "Can you do anything about the storm?"

Osias shook his head. "This is no regular storm. It is Korde, showing his wrath."

Draken shook the water off his cloak in the corridor and hung it by the door. "Excellent. I suppose that means he will chase us all the way to Monoea."

Osias gave him a rare smile. "You only did as I asked."

Draken strode the width of the cabin to peer through a crack in the shutter, then dropped down in front of it. A faint spray of water penetrated the shutters to dampen the back of his head and the ship rode another swell. He wondered if he imagined the voices of the shouting crew over the wailing wind. He hadn't felt this trapped since he was in the dungeons of Sevenfel.

Tyrolean cleaned his blades without missing a stroke. "Nothing to do but ride it out. Especially if such is the will of the gods."

Draken grunted, noncommittal. He was in no mood to talk philosophy or religion, not while being immutably dragged toward his fate. The gods had torn his life apart with their great hands and now they were dropping the pieces back to the world one by one, watching waves of destruction ripple out.

He dropped his head, trying to stretch the tension from his neck. If he could just be in the open sea air on a fair day, it might make this final journey bearable.

"The storm can't be all on your mind," Tyrolean said.

"No," Draken admitted. He avoided Osias's gaze. "Truth, I wonder if we're sailing into a trap."

"I like it less than you do," Tyrolean said. "But there's naught for it now."

Draken shook his head slowly and toyed with the hoops hanging from his ear. "King Aissyth can be . . . unpredictable. So I've heard."

Unpredictable enough to raise up his bastard cousin from enslavement to his own most trusted secret service, and then believe the lies framing Draken for the murder of his wife. He thought of his own recent sordid history, and how he'd followed the father he hated to a throne he never wanted. Unpredictability must run in the godsdamned family.

"I need ale," he said.

Osias nodded and rose. "I'll fetch it. I've made friends with the galley lad."

Draken watched the Mance go. "Thing is, I'm not sure why he's unpredictable, nor how to counter it."

"It's likely from answering the whims of too many others," Tyrolean said, the strap swishing along his blade. He held it up to check the edge. "Trying to please everyone. I've seen it done with commanders. They're the ones who tend to lose battles." When Draken didn't answer, he looked up. "What? No advice from your father's scrolls this time?"

Rain lashed hard at the shutters, rattling them. The whole world smelled of wet wool, salt, and sweaty, close men. Too close. There was no way to keep the truth from Tyrolean much longer. He would find out what Draken had been. Best to have it all loose now so he knew where Tyrolean stood, and to make certain he would care for the Queen afterward.

"Ty, there are things you should know."

"Such as?"

"Put the bloody swords down and I'll tell you." He waited while Tyrolean laid his weapons aside and drew a breath. "You know I wasn't born in Brîn."

"I remember." Tyrolean fell very still. He had learned as much when Osias had done the ritual to bind Bruche to Draken.

Draken inhaled, held it for a little. The words came out in a rush. "I am half Monoean."

The captain's lined eyes widened. "You're sundry?"

Draken bit down on his annoyance at the slur. "But royal blood, all. My father fled to Monoea when the Sword War turned against Brîn. I expect he thought he'd be received by the King and given asylum. I don't know the circumstances, but instead he was enslaved. Perhaps it was mistaken identity. Perhaps it was just compensation for being his own ruddy self. At any rate, my mother is the King's cousin."

Tyrolean sat very straight and stiff. He was quiet for a long moment. "He claimed he hid in the Dragonstar Isles. Where you said you were fostered."

"Osias encouraged me to tell the fostering story to match up with Father's." Bile pressed on the back of his throat. "When King Aissyth freed the slaves, my father worked his passage home, leaving me. Aissyth had me trained up as a bow-man by way of the Navy. I sailed a few Sohalias, patrolling and fighting through the Decade War. After the war he raised me to the Black Guard to help mop up."

"You're familial with the king?"

"Distant, but I was at court, aye. Until my wife was murdered." He paused. "King Aissyth convicted me and banished me to Akrasia for her death."

"Does King Aissyth know the new Khel Szi is you?"

Draken shook his head. "Truth? I don't know. And before you ask: no, Elena doesn't know." Tyrolean's mouth tightened, but Draken barreled on. "I held my tongue for stability's sake. Brîn would be in a terrible state had I not taken the Brînian throne. This you know. The truth would have undermined all we worked for in the battle against Truls."

Tyrolean stared at him. "I should kill you where you stand, if only for lying to our Queen."

"You'd execute me for lying to her, but not for *killing* her?" Difficult to say which made Draken feel worse. Killing Elena and bringing her back with Sea-born's magic had amounted to terrible, heartrending guilt and the torment of subsequent dreams.

Tyrolean's hands hung loose between his knees. He fisted and flexed them.

"I know you're faithful," Draken said, his tone tight, hands itching to reach for Seaborn. "You consider me an abomination. No better than a slave."

Tyrolean gave him a look. Unreadable. Wounded, maybe.

Draken laughed, rough. "Khellian's balls, I *was* a slave, first to Aissyth, then to my father, and now to my throne. So maybe the priests are right after all. If you must kill me, do it now."

Tyrolean rose to his feet. The sway of the ship didn't seem to bother him. In a moment he'd reach for his sword. Draken's fingers twitched. Tyrolean's swords still lay on his bench, but within quick reach.

"People have fought for you, died on your behalf," Tyrolean said.

Draken had killed dozens of Brînians for the simple crime of being abandoned by Akrasia during the Decade War, and dozens more had died on his behalf. Most of the women he cared for had died or suffered because of him. He suspected even Aarinnaie nurtured a death wish, and if the gods granted it, it would be in his service.

"I am sundry, truth. Heresy flows in my blood." He tried to keep control of his voice, but anger made it rise. "But you needn't trouble yourself with killing me. I am banished from Monoea. I will be executed when I arrive."

Tyrolean stared at him, but someone knocked, cutting off whatever reply he had fashioned. Draken cleared his throat and rose. "Come."

A galley lad, his face shadowed by furrowed brow and matted braids, clutched a pitcher of ale in both hands. He walked with his feet apart to keep his balance as the ship listed and set the pitcher on the railed table. There was a deep divot carved into the wood to keep it from sliding about. He backed out, head still bowed. Just as he caught the door latch his dark eyes caught Draken's. His whole face tightened as if in fear, and he darted through the door. It rattled as he slammed it behind him.

Cold sank into Draken's bones. "He heard us."

"He's just a lad," Tyrolean said. "He talks and they'll think he's telling tales."

Tyrolean poured out ale in the mugs and they drank, the only noise the waves crashing against the ship and the creak of the masts. Draken considered what would happen if the lad told what he'd overheard. But he was just that, a lad. Tyrolean was right. No one would believe him.

He cast Tyrolean a chary look. The Captain was another matter.

"I'd like to know more about your cousin," Tyrolean said. "Not much known of the King. Most Akrasians who come in contact with him have a nasty habit of dying."

Draken's heart lurched. He was responsible for some of those deaths. He forced his mind to Tyrolean's question. Truth, his cousin-King rarely exposed himself to outsiders. Maybe that was why this whole request for diplomacy didn't ring right. He wondered if the King even knew he was coming, if he was even still alive, if Monoea suffered from a real rebellion.

"The Landed courtiers are fierce for his pleasure," he admitted. Tension curdled in the muscles of his neck. Tyrolean watched him intently. Perhaps he really wanted to know. "There is much infighting. Elena's High lords are tame by comparison. But King Aissyth manages dozens of Landed lords and hundreds of minor landless. The hierarchy is rigid, locked in tradition. The minors chafe under the restraints of their positions, always have done."

"How are they raised up, then? Or are they?"

"Aye. They join the military. Unit commanders make more money on Ranking Day than a clean whorehouse on Sohalia Night."

"Is that how you achieved your rank?"

He felt as if Tyrolean wanted him to prove his quality, but he tried a weak joke instead. "I like to lie to myself and believe I was just that good."

"You must know the King in some ways better than his courtiers," Tyrolean said slowly. "Especially if you didn't try to get anything from him."

"From him? Gods, no. Even when he raised me up to his Black Guard, I took none of his favor for granted."

"And your wife? Did he have anything to do with your marriage?"

His throat tightened and he nodded, dropping his gaze. He wondered where her grave was, if someone had built an altar for her and kept it up. Her mother, perhaps. "Had Osias left it alone, Elena wouldn't even know I was alive."

"Hmm. I wonder. Elena might not have found you, but it's difficult to escape the sight of the Seven Eyes. You do have a way of landing on your feet, Your Highness."

"What are you going to do?"

Tyrolean snorted softly. "Who am I to destroy what the gods have wrought?" He sank down and reached for his sword and strap. "Born a Monoean slave, raised to a Brînian Prince. You'll make quite the cradle tale when it all comes out."

Draken shook his head and drank deeply of his ale, hiding his relief at Tyrolean's acceptance of his sordid past. "That'd be of more comfort if cradle tales weren't so often about the dead."

CHAPTER TWELVE

B y evening drink had muddied Draken's head and dulled the jagged edges of his worry. Tyrolean's blades, stored in a rack against the opposite wall, gleamed with fresh oil. He lay dozing on his bunk over Draken's, as self-contained as ever. Probably praying if he wasn't asleep already.

Draken sighed and hunched over his ale. Chill, wet air hissed through the shutters. Dried salt water streaked the wood beneath the window like tearstains. He tasted it on the rim of his earthenware mug and smelled it with every breath. It pervaded him with a sense of home and created an unaccountable longing for Bruche, his wit and rough wisdom. He'd considered his mind a noisy place when he'd carried Bruche inside him, but the swordhand had served the purpose of mocking him out of his own worries.

He'd kept the galleyboy running after more ale all evening. He hadn't noticed any more fear or shock from the boy, but he slowly considered that might be his blunted senses. He reached out and poured more, sloshing a bit on the table as the ship rolled over a wave. He could only pray for sleep. Gods knew it passed the time, not that he woke all that rested after tossing in his bunk all night.

The boat pitched over another, bigger wave, forcing him to grip the table to steady himself. Draken heard a low curse and something scrabbled outside his door. He turned his head to look just as it slammed open.

Akhanar Ghotze held a short sword as he entered. Three burly sailors crowded the corridor behind him. One of them pushed in behind Ghotze. The cabin went from stuffy to claustrophobic in an instant.

Tyrolean rolled from his bunk, landing on his feet and stepping toward his freshly oiled swords on the rack. Ghotze intercepted his progress with his blade, cutting the air between Tyrolean and his swords. "Not so, Captain."

Two of the sailors grabbed Draken and dragged him up from his bunk. His sleepy, drunken muscles barely tightened in protest as the sailors forced him to his knees before Ghotze. The cabin spun about him and his stomach did a lazy flip. He swallowed hard as Tyrolean demanded, "What are you on about, Ghotze?"

"We've heard tale that Khel Szi is not the man we took him for," Ghotze said, his tone tight. "That you're not Khel Szi at all."

"The galley boy. You sent him to get me drunk," Draken said. His slurred voice carried a note of finality, even to him. Perhaps his lies would kill him before King Aissyth got his chance.

"You're going to believe a lad over the word of your Prince?" Tyrolean glanced toward his swords and back at the captain. Ghotze's sword edged closer to his chest.

Draken drew in a breath, trying to clear his muddled head. He needed to stop Tyrolean trying to protect him before he got hurt.

"That boy is my grandson," Ghotze said. "And if the treachery he heard tells true, then my Prince, as you call him, is no Prince at all."

Draken set that aside with difficulty. One thing at a time. His bad knee ached sharply against the wooden floor and the sailors kept a painful grip on his arms. His mind protested putting together any coherent sentiments except to a vague curiosity about why he'd thought drinking himself into a near stupor was a good idea.

Where were his guards? Halmar? Gods, if they were dead . . . "My szi nêre?"

Ghotze straightened his back. "Locked below until we get at the truth."

Draken blinked blearily at him. The cut-metal lantern hanging behind Ghotze's head swung as the ship crested another swell and the flame flickered into Draken's eyes, blinding him for a moment.

"They're cooperating," Ghotze said. "As you should. We can end this quickly."

Depending on what Ghotze meant by *end*, Draken wasn't too certain cooperation was the best idea.

"And if he doesn't?" Tyrolean asked.

"Then we toss him over and let the gods sort it."

"Fools all, man!" Caught in a rare rage, Tyrolean took a step forward. "Are you trying to start war between Monoea and Akrasia? They're expecting him. They've threatened—"

"Back, Green." Ghotze's blade flicked across Tyrolean's bare chest. Blood sprang up on his pale skin. Just flesh deep, but Ghotze knew what he was about, damn him. Tyrolean lunged for his swords. One of the sailors holding Draken released his arm to go after him, tackling him against a wooden bench. Tyrolean went down hard with a grunt. Draken took the opportunity to wrench free of the other sailor holding him. Someone shouted and the boat listed enough to make his effort a clumsy scramble toward

Seaborn, looped on Draken's belt at the end of his bunk. The scabbard swung toward him. His fingers brushed the end of it as he felt a cold blade settle under his jaw.

Tyrolean snarled and tried to shove through the burly sailor without much success. Draken spat out, "Captain. Enough!"

Tyrolean was pinned to the bench by the sailor, still straining, his nostrils flared, his lined eyes white with fury. "Don't be a fool. Draken is royal and godsworn. People who mishandle him tend to meet bad ends."

"Enough," Draken repeated, breathless, his head pulled back to accommodate the sword at his throat. "Let me up, Akhanar Ghotze. I'll cooperate. Captain Tyrolean will, as well."

The sword backed from Draken's throat. Draken sank down onto his bunk. They kept Tyrolean pinned.

"Rorq, bind the 'Khel Szi' to the bunk post." Ghotze turned his hard glare on Tyrolean. "The Green can join the others in the hold."

Others? Had they taken Osias and Setia prisoner too? The Mance had his glamour; Draken prayed he'd made good use of it in time.

Rorq locked cold metal around his wrists, still scarred from shackling after his wife had died, and chained him to the post at the end of his bunk. Ghotze waved a hand at the dirty mugs and pitcher. Rorq took them away. Before he shut the door behind him, Draken caught sight of another guard waiting with bared blade outside. Not so alone then.

Tyrolean's nostrils flared. Draken held his gaze. "I'll sort this."

"Aye, Your Highness." Tyrolean gave him a stiff nod and didn't fight them as they shoved him out of the cabin.

Draken wrapped his hands around the cold chains and waited.

"You are no Khel Szi," Ghotze said, sliding his sword back into the tooled scabbard at his waist.

"Khel Szi was my father and my grandfather before him, and his father before him. Bastard I may be, but I never pretended any different."

"But you pretended the other half of your blood, aye? No one knows you're sundry." Ghotze reached out to touch Seaborn where it lay on the table.

Draken's fingers whitened on his chains. The rough metal scraped his skin and a tremor ran through him as it healed. Seaborn had a penchant for burning other people. It might cause Ghotze to think it was some magicks worked by Draken, though the sword had a mind of its own.

Ghotze drew it. The sword remained dull and dead.

Draken sighed in relief. "There is no law against sundry serving Brîn."

"Only the gods' own."

"The gods put me on the bloody throne," Draken snapped. Ghotze turned to look at him, eyes narrowed. Draken tempered his tone. "Akhen Khel wouldn't accept me had I not carried Khellian's blood."

"But you are Monoean. My grandson heard you say you would die if you return to her shores. That you are banished."

The boy had taken his care about listening.

No argument emerged from his drunken haze. And he was dead weary of lies. "The truth would only hurt Brîn."

"Brîn. Pah! It's your neck you're looking to spare, bastard. Your own godsforsaken honor, whatever there was of it."

Godsforsaken, indeed. How often in his early days after Lesle's death had he beseeched the gods for death?

Draken stared at the point of Ghotze's sword as it drew closer to his chest. He had no illusions his ability to heal himself would mend heart and bone. He couldn't make himself hate the idea. But the curved blade snagged Elena's pendant and lifted it. "This is a start. I wonder what else you're worth."

Draken shook his head. It was hard to hold up. "The gods chose me," he mumbled. "But I'm not worth that much."

"Then the gods can bloody well have you back. Rorq!"

The big sailor shoved the door open hard enough it banged against the end of Draken's bunk, jarring him and rattling his chains. Two more sailors followed close.

"Bring the sundry to the rail."

Draken's heart gulped blood and spit it back out chilled.

Ghotze turned away without a backward glance, still gripping Akhen Khel as he shoved past the sailors.

Rorq's face was hard and grim. "Come along, then." He reached for Draken's chains.

Draken lashed out with his bare foot and hooked Rorq's knee, yanking him off balance. The sailor crashed into him with a shout. Draken slammed his chain-wrapped fist into Rorq's nose, and tasted blood as it flicked across his face, sweetly bitter. Rorq screamed a strangled, wet scream. Draken growled and shoved Rorq off him, but the sailor came at him again, blood streaming over his mouth and chin, his mates on his heels. A fist found Draken's temple. The world whirled about him and pain slammed in close behind. The bunk behind him shifted with a heavy weight, or maybe it was the ship rolling over a wave. Abruptly, Draken gaped for air and his lungs seized. A thick arm tightened around his throat.

"Feeding the sea is all you're good for, sundry bastard." Somebody took off the chains. Draken lashed out again and struggled. The arm tightened on his throat. Black crept in on the world from all sides. The clink of the chains wasn't enough to keep the darkness at bay.

◆ ◆ ◆

You've things to attend, Draken. Awaken!

The harsh echoing shout made him twitch but pelting rain on his face and bare chest brought him to. *Bruche?*

No answer. Draken slumped against the rail. His ale-infused mind playing tricks again. His head hurt badly and rain soaked his head and back. Someone knelt by him, fixing a shackle to his ankle. He kicked out awkwardly, delayed by drink and lingering stupor. Something heavy held his leg pinned to the deck boards. The sailor at his knee scrambled back just in time, his work done. Groggy, Draken blinked down at a salt-pitted counterweight affixed to his ankle. Something about the whole thing seemed wrong. Wrong even beyond Ghotze's plan to pitch him into the sea.

He swung his head from side to side. He should have let himself sink the first time he'd been forced into the sea at sword point, in warm Khein Bay. It would have been a pleasant way to go in comparison to these storm-strewn waves.

"You could buy your way out of this," Ghotze said.

"Do it," Draken mumbled. "Kill me."

"Truth? No reason to spare you at all, then?"

Draken dragged his bleary gaze up to the Akhanar's face. "You're doing me a bloody favor."

"I wonder if the Queen would think so?"

That stung. His voice sharpened. "Do me a kindness and help me over the rail. Bad knee. Can't manage on my own with the counterweight."

Ghotze grunted, his brows lowered in a scowl. He looked comically confused. A humorless smile tugged at the corners of Draken's mouth until two sailors strode forward. Hands dragged Draken up and pushed at him, straining the ropes.

No, Draken! You—The voice broke. Draken had to strain to hear, difficult through his own grunts of pain and the voices of the sailors. *You will never . . . Elena, remember Elena . . .*

Draken blinked rapidly and uttered a wordless protest at the voice. *Bruche?*

He could join the spirit swordhand there. He wanted to go. Let the sea swallow him. It would be a relief. But one hand grappled for the rail; the other swung out and caught one of the sailors on the side of the head, finding a ropy lock. His fingers tightened on it like erring jaws on prey. The sailor shouted.

Another guttural, wordless growl burst from Draken's lips. If they were shoving him into the sea, he was damn well dragging one of them along with him.

The sailor snarled and tried to jerk free. Draken yanked back on him just as the other sailor shoved him harder. The sailor tumbled over the rail, past Draken. For a long breath he hung suspended over the sea as the sailor flipped over the rail with a sharp scream. His weight tore at Draken's grip. The hair dragged through his fist and wrenched free.

The sailor scrabbled at the air and disappeared screaming into the sea mist. He thudded against the side of the ship before the snarling waves swallowed him. The motion had pulled Draken down, bent over the wiggling rail. His head slammed against the edge where deck met hull. Pain burst behind his eyes but the icy spray kept him from blacking out. His waist was bent over the rope rail, locked into place by the weight on his ankle. Agony stabbed through his bad knee as the muscles tore and knit themselves as quickly. A great ocean swell shuddered through the ship.

Crack. The rope sagged abruptly, dropping him lower.

Draken gulped a breath of mist and salt spray. One hand, rubbed raw and stinging as it healed, still clung to the rope rail. His stomach and back strained against falling further. His head protested the rush of blood from hanging upside-down with epic, thought-clogging pain. *Let go*, he thought. *End this.*

Shouts penetrated the rain, his agony, and his groggy mind. Metal clanged. A deep voice screamed. Rain and briny spray ran into his nose and open mouth, making him cough. A sharp, high voice, unrecognizable through his coughing: "Ty! Get him up, damn you!"

Rough hands hauled Draken back up over the rail and dumped him onto the hard wood deck, slick with rain and a familiar, sickly-sweet reek that clotted in his lungs with every gasping breath. Rain pelted down clear and splashed back up crimson. Narrow, delicate bare feet stopped near his face. Small . . . the lad? His feet had been bare. No. That's not right. What was his name again . . . ?

"Seize the ship."

"Aye, Szirin."

Draken blinked and strained to see, but just got an eyeful of rainwater for his trouble. He squeezed his eyes shut against the sting. "*Aarin—*" Another burst of coughing cut him off.

"Up, Khel Szi. You've a ship to command." Strong, slim hands tugged at his bare arm, digging into his muscles. Her fingers felt like dagger points.

He moaned again and shoved to a sit, unable to pull free of her iron grip. Khellian's balls, she was strong for such a slight thing. "Aarinnaie. You're pulling on me."

"And you're drunk," Aarinnaie said.

But she let go.

"Damn it, Aarin."

"She won't let you go so easily," Osias said. "None of us will."

Draken wiped his hand over his eyes, clearing off the rain. Tyrolean appeared, his shirt plastered to his chest with the rain, blooded blades in each hand. Draken's szi nêre followed. Halmar's face deepened into a scowl. He eyed Draken and then his gaze passed over the bodies on the deck.

"Throw the traitors overboard, Halmar," Aarinnaie said.

Halmar looked at Draken, who blinked the rain out of his eyes and nodded.

"Aye, Szirin." Halmar signaled his men. They hefted the bodies of the two dead sailors, tossed them over. It was then Draken realized Ghotze was alive. Only just, gagging on blood from gaping chest wounds. Looked like Tyrolean's work.

Konnan looked at Draken. "Khel Szi? What of the Akhanar?"

Draken grabbed at the rail but had to try twice to get up. His knee, flexed the wrong way from the weight on his ankle, made him hiss in pain. The rope sagged under his weight. He grabbed a post instead and hauled himself to his feet. His knee gave way. He leaned his weight onto his other leg. Ghotze's mouth gaped and his eyes rolled as they followed Draken. His brown skin had taken on a greyish cast, stretched taut over his cheekbones, and his mouth gaped and worked. He grunted and moaned.

"Throw him in," Draken growled. "And get this blasted counterweight off my leg."

CHAPTER THIRTEEN

Ghotze floated for a moment, his arms waving, frantic and awkward. A fin appeared in the water nearby, and another. Froth splashed over a swell, sucking Ghotze under. Draken couldn't be certain in the infernal rain, but he thought he saw a dark stain rise from the depths.

Korde, drinking in blood sacrifice before Ma'Vanni scented the death in her realm? The god of death had ever been a hungry shadow. It had nearly been Draken who had stained the ocean. His whole body weakened at the thought. *Stop the blasted rain, then. You had your feast.*

He lowered himself to the deck, unable to move further with the weight on his leg. He had to sit in the wet for an eternity, shivering under an oiled cloak while Halmar sawed the ring from his ankle. Aparently the key had gone over with Ghotze.

Aarinnaie posted the other szi nêre on the anchors and confined the helmsman to his cabin and the other sailors belowdecks. The saw sliced his skin. He hissed in pain and bled on the already stained deck. Fortunately that and the shudder of the boat as it crested a wave hid the magical healing. Tyrolean leant his shoulder to Draken without a word, helping him limp back to the cabin. Once inside, Draken shoved him off and bound his already healed gash to conceal it. His knee hurt as if steel straps embedded in the muscle bound a stabbing knife buried inside it.

"This is yours, I believe." Tyrolean held out Elena's seal.

Draken slung it round his neck as he got up. Even dry trousers, warm under- and over-tunics, and a woolen cloak couldn't stop his shivering.

Tyrolean tossed him a blanket. "That went sideways from Sohalia quickly."

"Where are Os-sias and S-setia?"

"Sorting the crew."

Draken eased onto his bed, his back against the wall. The bunk posts were marred by the chains that had bound him there. "Need Gadye oscher wine." That stuff would sear him to his bones.

"I'll send for some." Tyrolean stripped his wet clothes and added hash marks on his muscled chest with a flinch. His kills. When Draken had first seen them, he'd thought them bragging notches. Now he knew them for penance. The Captain pressed a cloth to the small wounds until they stopped bleeding, dressed in dry clothes, wiped his blades clean, and re-sheathed them on his back.

Draken watched him. "Taking no chances, then?"

"The crew is likely loyal to Ghotze. And you'll need to decide what to do with the boy."

Draken looked at Tyrolean, wondering if he remembered another boy, one they'd been unable to save but whose death had led to Va Khlar's valuable alliance and friendship. "Ghotze is dead. Dead Akhanars don't pay their crew. Rather negates loyalty. Where is the lad?"

"In the hold with the men."

The door slammed open and Aarinnaie strode in. Her eyes were dark as storm clouds and her many black braids gleamed wetly. Curly sprigs sprouted from her hairline. Her sopping tunic and trousers clung tight to her narrow, muscled body. "What in the name of the Holy Seven was *that*?"

"I believe it was an attempted assassination," Draken said. "What are you doing here?"

She ignored his dry tone. "Saving your sorry arse." She poured herself ale, gulped it down, and eyed him over the rim of her mug.

"Not pouring one for me?"

"Ale already addled your wits, and you've little to spare."

Tyrolean opened his mouth to speak. Draken raised a weary hand to stop him. "I've no doubt you have many opinions on my lackluster intelligence, Aarin. Save them for when you've ample time to eviscerate me. Right now I'm more interested in the state of the ship."

"I set the szi nêre on the anchors and locked the helmsman in the aft cabin. The sailors are in the hold, anxious to a man. Halmar is outside your door. He won't leave you. We've barely time to sort this before we set sail again on the morrow." She gulped more ale and slammed the cup down. "Draken, damn you, what were you thinking?"

Thinking? He'd been identified, attacked, choked, and nearly tossed over the rail into the sea. Even Bruche had made an appearance . . . if he hadn't imagined it out of the drink. There'd been no time to *think*. "I—"

"Didn't. Obviously."

"Aarin—"

"Fools all! Did you not study on Ghotze and his crew? He loves money more than a sea captain should—"

"Akhanar," Tyrolean said. "He was a *fleet* Akhanar, Princess."

Aarinnaie shot the Akrasian captain a glare, barely missing a beat in berating Draken. "—and he's got more pirates on his crew than an island alehouse in Tradeseason. *And* he was hired on by Father. Didn't that raise your hackles even a bit? I know you know; I amended the bloody scroll you read with the truth rather than that glossed over gullshit the bloodlords compiled for you. Or are you too good to read your own reports now, Khel Szi?"

Draken stared at her, realized his mouth hung open, and shut it. He set his mug aside with a tiny thump. It was the only noise for several deep breaths, during which he tried to marshal his comprehension of all she'd just thrown at him, not to mention his temper. He started with the smallest issue first. "I assumed I would be rather hard pressed to find a sailor for my crew who hadn't dabbled in piracy. They are Brînians, after all."

"That's your Monoean blood talking. You are Khel Szi. You could have any sailor in Brîn." She shook her head and wiped at rainwater dripping down her face from her hair, seemingly oblivious to mentioning his heritage out loud in front of Tyrolean. "This makes no sense. How did Ghotze come to the point of actually throwing you off?"

Draken stared at her, bewildered. "What do you mean, how did he come to it? He was abundantly clear in his disapproval of my lies and sundry blood, as anyone in our godsforsaken, uncivilized hinterland would be."

"It seemed his intent all along," Tyrolean added. "He rid himself of any threat immediately, and it took no time for them to subdue His Highness and drag him to the rail."

Draken shot Tyrolean a sour look. Trust him to point out Draken's incompetence right when Aarinnaie was on a tirade about the very subject. "It didn't happen as quick as all that."

Tyrolean bowed his head to him, quite serious. "Ghotze's men subdued *me* quickly, Your Highness. You had no aid."

Aarinnaie heaved a long suffering sigh and dropped down onto the bench. "Stick to the damned topic. Do you two recall the bit about Ghotze loving money?"

Draken shrugged. "Retired pirates come cheap and a fleet Akhanar is paid well. What of it?"

"Not that well. Did you notice how old that counterweight on your leg was? Rusty. Convenient they had it soldered to an ankle-ring."

Draken shook his head; he was missing something. "What about it being old?"

"The ship is new. And another thing. Ghotze stuck us under this storm. Then when you finally get restless, the galleyboy totes ale to you unbidden all evening. Got you properly softened, I'd say."

"I'm not as dense as all that. I thought of it." Too late, but the idea had occurred.

Tyrolean narrowed his lined eyes. "You can't scheme a storm."

"I'd hate to insult Korde since you thought the storm is his fault." A humorless, smug smile tugged on Aarinnaie's lips. "If so, the Hungry God doesn't know his business very well. We nearly came out of it two nights ago. Ghotze's been dragging anchor since, letting the weather catch up with us."

Draken stared at her. "How in Khellian's name did you find all that out while you were hidden below?"

She shrugged.

Fools all, he should have known better than to trust someone his Father had relied upon. It meant going back over the entire staff and replacing it. Something to do when he got back. *If* I get back, he reminded himself. Dangerous, thinking of the future. He had a mountain to climb between here and there.

"So if not from Father, how did he make his money?"

She shrugged. "Bribery and smuggling. Any trader owing Father a favor used Ghotze and his fleet. After Akrasia started paying more attention to how many runs his ship made, Father raised him to fleet Akhanar. Not a bad plan, at first. Kept our lot protected. But between bribes, unloading fees, and sales levies in Brîn, Ghotze near destroyed wool trade between Akrasia and Brîn. That was when I was just a girl."

"You listened in to conversations not meant for you even then, eh? Good fortune for me you developed the habit early." What she was saying was starting to sink in. "It must be why Monoea starting breeding their own herds and developing their own loom shops. I recall some few minor Landless raised up during that time."

"Aye, Ghotze bled wool trade dry and turned to other markets."

"The Dragonstar Isles?" Tyrolean said.

She shrugged. Her eyes flitted between them and then rested on Draken as if he were the safer of the two. "Aye. It makes me think he worked it out you hadn't been raised there. At least it would make him curious about you, see if he could find some leverage from your past. He knows bloodlords from the Isles. Bloodlords like that lot you killed the other night in the alley."

"But Draken never did anything to Ghotze," Tyrolean pointed out.

"Never did anything *for* him, either. The last thing Ghotze wanted was an honest Khel Szi."

The truth was dawning. "No profit in it."

Aarinnaie leaned her head back against the shutter behind her as if it were suddenly too heavy for her to hold it up. "But there is good profit to be had from a Prince who is not who he says he is."

A chill weight settled between Draken's shoulder blades. No coin in him dead, though. "I was meant to beg for my life and barter with him, then."

"Aye, brother." This time her voice carried weary affection. "I should have acted sooner but it was all suspicion. Truth, I didn't put it all together until I saw you hanging over the rail. Ghotze didn't count on your being suicidal."

Draken leaned over his knees and rubbed his fingers over his face. They sat in silence until Tyrolean broke it. "Let the crew simmer in the hold for a bit, then?"

Draken turned this over and shook his head. "No. I think I should speak to them straightaway."

Tyrolean leaned forward, his forearms on his knees, and shook his head. "Something about this is all off. I saw part of what Ghotze did. It didn't look like a negotiation to me. It looked like a murder waiting to happen." He glanced at Aarinnaie. Her head still rested against the shutter, eyes closed, back straight. "What if Her Highness is wrong? What if Ghotze was meant to kill you? What would happen then?"

Draken's brow furrowed. "I don't know. I admit I didn't think much past my demise."

Aarinnaie opened her eyes. "The negotiations between Monoea and Akrasia would have been ruined."

"Especially if they really are rebelling and have some use for Draken."

"Aarinnaie could have negotiated," Draken said. "King Aissyth would respect your authority even if the Brînians do not."

"But Ghotze didn't know that. He didn't know I was aboard."

Tyrolean nodded. "So, beyond earning coin off your secret, which was a risky proposition at best, what did Ghotze stand to gain from your death?"

"Perhaps he worked for someone," Draken said.

Tyrolean arched a brow. "Someone who paid well to see Quunin attacked from the sea?"

"King Aissyth said once the most honest coin is made off war." The worst of the drunk had worn off, leaving him with a cracking headache. "I'd best go speak to the crew."

Aarinnaie rose. "What will you tell them?"

Draken thought about what he would expect to hear in this circumstance. He shook his head and heaved himself to his feet. His knee screamed at bearing weight. He winced and eased his weight onto his other leg. At least he'd worked out what not to say. "The truth, I suppose. Or some of it."

Getting down the ladder below took some doing. Halmar and Tyrolean insisted on going first as guards. They stood with bared blades, gazing impassively at the sailors around them. Ten in all, plus the lad. Six and the captain had died.

Draken's entrance was painstaking and slow, his knee screaming at its turn on the rungs. Aarinnaie followed, closing the hatch behind her against the stinging rain. She stayed off the hull floor, hanging onto the ladder. She wore a short sword strapped to her hip and her arms and legs bristled with sheathed knives.

The sailors rolled from their tight bunks to their feet, staring at Draken. He had a tough time reading their expressions amid the lines of cut-lantern light swinging across their faces, save the galley lad who sniveled and wiped his eyes with his fists, his face full of unbridled hostility. None knelt or bowed their heads or murmured his title.

"I care not for the past. I care not for those who are dead, and make no mistake, your Akhanar and his closest cohorts are very dead, as well as their purpose to kill me." He eyed them. "And I care for pirates least of all."

He paused, but none denied it.

"From this moment forward, you are mercenaries who answer to me. If I command you to work the lines, scrub the deck, or kill someone, you get paid the same: three Rare per day each, to be paid upon mine and my sister's safe arrival back at Brîn."

Eyes blinked, a couple of mouths fell open, others shifted on their feet and exchanged glances. He heard Aarinnaie's sharp breath. It was an exorbitant sum.

"But the King will kill you," Ghotze's grandboy said in a snuffly, weak voice. "I heard you say."

"All the more reason to keep him from it," Draken said. "You carry the royal house of Brîn on this ship. Our lives are in your very well paid hands."

He climbed the ladder, concealing a wince each time his bad leg had to bear his weight. He limped toward the Akhanar's cabin. Halmar followed close behind. "Are you with me, Halmar?"

"The sword chose you, Khel Szi," Halmar replied, his voice flat, his gaze unwavering. The man had never revealed whether he respected Draken, or even liked him. He'd sworn to serve the House of Khel, and it had to be enough.

Brimlud got to his feet as Draken opened the door, dark eyes shadowed under his furrowed brow. "You're alive, Khel Szi."

"I need you at the helm when we raise anchor at dawn."

"Who will captain the ship, if you don't mind the asking?"

Good question. "Who would you have?"

"You know ships. Fair more than a Nêre or Szi ought."

Draken had come by neither designation honestly, and everyone aboard ship knew his secret now. He shook his head. It couldn't be him. "I've never captained before."

Brimlud sighed, the old man's weariness apparent. Draken highly doubted this was the first mutiny he'd seen, though gods willing, it'd be his last. "I'll think on it."

His choice turned out to be Joran, a strapping young man of no more than a quarter century of Sohalias with braids down his back and muscles as thick as rigging knots. He was quietly deferential to Draken, who cared little whether it was because of the coin or actual respect. Before dawn Joran examined the maps, drew anchor, and got the crew setting the sails. By the time Draken was filling his alesick stomach with breakfast, they emerged from the storm.

The quiet was oppressive after days of battering wind and stinging rain. Only the slap of waves, creaking lines and wood, the drip of rain off the booms, and Joran's calm voice broke it as he strode about the deck seeing his orders were done.

The sea and sky lightened ahead. Behind lay the deep sucking grey of the storm. Seeing it at this distance locked the notion into Draken's mind that it was Korde's displeasure made manifest, no matter what Aarinnaie said of it. He stood at the rail on the quarterdeck, drizzle sparkling before his eyes as it dripped from his oiled cloak hood, and stared into that eerie, forbidding grey. His mind passed over the bodies of those who had tried to kill him, shredded into the bellies of great sea fish or yet drifting. And to Elena, who had escaped his thoughts for the better part of a day. Was she well? Cared for? Protected?

Aarinnaie joined him. "Joran has us in a tack toward course. Apparently Ghotze had us off, keeping to the storm."

"I'm still curious who is behind it all."

"Osias says he will quietly question the crew for more information. You know how the Mance are. Drag answers from you before you realize there's a question."

He nodded. "You've been on the sharp end of that."

Aarinnaie laughed. The nearest sailor glanced back at her. Draken couldn't read his expression. Somewhere between fear and admiration. "You as well, brother. For sevennight after sevennight, and you didn't even know."

He grunted. "I'd never even heard of the Mance until I got to Akrasia."

"Right. Father mentioned Monoeans are prejudiced against magic." She gave him a look. "A few thousand times."

He refused to rise to the bait. "Monoea is a cultured country, and faithful. We do not—"

"*We*, Khel Szi?"

Gods, it was as if he'd inadvertently accepted his fate. Born low, die low, he thought. "I am half-Monoean by blood, and fair more that by heart."

"And what of Brîn?"

He didn't answer. Brîn was . . . duty. He was of Brîn, perhaps more than any other place. But he didn't *feel* it the way he should. Except when it came to Elena, and she was Akrasia. Where that left him now, he had no idea. It probably would never matter.

"Will your royal Monoean blood save you from the King's blade?"

"No." A sail luffed overhead as the rain eased. The skies lightened to a cloudy white, like dull moonwrought. Finally. He slid his cloak hood back. "The King is the law."

"Meaning his people live by his whims."

"Truth, I'm likely to be thrown in his dungeon for a sevennight or more while he consults his lords over my fate. They will urge him to kill me." They'd never much liked him, the enslaved bastard cousin of the King. When he'd found Lesle murdered, he had reckoned it had been some worried Landed who'd done it. The Black Guard had afforded Draken many secrets about Monoean nobility. "I think—I pray—he considers well this time."

"This time?"

"It's always a game to see who can persuade the King best. This time I think they will be in accord. It might buy us time; more likely it will cost us."

"You should have told Elena who you are," Aarinnaie said.

"I'd be dead for the telling and where would Brîn be, eh?"

"You don't know that."

He snorted. "I think I do. Elena's lords hated me as well as King Aissyth's lords do." He thought of the flattering Ilumat, "watching" over his Queen and his child to be, and his stomach churned his breakfast. It wouldn't be so difficult for Elena to push aside his child for one got in marriage. Or to reserve his child for the empty Brînian throne.

Aarinnaie tipped her head, considering. A breeze caught her narrow braids and lifted a few of them. She tucked them behind her ear. In that moment Draken could almost imagine her as a small girl. Before she'd been taught to kill. When she'd been a harmless child.

Foolish, he chided himself. Aarinnaie was many things, but he'd lay out good Rare that she'd never been harmless.

"I meant for you to stay and help Elena as my regent," he said.

"A Szirin can't be regent of Brîn."

"Why not? Brin must live by *my* whim, aye?" His spirit felt a little lighter of a sudden. He decided not to wonder why.

A smile tugged at the corner of her lips. "Did you just say something in jest, Khel Szi? Ring for a scribe so we can mark the occasion."

His smile matched hers, slight but real. She reached out and wrapped her fingers around his wrist, then slid her narrow hand into his. Once again he was struck by how slight she was. So young. Yet strong. Powerful. Those little fingers had been bloodied many times.

"Tell me about your mother," he said. "Do you resemble her?"

She nodded. "I think so by the paintings, though I don't remember her. She died in childbirth when I was three. Our little brother barely lived a sevennight. Had he survived, he would be Szi, not you. The gods apparently did as they must to see you crowned at Brîn."

Truth, he wouldn't put killing a mother and child past the gods. They'd let Lesle die. He'd call it superstition if there hadn't been too many coincidences to discount it.

"And what of yours, Draken?" Her tone gentled. "Does she yet live?"

"Last I heard. I've never met her." He shook his head and stared out over the seas, searching for where the water met the skies. It was nearly seamless, but for a small shadowy bump. He frowned. "Is that land or another ship?"

"Looks like smoke," Osias said, coming to the rail.

Aarinnaie nodded. "I saw the maps. We're not due for land again until Monoea. We passed the Unmanned Islands. It must be a ship."

Draken turned back and squinted. He wished he'd brought his glass, but it was too valuable to risk aboard ship. "Akhanar?"

Joran strode closer. "Khel Szi?"

"Steer for that smoke on the horizon. I want to see what it is."

Joran gave the orders. The three sailors on deck went to tighten lines. Brimlud adjusted course at the wheel, and the sails swelled as a fresh wind filled them. Draken frowned as their speed increased.

"Almost as if the gods are blowing us there," he muttered.

Aarinnaie shook her head. "Not everything is a portent from the gods, brother."

He glanced at her. "Do you really believe that, knowing me?"

She laughed, but low and grim, her eyes locked on the smoke billowing into the quickly bluing sky.

CHAPTER FOURTEEN

By the time they gained on the ship, the smoke had lessened to ghostlike puffs on the sea breezes. A trade freighter labeled in Brînish as the *Sea Swallow*, it had taken on water and dragged deep in the sea. Ash from the burned sails still floated in the air. Blackened strips of cloth hung from booms. Bits of wreckage floated over the quiet waves. Despite repeated hails, no one responded.

Ghotze's grandson Treol shimmied up a mast, hand-over-hand like the fingercats in the Norvern Wildes of Monoea, and scanned the seas.

Draken called out, "Any of you know the *Sea Swallow*? Her owner? Her Akhanar?"

The sailors gathered on deck to see the wreckage. They shook their heads and mumbled denial. More than a couple sliced their forearms with a blade and let blood drip to the water, the Brînish offering to the gods in prayer their own ship remain safe. Tyrolean tossed coins into the sea.

"Not another ship in sight, Captain," Treol said, leaping from the lowest mast onto bare feet that thudded against the deck like hard boots. He took an awkward knee before Draken and kept his gaze somewhere around his stomach. "No living neither. Bodies are floating and seasharks are circling to the starboard and there's a big red-brown mark on the aftdeck."

"A mark?" Draken frowned and glanced up at the mast, wondering if he should go up to see it.

"It's a Brînian ship. See? Just there," Setia said as they sailed around the fore of the ship. The coiled snake banner of Brîn hung limp and torn from the rail. Her little hands clutched the rope rail.

"So you think Monoeans did this?" Tyrolean's sharp dark eyes missed nothing.

"Or pirates," Draken said. As they floated past the ship, a body emerged among the wreckage., It drifted face-down, arms and long hair wavering in the sea like bay grass. The bottom half of it was gone. Draken couldn't tell the race but the hair wasn't in locks.

126

"Never heard of a pirate who likes to leave evidence," Joran said, slipping a gaze at Draken.

"You would know," Aarinnaie said stiffly.

Joran tightened, but he said nothing.

"Aarinnaie," Draken said. "Joran is no pirate. Apologize."

She shoved a strand of hair from her face. "I won't. My royal brother had to buy your loyalty. You did nothing as Ghotze tried to kill him."

Her bottom lip pouted and her eyes widened. Draken sighed. It was probably the last thing some people had ever seen, that deceptively appealing, innocent look.

"*Enough*, Aarin," he said.

Aarinnaie shot him a glare, but she quieted.

"Shall I see the Szirin to your cabin, Khel Szi?" Joran asked politely as another body floated by. "I fear this will be ugly before it's done. Perhaps it's not for a female's, ah, gentler sensibilities."

Aarinniae released a frustrated growl. Draken held her gaze and shook his head very slightly. No wonder she kept away from court. She couldn't manage the least verbal sparring without lashing out. But he liked Joran so he kept his tone mild. "My sister doesn't have the usual gentle female sensibilities, Akhanar. It won't be necessary, thanks. Besides, I value her counsel."

To his credit, Joran hid his surprise well. He said nothing else. Draken's respect for his new ship captain notched up again.

"Some Monoeans know the Khel Szi would come this way," Aarinnaie said. "That ship captain, and her crew; the other ships. Do you think they killed all these people?"

"It's possible." His voice was quiet, no air behind it.

"To what end?" Tyrolean asked.

To start war in earnest? "I don't know. But I'm going over there and finding out. Joran, drop the skiff."

◆ ◆ ◆

The *Sea Swallow* had taken enough water she listed sharply. Climbing aboard from his skiff was a simple matter; the rope railings were only an arms-length away from the surface of the sea. He hauled himself up, muscles straining, and got his good knee under him. The other one bore his weight grudgingly. He hung onto the rail behind him and stared at the sloping deck. It was like any ship he'd ever been on, except for the rigging echoing in the silent death.

He heard dripping and climbing on his swordhand side; he glanced over. "Aarin!"

She pulled herself up, unsmiling. Her sheer undershift clung to her slight body. He could make out her ribs, her small, high breasts, the muscles in her shoulders. He averted his eyes.

"Are you capable of saying my name without sounding disapproving?" she asked.

"That was foolish to swim. There are biters in the water."

"They're busy with the dead. Besides, you need me," she said. "You value my counsel. Remember, my brother? My Prince?"

"Curse you, girl."

Draken walked up the shifting, sloping deck—well, hobbled. Damned knee. He aimed a brief scowl at the great stretch of blue sky, though the gods were sleeping. The healing magic that failed to mend his old injuries must be a reminder that he was ever the gods' tool: something to be kept sharp but always reliant on their goodwill. Beyond, smoke dissipated from a fire trough at the stern. The coals were burning down but ash nearly overflowed it. The wood stacked nearby was nearly gone. Someone had set a great fire to get attention with the smoke. Sea breezes dragged at the ash, spinning it to winddevils over the waves.

He climbed the few steps to the aft deck and stared at the sigil painted on the wood. The fresh sea breeze couldn't clear away the rotting smell of blood. The sigil was as wide as a man's height. Hand prints smeared the area around it. There was a big smear to the rail, as if a body had been dragged and tossed over. He thought of someone dipping their palm into hot blood pumping from a fresh wound, dragging it across the deck with purpose. He had seen enough horrors in war to forgo queasiness. But this . . .

"The boy spoke true. It is the Khisson House brand," Aarinnaie said.

Draken strove hard for indifference and failed, his jaw gritted. Aarinnaie held onto a mast and stared at him with dark eyes.

"It's a bloody fucking waste," he said, a low snarl. He glared at his sister. The assassin. The killer. The one who had once scoffed at the deaths of Akrasians and berated Joran for loyalty. "Do you see now what death is? Do you see how ugly, how careless? Blood runs red whether you're a friend or enemy. Bodies stink, no matter who you were. Whether you're Akrasian or Monoean or Brînian. King or slave. We all rot in the end."

"I know," she said softly. "I know."

He turned his back on her and limped down the small flight to the cabins, bracing himself against the wall to manage the sloping deck. She didn't follow.

The captain, who bore the shipsmark on his tunic, sprawled in his cabin. He'd fought but obviously been killed handily. They'd left him dead with his sword in hand. Deep slashes crisscrossed his throat and chest and face.

"Khel Szi?" Soft, meek. "There's something you should see in the hold." Still furious over the waste of life it had taken to draw the bloody sigil, Draken strode back, his bare feet falling hard and uneven on the sloped deck. Aarinnaie stood by the hatch, body stiff under her clinging, wet shift. She gripped the hatch so fiercely the flesh of her wrists strained against the knife sheaths strapped to them. She met Draken's gaze with stricken eyes, blinked rapidly.

Over on the *Bane*, Tyrolean remained on deck, still at the rail, watching.

The stink of death was stronger, drifting up in overpowering wafts. He steeled himself and went down a few ladder rungs. The smell thickened immediately, a gut-wrenching cocktail of bowel, sweat, blood, stale seawater, and burned flesh. Waves lapped the doomed hull. Chains clinked, muffled. The ship gurgled as it took on more water.

His eyes adjusted to the dim light faster than his mind adjusted to what he was seeing. The dulled edges of the forest took on the blunt sharpness of trees. Bodies. Everywhere. Packed tightly. Limp. Still.

Fatal visages ran from grim acceptance to terror. Blue eyes splayed nearly as wide as guts and throats. Blond hair splotched with black. Tanned skin now struck white, drained of blood. Fine woolen and silks stained crimson and brown.

The bodies didn't float in the stained water. Chains held them down.

Someone had walked among them and murdered them all.

He shifted, and his shadow with it. Sun lit a face . . . one he knew. She had been the wife of one of the Black Guards beneath him. Laryson, that was their name. He peered around and found the Guard. His head lolled, nearly severed from his neck.

It was several heartbeats to remember to breathe. Then he regretted drawing in another lungful of death stench. He started up the ladder quickly, stumbling over his bad knee, and then paused and climbed back down. Holding his breath, he reached into the brackish, boot-high water to grasp a cold, wet hand, and then another. No brands to match his. These were no criminals. But their clothing was fine. Minors, at least. Military. Maybe some Landed.

He had muck up to his elbows. Stained, oily, stinking seawater. He climbed back up, found the rain barrel, and thrust his branded hands in to clean them.

Aarinnaie watched him, one hand over her nose and mouth. It didn't muffle the edge of hysteria in her voice. "Were they all banished? Are they all criminals? There are so many. It can't be possible, can it?"

He shook his head slowly, willing himself to hold down the bile, to straighten his back, to shove the imagery from his mind. Blessed, habitual numbness settled in. But he'd never escape the memory of the stink. Those bodies could never be unseen again.

"Not criminals." At her frown, he added, "Military. Black Guards. Nobility."

She lowered her hand, clenching it. "This is a Brînian ship. Did our people do this?"

Draken wanted to dive into the sea and swim as deep and hard as he could, away. "There'll be fire-oil aboard. In the galley. Or on the aft deck for defense. Earthen jugs. Find it."

She stared a moment more before she went to find a jug and drag it back to him. He sent her after more and they slopped the acrid oil onto the deck and over the course sails before escaping into their skiff.

Despite its inevitable sinking, Draken wanted, needed the *Sea Swallow* to burn. He needed all evidence of the horror destroyed. At the moment he couldn't even think why, he just knew the truth of need in his bones. He threw his shoulders into rowing. Sea spray soaked them; a fine wind was picking up. After drying off, dressing in fresh clothes, and drinking warmed wine pressed into his hand by the well-meaning galleymate, he went to the cabin and found his bow. Back on the aft deck, as Brimlud steered them away, Draken lit arrow after arrow from the fire basin. For a little, the familiar bow in his hand was all he knew. Draw, release, the reassuring *thup* of the string against his wrist bracer. The deck and limp sails of the *Sea Swallow* caught. He shot until they were out of range. He watched the wreckage disappear into smoke and sea as they sailed away. Osias watched as well, wrapped in his white cloak, the wind tugging at his braids. He hadn't been talking much in the past days, as if he already knew the horrors floating on these waters, and those just ahead, in Monoea.

Tyrolean joined him at the rail. "Fine shooting, Your Highness."

Draken didn't answer, but he couldn't deny the relief of having a bow in his hand again, especially combined with the sensation of waves rolling under his feet. It gave him the reassuring sense of being a single stone mortared into a wall, rather than the keystone. This is who I am, he thought. A Monoean half-blood slave. A bowman. Night Lord. Khel Szi. If I die for it, so be it.

Tyrolean tried again. "Your sister is resting."

He relented without softening his stature. "Good."

Aarinnaie had made herself scarce, climbing up to the deck and letting Tyrolean wrap her in a cloak, obviously shaken by the carnage she'd seen. Draken didn't have it in him to comfort her. His mind was still wrangling with the possible costs. His life, most certainly. And maybe the others with him.

Gods protect them. Forget me. Protect my sister. My friends. These men.

This time he didn't have to try not to curse the gods as he prayed. He drew the sharp edge of an arrow across the back of his hand and let his blood fall into the sea. An offering to Korde. To Khellian. It was a bald-faced plea.

"Did you learn anything of use?" Tyrolean asked when he was through.

Draken grunted. Stared a few breaths longer. "The hold was full of Monoeans. Officers and nobles. Dead, all of them."

"Pirates—?"

"No."

Silence. "Who would do such a thing then?"

"Yramantha," Draken said.

Osias had shaken himself out of his reverie and joined them at the rail. "I think it must be. But I do not know why."

Tyrolean shook his head. "I don't know that we can make that conclusion. It's a big ocean. It could be anyone—"

"The sigil is the same Yramantha wore. The same as House Khisson. She knew I was coming this way. She's baring her teeth."

Tyrolean's hesitation told Draken the news had penetrated the stoic Captain. "How many?"

"Two hundred. Three. No brands. I checked." Draken's hands tightened on the rail. His own brands stood out from his skin in sharp relief, the scars pale, mottled, ugly. "They weren't criminals. They weren't slaves, or prisoners of war. They were a message from Yramantha for me."

CHAPTER FIFTEEN

"Come now, brother. Stand still. Nearly finished."

Draken shifted as Aarinniae inked a stern, stylized Khellian's mask in white and red on Draken's face. She cursed and reached up with a wet rag to redo the section he'd made her smear.

His black trousers were the loose, sashed sort. Seaborn was strapped to his waist and thigh by an embroidered leather belt. Thick moonwrought cuffs wrapped his wrists rather than his typical leather bracers, and over it all, the cloak given him by Elena: black wool adorned with two green stripes over each shoulder designating his Akrasian rank as Night Lord. A proper Brînian Szi would only wear boots in snow or if on a long journey, never into someone's home or to court. Despite the cold, Draken was bare-chested and barefoot, though he'd drawn the line at toe rings.

Aarinnaie reached up with the drawing stick and inked another narrow scroll on Draken's cheek. She squinted up at him, the tip of her tongue sticking out of the corner of her mouth, filled in a line beneath the moonwrought circlet on his brow, and stepped back.

"There. Quite stern and noble. The gods should be pleased."

"Would you know it's me? I'd like to buy a little time."

Aarinnaie shook her head, brow wrinkled, looking worried. "I don't know. I don't think so."

He turned his head as he felt the ship bump one of the huge outer docks anchored to the floor of Sister Bay. An ornate barge waited to pick them up and take them ashore. He'd seen it as they'd entered the harbor, which showed Yramantha had passed along the news of his arrival. But it had been two agonizing days of messaging across the harbor before they could settle on arrangements for his presentation to King Aissyth and Queen Bolaire. Somehow in the past Sohalia he'd forgotten how long Monoeans took to sort such things. He'd hoped the knots in his stomach would loosen once he was preparing to go ashore, but they were only worse. He couldn't keep his mind from jittering along the bumpy, shaded path to his death. Soon, he told himself. Surely it would be soon.

Aarinnaie's gown covered her throat to heel, though the fabric clung to her curves. Father, no doubt, had told her everything she should know about Monoea and proper etiquette. Once she had a cloak on, she'd be more than suitable. Released from the braids and thoroughly washed, her dark hair hung in miraculously sorted ringlets. Not proper to wear it loose in Monoea, but it would be in Brîn. Draken felt no little pride in her.

Curse the Seven that brought them to this moment, and all who had hurt his sister. She'd seen enough pain in her short life. She depended on him now and she might just lose him here. Watching his head get separated from his shoulders could be her undoing. Perhaps King Aissyth could be persuaded to execute him in private.

He touched her arm. "If it comes to violence, I'm certain King Aissyth won't harm you."

"He should be more afraid of me than I am of him." She straightened her back. "We should go."

"Wait. I want to ask a favor."

Her eyes narrowed.

"If they kill me, do not harm them. I'm here to avert war, Aarin, not make it."

"That sounds like an order, not a favor."

"Whichever will make you agree."

"Revenge appeases the lord god Khellian," she said. "Patron of our House."

"War would be a poor way to honor my memory. And I need you to go home, to explain to Elena. Let her hate me if she will. But don't let her start a war over my death. I'm not worth it."

She bit her lip, studying his inked face. "Where did you live? With your wife?"

"In Ashwyc City, near the palace."

"So you know them all."

"And they know me."

"You think they will execute you."

He was certain of it. "I don't know," he said gently.

"You have this ship. The men are yours to command. You could have gone anywhere. To any country. To Felspirn or Dokklok or the Filmun Straights. Anywhere *else* would have been safe. Instead you chose to come here."

Those places were further than the end of the world, far enough to be mythic.

"They threatened to kill Elena if I did not come."

"And Elena would have killed you had she learned who you are."

She knows who I am, Draken thought. Just not *what* I am. "And maybe she'd kill our child, as well. Or someone else might. Elena doesn't need my blood on her hands. This was my best chance to spare her." *To save her,* he almost could hear the ghostly voice of Bruche admonishing him. He sighed and said feebly, "They're waiting."

She blinked, a string of rapid movements. "I will do as you ask and forgo revenge."

His throat tightened too much to answer. Selfishly, he was glad she was here. A much smaller, nobler part of him wished she was safe at Brîn. She stood stiff in front of him, but then pressed her face against his bare chest, her fingers reaching up to grip the chain around his neck. He ran his hand over her curls, kissed her head, and set her back. "Put your cloak on, Szirin. It's time."

He walked her down the short corridor to the deck. The day was clear, fine, the air over the bay fresh but surprisingly cold. After having the warmth of the Akrasian day on his back for so many moonturns, and then the dampness of Brîn warming to Tradeseason, he was just remembering how chilly Monoea always was.

Sister Bay sprawled out around them, busy as usual. Dozens of ships anchored in the depths by the floating platform docks, and rowed barges ran their constant routes from the Outer Docks to the coastal docking districts. As a navy bowman, Draken had spent time in all the various docksides and trade districts, but especially at Coldbank, where the navy patrol ships docked. He scanned the ships there and found Yramantha's fleet of three. They drifted, no mark on them to betray what they'd done to their own people. *I'm here,* he thought. *As you bid me.* He wondered if he would see Yramantha. He wondered if he could keep from killing her if he did.

Aarinnaie's wide eyes took in the Seven Cities of Monoea from this close vantage of the Harbor, the great swath of land encircling Sister Bay packed to overflowing with buildings, roads, and people. Over the great, sheer Sevenfel Cliffs the gold-domed towers of the Palace Ashwyc glowed in the sun, blurred slightly by mists. Each city but two had docking districts: Ashwyc, the enormous palace and grounds built on the edge of the Cliffs, and Kordwyn, which sat behind Ashwyc and was all things bureaucratic in the kingdom: maintaining roads and byways, collecting taxes, trade licencing, policing the state. Despite the anxiety clawing at his gut, Draken smiled at his sister's amazement. He'd rarely compared his old and new countries, not wanting to dwell on the past too much since his exile, but Brîn was a village compared to the Seven Cities.

The barge captain, a ranked sailor in a bloodstone uniform, bowed to them deeply and welcomed them aboard. Draken helped Aarinnaie over the gap and handed her to Tyrolean, who seemed happy enough to take her arm and guide her into the comfortable lounge.

Halmar and three szi nêre accompanied him first, keeping close. The Brînians were all heavily armed with sword harness straps across their bare chests. Not a shiver among them, just proud vigilance. Tyrolean, Osias, and Setia followed, all regarded with naked curiosity. But soon the drums started, the oars caught the beat, and they glided across the bay.

The Captain saw them served warmed wine by a footman and then left them alone. "That's odd, his not staying," Aarinnaie said, reaching for her cup. Konnan gently took it from her and sipped from it himself before handing it back.

"He must have a good reputation to bring important diplomats to shore, but even so, a barge captain is too lowborn to make small talk with royalty," Draken answered. Also the captain didn't know Brînish and Draken hadn't yet decided whether a language barrier would serve or hurt his disguise, such as it was.

He didn't sit, but shifted from window to window. The shutters were open, admitting the view and the cold. Aarinnaie drank and got up to stand by him. He wrapped his arm around her shoulders, his heavy cloak enfolding her.

"No snow. It's a fine day." Though the air was cold.

"Snow in Trade?"

"Sometimes." Draken pointed to the greystone palace topped with golden domes and hung with banners atop the great cliff. "The royal palace. A city unto itself. Next to it is City Kordwyn. The other side, where there's so much open green between the walls, is Wyndam. Those are Landed city estates—the oldest, richest families. Below Wyndam, that great township is Newporte. And the other side of the Bay is Shadowcliff, Ostborough, and Coldbank." Where Yramantha's ships were docked.

"Why so many cities?"

He shrugged. "The cities started out as walled holdings, run by warlords."

She turned her head, looking at the dozens of docks along the coast. "At which dock will we land?"

"We'll go through Galbrayt's Gate in the big harbor with the stone piers and towers, just there below Wyndam."

"Where the Landed live," Aarinnaie said.

"Well done. Sometimes it's called Landed Gate."

"Galbrayt is a hero, aye?" Osias joined them at the window, eyes narrowed as he stared.

Draken nodded, though a chill prickled his back as he watched Osias peruse the Seven Cities. Osias had been bound by many spirits before Draken had broken his fetter. He wondered if they were still with Osias, or if they'd fled. He wondered if some of them had memories from ancient times, though it was centuries ago and in a different country.

"One of the Princes is named for him." The youngest.

More details of the Seven Sisters emerged as they drew closer: blocks and blocks of muddy streets and sharply peaked buildings, open squares for markets, roads winding near the Docksides, men and women working barges and docks and smaller freighters, fishers headed out to net the day's catch in the bay or open sea. The grey stone curving cliffs pocked with little alcoves rose like stern visages above it all. In the time it took to cross Sister Bay clouds had rolled in to smother what was left of the blue sky, promising a cold, stinging rain.

Draken's stomach tightened uncomfortably. His knee ached in the familiar damp cold, though it had been wrapped tightly and he'd had a Gadye potion to ward off the worst of the pain. His back was rigid enough to bounce a coin. He fingered the leather wrap on his sword absently, toying with the end that always came loose. Tyrolean spoke softly to Aarinnaie and the szi nêre, pointing out things of interest. None of the Brinians answered, but they stared. Osias and Setia stood at Draken's side.

The barge rowed toward the arch looming between the twin towers of Galbrayt's Gate. Dozens of bodies swung there, mangled by weather and birds. The breeze off Sister Bay turned them gently, revealing lank hair, tortured or missing limbs, gaping jaws. They ran the gamut from fresh to bird-picked. Draken's stomach convulsed around the wine he'd swallowed and threatened to spit it back up. Tyrolean fell silent.

"I thought Monoea didn't execute their prisoners," Setia whispered.

"They don't," Aarinnaie said.

"I wonder if they are rebels caught by the King or loyalists who would not bend to the rebellion," Osias said.

Draken swallowed hard. His voice was hollow. "King Aissyth would not break the laws of his lineage, not even for rebellion. That is not his work."

The bodies passed from view and the hollowness spread to his chest.

The Captain came to open the door, unsmiling and quiet. Or maybe he spoke and Draken missed it; all sound seemed to cease as he stepped off the barge. The land swayed beneath his feet and his limbs felt heavy. He paused to get his bearings. A Prince—Draken could tell by the twisted gold torq set with sky-stones about his throat and blond hair that matched the King's—approached them and bowed his head.

"Your Highness. I am Prince Galbrait. It is my pleasure and honor to escort you to the Palace at Ashwyc, His Royal Majesty's City." He spoke in flawless Brînian.

It had been a long while since Draken had seen Aissyth's youngest son. Galbrait had been dispatched to a military post in the Norvern Wildes as was commonly done with younger children to toughen them. Toughen him it had. He'd matured into broad-shouldered confidence. The sword at his hip was pragmatic rather than ornamental, the leather wrap on the grip stained black with sweat. His cloak was fur but his clothes and armor beneath were simple and fine.

Tyrolean stepped forward as they'd discussed. "Khel Szi, His Royal Highness, Prince of Brîn, and Night Lord for Her Majesty Queen Elena of Akrasia." Tyrolean spoke in a mix of Brînish and Akrasian as he indicated Draken.

Because he sat a throne, there was no need for Draken to bow. Galbrait bent in a bow and rose. He eyed Draken's four szi nêre and Tyrolean in his black armor and green cloak, then shifted his attention to Osias and Setia. Galbrait went rigid, enough that Draken thought he would recoil. Before Draken could wonder on it too closely, a smile twitched across Galbrait's lips. Brief. Unreadable. Diplomatic.

When he turned his gaze on Aarinnaie, the smile took on more life. "And you are?"

Aarinnaie's eyes widened at the mild breach of protocol.

"Khel Szi's sister, Aarinnaie Szirin, Her Royal Highness, Princess of Brîn," Tyrolean said. "And I am First Captain Tyrolean of the Akrasian Royal Escort, Your Highness, Special Envoy to Brîn. I serve the Khel Szi at Queen Elena's pleasure."

If Galbrait thought a high-rank Escort serving the Prince of Brîn was odd, he hid it well. "Khel Szi, Szirin, Captain . . ." Again his gaze flicked over Osias, likely not knowing how to address him or Setia, "It is my very great honor to greet you. Welcome to Monoea."

Greet. He said *greet*. Not *meet*. The knot tightened its bands inside Draken's ribs. He gave Galbrait a stiff nod and replied in Brînish, "The honor is mine." He glanced back at the Mance in order to introduce him, but Osias gave a minute shake of his head.

Galbrait gestured toward a carriage and several saddled horses flanked by a company of Royal Guards. Their heavy tack was familiar, causing a tug within Draken. "It is a cold Trade day, Szirin, and I've heard Brîn is milder than our Seven Cities. I brought the carriage for your comfort." Galbrait offered Aarinnaie his arm and helped her into the carriage. To her credit, she didn't smirk.

Draken cleared his throat and spoke softly in Brînish. "Setia, why don't you ride with Aarin?" The horses were all immense for her tiny frame and she wouldn't like being lifted up like a child, not in front of strangers. Konnan stepped forward to offer her his arm when Prince Galbrait didn't. Setia's dappled brow creased, but she acquiesced without comment.

Draken mounted the horse brought to him, a very fine kingstock Bay, distracted by the oddness of the scene. Why weren't the ladies brought horses? He'd never witnessed coddling them like that. Was it Monoean perception of Brînish culture? Truth, women had no right to inherit, but some few islander women fought alongside their men, and many certainly worked the same as or harder than men in the same trades.

Konnan fell back to ride behind the carriage. Halmar stayed with Draken. Galbrait mounted and indicated Draken should ride abreast with him at the head of the little parade. They started the sharp climb up the road that cut back and forth across the Sevenfall Cliffs into Wyndam.

"How was the journey, Khel Szi?" Galbrait asked.

"It went fair well, Your Highness," Draken said, gratefully keeping to Brînish since Galbrait did.

"We didn't anticipate your bringing your sister," Galbrait said. "A happy surprise. I hope we can make her feel welcome during her time here."

A chance to show some solidarity between Akrasia and Brîn had fallen right into his lap. What was one more twist of the truth when a man's whole life is a lie?

"It was Queen Elena's suggestion," Draken replied. "Aarinnaie has talents beyond what most men can imagine."

Galbrait gave him a look, brows drawn. Then his face cleared and he laughed politely. "Duly noted, Khel Szi." He changed the subject by pointing out estates Draken already well knew and explaining where the nobles' proper lands were in Monoea. Everything looked the same, brutally so. Draken had not been gone so long.

But fair long enough to make a new life. He longed for Elena's quiet presence and especially to be the man in truth she thought him to be. Then he remembered he probably wouldn't be a man at all before the sevennight was out, and he stiffened. Galbrait was too involved with his polite discourse about Wyndam to notice.

"The cliffs are called Sevenfel." They'd drawn close enough to see the funereal niches well. The nearest cliff climbed up, the road clinging to it. Each was filled with anything from bone fragments to grinning skulls to entire skeletons crammed in. It had been the war since they'd put any bodies in; Draken had been spared overseeing the crews of soldiers who severed heads and limbs from bodies to add to the gruesome testament to Monoea's military strength. There were hundreds upon hundreds of them and he felt as if he was seeing them for the first time.

"You don't ask about the skulls," Galbrait said quietly. "Everyone does. Do you know about them? Where you here at the Decade war?"

Dangerous territory, but not as dangerous as he was about to tread. Ashwyc City loomed ever closer.

"I know of the niches," he answered, matching Galbrait's soft tone.

Prince Galbrait glanced at Draken, likely wondering if the sight of his own people's remains exposed to the open air angered him. And it did, he realized abruptly. They hadn't fought for glory or riches, only for the yoke of Akrasia.

Chill winds whistled across the cliffs and cut through Draken's cloak. At least he'd brought his warm one. Elena's pendant felt like a piece of ice against his chest. Curse the Brînians and their brash habit of going shirtless.

Draken glanced back to see what the Mance made of the war prizes. Osias lifted his chin and scoured the cliffs with stormy eyes. As he passed beneath them, bones chattered softly in their niches. A flock of gulls cried out and soared away from the cliff top. Halmar remained as stoic as usual, but the Monoean guards shifted in their saddles, attention flitting from their charges to the cliffs.

Did they wonder why the wind seemed to barely touch the silver man? Would they accuse them of magicks? Surely Osias worked some eerie necromantic spell. Draken's hand strayed to Seaborn's hilt. The scabbard was warm against his thigh and the sword heated his palm. It did nothing to ease his stiff muscles.

Tyrolean glanced up and then bent to speak to Aarinnaie and Setia in the carriage. Draken felt a pang. It was right and good that Tyrolean keep close to Aarinnaie. But he couldn't help feeling his friend was already letting him go, moving on toward protecting his sister.

He reminded himself sternly that someone needed to look after her, and he trusted no one more than Tyrolean. It was his fault she needed protection. His stomach clenched again. Truth, she'd sneaked aboard his ship and she'd insisted on coming ashore. But he should have ordered her to hide aboard until the ugliness was over. Yet another woman in his life he'd failed to protect.

Galbrait had slowed his horse and gave Draken a curious look. He realized abruptly he must have stayed quiet too long for courtesy and tried to think of something to say. "You're too young to have fought."

"I was a child," Galbrait said. "But I dreamed of it, like we all do before we realize war is only ugliness and pain. And I remember the Night of Surrender."

Draken did too. He'd been called to greet his cousin-King and awarded his new commission with the Black Guard not soon after, all the royal family looking on. Galbrait had been there, a child Prince beneath his notice. And now Galbrait was a warrior to be reckoned with. A man wise enough to know what war was, and more importantly, what it wasn't. Draken didn't know what to think of his cousin. *Does he know me or not?*

He would know, soon enough.

Galbrait continued with the history lesson. " . . . and some of the bones are very old. No one alive remembers the cliffs without them. Legend says a long-ago King married a Blood Queen from Felspirn and she commissioned the niches carved into the cliffs."

Felspirn. Maybe Aarinnaie had the right of it. Maybe he should have fled to some far off land. "Have you been, Your Highness?"

"To Felspirn? I wish!" The Prince laughed again. "I've been on duty in the Norvern Wilds forever. I only was called back to court two sevennight ago. Father thinks it's time I marry." His lip curled.

Draken felt he could almost like the man. He had the sudden insight this was exactly as the King had planned. It sounded like Aissyth to send this younger, likable son to win the Brînian Prince over. It was oddly reassuring.

"Are you married, Khel Szi?" Galbrait asked.

Draken lifted Elena's pendant from his chest, curled his fingers around it. The familiar contours of Elena's face under his fingers soothed him. "My life is sworn to my Queen. We expect our first child before Frost."

Prince Galbrait 's brows climbed. He was a handsome enough man, with the perfect Monoean royal profile but for the lopsided bump on his nose indicating it'd been broken and a pale scar through the cleft in his chin. "Marriage must be different there. In your homeland . . ." He colored. "Forgive me. I pry."

"Not at all. Queen Elena and I cannot marry because of cultural differences and politics." Something even a Prince who'd been hanging around the Norvern Wildes for most of his raising up could doubtless understand. "I am her courtesan and subject. But my heart is fully with her, and hers with mine." At least until she found out who he really was. Draken cleared his throat, his attention drawn by a low rumble coming from higher in Wyndam. He lifted his chin to listen, but it remained the same. Must be the wind between buildings and walls.

Once they made the initial switching ascent through the notched cliff and passed through gates guarded by young Landed soldiers, the ground leveled out. Draken had passed this way hundreds of times in his life. At the clifftop it widened into a proper cobbled street. Great trees and stone walls rose on either side, protecting estates of the Landed. When they passed gates, he couldn't help but glance through them at the familiar houses.

"I'm attending balls at all of them lately," Galbrait mentioned. To search for a wife, no doubt.

"Does His Grace have someone suitable in mind for you?"

"A few." Another scowl touched Galbrait's lips and then he brightened. "Ah, Temple Ring. Nearly there, then."

It was on the tip of Draken's tongue to say he knew, but an odd reverant memory washed over him as the clean stone roadway opened up into the great circle—Sohalia revelries and scenes of daily market business.

Forty-nine great Everbloom trees had been planted thirty paces apart around the outer circle, trunks bigger than a man could reach around. Intricately carved gates, old enough to have been magicked before it was outlawed, and tall stone walls fronted the estates of Landed fortunate enough to live on Temple Ring. Narrower roadways, all paved in well-repaired greystone, led from it. They were dwarfed by King's Lane, the wide promenade that led to Ashwyc City.

Today it was oddly empty. Draken realized that a crowd waited further down on King's Lane. He blinked at the flower-strewn cobbles. Hundreds of nobles had gathered to greet their procession. As they rounded the Ring and came into view, a wave of cheers washed over them. Draken's horse tossed his head and snorted at the roar.

Galbrait shot him a grin. "I'd have told you but it was supposed to be a surprise. Not my idea . . ." He bowed his head, quite formally. "Welcome again to Monoea, Khel Szi of Brîn. Welcome to these Seven Cities. Welcome to Ashwyc Palace. We await you most eagerly."

We? Not the King? No wonder it had taken two days to arrange.

Galbrait spurred his horse into a prancing trot and a fresh, higher pitched cheer rose up through the nobles. More hothouse flowers were thrown before the Prince by dozens of giggling girls of marrying age. He surely was a favorite among them. The racket only slightly dropped when Draken urged his horse onto the lane. More flowers rained down, smothering the stone road before him. He lifted his chin and sat very straight in the saddle, the cold air sweeping his bare chest and inked face. His sword hummed against his thigh, as if it wanted to be freed of its scabbard. But drawing now would be an insult at best, worse: a death wish. Especially if the damned thing glowed like one of the Seven Eyes.

The last time he'd been here, they'd dragged him down to a prison ship in chains, shivering under a moonless night sky. He'd been too deep inside his grief and shock to feel frightened. Today, welcomed like the Prince he was, his insides wound into a sickening knot. The reveled greeting only made it worse. His szi nêre moved to flank him, drawing close as if knowing he needed their guard. Out of the corner of his eye he saw ladies leaning to speak to each other; others waved to him. Lords mostly stood quite still, examining him and his party. He could only imagine what they thought of this enemy Prince in their midst: bare-chested, scarred, bejeweled and painted up like some ruffian warlord.

Gold-peaked towers flanked the great gates of Ashwyc City, the stone and wood iron-banded to repel magicks.

Osias urged his horse closer and lifted his chin, indicating the rusting iron straps. "Superstition," he mouthed. His black moon tattoo stood in stark relief against his silvery skin and the grey air.

Tyrolean drew up on the other side of Draken, though he kept a pace behind. Draken nodded, slightly relieved at having his friends flanking him.

The gates hung open with an honor guard of perhaps two hundred soldiers in rows, faceless under full helms, every blade bared. This didn't alarm him; it was a typical Monoean greeting to display their weapons, a silent promise of protection rather than attack. Their swords and armor shone dully, reflecting the stormy skies.

How would Aissyth do it? Draken wondered. Slit his throat? Beheading, so his head will have its own niche? Or would he let Draken's flesh rot from Galbrayth's Gate?

His horse's hooves thumped over the big moat bridge along the outer wall— he'd never seen the bridge raised and wondered if it could be—and then inside, over another narrower bridge crossing the stream that used to run by his own cottage.

Hardy grass spread out on either side of the road, looking like an immense parkland interspersed with growing fields, pockets of trees, and clumps of cottages. On the windward side the land ended in a low wall at the cliff. But he turned inland, instinctively looking for his cottage where it sat tumbled over with flowers by the stream. It had been small and poorly placed, but it had been theirs. Not just anyone was granted land inside Ashwyc Palace City walls. It had been his cousin's greatest sign of acceptance, as much as he could do for Draken without causing a scandal.

He sought the familiar—the Everbloom with the broken top, the other with the old swing, and the three Spindle Trees . . . His heart clenched. The cow yard was empty but for weeds. A few flowers scrabbled a living at the base of the stone foundation. Nothing was left of his life here but a burnt out shell, a chimney, and blackened tree trunks jutting crookedly into the air.

CHAPTER SIXTEEN

The cutstone Palace walls, towers, and battlements were built on the highest cliff of Sevenfel, which grew from the lower cliffs as if shoved up from below. Draken didn't need his glass to know that bowmen lined the battlements with giant longbows more than sufficient to reach his location at the base of the cliff. More niches of death marred this face as well, though in the misty gloom rolling overhead, shadows concealed their occupants. Draken noticed his szi nêre and Tyrolean looking all around and followed their lead. He wasn't supposed to have been here before. The great stone towers with their golden domes atop the sheer cliff walls was such a feat of astounding, enormous architecture, few newcomers could resist staring. Some claimed it was the largest castle in the world.

Draken listened carefully as Osias passed beneath the cliff in case these bones would clatter at him, but the winds had kicked up too fiercely to hear. The cliff face and stone walls were as grey and forbidding as the soldiers who guarded it. Even the golden parapets were dulled by the clouds rolling from inland.

The roar of water grew as they crossed the ground at the base of Ashwyc Cliff. The river started higher, well past the Palace on gently sloped ground, and tumbled over the cliff into sizable freshwater pools. Draken stretched in his saddle to peer ahead, shading his eyes from the rain with a hand at his brow, but he couldn't see the river beneath the falls for the trees surrounding it, much less the bridge. A stinging rain began to fall. Everyone pulled their hoods up. Conversation fell off.

The horses walked through the vaporous gloom, mists wavering ahead like banes over Sohalia fires. Hooves echoed on the bridge, and then the carriage rolled over, nearly soundless. They started the long path upward, well-paved and walled as it crossed the easy end of the cliff and back again to nearly level ground.

Draken tightened again, seeing the familiar open maw of the gate into the palace proper. Spears stuck down from its mouth like jagged teeth, released by a wheel-and-weight system engineered by some long ago King. The Palace bridge was made of ancient slabs of blackened flagstone backed by more iron and wood so old it was petrified to stone-hard. The top was worn smooth by generations of hooves and boots and rough weather. An enemy ram would have to break through the stone as well as the iron and wood, providing they could build another bridge over the steep-walled river. Draken had only ever seen it up once, during the Decade War.

Inside the keep, Draken dismounted as a groom took his horse's reins. The cold air made his landing painful on his bare feet, though the szi nêre didn't seem to notice. Aarinnaie emerged from her carriage, lifting her skirts and letting Galbrait hand her down. For a moment she just stared upward at the walls and the castle, her hand resting on Galbrait's forearm. Then she blinked and took her hand back, turning her face toward Draken. The rest of the Monoean guards filed in under the gate. There was little sound but horses stamping and snorting in the wind. Galbrait had ceased his polite chatter and stepped away to speak to the guards at the great doors.

A dull clang, as if someone had rung a broken bell, echoed against the castle walls. Every head turned toward the gate. Draken's hand went to his sword and he turned, blood surging. The ringing turned to a rusty, stressed clanking as heavy chains protested movement. Aarinnaie moved as if to flee; Draken intercepted her. The steel spears of the gate crashed down.

"What is this?" Draken said to Galbrait. He kept a tight grip on Aarinnaie's arm.

Galbrait spread his hands. "There was some talk . . . it's for your safety. And ours. Brînians are not popular in Monoea, this you must know."

Draken narrowed his eyes. Tried to breathe. Think. This made no sense. "You didn't think to warn us?"

"We didn't think you'd come if you thought you would be locked in." Galbrait stepped closer. "Your Highness, please believe me. You are not a prisoner here. Indeed, you are very much the opposite."

Draken's nostrils flared as he exhaled. The gate had only been closed once in his lifetime, but he couln't argue that. His gaze flicked upward. No flag indicating court was convening. Perhaps because of the rain? It was dripping off his drawn hood.

"Are we for Court, then?" he asked.

"No. Father wishes to speak to you privately. Please. Come inside."

Privately . . . before court? Or in lieu of it? Their trunks were already being carried into the servant's entrance well aside from the formal one. Cognizant of the others watching, he guided Aarinnaie up the grand steps and out of the wet. The others followed in a tight knot. The steps were great slabs of white stone, reputed to have been part of a dowry of the Felspirn Princess. They sloped toward the middle, shadowed by grey grime that no amount of scrubbing could wash away. Draken flexed his hands as he climbed them. He had scrubbed them until his fingers bled on more than one occasion.

Inside, twin fires on opposite walls warmed the great entrance hall. One immense set of steps led to a rabbit warren of corridors and other steps. Another led to the grand public halls, the ballrooms, and Court. Draken knew them all, the servants quarters, which direction to the kitchens, how long it took to run a message from the King's study to the Queen's private chambers.

Swords and knives and shields strung with enemy colors hung high up on the great stone chimneys. A similar display filled the wall behind Elena's throne. There, magic kept blood dripping from one blade eternally. Here, the weapons were simply pieces of metal and wood that enemies had gripped as they'd died or surrendered. Draken rested his fingers on Seaborn's hilt. It might very well soon hang among the others, and Akrasia and Brîn would surely make war over it. My blade, he thought, his jaw set. Men might take it away, but the gods only awarded it once in a generation. Others were caretakers, not owners.

Servants waited but none of them relinquished their cloaks; despite the fires the air was damp and chilly.

Galbrait pulled Draken aside. "These guards will take the others to guest apartments, and I will see you to Father."

Aarinnaie gave him a sharp look. "It has been a long journey, Your Highness. Surely Khel Szi will be allowed some time to rest."

"A long journey means a long time for my father to wait, and he is not a patient man." A faint apologetic smile flickered and faded. "On Monoean soil all live by the whims of the King, not the Prince."

Whether he meant Draken or himself by the word Prince, Draken didn't know. He glanced about to see what Osias thought of their being separated but didn't catch his silvery head among the others crowding the hall. Had he wandered off? Setia stayed close to Aarinnaie.

"It's all right, Aarin. I'll go see the King and return to you soon." He didn't look at Galbrait to see if he gestured to reassure her. "It's why I'm here, after all." He dropped into Brinish. "Halmar, the szi nêre stay with the Szirin."

The words hung heavy on the air. If he were walking to his death, he wasn't going to drag his szi nêre along with him. Halmar met his gaze and dipped his chin, a slow gesture of respect and assent.

Satisfied, Draken turned with the Prince and walked down the long familiar corridor. They were almost certainly headed to the solarium, a feat of glazed horn windows and lush, indoor gardens that flowered in Frost and went to foreign heat-loving ferns during Trade Season. The King had liked to break his fast there sometimes but Draken had always thought of it as more the Queen's space. He smelled the earth and damp well before he saw the doors, and underlying it, an acrid smoke. His steps slowed without his meaning to.

Galbrait reached the doors ahead of him. "Just in here."

Draken entered and Galbrait closed the door behind them. The Prince stopped at the door. Draken's eyes narrowed. Blocking it. Galbrait gestured him on.

Draken stepped onto the paved path, examining the gardens, expecting damage, but only one section was truly gone and plowed under. The undergrowth, though . . . blackened corpses of plants curled against the ground under the larger ferns and small trees of the solarium, though he could see more sky then he'd recalled from before. The scent clogged his lungs. He coughed slightly and looked up, wishing for a clean breath. Condensation ran down the panes of horn and dripped from the leading.

"It was burned once before. You would have been a child then. You might remember."

Draken's attention snapped forward. King Aissyth stood on the path before him, several strides away. The king looked much the same: blond hair gone to mostly grey, beard concealing the recessed chin none of his sons inherited, thin lips pursed in a frown, eyes that had always watered at the corners. He wore a sword on his hip, as plain and useful as Seaborn, and chainmail peeked out from under his loose robes.

"You wear a sword in my presence?" Aissyth asked.

"It is not a simple sword to set aside lightly, Your Grace." Sometimes he wondered that the gods had not compelled him to keep the blasted thing on him all the time. But what Aissyth didn't know—

"No, I suppose it is not." The King studied Draken head to toe. "Well done. I wouldn't have recognized you."

"But you knew I was coming." He felt a bloody fool standing before his king, barechested, painted, Elena's moonwrought pendant hanging in plain view.

"Interrogating Yramantha proved very educational."

"She told you who I am." Yramantha, interrogated. Odd choice of word. She must be dead.

"And she told me of your involvement in the plot against me."

Draken coughed. The smokey scent made his eyes sting. "What involvement? I haven't been here since well before Sohalia last."

"The rebels mean to put you and your magic," his watery gaze flicked down at the sword on Draken's hip, "on my throne."

He stared. Shook his head. "That is ridiculous."

"Nevertheless, she was quite clear. It was then things started falling into place. Lesle's murder. Your complicity after a lifetime of bearing my faith. Your parentage . . . why my royal cousin would *ever* let a man like your father touch her. Your surviving exile . . ."

"Yramantha tossed me off her ship at Khein Bay with naught but the rags on my back," Draken said. "I didn't kill Lesle and I've long suspected my father of rape. Your Grace, I never asked for this sword or the magic—"

"Do not lie to me! I know you covet my throne—"

"I already have one bloody throne I don't want! Why in Khellian's name would I want yours?"

Thunder rumbled overhead and shuddered through the sheer horn windows. That seemed to stop Aissyth, but only for a breath. "The magic you used to kill Lesle has corrupted you. You think you can control it but it controls *you*. It craves life. Power. And it's found it in you. It's made you a living, breathing heresy and you must die before it takes further root in Monoea."

The finality in those sacrilegious words sent a chill through Draken. There was no guiding Aissyth out of his tangled web of reason. "You brought me here to kill me."

The King drew his sword. "It's a sight easier here than in Brîn. And killing you in self-defense needn't ruin relations between Akrasia and Monoea."

Draken's hand shifted to his sword, but he didn't draw. "And if I fail to fight back? If there is no self-defense in my death, only murder? Execution?"

Aissyth advanced. "My son is standing witness. He will back up my claim."

Draken made the mistake of glancing back at Galbrait. He was stoic by the door, his face a mask of judgement. The King swung in that moment, slicing Draken across the chest. He gasped as fire lit a path through his skin.

This was it, then. A few moments of pain and it could end.

But Elena flashed through his mind. Rain running down her cheeks like tears, throwing her arms about him, the swelling of their child under his hand. Her whispered plea to return soon . . .

In an instant his sword was in his hand and blocking the King's next strike. The longer blade clanged against Seaborn and jarred Draken's arm. He winced as the wound on his chest started to knit. The big paver shifted beneath their weight. He stumbled back. He would have thought it his imagination had the King not done the same. Excellent; unsteady ground plus an expert swordsman bent on killing him.

He unclasped his cloak as he switched his balance and strode forward two steps, meeting the King's next challenge. He had no armor, no way to block but with his sword. The King struck and he barely caught it on his crossguard, then shoved back as hard as he could. Awkward and not as powerful as he wanted, because the strike had been high-line. Still, it threw Aissyth's arm up and made him stagger back. Draken pressed again, taking advantage of the King's unprotected middle.

Seaborn sliced through the robes and into flesh. Draken followed the strike with another, pure muscle memory and trained habit. Blood gushed from the King's throat. He gaped and crumpled, robes furrowing around him. His sword thudded into the dirt to the side of the path and crushed a flowering fern.

Galbrait shouted and rushed him, but a guard hidden in the foliage reached Draken first. Moving on pure energy, no thought, Draken slashed hard at the only vulnerable spot in his light armor. The man's head tumbled off Seaborn and blood flowed as the big form crumpled.

"Life for life." Draken barely breathed the words but he felt the air shudder slightly. It was enough. He turned to face Galbrait, chest heaving, sword on guard, voice a low growl: "There. Your father lives."

Three more guards emerged from the foliage. The King moaned. Galbrait leaned back on his heels and his wide eyes shifted to his father, lying behind Draken.

Draken couldn't fight, unsure he could stomach more killing at the moment, much less magic. He spun to face the guards, lifted Seaborn, and flung it as hard as he could over their heads. If he never saw the thing again, it would be too soon. Slicked with blood, it silhouetted against the golden panes of horn before disappearing among the tallest trees and thickest foliage.

The guards flinched, which seemed to fuel their anger. One tackled him and they beat their fists on his back and head until flecks of light sparked in his eyes. He groaned and tried to lay limp as if he'd passed out so they'd stop, but they seemed to cease despite it. Shouts penetrated his pain. He dragged his head up to stare blearily toward them.

One of the guards was going for the king, seax in hand. It struck Draken as vaguely incongruous: royal guards were trained to the sword and didn't carry common weapons. Galbrait leapt forward and tackled him from the side. They tumbled into the ashy foliage, rolling on the dirt. Another guard strode forward and dragged the guard up, pulling him from the Prince's grip. Draken squinted. A crooked nose, plush, feminine lips, the right frame . . . gods, it was a son of House Rinwar, given to His Majesty as a guard. A solid strike to the temple made Rinwar fall limp. After Galbrait opened the doors and called out, more guards poured into the Solarium to see to the king and drag Rinwar away. There were plenty left over to give Draken a thorough beating.

CHAPTER SEVENTEEN

Gloom shrouded him as the door to his cell clanged shut and the guards carried off the torches. Draken closed his eyes, just breathing as the discomfort from the cuts and bruises turned to painful prickles and subsided into tingles as his wounds healed. The ground seemed to rock beneath him and his head spun sickeningly. He lay on his bad shoulder, rolled over onto his back to ease the chronic ache, and stared up into darkness. It was near nightfall, he thought. He wondered if any of the Seven were rising to see what had happened to their godsworn.

The gods had given him the sword. They had let Elena anoint him as Khel Szi. And then they'd sent him back here. They had ripped his life apart again, just as he'd settled a little, and let the shreds flutter down over the whole world. And now his sister and the others were in danger. . . . Aarinnaie must be frantic by now

Or killing someone.

Or already dead.

He groaned. His newfound ability to heal himself did nothing for the frustration that ached in his head like a spike.

"When we meet, Khellian, I will challenge you and you may destroy my soul for good." He cast a glare upward into the darkness over his head. "Or you never know. I might just destroy *you*."

A choked laugh answered his petulant growl. "What an amusing little flyfish you are."

Draken pushed to a sit. The effort made him pant. "Yramantha. How badly did they torture you?"

A beat. "Stop talking. They'll hear you."

"No one is down here." He strained to see in the blackness. "No one will come until it's time for a feeding."

"They don't often bring food down to this ruddy place."

149

He tried work out how long she must've been down here. Some nights, not quite seven, he reckoned. "Interrogations come more often. The King employs old prisoners to question his newer ones. I'm certain Grym earned his way out of chains on my back alone." He shifted his sore shoulder again, remembering.

"Stop. Just . . . stop talking."

Draken ran his hand over his face. He hated this, hated baiting her. But he had to make himself of some use to the King, had to prove he wasn't part of the rebellion if he had any hope at surviving. "Of course last time I was here, there were no traitors to distract them. They'll likely be far more interested in you."

Water dripped. Generations of damp running down cold stone walls. The incessant *plink plink plink* driving him mad as he lay beaten and broken in his cell. Licking the walls for a drink.

He pulled up his knees and rested his forearm on them."Why did they suspect you? Because you came to Brîn?"

"No. They accused me of killing the Princes. Someone lied. But I wasn't even in Monoea."

He frowned. Killing the Princes? "Were the Princes in the *Sea Swallow*?"

"Shouldn't it be called *Sea Swallowed* by now?"Another voice filtered through the darkness, low and far away. "Don't talk to him. He has magicks to trick you."

Draken frowned. "Rinwar? Is that you?"

"You know me?"

"I know your father. Why did you try to kill King Aissyth?"

A rough laugh. "Why did you *save* him?"

"I have a Queen and a country who needs me. His death does not serve them."

"Nor you, I assume," Yramantha said.

"I don't think my death serves anyone at the moment." Draken slid forward slowly so he didn't bang against the bars in the darkness. His eyes strained with trying to see. "There's a chance they'll take me first for questioning. Rinwar, if you tell me something, anything, perhaps I can spare you some pain. Better it come from me than you."

"Why would you do that?" Rinwar demanded. But there was a tremor behind his anger.

Because he was too difficult to kill. "Because you're too young and foolish to know what a real interrogation is, what real pain is." What true rebellion was. He bowed his head, letting the muscles stretch. They tugged painfully down his shoulder. He drew a deep breath, and then another. But they wouldn't release. Thom often rubbed his back and bad shoulder for him when it was sore with strain from the lists. He wished for his firm, capable hands now.

"I'm no child. I know what I'm doing—"

"No. You've no idea at all, or you never would have attacked the King. The very least difficult thing of all that can happen to you today is dying."

"The King was supposed to be dead. You were supposed to kill him."

"Why me?"

"I don't know. There was no time, no discussion. Father was adamant . . ." Rinwar's voice faded.

"Shut it, Rinwar!" Yramantha hissed. Draken heard Rinwar taking slow, careful breaths and gave the darkness a grim smile. Who needs magicks with a craven young lordling? He was under the boy's skin now, and hers. "Did your father know the Khel Szi is me?"

"An upstart Prince," Yramantha said. "Who won a civil war for your Queen. That's what they *thought* you were."

Not so far from the truth. "But then Lord Rinwar saw me come into Sevenfel with the Prince."

"He sent for me straightaway. There was no time to plan, to argue . . . Not that Father would listen anyway."

And here the lad sat waiting for torture.

Yramantha snorted softly and anger flared in Draken. "I saved Queen Elena. For that she demanded my loyalty. As well my father demanded I take his throne." Not to mention the gods and their bloody sword. "I know what it is to have your actions dictated by the whims of others, lad."

He heard a bit of shuffling: maybe Rinwar moving closer to the bars of his cell. That they each rated their own cell surprised Draken, and for the first time he realized the dungeon . . . this corridor at any rate, was oddly empty. "Where are all the prisoners?"

Another rustling of clothes; a shrug, maybe. Yramantha spoke. "Exiled. In the quarries. Working the King's Roads." She paused. "Executed."

Draken lifted his head. "*The King* is executing criminals?"

"We shouldn't be talking," Rinwar said.

"We're all as good as dead," Draken said. "Speak."

There was another long pause before Rinwar's rough voice came out of the darkness again. "Only those suspected of killing the Princes."

"Shut up!" A violent hiss. Chains clinked against bars in Yramantha's cell.

"Who killed the Princes? Which ones?"

"Prince Tryvann was found hanging in his rooms. His wife, too, and their children."

Draken's middle hollowed out. Assassination *inside* Palace Ashwyc? "What of Aissyth'Ae?"

"Missing these last three sevennight."

"His family? His wife?"

"All dead at the country Palace. But Prince Aissyth'Ae was just gone. It's said he must have gone off with someone he trusts."

Or he'd run . . . no. It wasn't in Aissyth'Ae to do that. He was not the most pleasant man, but he'd never been craven. Draken rubbed his head. Two attacks in palaces. No wonder Aissyth was mad with paranoia. "Who is doing this? Besides your father, who is involved in the rebellion?"

Yramantha made a warning growl. But she needn't have bothered.

"I don't know, all right? I don't know enough. Do you understand? It wasn't supposed to be like this, all that blood and Kupsyr on the ground without his head and . . . *You cut his head off!* Why did you do that? Kupsyr. He had only eighteen Sohalias and you cut his . . . *head* . . . it could have been me, it could have been . . ." Rinwar's shouts dissolved into blubbering tears.

Draken sank against the bars, listening to his wet sobbing. Gods, he wasn't made for this, questioning boys whose worst scandals should be with eligible girls at balls. But even as he let guilt overcome him, he took note: Kupsyr—the man he'd executed on Seakeep Tower. And now another son wasted by rebellion. Another Landed to add to the list of those King Aissyth would have to eradicate. Except there was no love lost between House Kupsyr and House Rinwar. Had it really taken mutual hatred of the King to bring them together? He couldn't quite believe that.

"Rinwar. Do you know my work for the Crown," he asked quietly, "before I was accused and exiled?"

It took some time for the sniffling to die down. "No."

"No, *Your Highness.*" It was the first time he had ever asked, insisted, on his proper title.

A penetrating pause. "No, Your Highness."

"What is your name? Your given name."

"Soeben, Your Highness."

Draken settled against the bars. They rattled slightly. Shivers were settling in. It'd be worse before it was over, if he was left here the night. "I was a Black Guard Commander, responsible for hunting down and eradicating my own kind. It is an ugly thing, Soeben, as you have learned this day."

To his surprise, Rinwar didn't snap back at him, but only released a breath. Both of them fell silent for some time. Draken pushed some straw together to soften the hard floor, ignoring the critters he sent scattering. He'd had worse accommodations. He struggled to stay awake, listening to the silence broken only by dripping and an occasional cough from Soeben or sigh from Yramantha.

His body ached and his mind strained with seeking a solution to his problem. The closest he'd been to death in a sevennight and he rather abruptly did not want to die. He could imagine Bruche's laughter at the irony.

He startled to rough voices and the clang of a gate. Torchlight made him blink and his blood freeze, until he realized it wasn't his gate that had opened. Guards pulled Soeben from his cell. The boy stumbled and turned his head to look at Draken before they pulled him over a short distance to an open area with a table. Draken sat up but remained silent. It wouldn't help to draw attention to himself right now and it certainly might hurt. He cursed inwardly, though. He'd had more questions for the boy and the likelihood of their ever being answered had just fallen away into the depths of despair—Soeben's, which was surely coming.

A man entered the room and Draken had to fight the urge to creep deeper into the shadows of his cell. Grym must've earned his freedom because he bore no shackles on his feet. His shaggy hair had been cut, slicked back into a neat dark tail, and his beard was gone. But Draken would recognize his pocked cheeks, crooked nose, and soft, sympathetic eyes anywhere. He'd stared up at them for long enough as Grym had torn out his fingernails, broken his foot, dislocated his shoulder, and sliced the delicate skin on his inner thighs. Grym had called Draken a challenge, and so he had been. Draken had extensive training to resist torture, and besides, he'd been innocent so he'd had nothing to confess. But Grym had not stopped until Draken screamed, and the next day he'd done it again, and the next again; until he'd been removed from the local dungeon and taken to the gaol at the docks after his sentencing.

Grym leaned against the bars, a torch in his hand. Draken had to duck his head; the flames stung his eyes after so long in the dark and the oil smell was rank. "You again."

Draken summoned a mild tone. "Aye, me."

"Eh, we're saving you for special." He jerked his chin at the others with him and Soeben's cell clanged open.

They tore Soeben's clothes from his body and shoved him onto the table. Two men held him on his back while a third strapped him down. Soeben struggled a little, but half-heartedly, as if he knew it was a losing battle. Grym watched, pale eyes narrowed.

When he was secure, Grym stepped forward and patted Soeben's chest over his heart.

Soeben shoved against the straps. "I am Landed. I am nobility. You can't—"

Grym shushed him with a gentle finger on his lips. "I'm supposed to find out what you told about the rebellion."

Told? Not what he knew . . . who had ordered this interrogation? Draken's gaze stayed riveted on Soeben and Grym.

"Such a pretty boy," Grym said, soft, coercive. "You'd have been a hero if you'd managed it, eh?"

Soeben's face hardened. Draken wouldn't have noticed had he not been watching so closely.

Grym saw it too. "Ah, then."

His hand trailed down to Soeben's fingers. His hand barely twitched but the boy cried out. His sharp yelp echoed echoed against the stone and bars. Grym pulled his hand away, leaving Soeben's ring finger sticking up at an odd angle. He yanked Soeben's House signet off the broken finger and pocketed it. The boy panted and turned his head to look past Grym into Draken's cell.

Yramantha made a noise of terror and he heard her scooting back across the rough stone and dirt.

Draken gave the boy a nod. He knew Soeben was a rebel, he deserved punishment, maybe death. But not like this, not with Grym, who was likely praying to the Seven the boy would last long enough to have some real fun. Not that it would stop him; Draken had seen Grym torture someone well past the point of breaking, of confession, past the point of the capability of speech.

Grym moved. Soeben grunted as Grym wrenched on the lad's hand, both arms corded. *Snap.* Soeben screamed, long, piercing. When he showed signs of slowing, Grym tugged on the broken limb, wrenching at it. The skin held. Grym reached for his blade. The screams resumed, broken only by wet gagging. Rancid scents of piss and puke filled the air. The arm hit the ground with a dull thud. Grym kicked it away, toward Draken's cell. One of the others cauterized the wound with a plank of metal, red hot from the fire. Soeben screamed breathlessly until it choked off. They slapped him awake and splashed him with water.

Draken felt his neck heat and his back prickle. His sword arm. Soeben would never fight again. Draken swallowed his bile. The boy would never do *anything* again, save scream.

Draken moved to the front of the cell, into the torchlight. They could see his face; they could recognize him through the smeared ink. He ignored them all for Soeben, unable to tear his eyes away. The lad's flowed with tears and bloody drool dripped from between his lips, but his jaw was set. Soeben turned his head and met his eyes.

Draken gripped the bars with both hands. *I will kill Grym. This I swear on my blood and my damned sword. He will die alone, desperate.* "I am with you."

CHAPTER EIGHTEEN

"*Draken?*"

The voice cut through the nightmarish fog of blood. He stirred, lifted his head from his thin, itchy bed of hay, so groggy his vision blurred in the torchlight. He reached up to wipe the back of his bumpy, branded hand over his eyes. Squinted and pushed himself to a sit. A cloaked figure waited on the other side of the bars, silvery and ghostlike. There was no mistaking that glow. A shadow a few steps behind it held a louvered lantern. It cast a sallow, surreal light.

"Osias," Draken said.

"Aye, and someone to help you."

The darker figure opened the louvers, shedding more light. Soeben lay strapped to the table in his blood and filth. A stinking, still shadow. Very dead. It also revealed the pale, aged face and shadowed eyes of an unfamiliar woman.

"Draken," she breathed.

Draken pushed to his feet. "My lady?"

For that was obviously what she was. Fine lace peeked under the hem of her long cloak. An intricate knot taming well-tended waves topped her head, the blonde partially slid into grey. He wished he were better clothed, not stinking in this cell with bits of straw stuck in his hair. "You know me?"

She nodded, wordless. Something crossed her face . . . anger? Terror?

"Who are you, may I ask?" Draken asked, taking a step forward.

She edged back from him, sliding on slippered feet.

He stopped.

"Lady Sikyra," Osias said. Lady Sikyra swallowed and glanced behind her at Soeben.

Draken looked at the still, battered body and sighed deeply. "I wish I could have done something. They seemed determined to see him dead."

"It is said he tried to kill the King."

Draken bowed his head to her, wondering if she was Soeben's mother or sister. "Aye," he said quietly.

Lady Sikyra fell quiet for a moment, studying him. He fought the urge to fidget under her gaze.

"You don't recognize me?" she asked.

"No, my lady. Should I?"

She blinked and lowered her head. "Forgive my stare. You look so very like your father. It's a bit of a shock."

Draken's heart skipped and slowed; his body fell still. The cold air started to penetrate. He stared at her, and she stared unblinking back. He swallowed, his throat tight. Osias reached between the bars and took Draken's wrist in his hand.

"You're my mother." He barely got enough air behind the words to be heard.

Lady Sikyra moved into action, reaching for the bars, the large round key in her hand. The bars clanked and she flinched, but she pulled them open. "Come. We must hurry if you're to escape."

He didn't move. "I can't."

"I can't leave you here."

He shook his head. "They have my sister, my friends, my guards. Hostages, if they aren't dead already."

"You cannot help them from a cell," Osias said.

"I can't just run off and leave them. I won't."

But she stood waiting. Eyes wide. Agonized. He wanted to reach out and touch her, prove to himself she was real. Instead he relented and moved forward slowly so not to spook her. She shuttered the lantern down again and led them not up the stairs, but back, deeper into darkness, deeper into the dungeon. He followed quietly, his bad knee stiff and aching in the cold, his bad shoulder tight. She gestured him ahead with the lantern and indicated narrow steps that cut abruptly between cells.

He gave her a look but he obeyed. The tunnel was black as pitch but for the shuttered lantern; dank, close, cold. His mother was so silent behind him that he glanced back to make sure she was still there. She glided in her slippers, ghostlike. His mind tangled with questions, but he buried them in the sick knot in his chest, where they'd lived his whole life.

Maybe he didn't want the answers.

The tunnel went up and a thin pool of grey light stretched toward them. Rain pattered as they exited the palace, the doorway old and sunken so that Draken had to duck. For a moment, he breathed. Sea air, crisp, wet. It cleansed his lungs. The backs of buildings faced them. His mother shut the thick, iron-banded door and turned toward its twin inserted nearby into the great wall of stone. A key, the snick of a well-oiled lock, and it swung open to reveal a narrow staircase, nearly as dark as the tunnel. Osias ghosted behind them.

"Was that Kordewyn?" he asked as they climbed. The next city over, if they had left the palatial city.

"Yes," she said.

They reached the top of the steps and entered a quiet back hall. A couple of low tables sat against the wall between doors. She touched his bare back to guide him. His skin quivered under her fingertips. She led them around a corner and through lacquered red doors into what must be her apartments.

He paused, feeling dirty in the opulence. Draperies woven in golds and browns cloaked the windows against the cold, plush rugs stretched across the smooth wooden floors, and the walls were covered in faded frescoes and ornate tapestries. The furniture was upholstered in soft fabrics. In the far corner, under a window where the draperies had been pulled to let in the sunlight, an unfinished tapestry filled a loom.

"I had a footman I trust bring you a bath and fresh clothes from your own things. Just through there. When you finish, you may eat. We've a little time before they start to work out where you've gone."

He felt his brows drop and he looked at her. She looked back at him with unsmiling patience.

"Aye, then. Thank you, my lady."

Osias followed him in without asking. Thick hangings cloaked the bed and a fire burned brightly in his mother's bedchamber. But no tub. He saw another open doorway and hesitantly walked to it . . . a small chamber with a steaming tub and another small fire. The room was cloyingly hot, welcome after the chill of the dungeon. True to her word, his own things were stacked on a table, Elena's necklace on top. He let his fingers trail over the chain, wondering how she'd managed it, but he was too filthy and sweaty to put it on.

He stripped and sank into the tub, letting the warmth seep into his skin. He picked up a stiff sea sponge and started scrubbing. The water quickly soured with dirt and ink. "You did this."

Osias wandered about examining things, his hands clasped behind his back. "You needed help and I found it."

"How did you know about her?"

Slight smile. "Did you think your past is too complicated for me to unravel?"

"Bruche told you." The spirit swordhand had been heavy on his mind lately.

"I still have my powers whether Korde likes it or not."

Draken stared at him. "Did he tell you before he left me . . . or recently?"

"He followed you across the sea. Very determined, Bruche. I've told him I thought it was time for his rest but he refuses to listen."

Draken sank back in the water with a sigh. He hadn't imagined it, then.

When he came back out, clad in his own loose trousers, long-sleeved tunic, and pendant, it was to find Sikyra had shed her cloak and knelt by the fire, poking it up. Food was laid but no servants were in sight.

"Please. Sit and eat. My cousin provided you little courtesy as of yet. I hope to remedy that."

Osias asked if he could smoke and Sikyra nodded. Soon the softly cloying scent of Gadye smoke drifted through the room. The Mance remained standing and apart, listening.

Draken sat, still cautious. The food was blessedly hot and delicious; he'd forgotten how much he missed the familiar grainbread, mutton, and shellfishes from the Outer Hills and Sister Bay.

"You should know. Earlier, with the king, was a ruse to draw the rebels out. My cousin simply took it too far."

He ate for a moment, quiet, trying not to think of Soeben, dead on that bloodstained slab. "The King is a crafty man."

"He has to be. His life is in danger, his whole line is threatened, and with it the world."

Cradle tales, Draken thought, but he didn't dare say it.

She sat across from him. "But don't blame him. It was I who thought to use you in this way."

He looked up at her, chewed, swallowed, said nothing as he reached for his cup. Halmar would be having fits, his eating without tasters. "You knew who I am?"

"That the Prince of Brîn is my son? Yes."

"How?"

"Your father made no secret of who he was, not with me."

Draken absorbed this, drank more wine. That tidbit could mean any number of things. No point in doing anything less than jumping in. He was back in Monoea, where someone might stab him in the back but at least they maintained no pretense that they were doing anything less. "Did he brag on his royal blood as he raped you?"

She reached across the table and slapped his cheek. Hard enough to snap his head to the side. Hard enough to make his eyes water.

"Is that what you think you are? Rape get? You should be ashamed."

He stared at her, stunned. It had been easier thinking she'd been raped, that she'd been the victim. Instead she'd broken strict mores without regard to consequence. Pleasure, then. That was all his life amounted to?

He waited for the sting, and his sudden fury, to settle before replying. "Aissyth's father banished you from court and left me a slave. What was I to think?"

She shook her head and sat back gracefully, her hands folded in her lap like sleeping snakes. "You think our King is so cruel to take my child and banish me from court after a *rape*? No. I was punished not for being a victim, but for pursuing a slave for a lover and daring to bear his child."

His brows climbed. "You mean to say you *loved* my father?"

"I mean to say I wanted him. And when I found out I was pregnant, I wanted his child."

An itchy apprehension spread through Draken. He had no idea what to say so he just reached for his cup again, downed the wine. When he lowered his cup, the pitcher was in his mother's hand, ready to pour. He held his cup out but didn't drink when it was full.

She set the pitcher down. It clinked, metal on stone. "You had a brother, did you know?"

Had. Past tense. Draken set his cup down and rested his hand on his knee. "You were married?"

"Of course not. Who would have me after I fouled myself with a Brînian slave and had a mixblood son?"

He couldn't really blame the court, knowing his father. Fouled, indeed. "Priests in Akrasia claim sundry are tainted. It's why they're enslaved there."

She snorted. "Priests and their laws. Don't quote them at me."

"That treads close to heresy," Osias said, though his tone was mild. He'd somehow managed to glide up to Draken's elbow. There was another chair, but he remained standing.

"What have the gods ever done for me? They stole my two sons. I've no use for religon."

"I'm the last one to defend the gods," Draken said. "What was his name?"

"Laethyn." Her voice lost its sharp edge. "A shooting accident . . . so I was told. It wasn't so long ago he died, not even a Sohalia before you left."

The name was familiar. A brother. He'd had a brother, here, underfoot at Ashwyc, and he'd never been told. "What was his work?"

"Royal Huntsman. The King was fond of him, rather as he is fond of you."

Draken snorted. "He has a funny way of showing it."

She ignored that. "After Laethyn died, I realized my mistake for keeping my distance. I realized what I was missing with you. But before I could get my courage up to approach you, Lesle had been killed and you were . . ." She looked down, smoothed her hand over her thigh.

"Exiled."

"*Gone,*" she whispered, her shoulders tight. "I had done nothing for you and it was too late. Aissyth had his hands tied once it was known how Lesle died. If he'd allowed you to stay, he knew you would stop at nothing to solve her murder. And if it all came out, his dissenters would have used it against him, accused you of using magicks, accused *him* of defending someone using magicks. They would have used you against him. He had to send you away to protect you."

"To protect himself."

"To protect the Crown," she said firmly.

It made a grim sense. Too much sense. He reminded himself that though she was his mother, he didn't *know* her. Was it truth? "Did King Aissyth get you up to this? Telling me?"

"No. He'll be angry that you know."

"Why?"

"Because it betrays how much you mean to him."

Draken snorted. "He banished me. He just tried to kill me—"

"I told you. A ruse to draw out the rebels."

"Brilliant. Even better. He *used* me."

"Kings always use people."

His wife was dead. Elena waited at home with his child. Men had died in the attack on Seakeep, good men on both sides. He shook his head. "I don't even know what you're trying to convince me of."

She leaned forward. "Help Aissyth fight the threat to the Crown."

He felt for the Queen's necklace around his throat and gripped the chain. "This isn't my kingdom any longer. This is not my fight."

"Perhaps not. But your new home is threatened by these Landed rebels. Ashen, we call them."

"Aye, I'm familiar. One of them enlightened me as to their interest in us. But Monoeans discarded magic long ago and have gotten on fine without it."

"Yes but these Ashen, they believe magic is the will of the gods. And they believe you're godsworn. They would make you an emperor if you let them."

"Nonsense."

"It's not. I've been studying them for Sohalias. Why do you think Laethyn died? A hunting accident, my arse. He was shot in the eye and the throat. *Two* arrows. They were trying to get me to stop investigating them for the King."

"Do you know a ship captain called Yramantha?"

"Yes, the same who carried you to exile, isn't she?" At his stare, she shrugged. "I'm nearly as invisible as servants. People talk around me. Yramantha is Ashen. Odd that. They usually only let men act. Maybe they thought since you knew her she could better persuade you."

A chill slid through him and cold sweat itched his back under his woolen shirt. They had gone to great lengths to get him to Monoea. "She threatened to kill Elena if I didn't come."

"They have the determination of the faithful and many blades on their side."

"Which sect?"

"Moonminster. You can pick them out because some have started marking themselves with ashes. And they wear a moon sigil on their tabards—three twined crescents. Shows how brazen they've gotten."

"Aye, I've seen it." He didn't know much about Moonminster Faith except that they were fatalists. He looked at Osias, whose smoke clouded the air around him.

The Mance shook his head slowly. "Fatalists who worship doctrine more than the gods."

Draken frowned. "There are temples in Akrasia, but Moonminster is illegal here."

His mother shrugged. "Last I heard, so was killing Princes and rebellion against the Crown."

He thought of the blood on the pavers in the courtyard at Seakeep, of war on his shores, of thousands of Monoeans invading Brîn and Akrasia. Of the Moonlings and Gadye captured and enslaved for their magic. Noble Akrasians fighting and dying. His own wild, gallant Brînians massacred. Even the powerful Mance couldn't fight off ten or twenty thousand Ashen if they dared breach the gates of Eidola. The Banes would overrun Akrasia again, destroying everyone and everything in their path.

"And if I refuse to cooperate?"

"They already threatened your Queen, did they not? How valid was the threat?"

It was a moment before he could answer. "They had her necklace and a lock of her hair to prove they could get close to her."

Her brows raised. "Impressive, though I doubt an Ashen could get so close to an Akrasian Queen. They must already have allies in Akrasia."

He glanced at Osias. "We'd thought of it but we can't work out who. Aarinnaie did uncover an islander nêre—a bloodlord—plotting against me. Shares that sigil with the Ashen. Harbors a grudge against Father—something political. And there's my inheriting out of wedlock." He set down his table knife. "Aarinnaie. The others. We have to get them out straightaway."

After a hesitation, his mother reached over and laid her hand over his where it rested on his knee, pale skin against dark, smooth against rough. Her nails were trim and neat, her fingers soft. He had to resist pulling his hand away, not because he loathed her touch, but because he feared she loathed his.

"Lady Sikyra," he said, not quite a question.

She gave him a tentative smile and for one horrible moment he thought she would ask him to call her Mother.

He willed his hand to relax under hers. "I don't know how to fight a Monoea that is determined to conquer Akrasia."

"How did you win your throne?"

A sore spot. His throne was neither earned nor won. "It was given me by my father and then by my Queen." And by the ruddy gods.

"And how did you win the heart of your Queen?"

His lips parted. Lies and subterfuge. At last he shook his head. "I shouldn't have done."

"Do your people love you?" she asked.

"Aye," Osias said. "They do."

Her gaze traveled over Draken's face, his locks, over his shoulders and down to their joined hands. "Talking to you now, it is made clear to me, for if I saw you on a road or at court I would not know you as my son. And yet, your manner urges me to love you."

He shook his head, bewildered. They'd only known each other a little while, less than a candle-burn. He didn't know if he could trust her. He didn't want to.

And yet something in him surged. "How? How do I beat them?"

"One word at a time," she said softly, her fingers squeezing his.

CHAPTER NINETEEN

Sikyra held out a key on a ribbon, the one from the outer doors. "Use this to make your escape. Do you remember the way?"

He nodded. "And how will you make yours, my lady?"

"This is my home. I'm not going anywhere." She gave a delicate shrug and rose to her feet.

He followed suit. It was past time to go. "Are my people housed in the guest corridors?"

"The one with the blue varnished doors."

He nodded. He knew it. "Will you come?"

"No, I cannot make an appearance where I might be seen. The King values my advice, but quite privately. I am still banished from court."

"Banished . . . yet you live in the palace." Skulking about in tunnels and secret staircases.

She gave him a sad smile. "It is the Monoean way, is it not? A lifetime alone for a few nights of pleasure?"

She took up his cloak and laid it over his shoulders, smoothing the fabric down over his back and straightening his damp locks. An odd, tingling warmth trailed her touch. The back of his neck heated.

"What will you do now?" she asked. "Will you help Aissyth?"

"I cannot. My loyalty is to my Queen now, and Brîn."

"Stop the rebellion here and it will never reach your shores."

He wanted to refuse her even as he thought he should ask her to come back to Brîn with him when this was done. But he had no idea if he would survive the day to do any of it. And would she even want to go? He faced leaving her . . . again. It hadn't meant much before, when he didn't know her. Now it was all changed.

He could see the beauty she'd been, the fine bones under her creased skin, the shape of her eye, the curve of her lips, her silky, fair hair. He wondered again what she must think when she looked at him. He was so different; his build, his skin, his hair, his scars. All of him.

He couldn't refuse her. "I'll do my best, my lady. Thank you." He dipped his chin to her, shamefully curt, and strode out.

He pulled up his hood, walking without having to think where to go. This time of year it was chilly in the corridors sometimes, for no fires warmed them. Many people moved between the rooms with cloaks on. Still, it would be best if he were able to reach his sister undetected.

"What will you do?" Osias asked.

He shook his head. "What do we really know but what she's told us? That this is a religious revolution? That the King was using me to suss out his assassin?"

"It worked. It makes sense."

"Rebellion makes no sense, not for the Landed. None of them are hungry or wanting."

"Except, perhaps, for religion. For magic."

He snorted. "And Rinwar sends his son to kill the King? To what end, when it announces his involvement?"

"Perhaps *because* it announces his involvement."

So lost in thought he'd taken them on a route near the great hall, Draken realized they were approaching guards stationed there. He grimaced under his hood, dropped his chin to hide his face deeper in its shadow, and started to turn back.

"Hie! Present yourself." Quick footsteps strode his way.

All his mother's effort for naught. The Guard would escort him back to the dungeon and the King would kill him quicker rather than later so he could not escape again. With a sigh, he pulled his hood back and faced the kings' guards.

"It's the Brînian," one of the guards said, his tone sharp.

They said nothing of Osias. He glanced around. He'd faded into the walls again. Damned useful, that. Maybe with all his magic he should have learned how.

Draken started to back away. The Guard followed quickly. He hurried after Draken, his hand on his sword hilt. Two other guards closed in as well. "Stop. We've been searching the palace for you."

"It's him, all right," another voice said down the hall.

Trapped.

"Truth? I'm honored," Draken said dryly. He'd only been gone long enough for a bath and meal. His last of either, he supposed. He stiffened, readying himself for rough hands on him again, readying himself to fight. He knew he should go quietly. It wasn't dignified, after all. Just let them do what they would do—

"Come. This way, Your Highness."

They closed ranks around him, though none touched him. They took him toward the guest corridor and, to his surprise, one of them opened a lacquered blue door and stepped back to admit him. Was this a concession of freedom or just a prettier prison?

He walked through to find Halmar and the other szi nêre flanking the door. They nodded to him as if nothing were amiss, as if the Prince hadn't tried to execute him, as if Draken hadn't spent the better part of the day in a dank cell watching a boy tortured to death. Halmar shut the door behind him as he entered.

It was a gracious, comfortable room in the Monoean style, with thick hangings flanking the windows, luxurious upholstered chairs by the fireplace, and a comfortable, sturdy dining set. Instead of frescoes, the walls held tapestries depicting Monoean heroes: Olyss, Cabe, and the martyred battle maiden: Aydra. Seaborn rested in its battered scabbard on the table next to a flat wooden box with black hinges. A scrollbox, perhaps

Prince Galbrait was at a window, his hands gripping the sill. Aarinnaie stood quietly at his side, her arms wrapped around her middle. Tyrolean had his arms crossed over his chest near the hearth. He wore all his swords. Setia curled in a chair staring into the guttering fire. The sun was slanting its final rays through the tiny leaded panes of glittering glass and the room was cold.

Tyrolean's frown eased, but only slightly. "Your Highness. You're back."

"Where is Osias?" Setia asked.

"Made himself scarce when the guards found me."

Prince Galbrait turned and strode toward Draken. He was unnaturally pale but for two bright spots on his cheeks. His shoulders remained stiff and tight. He moved like a career soldier with a score to settle.

But Aarinnaie pushed past him to throw her arms around Draken's neck. "Where've you been? Are you all right?" She set him back from herself, her hands on his shoulders, and stared up into his face.

"Well enough," he answered.

Her nose scrunched. "You smell . . . good. That's odd."

Draken ignored that, setting her gently aside to strap his swordbelt around his waist. Some of the tension in his body eased as the scabbard bumped his thigh. He gazed at the young Prince, eyes narrowed. "Where is your father, Prince Galbrait? I need to speak with him straightaway."

Galbrait shook his head, his pale lips a thin line.

"The King has gone missing," Tyrolean said.

Draken raised his brows. "Sorry?"

"The Queen, as well," Aarinnaie said.

"I'm in a cell for half a day and you *lose* the King and Queen?"

Galbrait strode toward the table, his body still tight. He undid the latch on the scrollbox and beckoned to Draken. "And we received this."

Severed hands from a man rested on a velveteen cushion. A ring with a skystone set in interwoven gold and moonwrought encircled one forefinger. The royal heir's ring. The wrists had been dipped in molten metal for caps and the skin heavily waxed, so that it flaked from the ring. Calluses from swordplay marred the skin between the thumb and forefinger.

Draken swallowed, noiseless, and willed the bile down. *Think, Drae. Think.*

Clean, even cuts. Done on a block, likely with a sword. Some ruddy rebel bastard had gone to the trouble to make a statement with these hands.

Death, he'd seen. Blood by the buckets. Screams and the feel of his sword slicing flesh. He had just watched Grym torture Soeben to death. But this formal presentation of brutality sickened him far more.

Draken forced his voice to sound calm, as calm as he could. He had no idea how well he succeeded. "That is Prince Aissyth'Ae's ring. But are we certain these are his hands?"

Galbrait stared at the hands and nodded slowly. "I gave him that scar, just there, on the fourth finger. We sparred before . . ." His voice caught. "Before he left."

Draken gentled his tone. "Was there a scroll accompanying this? A message of any sort?"

Galbrait let the lid of the box down gently. He shook his head. His white face had paled further, if possible.

"Tyrolean, see to a drink for His Highness, will you?"

Tyrolean moved to a low table where wine was laid. He poured two goblets, and pressed one into the Prince's hand and another into Draken's.

"Do you wish privacy?" Draken asked.

Galbrait's gaze slipped to Aarinnaie's face. "They may stay."

Tyrolean set the pitcher down with an audible clink after filling his own cup and downing it, his back to the room.

The wine was as cool as the room but warmed Draken's stomach. "Are there any other royals in residence whose safety should be secured?"

Galbrait blinked. "Um. It's awkward, but your mother—"

"My mother, aye," Draken said. "I've a feeling she can look after herself."

Aarinnaie blinked at Draken, speechless for once.

Galbrait nodded but kept his attention on his goblet. "I know Father trusts her as an advisor, but I don't know her. She was kept apart from us until the attack on Quunin on the coast."

Draken wondered what the Prince's opinion of the attack was, but now wasn't the time to ask. "I don't know her either, Galbrait. Don't worry about offending me. And yes, Aarin, my mother is here and we've met. We'll discuss her later." He stepped closer to the young Prince. "Have you any idea who took your parents? Who sent this?"

"Lord Rinwar comes to mind." Galbrait said. "If Aissyth'Ae is held nearby in Wyndam or down in Newporte, this could have been done and the box sent since the attempt on Father's life this morning." His gaze flicked up at Draken again and his face creased.

"I cannot stomach the cruelty of it, to take a man's hands," Aarinnaie said.

"I doubt he'll be needing them," Draken said. "He's surely dead."

She shot a worried look at Galbrait, obviously thinking little of Draken's blunt tone. "You can't know that, Khel Szi."

"No. He's right." Galbrait swallowed down his wine and set the cup down. "It is old custom, since before our time. They will keep his head to parade about. They wouldn't give up the proof that my . . . that the Crown Prince is dead. But he must be. I only wish I knew who is at the root of this."

Draken went back to the box and looked at the hands. Steeled himself and touched them. They were cold and stiff under his fingertips, but he couldn't tell if it was rigor or simply the effect from the chilly Trade air. The wax kept him from telling anything from the skin proper, making it difficult to place the time of amputation. He closed the box and latched it.

"My sense is we should assume this delivery was planned to coincide with my arrival," Draken said. "I'd wager the plans to abduct the King and Queen were supposed to happen a little later."

"Why do you say that?" Galbrait asked.

"Because spacing them out induces the most terror, as if troops are circling your position and hemming you in. Every time you think you're getting a handle on it, something else happens. Your father's little execution scheme today may have just bumped the schedule." If so, what was next?

"It must be *all* planned," Galbrait said, sounding defeated. "Killing Aissyth'Ae. Mother and Father . . ."

"Which means there's more to the plan," Aarinnaie added grimly.

Draken nodded. "They'd never go to all the trouble of abducting your parents and killing the Prince without the throne as the final goal. So if they've got the King and Queen, what is next?" He paused. His mother said the rebels wanted *him* on the throne.

As if managing the one he had wasn't trouble enough.

Everyone fell quiet. The fire snapped on damp wood, emitting a puff of black smoke. Halmar's bracelets clinked as he shifted his hand to rest on his sword-hilt. Aarinnaie broke the silence at last. "With the King missing won't rebels just march in here and take the throne?"

Galbrait snorted. It was half-hearted, but Draken was glad to hear it. There was life in the lad yet. "Ashwyc has never been taken. It's impenetrable."

"Unless they've already got people on the inside," Tyrolean met Draken's eyes. "As they obviously did at home. You've got to admit, this is frighteningly well-executed so far."

"There'd still have to be a bloody lot of them to take the palace." Draken set his cup down, the wine forgotten, and leaned against the table, his back to the box, his arms crossed over his chest. "But it makes sense. They need Ashwyc. They need the throne proper. No point in taking the King otherwise. He may well be a trade coin."

"We must fight this, but my brothers . . ." The bump in Galbrait's throat sharpened against his skin as he swallowed hard.

"Aye, Galbrait. It falls to you." Draken glanced at Tyrolean. "A friend of mine once told me it is honorable to fight in the light, not from darkness. You have that chance, here, now. Take the throne. You relinquish it to the King and no one else."

"And they will come and try to kill him. It will further draw out the rebels." Tyrolean nodded. "Very clever, my Prince."

Galbrait was silent for a breath. Two.

Draken gave him a level look "Your father would die to keep the throne in the succession."

"Is it so important it remain in the family, or is it about keeping it out of the hands of the rebel Landed?" Aarinnaie asked.

"Both," Galbrait said without hesitation—a history lesson driven into every Monoean. "Only a strong King ordained by the gods will keep the Landed and Minors from ripping Monoea apart."

Draken nodded. It seemed simple enough, but competition between the Landed and Minors was so ingrained in Monoean culture it propped the country up better than peace did. The entire economy was based on it. Inequality drove families to give their sons and daughters to the army and navy or to make names and coin for themselves in trade. It drove people to better themselves, as it had him. But that tension required a King as ballast.

"Then you *must* sit the throne as regent, in lieu of the King and the Crown Prince," Draken said. "It's the only way to draw the rebels out and end this."

Galbrait's eyes widened. "I cannot."

The gods chose his family as royals and then let it come to this? No. Too cruel, surely. But he felt dragged into their schemes even as he spoke. "You must. Your father is gone. The Crown Prince is dead. You're the only one of your line here."

"There's you," Galbrait pointed out.

"I am a second cousin and a bastard, *and* disowned. It cannot be me." He sat down and laid his arm on the table: the kindly uncle. "Galbrait. If you want your Father back, you must bring the rebels to battle. The best place to do that is here, where you have a measure of control. You can trap them here and kill them all. You have a chance to end this."

Galbrait pursed his lips, looking abruptly like a petulant child. "But how? They won't just come here because we call them."

"No. They won't. We must devise a ruse." But what? He couldn't count on Galbrait coming up with anything. He was still a boy really, no real perspective, no older than Soeben Rinwar had been. And look where idealism and stubbornness had gotten Soeben. A boy, dead before his time, and . . .

Draken narrowed his eyes at Tyrolean. "Once we gave Gusten VaKhlar's body to his father, our enemy, and made him our friend. Do you remember, Captain?"

"I remember you bargained well with that death," Tyrolean said. His expression was set, hard.

"The gods know me and yet they chose me," Draken reminded him.

Tyrolean spread his hands. "I said nothing of it."

"You didn't have to." He turned to Galbrait. "Have Soeben Rinwar prepared to be moved. A carriage and your best horses, something worthy of the dead son of a Landed family."

Galbrait shook his head. "Moved? Moved where?"

"I'm taking Soeben home," Draken said.

CHAPTER TWENTY

Draken had to reassure himself Galbrait still had command of the palace, and the only way to do that was to get the Prince out among the courtiers and sitting on the throne. A few important Landed believed to be loyal were rounded up to see him placed there. Draken held to the background, despite Galbrait's protests. Enough people knew who he was, and he'd only serve as a distraction. Rinwar was noteably not in attendance, though he had been invited. None wore ash on their foreheads.

Galbrait wore a fine court jacket, loose about the neck to keep his torq in plain view. He looked very young to Draken, standing on the dais, but he composed himself well.

He was honest, to a point. "My brothers are dead, and their wives and heirs. My father is missing, feared abducted . . ." He looked around at all of them and let that sink in, as well as the unspoken next leap that the King was dead. "My mother-Queen is quite indisposed." Better to let them think she was languishing in grief rather than separated from her head at this point. It might reassure nobles not in the know and draw out rebels who knew he was lying.

"There is no one left but me. I will resolve these issues as best as I am able. Do not fear. Your Prince, despite rebellion and attacks, is still with you."

His gaze slid to Draken's face, and then he seated himself on his father's throne.

The Landed rattled their court swords in their metal scabbards—typical, benign approval, but plenty of lips bent to whisper in ears, as well.

Tyrolean leaned toward Draken. "That went fair well. Perhaps it is a sign we are in the right on this."

"The day is not ended. We still have to see Rinwar."

✦ ✦ ✦

"Absolutely not, Aarinnaie."

"But I'm the best choice to go with you. No one will suspect me."

Draken shook his head. "It's too dangerous."

"Not for me." She growled softly, nostrils flared, fists clenched. Setia, standing just behind her holding her cloak for her, shied slightly. As well she should. Aarinnaie's anger was a palpable thing. And Aarin had a point. Truth, she had once singlehandedly killed two well-armed Escorts, had survived a battle full of rabid Banes, had saved Draken's life more than once. She could defend herself well enough. But everything in Draken wanted to protect her, keep her safe.

He tried again. "We can't both go; Brîn might be left without an heir."

Aarinnaie scowled. "So let me go in your stead. You're the Szi; I mean nothing to our people and even less to these."

He hadn't wanted to tell her this. He could guess her reaction. "I, ah. Left instructions that you were to take my place on the throne should anything happen to me."

That silenced her. But only for a moment. "Oh, Draken, you *didn't*."

"I did and Elena agreed. You're not even supposed to be here, remember? And I'm supposed to be dead by now. I need someone with Khellian's blood to succeed me or Brîn reverts fully to Akrasia. That would start civil war, as you well know."

"I won't . . . I can't! I'd be no good at it and, and I'm female . . . and . . . and I don't want to."

"Time to grow up and drop the spoiled façade. You're as allied with Elena as I. She would accept you and make the people follow. And Brîn must get over their unfair female inheritance rules at any rate." He shot a glare at Galbrait, which admittedly the Prince didn't deserve.

Galbrait bowed his head, cheeks flushing. Monoea allowed both sexes to inherit equally, though some men thought women too prone to delicacy and illness to lead Landed families. The King was one such man. However, Aissyth had three sons and a bevy of grandsons, so his views were—had been—moot for the next couple of generations.

"Stay here and protect the Prince." Galbrait's brows raised. Draken ignored him. "And put on something appropriate. You can't fight in that gown."

"Please, Szirin," Galbrait said. "I could use a friend at my side."

That did it. She fair fluttered her lashes at Galbrait and acquiesced to Draken with barebones courtesy. The gestures were so opposite Draken reckoned one was a ruse, but he couldn't figure out which, nor why. She disappeared into her rooms to change, Setia at her heels. With Osias still missing, Setia had little to do but return to her much earlier role as lady's maid.

As Halmar reapplied the ink to Draken's face, Draken asked him, "How long do you suppose she'll stay mad at me?"

"Szirin leans more toward revenge, Khel Szi," Halmar answered in his rumbling voice. Konnon and Galbrait chuckled low. Tyrolean, however, did not, and said nothing as they mounted and rode behind the golden carriage carrying Soeben.

"She'd drive you mad, Ty," Draken said. "I wouldn't wish her on an enemy, much less my best friend."

Tyrolean returned an unreadable look. "It's a risk, bringing the dead boy back. Rinwar is a rebel, aye?"

"I know Monoea, Captain," Draken said, and he hoped it was true. "If we held Soeben from his father, it wouldn't be looked at as a bargaining chip but as a threat. Or worse, an insult."

"Is bringing the dead lad not a bribe of sorts?"

Draken gave him a grim smile. "Monoeans prefer to call bribes 'acts of good faith.' Whatever it is, I have to befriend the rebels to stop them."

"I see," Tyrolean said, though it was clear by his frown that he did not.

The Rinwar estate in Wyndam was no Ashwyc Palace, but by any standard it was huge, constructed of square-cut stone and a few real glass windows. Iceflocks bloomed alongside other early Tradeseason blossoms. He was grateful the unseasonable cold diluted their heady scent; Lesle had planted their cottage over with creeping flowers and the last thing he wanted at the moment was a reminder of her. Two wings of the building sprawled out hundreds of paces in each direction, fronted by terraces, and surrounded by lawns. The formal gardens were trimmed so sharply it set his teeth on edge.

Two decades of Rinwar's hirelings stood in formation before the villa in honor of the return of the House's dead son. Most were older, unwealthy minors gone mercenary after their stints in the military. Draken set his expression to properly regretful, resisted the urge to lay his hand on his sword hilt, and dismounted. He wished he had his armor, but that would have given the wrong message. Tyrolean wore his, as he was acting as a guard.

The yard was quiet, only a slight cold breeze rustling Draken's cloak and the far off sound of the ocean, so familiar it made his throat sting. He pushed ahead of the others and went to stand before the carriage. The horses snorted and stamped, then settled.

Lord Rinwar, the only man old and dressed well enough to be Soeben's father, stepped forward from the group gathered there. He wore his house sword, long enough to require a leather baldric embroidered with the three twined moons. The ash smeared on his forehead made crude contrast to his finery. A woman had been holding Rinwar's arm; she released it, staring at the carriage. Also marked with ash, her face was flushed and her eyes were red. Soeben's mother. Draken felt a stabbing sensation in his gut, sick and piercing. For the first time that day, Elena flitted through his mind—her strained face and voice when she'd been in pain and and in fear of losing their child.

If you ever loved me, Khellian, Draken thought, *slay me now and spare my heart the loss of my child.*

He strode forward to greet them. Rinwar, too, only had eyes for the carriage. Despite careful study, Draken saw nothing but grief in that drawn face. If he had anticipated his son's death, he was as good an actor as any Newporte street mask. Rinwar's lands were large but unimportant, very unlike the slight, older man standing here. Draken was willing to wager Rinwar hadn't been to the Norvern Wildes and the city of Wildefel since he was a very young man. He blinked at Draken, apparently too stricken by the death of his son to hide his astonishment at Draken's uncultivated, inked appearance. Of course, according to Soeben, Rinwar had seen Draken's entrance into the city.

"I am Khel Szi of Brîn," Draken said in Brînish and then repeated the phrase in Monoean. He met the man's gaze squarely.

"I know who you are, Draken vae Khellian. You recall my lady wife, Lady Faizen."

"I do. This is First Captain Tyrolean of Akrasia, Special Envoy to Brîn. We bring your son, our heartfelt sympathy on his loss, and a message from His Highness Galbrait, Prince and Lord Regent of Monoea."

Rinwar's thin-lashed eyelids fluttered slightly. "Regent . . . ? What's this about?"

"Perhaps this is best discussed in private, Landed."

"Yes . . . of course. I am remiss. Please, come. My wife will see to Soeben."

Draken turned to the lady and gave her a bow after Akrasian custom, taking her outstretched, cold hand and touching his forehead to it. Something he normally only did for his Queen, but the woman had just lost her son. "My lady, please accept my condolences. Your son was very brave." He paused. "It may be best if others care for him before you release him to Ma'Vanni's embrace."

She swallowed. Tears welled in her eyes. "Was his passing peaceful, Your Highness?"

Truth was integral to his scheme, though he cursed himself inwardly before saying very gently, "I'm afraid not, my lady. He suffered to the last. But he was never craven."

The lady's lips parted in a strangled gasp and a few women came to lead her toward the carriage. Rinwar, paled, turned, and led the way into his manor. He barely gave them time to look around; Draken got a sense of cold opulence in stormy shades of blue and white before Rinwar brought them into a smaller private salon with a desk, darkened by heavy navy drapes and grey stone walls. Draken and Tyrolean exchanged glances. Ground floor, so the windows might provide escape if needed.

"Drink?" Rinwar poured without glancing back for an answer and brought them each a fine spun-glass cup. He didn't take one for himself.

Draken and Tyrolean accepted the cups without lifting them to their lips.

"You have my condolences on the loss of your son, Landed," Draken said.

Rinwar snorted, though it didn't have the weight behind it that it might ordinarily. "Indeed. He was meant to execute the King, I was told. But what I don't know was why."

Draken ignored the lie. "Soeben turned on the King when the King was fighting me . . . I was forced to magick the King back to life. Soeben survived his capture and was sent to the dungeon."

"Magic?" Rinwar sounded startled. Reports of what had happened hadn't reached him then. "What did you do?"

"I saved him. That's all you need know."

Rinwar's gaze flicked downward. To Seaborn, where it rested on Draken's hip? "Were you with Soeben when he died?"

Was Draken imagining the sorrow had faded from those narrow, thin-lidded eyes? "I watched the King's sadist torture your son to death. It took the better part of the morning."

Rinwar winced.

Draken pressed a little more. "Before he died, we spoke, Soeben and I."

"What did he tell the sadist?"

As he thought, Rinwar was worried about his rebellion. "Far less than he told me."

"Damn you, man. What did he *say*?"

"Fair enough to implicate you, which should prove I am not trying to make an enemy of you, Lord Rinwar. Actually, I myself am none too pleased with the King at the moment."

"I imagine not. I heard you were to be executed, too." Rinwar walked back to the table with the wine, poured out one for himself from the same pitcher, drank it down, and poured it again.

Tyrolean visibly relaxed, drank some of his, and exchanged cups surreptitiously with Draken while Rinwar's back was turned.

Draken shook his head at Tyrolean's tasting for him and set the cup down. "Landed, since the King is missing, my only recourse is to deal with his youngest son—"

"*Missing?*"

"Please do not think me a fool. You know the King and Queen are missing, and I know you most likely had aught to do with it. As I said. I tire of pretense. Let us speak as equals, though I lower myself to deal with Landed when I am a Prince."

He let the last word sit in the room, heavy on the air. Tyrolean managed not to gape at Draken's uncustomary arrogance. Rinwar, not so much. He sputtered. "What—just *what* are you accusing me of?"

"I see where Soeben got his tenacity from," Draken said. "A shame it only prolonged his suffering."

Rinwar scowled but gave up his protest.

Odd, that. Draken didn't look at Tyrolean. If he did he might falter. "Destroy the Crown, kill off the royals. I have no claim to this throne. I care not."

Rinwar grunted. "As if you don't want a taste of revenge."

"It is sweet. I admit it. But I also look to Brîn's wellbeing. Rip this country apart if you wish, only do not touch mine. If you agree, I will help you."

"Monoea is your country."

"The better part of my blood is from Brîn. Aissyth proved that when he banished me from Monoea."

Rinwar relaxed a little. Here, Draken thought, is a man who is only comfortable when owed a favor. "Refreshing to deal with someone so direct. Aissyth has long been weak."

Draken tried to keep his voice mild. "History has plenty of weak kings, and yet things do turn for the worse when there are none."

"Indeed. I wonder that Aissyth cannot disprove our history." Rinwar drained his cup and poured yet again. He breathed heavily through flared nostrils. Draken waited. Rinwar obviously wanted to openly slander the King. "What do you suggest?"

Now, at last, they were getting somewhere. "I can get you into the Palace."

"How?" Rinwar demanded.

"Have we a pact or not? My help in your rebellion in exchange for leaving Brîn and Akrasia alone."

Rinwar squinted at him, considering. At last he sighed. "Yes. We've a pact."

"Swear it on our blood." Draken drew his blade and sliced his palm, shallow but stinging.

"That is magic." Rinwar didn't show the typical Monoean disdain.

"Aye."

Rinwar did as he was bid, cutting his palm and letting their blood mingle. The cut hurt only a little, but Draken felt a slight wave of nausea roll through him as the cut healed, as if the ground shifted slightly under his feet.

Rinwar frowned. "How do I get in? And will it accommodate my troops?"

"Aye, though it'll be slow going. There are two ways. Steps from the outside to some residence apartments, and a small tunnel into the dungeons." His mother would kill him if she knew. "Careless of the King, really. But the difficult bit will be getting into the city proper."

Rinwar flushed red. "I thought you had a way into the city, Gods curse you!"

"They already have," Draken said. "It's a problem, not impossible. I've a way inside, don't worry. I'll lead your men."

Rinwar's eyes narrowed. "Why would you go back there?"

"As I said, I want Brîn free of your troubles here. Also, I've unfinished business at the palace."

"Which is?"

"My own to know, my lord." Draken was not going to forgo his vow to Soeben. Besides, they'd need every man to fight the coming attack on Ashwyc.

Rinwar grunted, obviously displeased but not enough to argue. "I'll just ring for my captain and you can explain the details."

Of course the Landed Lord wouldn't be fighting himself. Draken supposed he should have thought of it. He'd have to kill Rinwar here, without his men knowing, before he and Tyrolean led them to their deaths inside Ashwyc.

"Is the King dead, my lord?" Tyrolean, his voice quiet and calm. A simple question, but it set Draken's heart racing.

Rinwar held a long moment before relenting. "I suppose it's rather time he was."

"Why keep him alive?" Draken asked.

"It's not sentimental, if that's what you're wondering, though we are cousins. No, once it's done, it's done. The King will be of no more use to me."

The narrow doors slammed open. Lady Faizen. "He murdered our son! Kill him now, my lord, or I will."

Two bright spots of ire marred her pale cheeks. She had blood on her bodice and skirts and brought with her the faint scent of death. Damn, she'd opened the casket and touched Soeben. Draken shot a glance at Tyrolean. The captain's lips tightened and his eyes narrowed. His hand crept up to rub his chest, a sign he'd be going for his swords soon.

"Faiz—" Rinwar began, but the lady interrupted him.

"They tortured him! Soeben is dead, his body ruined!" She turned on Draken. "You were there."

She knew he bloody well had been. He just looked at her.

"And you did *nothing*?" Her voice shrilled.

"His Highness was locked in a cell at the time," Tyrolean said.

"You . . . You should be dead. Not Soeben! Why are you even free? The King wanted you executed—"

"It was a ruse," Draken growled. "To draw the rebels out. To gain information." To see if you Ashen want me for my magic.

"Rebels—but Soeben had no part in that!"

So she did know of the plot against the crown. The deathblow to Rinwar's innocence. Draken's mind raced. How far did this stretch? How many Houses?

Grieving parents or not, he wasn't about to gift them with the truth of Soeben's confusion and innocence, his sense of betrayal. They deserved none of it. He could only pray they died thinking it was all their fault. Right now it was the best he could do for the boy.

"He most certainly did, thanks to his Lord Father. I heard all he said as they tortured him. Not that he talked much amid all the screaming. But it was enough."

Lord Rinwar shouted something inarticulate, drawing the sword at his belt. But indignation carried Draken through. Soeben could have been spared pain and death had his own father not used his compliant nature and youth against him.

Lady Faizen gave an inhuman hiss and launched toward Draken. He started to lash out at her, defending himself with his fist, trying to catch the knife. But Tyrolean was quicker; he caught her around the middle, trapping her arms against her body with one strong arm and dragging her away. She screamed as he wrenched at her hand with the knife; it clanked against the floor.

"Drae, look to the lord!" Tyrolean said.

Draken spun, drawing as he did and bringing his opposite arm up. Rinwar's sword crashed against his bracer. Draken growled in pain as the impact shook through his arm and weakened shoulder. Rinwar pressed his sudden advantage, snapping his blade up. Draken jerked back just in time but the tip of the blade caught his cheek and left a stinging cut that poured blood.

He closed in, driven by fury, and risked taking a strike by lashing out with his fist and catching Rinwar by the thick, ornate tie on his shirt. He jerked Rinwar closer, stealing the advantage with his shorter sword, and drove his blade into Rinwar's side.

Rinwar gasped and coughed, a strangled sound of agony. He fell against Draken, who bore his weight to the stone floor. Lady Faizen screamed, but it choked to a stop.

"Your Highness." Tyrolean, calm. Almost placid.

Draken turned to look at him. The Captain held a dagger tight under Lady Faizen's chin.

"If you would die this day, my lady," Draken said. "By all means continue screaming."

Faizen swallowed, which made her skin press harder against the blade. She winced against Tyrolean, but her struggles faded.

"That's better," Draken said. "Hold her, Ty. She may be of use. If she is not, or if she fights you, kill her."

Draken shoved Rinwar away. The motion dragged the sword out of his body. Draken climbed to his feet, suppressing a wince at his aching body, and crossed the room to bar the door.

"You've killed me," Rinwar gasped. He rolled his eyes toward his wife, who stared back at him, horrified, from Tyrolean's grip.

"Not yet," Draken said grimly. He went back to the lord and knelt on one knee. "Where is the King?"

Rinwar's lips parted. He coughed. No blood. Yet. He'd taken a severe gut wound . . . it would take some time, perhaps even some nights, if properly tended, for him to die. Draken had some time yet.

"Speak," Draken said, "or suffer. It matters little to me. I will comb this fastness to find him."

"Not . . . not here." Rinwar's gaze skittered away from Draken's. He blinked rapidly.

"You're lying."

"Tell him, please . . ." Lady Faizen swallowed. "Please let us go."

"Silence her, Ty."

Tyrolean slid his free arm up around Faizen's throat beneath the knife and squeezed. She pried at his arm with her fingers, making airless noises of protest, but the struggle made little difference to his taut muscles. The acrid scent of urine filled the room and soaked her skirts. She kicked a couple of times and then she slumped against him. He still held her in his arms, his inscrutable stare on Draken.

Draken couldn't even pin this one on the gods. *This is the ugliest thing I've made him do*, he thought. *I've lost him as a friend.* And yet, Soeben's screams still haunted his thoughts as well. His parents had sent him to a horrible death. Not the King. Not Draken.

"You've killed her! Bast—" Coughing broke the word in half. Blood sprayed from his lips.

"A blood choke, only," Draken said. "So far. Let's start simply. Is the King here, in Wyndam? On your grounds?"

Rinwar stared at his wife, stricken.

Draken would have sworn before this day that there was no love lost between the two. He'd seen them before and they treated each other with perfunctory courtesy, nothing more. However, Faizen knew about the rebellion. They shared children and were grieving Soeben together.

At any rate, he needed to find out all he could, very quickly.

Blood seeped through Rinwar's fine linen shirt and woven court jacket. It had been a clean, quick stab, leaving the man with internal bleeding but little enough coming out. Draken nudged the wound with his boot. Just a little. Just enough to get his attention. Rinwar gasped a cry and his watering eyes locked on Draken's.

"Stay with me, Rinwar. Is the King here?"

Rinwar's chin twitched in an unreadable gesture.

Draken turned his head and nodded to Tyrolean. Faizen was just stirring. Tyrolean let a slight grimace pass, but he obeyed. His arm slipped up again around Lady Faizen's throat and tightened again. She went limp in his arms, but his grip didn't lessen.

"No! *Stop* . . . stop. He's here." More blood coughed up from between his lips, scarlet against the dark floor.

Tyrolean let his arm relax.

"Where, exactly?" Draken asked, gripping his sword but not moving it. His heart pounded and his blood roared. They'd made too much noise. They'd taken too much time. Rinwar's men would be upon them at any moment. The sword heated in his hand. It glowed faintly in the candlelit gloom, black lines wavering beneath the surface of the metal.

Rinwar was silent, but his mouth worked. His hand came up to grip Draken's wrist. Finally he whispered, *"Down . . . down."*

"Is there a dungeon here?" Tyrolean asked.

"Most of these old places have them." The walls around the fireplace were black with ancient soot, and these windows had thick shutters rather than glass. It predated Ashwyc Palace, surely. Wyndam had existed when Monoea wasn't a single country, but warring citystates filled with lords who abducted, tortured, and killed for power. This house belonged to the oldest family so it must have existed back then.

"Is it you at the head of this rebellion, then? You, Rinwar? Does it stop with you?"

Rinwar huffed air, drawing Draken's eye. He moaned once more and fell limp. His eyes were wild and white in their death stare.

Faizen moaned. Her mouth worked and her eyelids fluttered. She swallowed and said wetly, "You've killed him. For this, at least, the King must die. If I'm fortunate, he already is dead."

"That's treason," Draken growled, and not even very *good* treason.

"I would rather die a traitor to this crown than in service to it."

Tyrolean tightened his grip and laid the blade under Faizen's chin again. Unflappable, hard: "Your lord is dead. Save yourself, my lady."

Draken met her wild eyes. "For your family, if nothing else."

"There's nothing left," Faizen husked out.

"Your son. Your daughter. Soeben's memory—"

"There's nothing left! You've stolen them all!" Her tongue flicked over her quivering bottom lip, she drew a breath, and thrust her body forward.

Tyrolean kept the edges of his blade as thin as the edge of a fine Crown scroll. The gash it caused in her throat was brutal, quick, and gaping. Maybe even she didn't expect it to happen so quickly; gaping lips and flaring nostrils tried to draw futile breath. Blood gushed down her front and over Tyrolean's arm.

Tyrolean let her down, gently, his back bent at an awkward angle. She tumbled to the floor as her heart pumped its last, one fist curled by her pale face.

It was several heartbeats before Draken remembered to breathe.

Tyrolean set the blade next to her on the floor, rose to his full height, and pulled his bracer off. His sleeve was soaked with hot blood, stinking of rank salt like the sea. Draken wondered if there would ever be a night he didn't fall asleep with that scent in his nostrils, with death in his lungs.

"Tyrolean."

"We must find the King. We must end this." Tyrolean cut his bloody sleeve away with his knife.

"This was supposed to be a godsdamned diplomatic mission. We had a pact, Rinwar and I. I could have stopped this." The tinge of desperation stained his voice. Draken wondered where it came from. He felt vacant inside.

"There was nothing to be done. Let us find the King and quit this place." Tyrolean's words sounded as empty as Draken felt. Banal; a pacification. Nothing more.

"Aye. Let's do that." A pounding on the door jolted through him, prickling his skin like nearby lightning. Someone shouted, "Rinwar! My lord, open the door!"

Tyrolean met his eyes. "Rinwar's men are here, Draken. Will you lead, or shall I?"

Draken. Not Khel Szi. Not Highness. "I will. This is my fight," Draken said. "How many do you think there are?"

The doors pounded again, and strained against their bar. Someone clever slipped a blade in the crack between them and shoved up against the metal latches.

"Enough to kill in the light." Tyrolean yanked his blades from their scabbards and turned toward the door.

He was right. There'd been enough killing in shadows to last Monoea a generation. The latch flipped with a scraping creak and the doors burst open.

CHAPTER TWENTY-ONE

Less than an army crowded the corridor outside Rinwar's study, but too many to count in the ensuing chaos. On dual instinct, Draken and Tyrolean kept the fight to just inside the doorway. Crowded by the doors and flanking tables, it created a sieve through which opponents could only attack them two at a time. Draken had the front line; Tyrolean just behind him. Tyrolean was a cyclone of blades, silent but for the whistle of steel on air and the dull thud when they achieved a hit. Draken fought slower, grunting as he drove Seaborn home.

Magic fair hummed through his blood, a tantalizing drag to wring life from death. His lips parted, wanting to whisper the words.

This is new, he thought, startled.

The hesitation cost him a strike and slowed his defensive move. A blade caught the bicep of his free arm, slicing deep, stopping at the bone with soul-shuddering intensity rather than pain. His opponent nearly slipped through. Draken growled and struck, almost feeling as if the sword were leading, or as if his old swordhand Bruche guided his arm. Maybe it was muscle memory, but his blow knocked his attacker's attempt at a guard and caught the man across the throat. Blood gushed from his jugular and the man fell before his expression could register surprise.

The next one was big enough to bear a two-handed sword. It was too big to wield in the close quarters of the doorway and corridor; he shoved past Draken with a growl and went for Tyrolean where he had more room. Draken let him go; he had to. He could only pray Tyrolean had his back.

His arm seared where the cut healed itself and vertigo clawed at his head. Draken had no time to think of why. The last man forced immediate battle as Draken was shoved back. He was wiry and strong, every blow too precise for Draken to defend against for long. Urgency from exhaustion, from knowing he wasn't good enough, from knowing more guards could come at any moment, caused Draken to take extraordinary chances. He was vaguely aware of taking cuts; he came at the wiry fighter hard and fast, letting him inside his guard, blocking with his braced arm. The bone ached from taking so many quick blows.

He drove the wiry man back, punched him in the face as the man's blade sliced in the gap beneath his breast plate. They were too close for the strike to get enough momentum. It merely stung rather than gutted. Draken punched again with his bracer. The wiry guard stumbled back, falling against the opposite wall in the corridor. Draken sliced his throat and spun, remembering the one that had slipped by him.

There were two Ashen. Though one was only tall as Draken's chin, he had Tyrolean well-engaged with the help of the brutally huge compatriot. The Captain was doing his best, fighting with both blades in tandem. But he was faltering. Draken had never seen that from him before. Then he realized Tyrolean was bleeding from a cut across the chin and another along his chest. Someone had gotten past those rapid, agile strikes? A second shock of the day. Or perhaps the tenth. Draken had lost count.

Tyrolean caught the big man's sword with his smaller one and shoved him toward Draken, who could barely believe Tyrolean's tempered Gadye alloy held against the heavier two-handed blade. Ty followed with a hit to the thigh—not a killing blow, but damaging enough to make the big man growl in pain and waver.

Draken's arm stung deeply but he ignored it and shoved his sword well within the big man's reach, more to draw his attention away from Tyrolean. He had all he could do to temper attack from the nimbler, smaller Ashen.

With the stench of blood and loosed bowels filling his lungs, Draken surged forward, following his attention-getting strike with a more effective one. Seaborn clattered hard against the big man's blade, knocking it aside. Seaborn flared; the big man's eyes widened. But the big man hadn't started fighting yesterday; the great sword came back at Draken with shocking power, if not speed. Draken had to lift his arm to deflect the blow, but he misjudged. Too early. The big sword skipped off his elbow and stabbed through the leather breast plate, crunching ribs and driving deep through flesh and organs.

Draken coughed, stumbled. Seaborn flared hot but it fell from his hand as his whole body seemed to fail at once. He didn't know or realize he fell; he was just *there*, his head twisted at an odd angle against the thick leg of a table and aching as if a bane had crawled in there and scraped the inside of his skull with its claws.

Something glowed from the corner of his eye; his hand crabbed toward it and caught the crossguard of his sword. His fingers worked until the familiar leather grip was under his hand. But he was too weak to grasp it.

The big man knelt on one knee, lifting his sword in both hands. Pointed down. At Draken's heart.

A shout made the Ashen look aside; a thud as a man fell, and then abruptly, something inside Draken surged. Everything shuddered violently. He heard a great *crack*, as if a giant had splintered a mountain in two. Every wound, especially the deep one in his side, consumed him with astonishing pain. More, smaller noises, crashing and the rupture of stone. He only barely registered the big man's head separating from his shoulders, and Tyrolean's crossed blades. He was bloody across his front and to his elbows. Draken heard his name, vaguely, and the world stuttered into darkness—

"Draken." Someone hook him, a strong hand on his shoulder.

A white light glared into his eyes.

Draken heaved a breath and coughed, but only because his throat was dry. The light blinded him. He squinted into it, tried to speak. Another cough.

The strong hand cupped the back of his neck and lifted. A cup was pressed to his lips. Cool wine mixed with liquid grain, the sting of alcohol on his lips. He coughed but gulped it down. Realized his fingers encircled the familiar leather wrapped hilt of Seaborn. His thumb shifted over the loose end of leather and he released it.

The light faded. He blinked. Osias bent over him, holding the cup to his mouth, his strong hand gripping the back of Draken's neck. Their faces were very close, the moon on his forehead looking like a black hole, as if his flesh didn't exist there. Like it was a hole to nothing. Like the Palisade. The sensation made Draken feel ill. He let Osias slide from focus. Beyond him, Tyrolean stood, chest heaving, covered in blood.

Abrupt lucidity left him reeling. Torturing Rinwar. Lady Faizen throwing herself on Tyrolean's blade. The fight, the sword crashing into his side. His fingers fumbled for his ribs but Tyrolean pulled him up to a sit.

"That is very good wine," Draken said.

"Is there something you want to tell me, Your Highness?" Tyrolean said.

Draken looked down at his chest. Drying blood caked it. His shoulders tightened. The one still suffered a deep twinge of pain, as it had for moonturns, since it had been dislocated in a fight. His tone was acerbic. "The gods see fit to heal a deathblow but they fail to fix my sore shoulder."

Tyrolean's brows raised. "The gods?"

Draken twisted free of Osias' grip, grasped the table leg behind him, and levered himself upright. His knee protested vehemently, resisted straightening, tight as usual. It'd loosen in a dozen steps. "Khellian's balls, you're bleeding a river, Ty."

"I've had worse." The shortness in his tone betrayed his pain. "You want to tell me what in Korde's sour heart is happening to you, Draken? I thought you were dead."

Draken didn't answer. He was too busy staring around at the room. Jagged cracks split the walls. One pillar supporting the mantle had crashed to the floor. Shutters hung askew from lopsided windows. Icy draughts leaking in cleared the room of some of the death stench, but an undercurrent of broken stone and dust thickened the air. Every table looked as if someone had swept their items to the floor, which was liberally distributed with blood, shards of pottery, scrolls, bodies, and weapons.

Draken frowned. Something was missing among them. "Do you notice none of them have the ash marks like Rinwar and his wife." And his son.

"I was too busy noticing your mortal wounds knitting themselves," Tyrolean said.

"And the earthquake as they did so," Osias said.

Draken stared at Osias. His healing caused an earthquake?

The Mance toed a crack with his boot. "See? Just there."

Cracks in the stone floor radiated out from where Draken had fallen. He blinked and stepped away. But the ground stayed still.

"How long have you known?" Tyrolean watched Draken, his face blank, betraying nothing.

He reached for the wine and poured it over his sword, drying with layers of blood, then scrubbed it on his discarded shirt until his hands stopped trembling. The normal activity of cleaning his blade calmed his shaking, but not his mind. What in Seven Bloodied Moons had happened to him? Healing minor cuts was one thing, but he should be dead . . . had been as good as. Some feral magic was at work within him. He gave Seaborn a suspicious look even as he cared for it.

"Some sevennight now. I had no idea it would come to this, healing a death blow." He should have told Tyrolean, Elena, someone. "Is it the sword, Osias?"

"Aye. And no. Akhen Khel and its magics are wrapped up within the will of the gods. You are truly godsworn, Draken."

Tyrolean's face was blank, betraying nothing about what he thought of any of it. He busied himself cleaning his swords with the cloak of a fallen Ashen. There was no way to escape but together. Draken was willing to wager the City of Brîn that Tyrolean wished things were different.

"Why are you here, Osias? How?"

"I thought it prudent to investigate while glamoured. Listen well, because we've not much time. This villa is filled with Ashen, or their mercenaries at least."

"Listen to what?" Draken asked.

"Rinwar is leading the rebellion."

Draken's shoulders sagged with relief. "Excellent. We've just cut off its paws then."

"No. Not this Rinwar," Osias said, gesturing to the dead one. "His elder brother. A Moonminster priest."

Tyrolean gave an uncharacteristic groan. "We're in the right family then."

"Aye," Osias said. "Just not the right man. And more bad news: rumor says he's left for Akrasia."

"Akrasia—?" Draken shed his bloodied cloak, but the rustling failed to overcome the echo of voices from down the hall. "Wait. Is that shouting?"

"That way." Tyrolean led them in the opposite direction down a long corridor. "I saw stairs as we came in."

"These big old places have a half-dozen flights at least, for servants and guards and the family. We need a back stair." And a bow, to fend off more hand-to-hand fights.

"Osias? Do you have your bow?" Tyrolean said.

The Mance produced his longbow out of rippling air. "Aye. But I used the last of my arrows getting inside this place."

What he wouldn't give to run across the armory, which might not be in this building at all. He longed for his own Citadel, or even Ashwyc Palace, which he knew better than this place he'd only ever been in a few times, and then only in the public areas for parties or to accompany the King on Black Guard business.

"This one?" Tyrolean indicated a narrow flight.

"Aye. It'll have to do." Though he had no idea where they led. They went down the stairs at a good clip, though he let Tyrolean and Osias go first because his knee was still stiff.

The voices closed in on the top of the stair as they descended down into darkness. Draken put his sword in its scabbard to hide its light and they moved carefully down, as silently as they could. The skin on the back of his neck crawled. He kept imagining an arrow piercing his bare back.

"Let's see how you bloody magic *that* away," he muttered to the gods, annoyed at his nerves. He'd been in enough battles and tight spots to remain mostly calm. But fresh tremors in his fingers skittered up his arms and settled in his chest. He tightened his grip on the sword, trying to will strength into his body.

"Be easy," Tyrolean said softly.

"A light, Khel Szi," Osias suggested.

Draken glanced back. The voices from the top of the stairs had faded, but it didn't mean they weren't being followed. Still, they wouldn't get far in this pitch stairwell that smelled of dust and death. He drew his sword again. Seaborn's faint halo broke the darkness, revealing more steps, reflecting off Osias' silvery hair.

After two turns at featureless landings, they reached the bottom of the flight and paused. They were far underground. Osias lifted his head and sniffed. The air was stale and cold. Torch-lit corridors ran in four directions.

"We could easily be trapped down here," Tyrolean said.

Draken nodded, grim. "Or lost. But we came to find the King. I fear we don't have much time. The rebels will know soon that Rinwar is dead."

Tyrolean nodded. After a moment of recounting their turns and rectifying them with the layout of the house above, Draken nodded at the corridor he thought may lead inward; surely they'd hold the King deep in the bowels of the villa. They walked quietly for some time. Their soft footfalls and breath were the only sounds. Sweat broke out cold over Draken's skin. Tyrolean must feel it too; his skin gleamed damply pale in the dim light, ghostlike. That turn led to a dead end. Draken kicked at a bit of rubbish—remnants of cloth and a broken basket—in frustration.

"So we go back, then," Osias said.

There was nothing else to do, though Draken silently cursed the waste of time. They turned and went back to the crossing, treading softly lest the guards were waiting for them. But it seemed deserted.

Draken shook his head. "Maybe we're wrong. Maybe no one ever comes down here."

But Tyrolean glanced about, gestured down another anonymous corridor, and Draken and Osias followed.

"It's odd. Rinwar made little effort to hide his actions, nor did he fight back terribly hard," Tyrolean said at last, very softly, "The whole thing was rather too easily done."

Draken snorted. "Speak for yourself. You didn't take a sword in your gut."

Tyrolean cast an inscrutable glance over his shoulder. Draken couldn't help wondering if he wished the sword had done its job.

"I think Rinwar was curious over what you had to say," Osias said. "It is my sense Monoeans don't take to outsiders easily."

"They don't take to *themselves* easily," Draken said. "That I took an interest in the rebellion, even for selfish reasons, had to intrigue him. He must have thought he could use me to his own end."

He thought again of his mother telling him the rebels wanted him on their throne. He shook his head. Magic or not, it made little sense. Still, he felt an odd urge to share it with them. Before he could speak, though, Tyrolean did.

"You brought him his dead son."

Draken grunted. A habit he'd like to quit, parleying with dead sons. "I owe you an apology, Captain. I asked you to do an ugly thing back there."

"It's an ugly world," Tyrolian said. "You must have hated living here."

"Not so long ago I thought the same thing about you and Akras—"

Tyrolean stopped walking and lifted his hand to his lips for quiet. Draken slid his sword into its scabbard, shrouding them in darkness. Clinking ahead. Regular intervals.

"We're coming up on something," Tyrolean said softly, not quite a whisper, which would carry in the quiet better than his deep voice. Two hushed whispers as he drew his blades.

Draken lifted his chin and sniffed. Tyrolean was right. The air tasted of sweat and fear. A slight draft brushed his cheek.

"The dungeon," Osias whispered.

Draken could only hope.

And he was curious, if he bothered to admit it to himself. Landed had people who answered to them, which meant holding cages. But it was against the King's law to have a proper dungeon, with torturing equipment and sadists. Would Rinwar have followed that law?

Draken drew Seaborn for light again, and they crept on. A noise, a low grunt, raised their weapons and hackles. Draken pushed ahead. He wasn't going to let Tyrolean take the lead in this. Draken had agreed to find the King, to help Galbrait, his old country, and keep this war from his new one. If there was a fight coming, Draken would take the first leap into the fray.

The corridor narrowed, the walls chiseled from the rough, cold bedrock that Sevenfel rested on. It felt as if it weighed on him, as if the whole thing might come tumbling down. A few cracks pierced the stone, seeping dust and scree and water like blood from a wound.

A clink. A wet cough, almost a sob.

Draken strode faster, his arms in fight position. The corridor ended at a T; he paused before broaching the intersection and listened again. Tyrolean tipped his head toward his swordarm and Draken nodded. They rounded the corner, side-by-side.

A guard stood where the cells started; he was armed and alert, a seax in his hand. He leapt instantly to action, bringing his blade up to stab. Draken darted in and thrust him back with a forearm against his chest. The blade nicked Draken's shoulder on its way down, but he ignored it, bringing Seaborn around to slash open the guard's stomach. He shouted in pain and staggered back against the bars behind him. Draken snarled and stepped closer to finish the job, but a shout stopped him.

"Leave him. Here!" Tyrolean, breathless.

The guard wasn't going anywhere. Draken spun and rushed after Tyrolean, who was fighting against two more guards. Draken killed one of them with a growl and not one shred of regret; the man's sword was about to decapitate the Captain. Tyrolean finished off his and they huffed, staring at each other. Even more shouts were echoing from back the way they'd come.

"This is a death trap," Osias said.

"Draken!" A hissed, anguished whisper.

"Your Grace." Draken strode for one of the cells, getting his first real look at the place. Rinwar had not resisted putting in torture equipment, but it was blackened and dusty with age.

Except for one rough table. Draken swallowed, sickened. The Queen, her gown ripped from her body, her chest bloody, her lips open and staring. Tyrolean ignored the dead Queen and started searching the guards for a key to unbolt the King's cell. The man Draken had injured cried out hoarsely as Tyrolean pawed at his clothing. He found one and tossed it to Draken. "Your Highness? Shall I kill him?"

"Yes! He tortured and raped my wife!" The whites of Aissyth's eyes glared in the gloom, his chest heaved, his hair and clothes were disheveled and bloody.

Tyrolean tightened, glanced at Draken.

"Do it." Draken turned away from the aborted cry, the wet sound of Tyrolean's blades ruining flesh. He unlocked the King's cell and let him out. "Are you unhurt, Your Grace?"

Aissyth grimaced, shoved past Draken, and went to his wife. He laid his hand on her bloodless cheek for a moment, then tried to cover her legs with the shreds of her gown.

"Your Grace," Draken said, as gently as he could.

"So much blood," King Aissyth said.

From the Queen, from the dead guards. On his own chest. Draken barely noticed it anymore. "Your Grace, we must go."

The King kept trying to cover his wife, to kiss her cold lips and stroke back her hair.

More voices, footsteps. Draken took the King's arm, quieted his motions, and tugged. Aissyth looked up at him, agony stripped bare. For a moment Draken wondered if he knew anything but his dead wife, if he remembered he was in an enemy's dungeon, that danger was coming.

"Draken, his wife is dead."

"So will we all be," he retorted, tugging on the King's arm. "Your Grace. We must go."

"But . . ."

"We'll return for her when we've put down the rebellion."

Aissyth nodded and allowed Draken to lead him. Sounds echoed from where they'd come. He led them deeper, past more torture apparatuses. The Wailing Woman. The Tall Man. The Immobilizer. Cracked leather straps dangled from the ceiling. A board of blades, pliers, and other cruel devices. A few were missing from pegs, left scattered around the Queen's body.

They strode past these and the cells, all empty. The sounds faded behind them into their own huffing breath and quiet footfalls; even the King knew to walk softly, though he still had a bewildered air. After a few turns, Draken realized maybe they wouldn't be trapped down here after all. He signaled them to stop. They needed to regroup, to plan. "Your Grace, do you know the way out?"

Aissyth frowned. For a long-held breath, Draken was certain the King was still too stunned to answer. Tyrolean gave him a look from behind Aissyth.

"I've only been down here once, but I'm certain there are a couple of back ways in. It's how these dungeons were built, so one could escort prisoners in and out without going through the main house." He caught Draken's eye, momentary shrewdness overtaking grief and confusion. "The Palace is the same, as you saw when your mother brought you out."

Draken eased a breath. "As you say, Your Grace."

"I'll check to see if we've lost them." Osias turned and scouted back the way they'd come. Within a breath he'd disappeared completely into the shadows and stone.

The others stood quiet for a moment, Draken wondering if they'd ever find a way out of this warren of corridors. He wondered who had dug them and how many people had been worked to death in the process. As a slave in the Palace, he'd been worked fair hard; by now he supposed he'd be dead if it had gone on. Most slaves didn't live very long. He thought of his father, some nights too exhausted to be angry. No wonder he looked so decrepit when they'd last met. The Monoeans must have worked him hard and long. He squashed the twinge the thought caused and looked at the King.

"Did you know my father was Prince when he was a slave at the Palace?"

Aissyth blinked, didn't meet his eyes. "Not at the time. I heard rumors later, from the trade routes. It seemed . . . incredible, really. Too incredible. I disregarded it."

A lie, and badly told. One that kept Draken from tempering his hard tone. "Why did they torture the Queen?"

The King flinched. His face greyed in the torchlight, shed its rosy glow.

Draken stepped closer. "*Why* did they torture her?" They had wanted something from the King, he was certain of it. Information, maybe.

Aissyth hissed through his teeth. "Orders. They wanted me to sign orders. My last as King, they said."

"Who? Rinwar?"

The King said nothing.

Impatience reared like a demon inside Draken. He gripped his sword and it heated in his hand. The King holding back on him now? After all this . . . after all he'd done? "This has something to do with me."

"It has everything to do with you." Aissyth drew a breath. He seemed to steady as he released it. A trace of the old, hard King bared itself. "They were orders to attack Akrasia."

A beat. Another. "Did you sign them?"

Aissyth flinched. "She was my wife. And they killed her anyway."

Draken stared at him, bewilderment battling with urgent fury. He shoved it all down as soft, quick footfalls came their way. Osias, moving at top speed but not breathing hard. "They come."

"How many?"

He shook his head. "A dozen, perhaps? Or more. In any case, we must move."

At the moment, Draken just cared whether they'd have to fight again. But in the back of his mind, things weren't adding up. They raced down the corridor, took a turn, and another turn. The musty stink of death permeated the air, growing with every step. The torchlight died out. Tyrolean uttered a rare curse. Draken echoed it and drew his sword. He unleashed some of his carefully suppressed anger and the sword flared.

Its light revealed dusty bones scattered on the rough stone floor, and several bodies hanging from shackles. A dead end.

CHAPTER TWENTY-TWO

D raken wondered if he would ever escape the sound of boots coming after him from the dark. But then, they were fair trapped, so it was likely. Just not the way he'd like.

"Ideas?" He looked from the King's pale face to Tyrolean's set jaw.

"That last turn was a T. It'll make a bottleneck. If we can fight our way past them . . ." Tyrolean shrugged and Draken took his meaning. It was unlikely at best. Even Osias looked grim.

"They'll have arrows. We cannot stay here," Aissyth added.

"We go back then, to meet them. On the offensive." Draken shoved ahead of them and took the lead. At the moment he knew only to protect the King. If Aissyth could escape—it would be a long road to the palace—but if he could escape, then he could set Monoea right. Surely if he were free, Aissyth would stop the attack on Brîn. Stop war from breaking out again.

A flaw in his logic niggled at him, but he was too busy to pay it much mind. He raced down the corridor without looking back, the walls feeling close and dirty in the eerie white light of his sword. Godslight, he thought, pure and bright and small against the darkness. It reminded him of Zozia alone in the night sky.

Seaborn's light cast jolting shadows against the stone, moving like a flickering candle as he ran. He caught a glimpse of the shape of a man with a horned helmet, rearing against the stone. *Khellian*. It made him falter and redirect the light off the flat of the blade. Seaborn's light flashed over mere stone. Nothing. A trick of the eye.

He pushed on—shadows couldn't kill him. He made the mistake of letting his gaze connect with the sword's light. It blinded him for a moment. He peered past it, still running.

The shadows ahead resolved into actual men with swords.

Maybe it was Seaborn's light, but they hesitated. Draken killed two of them before they got a chance to attack. A tiny ripple of relief pierced the battle haze that he still knew Monoean light armor well enough to penetrate it without much thought. Then he was full-on fighting, swinging until his arms ached. Men kept coming. His body tired, slowed. His opponents took advantage of it, striking and cutting him. Never enough damage to bring him down, but enough to wear on him. He could see only by the light of his sword. It cast a vicious bloodstained glare on his opponents, demonizing their features. The fighting was hot, dirty, wet. More than once he stumbled over a body and had to fight his way back up from his knees. Shouts and noises blended with the cacophony of blood roaring through his veins. His shoulder ached. His bad knee throbbed. Only furious madness drove him, but it, too, began to flag. His body couldn't move as fast, he couldn't swing as hard—

Somehow he knew when the King fell, some otherworldly awareness of his surroundings thrust upon him. Seaborn plunged through the leather plate of day armor on the man facing him. He growled and shoved the dead man aside, blood slicking his free hand—

A high-pitched screech broke through the haze.

Khel Szi!

"Draken." Osias.

He blinked and stopped swinging. Seaborn's red-stained light revealed a slew of bodies—what felt like a dozen but in truth were eight, and buckets of blood. He swallowed, willing himself calm. No reaction. Not even on the inside. Especially not on the inside.

Someone picked her way across the nearest body and leapt against him: arms locked about his neck, a slim, strong body pressed against his. Her weight nearly knocked him off balance. He turned his head and drew in her scent, still familiar despite the blood. Or maybe because of it.

"Aarinnaie," he whispered. Weariness and relief surged through him.

"I thought—I thought you—" A sob choked off her words.

"I know. Hush now." Draken didn't have the heart to chastise her for coming. He pushed her away gently, toward Tyrolean, and lifted the sword to shed its dim, blood-slicked light, searching out the King in the tumbled wreckage of bodies. Halmar appeared with a louvered lantern and Draken lowered his blade as yellow oil light revealed Aissyth sprawled across the floor.

Draken knelt and laid a hand on Aissyth's shoulder. The King had suffered a gash across his chest that was deep enough to let bone shine through, and another stab wound that must have pierced a lung. Blood spread from his body in a slow pool. Red spittle stained his lips. He was still warm, but no pulse beat beneath his skin.

"Cousin," Draken whispered and bowed his head.

A high-pitched gasp made him turn. Lady Sikyra was picking her way quickly over bodies and pushing her way between Draken's wary szi nêre. Konnan stepped in front of her.

"Let her pass, Konnan."

Halmar offered his hand. She took it without looking at him and let him guide her to Draken.

"My lady," Draken said, his voice rough with fresh shock at seeing his mother wearing trousers and bearing a bloodied seax. "Why are you here?"

"You must go. Galbrait is injured," she said. "Back down the corridor."

"No!" Aarinnaie cried, and started back.

"Halmar, stop her," Draken said. "I'll go." They couldn't count on the corridor being secure. Damn Aarinnaie. She should be at the Palace, safe; no. At home. Anywhere but this dank tunnel where a nation had died.

It was Tyrolean who reached out and neatly gripped Aarinnaie's arm. To Draken's surprise, she didn't resist him. Draken pushed by them all as Halmar gave Konnan a few terse instructions. Konnan stepped past Aarinnaie and trotted back down the corridor after Draken. He heard his mother's moan behind him. "Oh, Aissyth. No. No, my King."

Draken hissed a curse. Something old and dark and ugly reared inside him. All this blood and torn flesh and machination would only lead to more war, more death. In one day the direct line of Monoean kings had been eviscerated.

Galbrait sprawled, eyes open, moaning wordlessly. He'd been stabbed in the gut. Setia knelt by him, one hand holding a torch for light, the other pressing a folded cloak against the wound. But anyone could see it was futile.

He knelt by the young man. "Be easy. We'll get you out of here." But he had no idea how, not alive at any rate. Blood ran from Galbrait like the Eros swollen with Newseason rain. He'd given as good as he'd gotten, though; two house guards sprawled nearby.

Galbrait swallowed and coughed blood. He gasped, *"Father?"*

After a hesitation, Draken shook his head.

Galbrait moaned again. Draken closed his eyes, wishing he could shut off all his senses to the brutality of their surroundings, of their situation. This young, dying man was now King. In a few breaths there would be no more kings. He shuddered, unable to shrug off the old stories of chaos should all the kings die.

"Khel Szi, we cannot stay here."

"Why did he come, Konnan?"

"He insisted, Khel Szi, when Aarinnaie did. You were too long away without guards."

Draken lifted his head and stared at the young szi nêre until Konnan's dappled forehead wrinkled. But it wasn't his accusatory tone on Draken's mind. Gods, the orders to attack Akrasia. Soldiers were probably already on the way to the docks at Cold Bank. The King and Crown Prince Aissyth'Ae were dead, and now Prince Galbrait was lost to them as well. There would be no royal orders to halt the attack.

Aarinnaie had escaped Halmar's grip, though the Comhanar followed close behind. "There is a way to save him," she said softly.

"*What?* Aarin, no—"

"It's simple enough, Khel Szi. Find a guard and kill him for Galbrait. They're all rebels anyway."

"We don't know that." He glared at his sister. Halmar dipped his chin, drawing Draken's eye. "I fear it is a moot point. He won't last but a few dozen more breaths, Khel Szi."

"No—no magicks—" Galbrait cried out and coughed. It died away as he fell unconscious.

Draken couldn't slip his sword into this young man's heart, even if it was going to stop beating soon. "At any rate, it's out of the question. There's no time. We must focus on escape. There's little chance we'd capture a guard in time; there are too many of them and they won't patrol alone. And the King would not have condoned saving even Galbrait with magic."

"You aren't saving Galbrait," Aarinnaie said. "You're saving Monoea and Brîn. Think. As King he will owe you his *life*. We never need fear Monoea again."

"Aarin, enough!" Damn, his voice was rough again. He cleared his throat and reeled in his impatience. After all, she didn't know about the impending attack. "They made Aissyth sign orders to send ships to attack Akrasia. We've little time to stop them."

"Korde has surely damned us, then. If the ships leave we've no prayer of catching them, not with the Trades behind them," Tyrolean said.

"Nor can we warn Brîn," Halmar added.

Osias shook his head. "We must get to the docks and try to stop them somehow."

Draken looked down at Galbrait's still form, breath barely moving Setia's hand resting on his torn body, and he thought of Aissyth. His cousin-King had held the safety of Draken's people in his dead hands. "Aissyth was going to reverse the orders."

Sikyra pushed closer. "Galbrait yet lives, the rightful King. He can stop the orders. Kill me for him."

Aarinnaie shook her head. "My Lady, no. That's not what I meant—"

Sikyra ignored her. "Please. Draken. Let me do this for him. For you."

He stared at her, incredulous. "For me?"

"For your people. For all the people."

Gods, do not ask this of me. He shook his head, wordless.

"You must. Please, Your Highness." She stepped closer and looked into his face. Concern and age lined it. "Let me do this thing for you, for all I have not done."

"Your death is no small thing," Draken said.

"I am small compared to the Crown Prince, to the King, to the entirety of your people," Sikyra said.

The words escaped before he could stop them. "Not to me."

She drew in a sharp breath. Her eyes glistened in the torchlight. A wavering smile crossed her lips. "Aissyth once saved my son, Draken. The least I can do is return the favor."

Draken blinked several times, drew a sharp breath. Again words escaped him without his meaning to speak, as if whatever god owned this cruel jest had taken possession of his tongue. "You're certain of this?"

She reached up to touch his cheek. Her hand was cool, smooth. "I've known no truer thing since I heard your first cry."

He eased a breath from his chest and looked down at the Prince. Osias knelt by him and felt for a pulse. "If you do this thing, you must do it quickly."

Sikyra spoke again, softly, so that maybe only Draken could hear. "Let me help you this one time. Revive Galbrait. Help him stop the war between your nations."

Your nations. None were his, not by rights. No amount of magical approval from the gods made him anything but what he was: a half-breed ex-slave bastard with more blood on his hands than a Monoean sadist.

A pall of silence held reign in the tight, bloody tunnel. The only thing breaking it was the rasping, weak breath of the dying Prince.

He gave his mother a look, maybe pleading, maybe vacant, if how he felt was any judge. She'd taken hold of his arms, her hands slim but strong on his biceps. He pulled free gently, turned, and thrust Seaborn into Galbrait's chest before he had more time to think about it. Seaborn flared in his hand, shedding cruel godslight over dirty, strained faces. He wondered if any of them were breathing. He certainly could drag no air into his aching chest.

He turned back to his mother. His eyes stung, cold sweat prickled his back.

"Aissyth spoke true. You deserve more. You always deserved more. You're a good man, Draken."

He just stared at her, unable to speak. She couldn't be further from the truth, but even *he* wasn't dishonorable enough to dissuade a mother's delusion of his son's worth at the moment of her death. She deserved at least that.

She reached out and straightened Elena's pendant around his neck, looked at it. "This is your Queen?"

There was no air behind his answer: *"Aye."*

"Your lover?"

He swallowed. "She is with child."

A tremulous smile flitted across Sikyra's lips. She squared her shoulders. "Now, my son."

His stomach twisted painfully, every part of him screaming to stop, not do this. Draken took her by the shoulder to brace her, met her eyes. She gave a little nod and reached up to wrap her fingers around his wrist. How could he think of killing her? But his arm was already pushing forward. The point made a little wet sound as it split her flesh. Seaborn slid inside her chest, fitting there as if she made a new, clean sheath.

"Life for life . . ."

Her lips parted. His hand tightened on her shoulder as her weight leaned into the blade. She blinked, her focus slipped away, staring into some unfathomable darkness beyond, and she slumped against him.

He swallowed back the bile and closed his eyes. Someone . . . Halmar . . . pulled her away gently, leaving Seaborn in Draken's hand, glowing with magic through the blood. Scrolling lines crawled across the blade as the magic took hold, and then faded just as quickly. Elena's pendant lay cold against his chest; Seaborn weighed heavy in his hand. He felt the ghost of his mother in his arms, heard the echo of her voice in his ear.

He heard a cough, looked up. Halmar laid his mother gently down on the floor.

"Father?" Galbrait, his voice whispy, but he was moving. Breathing. Tyrolean knelt by the Prince and spoke lowly, something Draken couldn't hear.

Draken stepped back, looked fruitlessly for something to clean his sword of his mother's blood as if it would cleanse his soul of it.

Aarinnaie moved to his side and wrapped her hand around his wrist. "Be easy, brother," she whispered. "You did as you must."

Everyone watched Galbrait, but Draken stared at his mother, limp on the floor. Halmar started to lay a cloak over her; Draken shook his head. It was no use now. The ugliness of her death was locked into his mind's eye.

Galbrait sat up with Tyrolean's help and looked around at the carnage. "What happened?"

"You died. Draken brought you back," Aarinnaie said.

Galbrait blinked at her, and then turned a narrow-eyed gaze at Draken. His hand traveled over his middle, where the wound had been. "What? How?"

Draken ran his hand over his forehead and hair. It was sticky with sweat and worse. He needed another bath, badly. "We don't have time for this. Galbrait." He did his best to gentle his tone. "Your Majesty. Your father is dead. You are King."

He waited for the news, and all the meaning it carried with it, to sink in. Galbrait gaped at him. No tears, no anguished cry. Whether he'd loved his father or not, the Prince knew it wasn't the time. "Mother?"

Draken shook his head. "I'm sorry."

Galbrait started to climb to his feet. Tyrolean grabbed his arm to steady him. "Be easy. You've had a shock."

Galbrait shook loose, passed a couple of moments swaying, and swallowed when he saw Sikyra laying dead behind Draken. "Your mother died as well."

"We must go," Draken said. "Down to Sister Bay."

"To the Bay? No, I have to go back to the Palace, to, to . . ." The Prince swayed a little again and this time didn't shrug off Tyrolean's arm under his. "To take command."

"First, Sister Bay," Draken said firmly. "Your Father ordered warships to depart for Akrasia. You're the only one who can stop them now."

"He . . ." Galbrait shook his head. "I cannot. I must get back to the Palace. The Ashen will go there."

"No one has breached Ashwyc since it was built." Despite his trying to arrange that very thing today, Draken had no time to argue with a Prince who had brought a stubborn streak back with him from the dead. "Tyrolean, see to the Prince, will you? This way."

He turned, looked down at his mother once more, fixing her features into his memory, swallowed hard, and walked on, sword out, ignoring Galbrait's protests.

CHAPTER TWENTY-THREE

Newporte's crooked buildings trapped the unseasonable chill alongside the scents of trash, rotten fish, and stale cooking odors. Every nose was red and snuffly. The poorest city in Sevenfel, her narrow streets were mostly pedestrian, clogged with the usual Tradeseason crowds. Pavers and cobbles had buckled from the constant freezes and thaws. It seemed someone was always tripping in front of Draken. He kept compulsively glancing toward Sister Bay, scanning the fog-clad waters for the *Bane* and for Monoean warships setting sail. But he could make out little through the low-hanging haze.

Galbrait didn't help matters. They'd stripped him of his bloody shirt and wrapped him in a serviceable, fairly clean cloak from one of Rinwar's dead guards. It covered his torq but couldn't hide his obvious impatience, which lent itself to the haughty manner of the Landed. He shoved between the people and kept close enough on Draken's heels to trip over them. The rest of their little party looked ragged and battleworn, even Osias, though they'd managed to wipe off the worst of the blood.

"This is madness," Galbrait said. "It's too late. It must be. We spent half the day fighting already and now this," he gritted his teeth and edged between two women dragging stubborn goats, "We'll never make it in time. And why would they listen to me anyway? The King is dead and—"

Draken lifted his hand to his mouth. *"Shh."* Tyrolean glanced around to see if they'd been heard, but the people were all muttering among themselves, taken by their own concerns.

Galbrait gave Draken a look, abashed, wounded.

Draken relented, quietly. "You're our best hope."

"Aissyth'Ae—"

"Is dead," Draken said through gritted teeth.

Galbrait winced. "We don't know that. And we don't know if the Landed's battle commanders will accept my orders any more than they accepted Father's."

Gods, had he taken no truth from those gilded, waxed hands? But Draken couldn't get into that out on the street. His patience ran out. "Aye, it's a point. You're certainly more hindrance than help to me at the moment."

"You can always kill him again," Aarinnaie suggested in a syrupy tone.

Her upset from the tunnels seemed to have dissipated in the open air. Or maybe it was pure bravado. Whichever; he appreciated her steady hand. He couldn't manage another panicked royal at the moment.

Galbrait frowned, but he stopped talking.

Tyrolean pushed closer. "We've followers."

Draken nodded. He'd left the watch to his szi nêre, and had guessed as much since Halmar had bid Konnon to drop back several paces as rear guard. "Keep close, Aarin."

She gave a haughty sniff, but did as he asked. Konnan and Halmar brought up the rear, and Osias strode ahead to take the lead, Setia at his heels. Maybe the Mance could suss out the best route or something.

"You, as well," Draken muttered to Galbrait. "You'd make a pretty prize."

Galbrait snorted, his hand shifting to his sword hilt. "I'd like to see them try."

Draken returned his attention to avoiding errant cobbles. Invading Rinwar's house and killing masses of guards, not to mention dying and being brought back to life, seemed to have unreasonably emboldened the young Prince. Draken hoped there wasn't a heavy price to pay for that audacity later. Of course, with the gods in command, tarrifs on confidence always ran high.

And magic as well. The memory of his mother dying in his arms stabbed at him. His blade slipping through her flesh, her warm hand on his cheek and her weight slumping against him, her last breath whispering between her lips. His stomach twisted. Gods willing, he'd already paid his due.

Draken looked for the tall cargo lifts and masts marking the harbor and cursed softly; it was easy to get turned about in Newporte. He wondered if there was a straight road or alleyway in the whole damned city. Just there . . . he led them down an alley, the stink of food cooking and ales brewing assaulting them as they passed. Aarinnaie wound her scarf around her face. Just as well. He didn't want her challenged and she might well be, foreign and slight and bristling with enough weapons to turn heads. He'd hate for her to hurt anyone.

The alley ran long and in the correct direction. He wondered if it were better to stick to it as long as he could or rejoin the crowded streets. Alley, he decided. It was quicker and they could likely best anyone who attacked.

"Heed, what is this?" Galbrait slowed his pace.

A wagon with a broken axle blocked the alley. About a dozen people stood around it, using it as an excuse to take a break and gossip.

"Go back, Khel Szi?" Halmar cast a glance over his shoulder. Their followers, a few youngish dockside toughs, hadn't dared the alleyway yet.

"No. Through. We'll have to move the bloody thing."

Truth, it'd be a service. The wagon blocked most of the narrow road, too. He tried to shove between the edge of the wagon and the corner of the building, but couldn't fit. The people around it stared at him, quieting. For a moment surprise took him. Newporte was used to foreign traders eating, drinking, and whoring in town. He'd rarely been stared at down in the city. But then he recalled his face had been inked again and his cloak parted to reveal his bare chest and expensive moonwrought pendant. He doubted he looked a typical trader, even in Algir on the Hoarfrost in Akrasia, where many rich Brînian traders anchored at port during Tradeseason.

"Need help?" Galbrait asked them affably.

The people gave him blank, confused looks.

Draken thought about what they were seeing. Obviously well bred, lordly features, body broadened by good food and strength training, cheeks blooming with good health. He'd slipped into his noble persona as easily as throwing the stolen cloak over his shoulders. He wore it well. Draken wondered if he'd ever radiate nobility as Galbrait did. Royal blood might run through Draken's veins, but it hadn't been instilled in his body and manner. Still, the men and women by the wagon must be wondering what a Landed must be doing down in Newporte with a foreign party.

Draken jerked his chin without waiting for an answer to Galbrait's friendly offer. Halmar and the other szi nêre shifted forward. They braced their brawny bodies, blood-stained but stinking no worse than the locals, against the wagon and shoved.

It moved only a hand's width before snagging on more heaved cobbles.

"We'll have to lift it, Khel Szi," Halmar said.

Draken scanned the faces. Most were ruddy from the cold. Noses ran and a few of them coughed. "Who owns this wagon?"

A paunchy man with narrow shoulders shifted forward, rubbing his sleeve across his veined nose. "S'mine . . ." His bemused, rheumy gaze flicked over Draken and he settled for, "my lord."

Draken was used to such examinations from a lifetime of being the only citizen with dark skin at court. This time he was bare-chested, speckled with blood, face ink likely smeared. He spoke before Tyrolean could jump in with an admonition to address him as Prince.

"We'll need your help," he said to the gathered people. "It must be lifted and moved to the gap in buildings there." He directed them with his bloodstained fingers until he felt they had sufficient manpower to move the thing. "No Ty," he added quietly in Brînish. "Watch the Szirin."

Tyrolean nodded. Aarinnaie's hood and scarf hid the scowl that was surely there. A few questioning gazes went her way; doubtless the locals thought her a stolen whore or some other slip of trouble. Galbrait gave Draken an unreadable look, but climbed over the wagon in order to join the Monoeans.

They shifted into position, no one questioning. Others cleared the road so they'd have space to work. Together they heaved, grunting, shifting the awkward burden back from the entrance to the alley. Even the wheels on the working axle didn't move easily. After what seemed to take the whole bloody day, they got the wagon out of the way of the alley and most of the road. Someone brought out a flask. Harsh on the throat but everyone had a swallow. To do less would be the height of rudeness. As Galbrait drank, his collar separated to reveal the skystone torq about his throat.

The man next to him stepped back, blinking. "Your Highness. I didn't know or I would have given you proper respect."

Draken suppressed a curse.

"I'm on an errand for the Crown, one that requires my obscurity. I trust you will keep my presence secret?" Galbrait forced another smile. The people murmured amongst themselves. The man nodded, gaping, then backed another step and dropped his chin.

The Prince handed the flask back to its owner and turned to go. Draken nodded to the men and strode after him. The others hurried to catch up. Aarinnaie stayed quiet, but she kept close on Galbrait's heels.

"I'd have given the man with the broken wagon a coin to have it repaired, but surprisingly, I forgot my purse." Galbrait glanced at Draken, who gave him a perfunctory nod.

"Money won't buy your way out of a battle," Draken said.

"Not always, no," Galbrait replied.

"Do you think they will stay quiet?" Tyrolean asked Draken quietly as they broached anther alley.

He snorted. "No. We must hurry before their tales catch up to us."

They were still so far from Cold Bank. If people learned of Galbrait's presence in Newporte, they could do anything from mob him admiringly to attempt abduction. At best, they'd slow their progress to the docks. Draken strode on, suffering the terrible certainty they were already too late.

✦ ✦ ✦

Draken could barely see ten steps ahead. Fog from Sister Bay closed around them, blurring Newporte's dirty edges, smothering some of the foodstuff and rubbish reek with sea scents, and seeping against Draken's bare skin with an icy breath. He wished he was able to buy a woolen tunic or cloak, but like Galbrait he hadn't brought any coins to his battle with the Rinwars.

This close to the water lapping against the piers, the fog swirled and shifted like live things watched them from within it. They found a dockmistress at one of the ferry piers. The woman was pale as whitecaps with raw spots on her cheeks from the chill wind coming off the Bay, and she didn't rise from her bench inside its protective shed. A big shapeless cloak was tied under her chin. She clutched it closed, but it didn't hide her fever-tremors. She sniffled at them and frowned.

Draken frowned, too. She ought to be abed. He thought of the snuffling wagon owner and the other coughing locals. Was the whole of Newporte ill? "Coldest Tradeseason I can remember. Everyone's got chest-rot."

The woman nodded and pulled her cloak about her a little tighter. She asked in a croak that set her coughing, "What is your need?"

He waited for her coughing to subside. Behind him, his szi nêre shifted uneasily. He sighed, wishing he had time for subterfuge. Doubtless his presence here and word of his business would fetch good coin from the right people. Not to mention Galbrait's presence. "I heard warships are sailing for Akrasia. Have you seen any such activity at Cold Bank?"

"Can't see 'crost Sister," the woman replied and pursed her pudgy, chapped lips.

Draken got the idea she might be trying for a bribe, but was too careworn to sweet-talk her. Maybe she just had poor vision. He laid his hand on his swordhilt and stepped closer in case she did. "No word, then?"

She blinked up at him and lowered her gaze. "Odd thing. Twenty-two house soldiers paid passage to Cold Bank early morn. Didn't ask their business, but they were kitted for travel."

Aarinnaie pushed forward. "House soldiers . . . mercenaries, you mean?"

The dockmistress furrowed her brow. "Mercs are illegal in Sevenfel."

"Minors, she means. What colors did they wear?"

"Brown and white for two, the rest in gold and green. I can't match colors to Houses though. Ruddy Landed all look alike to me." Her gaze skipped to Galbrait as if she were daring him to speak out against her slight. He merely cleared his throat and kept his gaze on the sea, as if he could make anything out in the fog.

"No matter," Draken said grimly. "I can."

Rinwar was gold and green. Brown was a House called Lagun. Old. Powerful. They'd been in debt trouble far before Lesle's death, so Aarinnaie wasn't so far off in her assertion. Mercenaries, indeed. He wondered what it had cost Rinwar to secure two House decades. And now he was too dead to benefit. Of course there was his brother-Priest.

"Are we off to Cold Bank, or may I go back now?" Galbrait, his tone bordering between petulant and furious.

Draken ignored him. "Thanks very much. Is the ferry on offer? We'd like passage across the Bay."

"It's just there. Five pierced each." Steep fare, even if they were just bloodmetal with holes drilled into them to lessen weight and value. It didn't matter at any rate; they had no coins with them.

Draken glanced at Galbrait. The Prince heaved a sigh, pushed forward, and tugged at the laces on his cloak to reveal his skystone torq. "I am Prince Galbrait and I must commandeer your ferry. I've no coin on me now, but you'll be well compensated, I swear it."

For the first time the dockmistress sharpened. She started to kneel but Galbrait shook his head. His words were as polite as his tone was short. "No, I pray you rest, mistress, and forget you saw me altogether."

Crooked yellow teeth tugged at her bottom lip, but she nodded. "Yes, Highness. It's just there, at the end of the pier. My old Lene will see you across. Tell him I say to leave straightaway."

"Thank you, mistress," Draken said, dipped his chin to her.

After a clipped conversation with the greying ferryman Lene, who lisped accommodatingly through his few teeth, they were underway. Three hardened men per side rowed the ferry barge. No winds had cleared the fog nor moved ships about by sail, and the air over Sister Bay was a seeping damp that seemed to slow a man's very marrow. Gradually a faint glow pierced the fog high on the far hillside; the signal tower at Cold Bank. After he saw it, Draken took cover in the drafty shelter. He sat quietly wrapped in his cloak, thinking.

"Poor quarters," Galbrait said, shifting closer to him. He didn't seem to know where to put his gaze.

The ferry didn't compare to the royal barge that had carried them through Traitor's Gate; cold air whistled through the cracks of the shuttered, dirty room. Draken grunted. "I've had worse."

"Recently, and under my family's hospitality, too."

Draken's brows pressed together. Thoughts of his mother didn't stray far. "My family, as well. We're cousins, aye?"

Galbrait nodded, thoughtful. "And if Rinwar's ships left already? Have you thought of it? What then?"

Besides his mother, he'd thought of little else. "I have a duty to try to stop them, or, barring that, I must warn my Queen attack comes and fight on her behalf."

"But if the Landed sent only a few ships—"

"They won't have done." Draken noticed Tyrolean was paying close attention and shifted to address him as well. "They will not have wasted such effort with only a few."

"But last time you said there were only three."

"Last time, your father argued against attacking Akrasia. This time, things are different. The Landed have taken control of the Crown."

Galbrait's lips tightened. "You attacked *us*. Father sent a retaliation."

"We didn't attack you."

"It was a Brînian ship!"

"Stolen or hired by someone else, certainly not ordered by me nor Elena."

Galbrait grunted, frowning. He couldn't argue against that; he had no proof. Problem was, Draken hadn't any either. Draken shook his head, weary. It was exactly as whoever had sent the ship to attack Monoea had wanted. Doubt seized the truth like a chokevine.

"A cousin of the Monoean Royal House is Prince at Brîn," Aarinnaie said quietly, her dark eyes on Draken's. "If the goal is to kill off your royal family, they're going to want you dead." She glanced at Galbrait. "Both of you."

"And so I would have been," Draken said, "had Soebon not tried to gain his father's favor by going after the King."

Lene knocked and stuck his head in the door. "We're nearly there."

Draken got to his feet. "Do you see warships berthed?" He pushed Lene aside without waiting for an answer and went on deck to look. His shoulders slumped. The docks were empty, as were the moorings. The vacancy was suspect in itself; on any given day there should be ships here. Unless several had just departed.

He said nothing else until after they reached the pier. Once there, he stood on the end and stared hard out into the grey, misty open sea. He couldn't even make out dark dots that every sailor could identify as a ship. A dock boy made quick worth of the truth.

"How many ships were there?" Draken asked him.

"Twenty, I reckon, my lord, but there was word of more."

Twenty, he thought. *I have failed.* Failed in negotiation, failed in keeping his old King alive, failed to protect his mother. Now he was about to fail Elena and Akrasia as well. He should have told Elena the truth about him, let them execute him as a liar and a traitor to Akrasia. At least then another diplomat would have been sent and negotiations wouldn't have been muddied by his past and his lies. He wouldn't have lived to have been manipulated by the Ashen.

Draken looked again out to sea and then trudged back up the pier toward the others. The mists were just clearing enough to see the *Bane's* masts poking over it. Still there, then. He hadn't realized until just this moment that he'd suspected his mercenary crew would desert him. That was good. It didn't make up for the news, but it was good.

"What did the boy say?" Galbrait asked.

He sighed and couldn't help peering out toward the open sea again. Nothing. The ships were gone and they had little chance at catching them. Even so, what use would the *Bane* be against a fleet of twenty? "He said Monoea and Akrasia are at war."

CHAPTER TWENTY-FOUR

"What will you do now?" Aarinnaie asked Draken, tying a scarf over her head. Coiled sprigs had broken loose and she brushed them away from her eyes.

He could sail after them, try to warn the Queen. But how would they get past an entire fleet without suffering attack? Draken turned to Galbrait. "Will you fight this? Will you send ships after them to fetch them back?"

Galbrait's jaw tightened. His hand crept up to worry the royal torq about his throat.

"They are your people, as well," Draken said. "Akrasia has a lot of life in her army; Brîn's navy is still very good. Whether they win or lose, many people will die. Your people and mine."

The Prince peered up at him. "We don't even know if they will obey me as King."

"We'll have to go to the Palace then, and find out. Halmar, you and the nêre take Aarinnaie, Osias, and Setia back to the *Bane*."

Aarinnaie sputtered. "Draken! I'm not going to sit on that boat and wait like—like—a good little Szirin doing needlework while my brother goes to battle!"

"It's not a battle, Aarin. I'm escorting the Prince back to the castle to help him make orders that can stop this attack. You're not the emissary here. I am."

"I'm not a fool, brother. It is no safe thing you do."

"I told you before, someone must go back in my stead. And we owe the crew their payment. You must see to that as well." *If my head should end up in that wall*, he added silently.

She bit her lip and stared up into his face. Only he knew her well enough to realize it was anger, not worry or frustration.

He glanced at the others and took her a little aside, his hand resting on her narrow shoulder. There might not be time to speak later. Galbrait's worry over

whether his orders would be obeyed reminded him that the only way to defeat
a powerful enemy was to turn its strength against it. Monoea was strong in
leadership and unquestioning discipline. But the problem with unquestioning
discipline was that a soldier who only followed orders had no grounding
without those orders.

He spoke lowly. "If I don't return with you to Brîn, seek out the highest
Landed among the enemy and kill him and all who are his closest advisors.
There is a priest named Rinwar. Killing him will be your best chance at driving
them off."

She stared up into his face and gave a tight nod. "I will," she said softly.

He released her and turned to Halmar. "Despite her charms and persuasive
abilities, Comhanar, I expect the Szirin to be taken to the *Bane* and kept safe
until my return or the deadline for it has passed. Will you see this done?"

To his credit, Halmar didn't smile, and to hers, Aarinnaie only sighed noisily.

Osias smiled, though. "Setia and I will be glad for her company."

Maybe that was meant to be encouraging, but Osias hadn't offered to come.
It was hard not to think Osias believed the mission doomed.

Draken looked around for Tyrolean's lined eyes. "Captain?"

"With your leave, I will attend you, Your Highness."

Draken nodded. He'd asked too much of his friend already, but he couldn't
deny his relief at Tyrolean's crisp reply. He raked a hard stare over Halmar
and Konnan to ensure their cooperation in protecting Aarinnaie. Their
crisp nods reassured him. Aarinnaie said something but the winds whipped
it from his ears. It didn't matter now. All that mattered now was getting
Galbrait back to the Palace. He needed to find a dock and quick passage back
through . . . through Shadowcliff. His hand dropped to the key lashed to his
belt. Through his mother's passage. Though he very much did not want to go
back through there.

Stomach knotted with worry over the impending attack on Akrasia and
unshed grief for his mother, he secured a small craft at the next dock. The
skiffer aboard mentioned payment and Galbrait yanked at his cloak collar
to reveal his torq, apparently having lost his patience with playing the com-
moner. Eyes wide, the skiffer dipped a knee to his Prince and fell to hurrying
his oars along.

Galbrait gave Draken a curious look when he heard the request to land at
Shadowcliff. "Not Galbrayt's Gate?"

Draken couldn't explain, not with so many close ears. He could trust no one,
not even Galbrait. He pulled his hood up against the cold and hid his face,
cutting off further conversation.

Ghostlike mists thickened, if possible, as they rowed toward the Great Pier. No moonlight pierced the fog over Sister Bay, as if war was the only thing that could obscure the gods' light.

They sat stiff and silent as choppy waves shoved the skiff about, challenging the oarsmen. Constant spray off the bow left them damp and chilled through. Draken huddled in his cloak and stared at the growing puddle seeping through the hull, his mind swimming wilder than the currents in the rough bay. For the first time he let himself think of his mother, really think of her. He'd known her less than a day and she'd not only saved his life but given hers for Galbrait. But why come forward now when she had ignored him his whole life? Was it because of his brother dying? Had she meant for Draken to be a half-rate replacement? That stung a little, even though from the short bit they'd talked, he didn't really believe it. But he couldn't know for certain. It all begged the question: who was she, really? There was so much he didn't know and the people who could tell him were dying at an astounding rate.

"Your Highnesses," Tyrolean said.

Draken gave a mechanical nod. They were nearing the Great Pier at Shadow-cliff. The sea had ever been blackest here, shadowed by the great depths against the greystone cliffs the city was named for. At the moment it reflected the grey of the swirling fog so that if Draken looked down he could imagine misty faces staring back at him. As they entered Shadowcliff's harbor, floating piers cut the spray and waves. Other ships, lit by lanterns prow and stern, drifted by.

Once off the skiff, Draken walked quickly, the Prince and Tyrolean hurrying behind. The skiffer was already gossiping to his cohorts on the Pier and eyes followed them. Bad enough Galbrait's appearance in Shadowcliff would churn the rumor mills, but if it got out that the Landed had taken their King to war, there'd be panic and rioting in the streets. He glanced at Galbrait, his youthful face still smooth, and wondered if he were as determined and hard as his namesake, General Galbrayt. He had a bad feeling they were about to find out.

The fog made traveling quickly hazardous, even by foot. Gossiping clusters of people crowded the steps, moving slowly up and down the slick stones. Some just plain stood to one side as if they could wait it out. Draken chafed at their slow progress, though he couldn't fault them. Much like the ones in Newporte standing about the broken wagon, overworked people enslaved to meager survival took every opportunity to rest.

Tyrolean kept close, but he needn't have bothered. The citizens barely glanced his way, marking him as a foreigner coming to trade. Close enough. They just didn't realize his goods were life and death.

That image disintegrated when they met the gate guards at Kordewyn. First the queue—and Draken had considered the steps slow-going. He shifted from foot to foot and constantly glanced back down into the fog concealing the city. Darkness crept through it as nightfall encroached on Sevenfel. Daybreak would not be far behind. "Gods forbid we don't make dayclose."

"It's Tradeseason," Galbrait said. "The merchants are open in the night."

Right. He'd forgotten.

Someone turned their head at Galbrait's voice. Maybe it was the accent, or his handsome features, bruised on one side. Draken leaned close to Galbrait. "We'll never get there at this rate. Tell them who you are."

Galbrait looked back at him, brows raised. Draken just looked back at him. The Prince hissed a breath and undid the top ties on his cloak so his torq showed, and called out, "Make way for business of the Crown. Make way!"

Heads turned, protests sounding and dying as people realized who Galbrait was. Everyone knew the torqs the royals wore—all of a kind, twisted precious metals with skystones embedded in the ends. Draken stared down the people just in front of them, and they shifted to one side as best as they were able; the path sloping up to the gate was barely five shoulders across. Slowly, they were able to shift their way through the crowd and reach the gate. Word had preceded them and the guards studied Galbrait, albeit politely.

"Gods spare me, he's on a bloody coin," Draken said. "Let us pass."

The guard, his belly straining the straps of his armor, turned to Draken. "And you are?"

"Khel Szi, Prince of Brîn," Galbrait said. "And this is his Captain and guard. Let us pass, soldier. Do we look as if we're out for a leisurely stroll to market? Your delay could cost us all far more than your own position here."

Galbrait's authoritative ring did it. Or perhaps it was that his cloak had parted to reveal the blood caked on his skin. The guard stepped back with a bow. But it had been long enough for people on the inside of the gate to grasp that they were looking at not only their own Prince, but also a foreign one. It would only take moments more for them to realize they were largely unprotected, though Tyrolean was an imposing presence. Draken hurried Galbrait along, steering him down streets and alleys toward Ashwyc.

"Do you know where you're going?" Tyrolean asked.

Not exactly. "Aye. This way."

Draken didn't know Kordewyn well, having had few reasons to walk through the Merchant City even when he'd made a home at Ashwyc. He'd never spent much time in this staid borough where coin was the only measure of man's worth. A thought almost made him smile: Va Khlar could show these Kordewyn merchants a thing or two about trade. He suppressed it, and the vague curiosity of whether he'd see the Reschanian trader-lord again. This night he had to make his way more by instinct; the fog and falling darkness concealed the grey cliffs and walls of Ashwyc. Not even a glimmer of moonlight shone through or reflected off the golden tower domes, though oil lamps burned dully against the miserable damp.

At the second dead end that didn't finish in the cliff he growled in frustration. "It's no use. How am I supposed to find it in this ruddy fog?"

"Find what?" Galbrait asked. "Where are we going?"

"Doors. My mother took me through two doors in the cliff—entrances to Ashwyc."

"Why didn't you say so? They're this way." Galbrait led the way back out of the alley. "But they'll be locked."

Draken produced the key tied to his belt.

Galbrait's eyes widened. He trotted down the cobbles, heading inland. "Excellent. I've one too, but not on me. Who gave it to you? Your mother? She must have been more friendly with Father than I realized—"

"Draken," Tyrolean said lowly.

Draken glanced back at him and caught sight of a man-shaped shadow trailing them. It wavered back, into the fog, and disappeared. But now that he knew what to listen for, he heard bootsteps as well—more than one pair. Far more. He groaned under his breath. "Can't we do one bloody thing without someone trying to accost us?"

"We did just walk all the way through Newporte," Galbrait pointed out in a low tone.

"Took them that long to catch up to us," Tyrolean muttered. They walked faster. The boots behind them rapidly sounded too many for them to take on just the three of them. Man-shapes emerged and retreated into the fog, hiding their true numbers and identity, if not their intent.

"Maybe they're not after us," Galbrait whispered.

"No, they are. They just don't know how many we are or they would have attacked by now," Tyrolean replied in a low tone.

"Or they want to follow where we're going." Draken hissed for quiet. How well known were these doors into Ashwyc Palace? Were they rebels, seeking a way in?

Galbrait slowed to study a building. Wrinkled his nose and shook his head before trotting to the next intersection. Tyrolean and Draken jogged after him, barely close enough to see him dart around the corner. The footsteps quickened behind them.

They were about to be trapped. Draken broke into a run, shoving past the Prince. He almost ran headlong into the grey cliff, strode along it, running his hand along the stone and peering at the seemingly blank wall, until he found the doors. He felt all around one to his swordhand side, peering down. Where a lock should be was just an iron plate. Damn, damn.

"Draken. Hurry." Tyrolean's swords hissed from their scabbards.

Draken sidestepped toward the other door. Fumbled his fingers over the iron and found a keyhole. He didn't answer, too busy yanking the key from its cord and fitting it into the lock.

As the key turned, a knife whistled by his ear and clattered off the door, and then another sank into his shoulder, knocking him into the wooden door. His breath whooshed from his chest. "Bloody Seven—" A gasp cut him off as Galbrait yanked him back.

Draken heard the click of the lock and the door swung wide. Torchlight vaguely lit the steps and mists swirled in. Galbrait snagged the key but it slipped from his fingers and jingled against the cobbles. More pounding boots and a shout.

"Go—go!" Tyrolean, pushing them through.

"The key!" Draken said, turning in the doorway.

"I've got it." Tyrolean kicked at the ground and the key sailed through the doorway to clatter against the steps. "Inside!" He shoved at Draken, who stumbled back against the steps and sat down hard. Between that and his flesh doing its level best to heal around the knife, he yelped in pain. The door slammed shut just as the familiar vertigo sensation overcame Draken. The world spun and rocked and showered them with dust. Draken swallowed hard as his empty stomach twisted.

Fists pounded the door and heavy voices shouted, but it was too late. Every instinct made Draken want to scurry up the steps, escape their attackers who were so close, but the knife in his shoulder had other ideas. He hunched over, trying to breathe. Every motion seemed to make the blade burrow deeper.

"You were hit?" Tyrolean asked.

"Aye." A breathy whisper.

Tyrolean grimaced, but he reached around Draken and pulled the blade out. His skin sealed quickly. The world rocked again, mortar crumbling down from the stone walls. Draken groaned at the sharp burst of pain and subsequent nausea. All he needed was retching on top of everything else.

"Easy," Tyrolean said, his hand on Draken's good shoulder. "Where are we?"

He rubbed his hand over his face. A nearby torch smoked softly, yellowing Tyrolean's pale skin. "My mother's quarters are up these stairs."

"Someone's coming!" Galbrait hissed from midway up the stairs.

Tyrolean took the steps three at a time to grab Galbrait's arm and pull him back down into the stairwell.

More bootsteps keeping time—Draken thought he could learn to hate that sound—made them cringe back. He grabbed the torch and extinguished it against the wall. It snuffled out, smoking and oily. They sank back down the steps, quiet in the darkness of the stairwell, though a torch at the top clearly lit a line of marching soldiers carrying seaxes. Draken's eyes narrowed. They weren't wearing the King's bright blue but some muted color not illuminated very well by the torchlight. Save that, Draken concentrated on not breathing. When they'd gone, Galbrait rubbed his hand on the back of his neck and hissed. He'd probably noticed the same thing.

All seemed silent at last. Draken's voice was gruff but he touched Galbrait's shoulder. "Let's go to my mother's quarters. I don't think anyone will think to go in there."

The hearth was cold. She'd left their tea things out. His clothes from the dungeon, his Brînian things, had been carefully folded and laid on a side table, despite their filthy state. The ordinariness of the scene made his throat tighten. Maybe she'd meant for a maid to repair and clean them.

Tyrolean gave him a nod and eased past him. He strode about, checking things, and nodded them inside. "It's clear. Empty."

Galbrait cleared his throat as he shut the door behind them, and rubbed his hands over his face. "We both lost our mothers today."

The Prince's naked grief reminded him he'd never had Sikyra as a mother. He felt a pang at killing her, but her loss didn't belong to him. Maybe it belonged to a dead brother he'd never known, or to the royal family. Or to no one. He didn't know.

He laid his hand on the Prince's shoulder, rubbed, and released him. "We have bigger problems. The Palace is taken. Those were some Landed color, not royal."

"One had the ash mark, too." Tyrolean gestured to his forehead and shut the drawer he'd been looking in. He moved to the next one, and the next.

"We have to leave the palace, Galbrait," Draken said.

"What? We just got here."

"It's over."

Galbrait turned on him, fists clenched. "You cannot mean that."

"Stay if you wish. The only reason I'm here is to stop the attack on my people. That's no longer possible. Ashwyc is taken, your country is at war, and the ships, quite literally, have sailed."

"That was very well put, Your Highness," Tyrolean said. He moved a chair from in front of a wardrobe and opened it.

Galbrait's mouth snapped shut. He glared at Draken for a heartbeat, two. Draken ignored him and went to the cold tub to wash up. The water was dingy from his previous bath and icy cold, but at least it hadn't been drained.

"Galbrait, if you're coming with us, clean up. We'll need to get back through Kordewyn and I don't trust them letting us pass through in our filthy state again. Then we'll see to something to wear." That would take some doing. Draken frowned and splashed himself again and reached for a towel to rub off the worst of the blood and sweat, his skin chilled. He scrubbed it over his face.

"Draken."

Draken lowered the towel, frowning. "Ty, you needn't bother. These are a lady's quarters—"

A rare grin from Tyrolean as he held out a black shirt. "Will this suffice?"

The wardrobe was stacked full of folded clothes, silks, linens, gowns, shirts, trews . . . Draken cocked his head and stepped closer. A wave of memory swept through him, almost making him sway. He recognized the shirt well enough. Black, woolen, and warm, perfect for slipping through misty woods hunting Brînians.

"Those are *my* things."

A few steps and he pulled out a blue gown. It flowed from neat folds, linen to keep it from creasing crumpling on the floor. Floral scents emanated from it. The air was a sharp blade in his lungs. "This belonged to my wife."

Tyrolean stilled. "Draken—"

"Her name was Lesle," Draken said, crushing the fine fabric in his fists.

◆ ◆ ◆

"We'll have to go back out the way we came," Draken said.

He'd dressed silently in his old things, immersed in the memories raised by scents: Lesle pressing her cheek to his after he'd rubbed in mint oil after shaving, his under-Captain's wry sense of humor. Tyrolean changed too, and Galbrait, all in Draken's old clothing and cloaks. The things were a bit big on Galbrait. Draken avoided looking at his companions too closely.

"I cannot just leave the Palace," Galbrait said. "That's surrendering."

"It's not surrendering. It's escaping," Tyrolean said.

"Galbrait, you must come. It's not safe for you here any longer. I'll get you to the *Bane* and we'll sort out where to take you from there."

Galbrait stood for a moment. "But I'm King."

"Aye, you're King. But Monoea already has one dead King. It needs you alive. Perhaps we can arrange for passage upcoast to the Wyldes. Surely you've still some allies there from your posting."

Galbrait's brow furrowed and he nodded.

"Good lad. I'll lead, then." Draken pushed past him. It was a quick jaunt to the door. One sweep of a torch and they found the key, tipped against a stair riser.

There was no keyhole, just a handle for pulling the door shut behind oneself. Draken swore, thinking of the other door with the black metal plate. "Whoever heard of a door that locks only from the outside?"

"I thought you said you used this door before?" Tyrolean said. He had his swords out and his back to them, watching the stairwell. Galbrait shifted anxiously from foot to foot, glancing between them.

"I did. My mother did it last time, though, and with all the commotion before I didn't think to examine the doors closely."

"You used the dungeon corridor to get out," Galbrait said.

"Aye. You knew these doors. You didn't know this one only unlocked *outside*?"

The Prince shook his head. "I'd seen them from Kordewyn before. But I've never used them."

"Right. We have to go down to the dungeon then, and use that door. I know that one works, I saw it done."

"And if we run into a company of rebels?" Galbrait asked.

"We'll have to be better than that. Come."

His mother's corridor was empty, as was the steps leading down. She had lived in a largely unused wing of the Palace, surely placed near those doors so she could come and go without others paying her mind. It made sense. Draken wanted to quit thinking about her life here in the palace, wanted to stop wondering why she'd kept all his and Lesle's things, about his dead brother, about how closely she'd followed Draken's life. Truth, it replaced his anxiety with a dull regret—better to stroll through enemy territory with.

Even the cells were empty. He wondered what the Ashen had done with all the loyalists. Killed them outright, perhaps. They saw no one as they moved between the cells and grisly accoutrements, still stained with fresh splatters of Soeben's blood. His breath hitched. So much death in a day: Soeben and Prince Aissyth'Ae, the King and Queen, his mother, the Rinwars.

Once Osias had commented on his long association with death. Was he meant to watch the gods amuse themselves with the lives of those he loved?

Voices ahead of them, muffled by stone, interrupted his theological deliberation. He lifted a hand but the others had already paused. He couldn't make out the words but it could only be Grym and the other guards. They couldn't make it back to the steps in time. The bars on the cells wouldn't hide them and it would be easy enough to trap them inside. And deliberation about death aside, he still wanted to kill Grym, even if he had to frame the opportunity in defense. He gritted his teeth and drew Seaborn.

Their quarters were tight in the narrow space between cells, filled with tables for torture and other equipment. He and Tyrolean would be all right with their shorter blades but Galbrait could have a difficult time with his longsword.

Galbrait—of course. Maybe Grym would listen to his Prince.

Grym came noisily, talking casually, as if he knew there would be no one to meet him and his cohorts. Indeed, all the cells were empty. Draken had a moment's puzzling over that again before the torturer stopped, staring at him.

Three guards in blue followed Grym. One of them spoke. "Aside, sadist, and let us at the Prince."

Grym scowled over his shoulder at them. "This Brînian is mine. He escaped. The King said any who escape are mine—"

"What King Aissyth says no longer matters," Draken said. "He is dead. Stand aside for your new King."

The guard shoved Grym aside and pushed by him. His tone changed, abruptly conciliatory, and he dipped his chin to Galbrait. "Your Highness, if you'll just come with me, we'll straighten out this misunderstanding."

Misunderstanding? Draken's brow creased. He raised Seaborn. "You'll have to go through me."

"And me." Tyrolean.

"Don't make me cut you down. You are not his guard; I am. Stand aside, Brînian."

Grym backed a step, bumped into the guard behind him, was shoved aside. He stumbled against a grisly, stained table with gears attached to shackles.

Seaborn flared in Draken's hand, drawing the guard's eye. Draken thrust forward with just time to wonder if he would curse the warning the sword gave his opponent or whether it would serve as distraction. Distraction for the first guard; Draken slashed twice and the man lay dying at his feet, gagging on the blood pouring from his throat.

But it was Draken's turn for distraction; the smell of blood here brought the echo of Soeben's screams. The next King's guard leapt over the first, coming at Draken with his sword on high guard. Draken struck upward belatedly and the King's guard easily blocked him and struck, not at Draken, but at Seaborn itself.

The shock of the blow jolted through Draken's arm and resonated through his whole, exhausted body. His fingers loosed their grip and Seaborn flew in a sharp arc to clatter against the bars of a cell. With the torture table at his back, and Tyrolean, Draken had no retreat from the soul-shuddering pain of the blade slashing at his flesh. A deep shout of fury from Tyrolean. Black depths colder than the open sea. And then nothing at all.

CHAPTER TWENTY-FIVE

Draken opened his eyes in a small little room, windowless, his arm shackled to a thick bed frame. Tyrolean sat next to him, scabbards empty, one arm shackled to the opposite corner of the bed, the other resting on his upraised knees. Elena's necklace was gone. He had a fresh bruise on his jaw. Draken wondered if it were nightfall. He hoped Aarinnaie had gone, the *Bane* had sailed. It wasn't safe for her here.

"Why didn't they kill us?" he said, voice hoarse.

Tyrolean shook his head. "They must need us."

They sat in silence for a bit, listening. No sounds. "Have you ever been caught and chained like this before?"

"No. My life was quite ordinary before you came round," Tyrolean answered.

"I owe you an apology, Ty. I never should have allowed you to come, and certainly not without your knowing the truth about me."

Tyrolean regarded him for long moments before speaking. "Has it occurred to you these things happen because of who you *are* rather than who you were?"

"And just who am I? A half-blood liar with middling battle skills and a sorcerous sword." Actually, not even the sword. They'd taken Elena's pendant, too.

"You are Prince at Brîn and Elena's highest lord. You also have a distinct habit of talking your way into unlikely favor. If they kill you, Elena is likely to attack Monoea."

"The Council Lords will talk her out of it. Aarinnaie—"

"Could talk her way out of attempted assassination on the Queen, but no one can sway Elena when she is determined thus. And she will be, should you not return to her."

Draken groaned. His head hurt. They must have smacked him on the temple to knock him out. "I shouldn't have let her raise me up." In hindsight, letting his ruddy father kill him would have been the better tactic. Of course how many times had he faced death and come out on the other side? He couldn't fathom Elena sending Brînians and Akrasians to die for him in a futile war. He swallowed, waited until his voice approached some semblance of normal. "She'll be rather too busy defending Akrasia from the galleons already on their way."

Someone pounded on the door, making them both start. No voice, just the pounding. Then the latch rattled and it swung open. Draken blinked, though the torchlight beyond was dim. As his eyes adjusted, his stomach sank. He could make out Grym's lean, bent form anywhere. No one spoke as two brawny guards with ash marks strode in, unchained Draken, and hauled him up and out.

They'd brought him to Galbrait's personal quarters. Draken's brow furrowed. Did that mean Galbrait was dead? Most likely.

Their weapons—Tyrolean's, his, and Galbrait's swords and knives—lay in an unceremonial bloodstained heap on a side table. All the comfortable sitting furniture had been shoved aside. A dining table had been converted to a torture platform. Bolts and ropes and blood marred the glossy surface. A brazier burned nearby, red hot implements stuck into the coals. Grym wore Elena's Night Lord pendant.

The Ashen dragged Draken toward the table. He instinctively struggled and nearly broke free. The Ashen grunted and dug their fingers deeper into his straining muscles. Instead of dragging him up, they forced him to his knees before the table. He started to struggle again but one of them slammed his studded gauntlet into his head. The world tilted as they yanked his wrists toward the thick table legs to affix them there. His stomach swam and the dim light swirled into a thousand colors.

His bad shoulder tightened in a spasm as they pulled it forward to bind to the table. Abrupt pain sliced through his fugue. He thrust himself forward, bounced off the table, and jerked back, wrenching himself free of their grip. He cradled his bad arm against more stabbing pain, but his free hand knocked a guard back. Despite the pain, his body was fair rested, at full strength. He lurched to his feet and twisted back, toward his sword. He reached the table, scrabbling for it. One of the blades sliced his finger and it stung as it healed.

Grym shouted something indecipherable, and one of the Ashen snarled back at him. Draken growled and reached for Seaborn. His fingers closed on the familiar leather as hands pulled him back. Draken's arm arced in a strike, holding Seaborn with only three fingers. The flat of the sword crashed into the guard's bare head so hard it nearly made the sword leap from Draken's hand. The other Ashen yanked on his other arm, drawing a sharp groan as his shoulder protested.

Draken swung the sword around and the flat caught the Ashen on the arm. Just a shred of a hesitation before the Ashen reached for his sword. It was enough. Draken wrenched free of him, his arms flying up into a high guard and bringing the sword down. Seaborn skipped off his armored shoulder to cut through the flesh of his neck.

The Ashen toppled. Sparks flew from the brazier as he fell into it. He was too busy dying to care.

Strength and certainty surged through his veins. Draken spun to advance on Grym, who cowered, brandishing his knife. Draken smacked at it with the flat of his sword. It clattered away. Grym shrank back. Draken grabbed him by Elena's necklace and pulled him closer.

"Where is Prince Galbrait? Is he dead?"

"I-I don't know. They took him—"

"Liar!" Draken pressed his blade under Grym's chin. The sadist stepped back again, but Draken followed, the need for answers and the lust for blood warring in his veins.

"I finished with him and they took him."

Draken narrowed his eyes. "Finished what?"

"Reminding him of his duty."

Duty? Via torture? Draken blinked and Grym tried to step back again but ran into a bench pushed out of place to make room for the big table. He fell back, hard. Draken followed with his sword, piercing through bone and chest, blood-scent filling his lungs.

He drew a breath and coughed. It seemed to echo in the still room. Grym lay sprawled on the bench, a heavy weight dragging down the end of Draken's sword. He pulled the blade back with a sucking sound, grotesque against the overwhelming silence. Then he reached down and pulled Elena's necklace from around Grym's dead neck and laid it over his own.

Smoke laced the smells of carnage. Had he truly managed to kill them all? He blinked again and turned slowly. Red-hot brands and iron pokers had spilled onto the stone floor. Fire licked at draperies, lit by the toppled brazier. The air was quickly becoming choked with smoke.

He cursed and strode to the servant's door, worked the latch and yanked it open, but wasted no time in going back to search for keys to the shackles. They had fallen under the table. He bent, wincing as he rested his bad arm on the table to steady himself.

Tyrolean eyed the carnage after Draken unchained him. "You didn't exactly talk your way out of this one, Your Highness."

"Talking is overrated." He picked up Galbrait's sword and slung the belt over his shoulder.

"And the fire?"

"Let the place burn. I know where Galbrait is. Come."

Tyrolean and Draken kept their swords at the ready. Draken felt naked in the wide corridor leading to the Throne Hall. He ducked in a back way, into a servant's side room to a little used stairwell that led to the nursery quarters. He used to come through here on errands as a young slave and marvel at the soft beds and toys—actual *toys* for the young royals. He felt now as if the ghosts of the dead Princes might linger, drawn to happier, safer times.

The narrow, winding servant's stair led away from the primary living quarters into a small private room that had been used to stage meals and events for the Princes in their private quarters. Draken had spent enough time there as a young slave that the room felt odd without the bustle of kitchen-maids and footmen. But empty it was, and had been for a long while, if the dust and cracked windowpanes were any indication. Draken frowned. He never recalled seeing the Palace in such disrepair.

Tyrolean's bemused voice broke into his musings. "Not here."

"No, curse it. I thought he would be."

"I suppose there's no chance you're leading us any closer to escape?"

"Galbrait is King. The Ashen want to make a puppet of him. I cannot leave him to that."

"With all respect, Your Highness, why not? I'm here to protect you, not rescue beleaguered foreign Princes."

"It is the gods' will he should rule; his line goes back through the ages."

"I recall you arguing once against such a qualification for yourself."

Draken sighed, impatient. "If Galbrait dies, his line dies with him, and that is going against the will of the gods, or so Monoeans believe. I don't think even the Ashen dare to spite them."

"No. You're the only one who does that." Tyrolean's lips twitched in something like a grin. "How is it you think we're going to rescue Galbrait? He'll be under significant guard."

Draken barely heard Tyrolean for the footfalls outside the heavy door. He lifted his hand to his lips to silence the Captain. Muffled voices and boots on stone passed by the door. After they were gone, he lowered his voice and met Tyrolean's gaze with a frown. "It's a concern, truth."

Maybe the Prince was too injured from torture to keep under heavy guard, which would make getting to him simpler but all the more difficult to rescue. Hauling an unconscious or injured charge through the Palace unnoticed would be damned impossible. How would he get there with Ashen clogging the corridors, much less get Galbrait back out? Maybe he'd just have to drag him out the bloody window . . . He stopped to think a moment. Of course.

"We've no hooks, I'm going to have to do this freehand."

Tyrolean arched a brow, which served to make his lined eyes only seem more elegantly expressive, despite the dirt and blood splatters on his cheek. "Do what, Your Highness?"

"Use a servant's passage way to get to the King's quarters and then get Galbrait to climb out the window."

"Won't they find you?" Tyrolean shook his head. "How do you even know where to go?"

"I know every bit of this palace, moreso even than the royals. I was a slave here. Truth, no Landed or Minor Ashen would know the passageways like I do."

Tyrolean opened his mouth to protest; Draken shook his head. "I want to keep you in reserve should I be captured."

All was black night outside, and still cloaked in fog too thick for the Eyes to penetrate. At least they had decent cover. Draken drew his blade and tapped the pommel against the hornpane window, spreading the crack. A horn fell to the wiry, thorny shrubs below, about a man-and-a-half of distance. Beyond, the sky was rapidly losing its glow as the sun retreated before the nightly onslaught of the Seven Eyes.

Tyrolean went to guard the door as Draken worked on the window. The cracks spread to the sill and glazing. He gingerly pulled the thin pieces away and set them on the floor. It took a little time, but it cleared a big enough opening for Tyrolean to climb through.

"You go down. I'll go to the King's quarters. If he's not there, I'll come down." Draken paused, sheathing Seaborn to give himself something to do. There was much he could say in this moment, or nothing. He chose the latter. "Do not wait too long on me. You can make the *Bane* by dawn."

Tyrolean held his gaze for a long moment, and gave him a nod. "Aye, Your Highness."

Draken felt the same relief he'd always felt in the Captain's presence; they were soldiers together, first. Lies meant nothing next to the blood they'd spilled together. He pushed through the concealed door into the passageway that led to the King's quarters as Tyrolean climbed down to the ground.

CHAPTER TWENTY-SIX

L ike the staging room, the passageway was dingy, unlit, and dusty. He shook his head. Since when had the servants quit using it to serve the King unobtrusively? Had the knowledge of the passageways faded with slavery? He had a moment's fear the door leading to the king's chambers would be barred, but the hidden wooden panel slipped open and caught on a rug that hadn't been there when he was a child.

Beyond that, the King's chambers hadn't changed much. The grey misty light from the windows, the Eyes faintly glowing through, shone in on the room. Drapes the color of dried blood shadowed the raised bed. Several chairs surrounded a cold hearth with an opening taller than Draken. A desk with a couple of scrolls and a scattering of gold coins took up the nearest corner. A weapons rack hung open and empty. The doors to the outer chamber were open, as well as a narrow entry to a dressing room. All lay silent and still.

Despite the shadows and walls concealing his view, Draken had no instinct to search the place. It seemed empty. A breath pushed from his chest, fueling a whispered curse. He turned to go, starting to sheathe Seaborn, then thought better of it. He swept the gold, enough to feed several families well for a sevennight, into his hand and opened a drawer in the desk, hoping to find more. A small scratching noise made him look up. Seaborn was in his hand before he realized.

Another scratch, and then silence. An animal, perhaps; a rock-rat sniffing out crumbs. But he eased forward just the same, unable to not hope.

A huddled form cowered in the corner behind the big bed, arms wrapped around up-drawn knees, chin tucked to chest. Faint moonglow lit blond curls.

"Galbrait," Draken whispered.

The Prince wedged his long body deeper into the shadowed corner, if possible.

Draken tied the bag of coins to his belt and knelt on his good knee. After a hesitation, he reached out to lay his hand on the Prince's shoulder. Galbrait trembled under his touch. Gods, what had they done to him? "Galbrait. It is Draken. Show me the damage."

The Prince lifted his head. One eye was so bruised it had swollen shut and that cheek had been sliced deep enough to need stitches. The cuts still oozed blood and it had dried stiff along his hairline. He relaxed his grip on his knees enough to let Draken see his bare chest bore similar cuts, deep enough to bleed well but only through flesh, not scoring bone. Not life threatening, unless swordrot set in. He needed treatment soon, a salt bath, alcohol, and stitches. He wouldn't meet Draken's gaze.

"I'll take you out of here," Draken said.

"I cannot . . . I must stay." Galbrait shook his head.

Draken ignored that. The internal bar on the door had been removed; the more sophisticated lock had been smashed and disabled by a hard blow. He didn't dare test it, but he'd lay good rare it was barred securely from the outside. He heard soft voices in the corridor, the shifting of someone in leather boots. Guards. He cursed under his breath, pulled the inner doors shut to muffle their voices, and returned to Galbrait. As he approached, Galbrait shuddered and dropped his head again. Damn, the slightest noise had him cringing.

"Look at me." Draken tried to steel his voice to calm. "What did they tell you?"

Galbrait 's good eye blinked and skittered from Draken's intent gaze. His voice was dull, flat, the words rote. "My brothers are dead. My family are all dead."

"I'm not dead, cousin. I am here, with you. What do they want from you?"

Galbrait blinked and looked up at him. His voice strengthened, but also sounded more desperate. "Not me. They want you to be King."

Alarm breathed on the back of Draken's neck. "Ashwyc is taken, and when news spreads, Sevenfel will erupt. Prince or King, you cannot stay here. You must come with me."

Galbrait swallowed. His shoulders came up as if the motion pained him. Seaborn's light betrayed the ligature marks above his torq. Grym had nearly strangled the lad. "I can't. Don't you see? I must take the throne, even . . . even . . ." A strangled cough cut him off.

Draken cast about the room for water, wine, anything. A tray on the low table by the hearth. Maybe from last night. He strode to it, poured out cold red-tea, and brought it back. Galbrait didn't reach for it. Draken lifted his hand and pressed his fingers around the cup. "Drink."

The Prince coughed as he tried to swallow it down, and gagged a little. But he drank. "I cannot leave the Palace."

"Just for a little—"

"No. A King has to be here. You know that. You can't make me go or there are no more kings." His eyes were wild, his voice frantic.

"Be easy. That's just legend. I'm taking you to help you, aren't I? Together we'll get Monoea back," Draken said, though the shreds of an idea were occurring that had little to do with the Monoean throne. "But we cannot do that cowering in this corner."

Galbrait licked his bottom lip and winced. It was cracked, stained crimson from the bruising and the red-tea. Fresh blood trickled down his chin.

"Are you a child or a man, Galbrait? A coddled Prince or a King? Here, now you decide which you shall be."

Draken dragged his thumb over the loose bit of leather wrap on his sword grip. The metal pommel warmed against his hand. He couldn't allow Galbrait to sit the throne as a puppet. He couldn't leave him here. The city would erupt with him gone and presumed dead, but it would give the Ashen remaining here something to deal with.

The Prince pushed his shoulder against the wall, as if he'd like to disappear within the stone. Tears slipped from his good eye, glinting against his cheek in Seaborn's unforgiving light. He drew a shuddering breath. It whistled faintly in his chest. But he didn't fight as Draken pulled him to his feet.

"Can you still climb the walls as you did when you were younger? Can you escape the City?"

Galbrait's lips twitched in pain as he got to his feet. "There's a gate . . . in the woods, inside a springhouse. Leads to Kordewyn's park. It's quite hidden. Only opens from this side."

Draken wasn't surprised. The royals wouldn't leave themselves with no escape from the Palace City. Since discovering the doors, he'd wager a half-dozen such gates existed. Draken strode to a wardrobe and tossed him a shirt. "Get dressed. It's cold."

Draken cracked the transluscent horn panes, pulling them free of their leading, which tore aside easily enough. Galbrait pulled his father's shirt on, buckled on his sword brought by Draken, and slung a cloak over his shoulders. He edged down the wall, holding onto the stone with his fingertips. Draken held his tongue despite the painfully slow pace. He'd closed the shutters over the broken window. Let the bastards wonder where the Prince had gone, at least for a few breaths. They needed every stride of a head start they could get.

CHAPTER TWENTY-SEVEN

The fog was starting to dissipate, letting the Eyes shine their cold light into the alleyways and streets of Kordewyn. It was active, but quiet. Everyone was wrapped in cloaks against the damp chill as they hurried to their destinations.

Grand merchant houses with shuttered windows presided over deep vaults piled high with gold and coin. Draken had heard once that a Wildes pelt trader had a vault so overflowing that he'd buried his cheating wife and her lover alive in it, to suffocate and die under the weight of all that gold. Despite abundant witnesses and an alleged drunken confession, the pelt trader was so influential no one had ever bothered digging them out.

The city gates were open but still well-guarded. Draken watched them from a distance, thinking of their followers from before. The last thing he wanted to do was alert the city that the Prince . . . the King . . . was wandering Kordewyn at night.

"Draken." It was the first word Tyrolean had said since they'd met him at the bottom of the Palace wall, darted across the grounds, and stole through the woods to the gate in the springhouse.

He looked at Tyrolean and shifted his hand from his sword hilt to tuck a thumb in his belt. A stiff expression concealed Tyrolean's worries; Draken matched it. Galbrait looked like a broken horse. His shoulders sloped under the King's fine shirt and cloak, his blonde hair still matted with blood, his bruised face tipped to the ground. Occasional shivers took hold of his body. Shock, maybe. In a day the Prince had lost his King, his family, his dignity under torture, and his throne. Draken reached up and pulled the Prince's hood up. Galbrait didn't lift his head.

He thought what to say to comfort him but came up empty. The torq was hidden by his cloak and the bruising concealed his identity well enough—King Aissyth would barely have recognized Galbrait if he'd still been alive to do so.

The thought sent a wave of impatient anger through him. What in Khellian's name was Draken to do with the Monoean Crown Prince? Was he to stay here and stop this bloody revolution when all he wanted to do was set sail for Akrasia, for Elena, and spare them the coming war? He cast a resentful glance skyward, but Khellian hadn't appeared, and wouldn't until Zozia had passed the zenith during Trade. The war god never gave Draken any answer but killing, at any rate.

Then he had the same disconcerting thought as before. It lit a fire of nervous doubt in his belly, something that made him feel as if he might split in two. There was a way. He could use Galbrait . . . he still needed the Prince to save Brîn and Akrasia.

"Are you well, Your Highness?"

Likely Tyrolean thought Draken was about to lose it, go mad or worse. Draken sighed and tried to look in control, since he couldn't manage Princely at the moment. Manic worry felt like the slithering of a bane through one's veins. Succumb once and he was fair vulnerable ever after.

"I'm all right," he said. "Come."

◆ ◆ ◆

When they reached the guard, he gave them a tired look and then straightened with a frown. "You're Brînian." His eyes narrowed. "And Akrasian. What business had you in Kordewyn so late at night that you're skulking through the gate now?"

Draken held his temper with some difficulty, gripping his belt rather than letting his hand stray to the hilt at his side. His fingers bumped into the bag of coins tucked between his waist and the leather. He pulled it out, digging within, and drew out a gold King. "I'm rather in a hurry and my business is my own matter."

"And who's that?" the guard gestured with a sharp jerk of his chin at Galbrait, still huddling in his cloak.

"My guide."

Galbrait sneaked a glance up and the guard sniffed at his battered face. "Must've done you a wrong."

"A bad night at the tavern." Draken sighed. "We're just trying to get back to Shadowcliff."

"What's the hold-up?" Someone shouted from behind. "Rumors Ashen have taken the Palace and you're trading crow stories?"

Rumors, eh? That was quick. Almost as if it had been deliberate. Draken's eyes narrowed and he looked at Tyrolean. The Captain's jaw twitched. If rumors had escaped those secure stone walls, how long would it take for Sevenfel to erupt? By daylight and no later. The earliest marketeers and cooks were already rising.

"Heed, keep quiet! It'll take what it it takes." The guard scowled down at the King on Draken's palm and muttered, "Two."

"*Two?*"

"Each."

A shaggy highwayman in the Norvern Wildes wouldn't ask a fare so high from a coddled Landed lady caught unawares without her guard. "Four total and not a Prince more." Truth, he had no silver, only Aissyth's gold, and if they were held up much longer it'd take them past moonfall to make the *Bane*. They might need coin to buy passage on another ship.

The guard bared his teeth in a hostile grin, closed his burly fist over the coins, and let them through, though Draken felt his eyes on his back. The steps into Shadowcliff were empty but treacherous—so cold the damp had become a veneer of ice. Several times Galbrait slipped and Tyrolean had to catch him under the arm.

Tradeseason days started early in all the burroughs. Shadowcliff, by the time they descended the steps, was full of tradespeople. The buildings were all low and crowded, stalls and tents set up anywhere they could fit. They ran across several groups of guards, mostly city forces there to keep peace with so much coin floating about during trade, and all manner of races. Bare-chested, well-armed Brinians, an Akrasian half with lined eyes and Gadye braids binding back her dark hair, merchants from Felspirn robed head to toe and Straits traders in their red-stained leathers. No one paid them much mind beyond the Brînians, who were probably wondering why Draken wore local attire. But as they made their way through the warren of streets hemmed in by lowslung buildings, Tyrolean grunted. "Royal guards behind us, I think."

Sharply. "Following us?"

"No, Your Highness. I don't think they've seen us yet."

Galbrait, who'd been shuffling along with his head down, albeit keeping pace, slowed and looked back. Draken grasped his arm and shoved past a couple of dockers to get some distance. "No. Do not look."

"But they can help us. The royal guards are all loyalists."

Draken snorted softly. "It's not as if that garb is tattooed on. They could be Ashen in disguise."

Galbrait kept looking behind them and Tyrolean kept close, doing his best to stay in between the Prince and the guards. Draken concentrated on leading them to the harbor. Shadowcliff he knew as well as his own hand.

"We won't make it. The sun's up." Galbrait spoke sullenly, cuts slurring his words worse than Halmar's lip rings.

"Shut it, Galbrait," Draken growled.

Again, there were too many ships moored in the center of Sister Bay to pick out the *Bane* from among them, even with the rising sun setting the watery horizon aflame. Draken cursed low, impatient.

"Be easy, they won't leave without you."

Draken shot Tyrolean a look. "I gave them orders."

Tyrolean shook his head as if he already tired of the conversation. "Halmar might go so far as to let you wander Sevenfel alone, but he would never leave his Khel Szi to the mercy of Monoea. Not to mention Aarinnaie gave in to you far too easily to trust."

"There is that," Draken said. All of which could bring in a new host of problems. The *Bane* was surely known. Ashen could surround the ship.

"If we're stuck here, we should ask for their help." Galbrait started to turn round and lift an arm as if to hail the guards. One of them looked their way, though Tyrolean snapped his arm back down as if it were the lever on a well-oiled latch.

Galbrait yelped, frustrated and impatient. Several heads turned from the docks and on shore, saw they were foreigners, and looked away. One of the guards glanced their way.

Galbrait opened his mouth to speak again, but Draken backed him a couple of steps behind a dockshed and jabbed his fist into the Prince's stomach. The Prince bent over with a sharp grunt and Draken brought his knee up. The collision of knee to forehead made Galbrait drop to the wet wooden dock like a lumpy bag of mortar.

"That wasn't very nice, Your Highness."

"I've never pretended to be nice. Help me up with him."

"It's almost as if he wanted to get caught."

"I noticed." They hauled him up between them. Galbrait swung his head woozily, but he didn't fight them. Nor did he help; he was almost a dead weight with dragging feet despite a vague mumble of protest.

They walked as quickly as they could. Draken had to keep tight control of his emotions lest he dump the Prince and race down the pier in a fit of anxious impatience. He kept telling himself they could find passage home, he was a Prince with means, he could take his pick of the uncouth ship captains that populated every port. But it was difficult to believe while hauling the beaten, bloody Crown Prince of Monoea to tremulous safety during a burgeoning revolution.

A couple of whispering ladies eyed them; Draken worked up an even tone to apologize for his friend who had drunk too much at the tavern. They giggled and hurried on, adding to the throng behind them. Draken saw a small craft waiting for a lease and dragged the Prince onto it. It swayed under their weight but he let Galbrait fall to the deck a little harder than necessary. The Prince groaned and shifted but didn't lift his head.

"Drunk?" asked the skiffer.

"Got into a little trouble with the local guards. Get us out of here and there's a gold King in it for you. There. To the moored ships off Coldbank."

"Straightaway, master!"

Draken stared out where the *Bane* should be. A vague forest of masts shifted in the gathering gloom as the skiff pushed off. Behind them, fog and smoke layered the sky and drifted to taint the sea air. He wondered if Elena was all right. He wondered if the *Bane* would still be there. But mostly he wondered if he'd ever live to smell air cleansed of war and death.

◆ ◆ ◆

"It's about bloody time," Aarinnaie called, shrouded in a cloak against the cold.

Halmar's hulking figure lurked behind her, new sunlight glinting against the flat of his sword and on the moonwrought pierced into his skin.

A slight smile cracked through Draken's anxiety. Aarinnaie sounded uncharacteristically worried. He gave the skiffer two of Galbrait's kings, leaving him bowing and sputtering. "Master . . . my lord . . ."

"You did not see us. We were never here."

The skiffer blinked at him. "Of course, I—"

"Go." He turned away and hauled Galbrait upright. The Prince moaned and peered at him with his good eye. The fresh bruise from Draken's knee was blooming on one side of his forehead. "You hit me."

"Don't make me do it again," Draken said. "Halmar, a hand?"

Two sailors set the wooden and rope dock-steps in place as the skiffer bid his oarsmen to row away. Halmar strode down, his weight shifting the dock. It earned him a scowl from a sailor fishing at one end. He hauled Galbrait over his brawny shoulder as if he were a boy and strode back up the steps.

"Put him in the bunk in my cabin," Draken said. "Aarinnaie, watch him. I'll be along in a moment . . . what?"

"You have different clothes on," Aarinnaie said. "What happened?"

"We ran into some trouble."

Osias was watching with narrowed eyes, his double-bowl pipe smoking in thin streams. He looked too pale to be pretty as usual, his features hard and jagged in the new sun.

"I'll tell you all in a little; first I must speak to Akhanar Joran so we can launch as soon as possible."

She bit her lip, but followed Halmar into the cabin. Draken drew in a breath, intending on finding Joran, but instead he leaned back against the rigging. Tyrolean lingered near, watching Sevenfel.

"An interesting city," Osias said.

"If it survives this." Draken frowned, but he didn't look back. He'd lived most of his life in Sevenfel but it never had felt like home. Even Lesle seemed a dream. He rubbed his fingers together, thinking of her silken gown. He had trouble recalling her feel, her scent, her voice now. It all had been replaced with more recent memories of Elena.

Who would soon be fighting a battle because he'd failed here so miserably.

"Setia and I'll see to the young Prince, Draken."

"Fine. But be aware, he's as much hostage as anything, even if he doesn't know it."

"Be easy. We're going home." Osias touched his shoulder and disappeared into the cabin, trailing Gadye smoke that seemed to tug deep on Draken's lungs.

He closed his eyes, but felt nothing but the familiar sway of a ship's deck, the endless, soft lap of water against the hull. "Maybe Aarin was right. Maybe I should sail off. We could go anywhere."

"And let Akrasia suffer attack with no warning?"

"We're too far behind to warn them."

"We aren't too far behind to help."

Draken opened his eyes, snuck a glance at the stoic Tyrolean. His dark eyes reflected the rising daylight. It made Draken think of Osias. "If I go back, she may well learn the truth about me."

"Perhaps that is for the best," Tyrolean said.

"I am heresy, embodied. You of all people know that." Tyrolean spent more time praying than anyone he knew.

Tyrolean shrugged, though stiffly, as if his shoulders pained him. Doubtless they did. They'd seen a lot of swordplay. "Perhaps. And yet, the gods chose you to carry their sword. They help you live, again and again, no matter how many times you try to die."

Draken grunted. "You always say that when you won't indulge me in an argument."

"Or your self pity." Tyrolean slapped Draken on the shoulder, a rare gesture. "Go speak to the Akhanar Your Highness. Take us home."

CHAPTER TWENTY-EIGHT

Draken stood at the prow of the *Bane*, his hands resting on the rail. Joran knew his business. They'd had to sail upcoast to catch the Backtrades and now, a sevennight later, a fair wind blew them toward Akrasia, though not fair enough to catch the Monoean fleet. The *Bane* was quick, but not quick enough to catch twenty galleons with a whole day and night head-start. And he had no idea what they'd do if they caught them anyway. It'd be like a bloodfly taunting a herd of lions.

His fingers tightened on the rail, thinking of warships rounding Akrasia, searching out Khein or maybe going downcoast around to Brîn. He wondered whether Elena was still there, or if she'd gone to Auwaer as he'd asked. Twenty galleons meant at least six-thousand men, and he had a bad feeling more would follow, and more after that.

"Akhanar Joran says he'll drop anchor at Khein, Khel Szi." Aarinnaie eased up next to him and laid her narrow hands on the rail. They looked incongruous next to his, completely unrelated. Once again, he wondered how they could be so bloodstained when they looked so delicate.

"Aye," Draken answered. "Most of my troops are at Khein."

"Your Akrasian troops." Her voice held the tinge of insult.

"They far outnumber my Brînian soldiers, this you know." The treaty with Akrasia held Brîn to an active army of about three thousand.

She shook her head. "You're still Elena's creature, after all this."

Draken arched his brows.

"I only mean that in this, you should be King."

That sounded too close to what the Ashen wanted. "I control Elena's army," Draken said. "That's quite enough."

Aarinnaie scowled.

He sighed. "Elena is a good Queen. She was raised to rule, Aarin. I wasn't."

"When are you going to realize that you weren't raised to it, but born to it?"

Draken just shook his head, feeling weary. He was far more suited to the thick of the battle than the strategy tent. "How is Galbrait? Any change?"

"I think he would starve himself to death on that bed if not for Setia coaxing him to eat."

He slipped her a sideway's glance. "I understand you've been instrumental in his care, as well."

A delicate shrug. The day was clear and warm and her shoulders were bare. Fine muscles corded under her skin, darkened from days of sunlit sailing. "The Mance and Setia know how to handle him better than I." She tossed her curls, drawing the eye of a sailor. He saw Draken watching him and turned away. "I've little use for such weakness," she added.

"Grief is not weakness, Aarin. Does he know he's a hostage?"

"I don't think so. We're being too nice to him. But he is angry with you," Aarinnaie said. "He realized you have him by the stones."

He snorted to hide a grin. "I've got to get you off this ship. The sailors are a bad influence."

A smile quirked her lips. "If Monoea is in civil war, Galbrait won't be able to live with himself."

"He's going to have to learn to, if he is to survive this and take back his throne," Draken said. "At least he is alive, and his own man, free to make his own decisions."

"Indeed. And if that decision is to turn right back round and go to Monoea as soon as we land?"

He gave her a sharp look. "Has he suggested it?"

She shrugged again, more at ease. One-upping him seemed to relax Aarinnaie. "Not in so many words," she said. "I know you think he's the only one who can stop the attack."

He rubbed his fingers over his unshaven chin. "I'm also saving his life."

"*Please*. I don't fault you for it. Brîn is my home too." Sly smile. "And I hate Elena less than before. She is carrying my niece after all."

"Certain of that, are you?"

"Thom mentioned something."

Draken's eyes widened, wondering if she was teasing him or if the Gadye had actually spoken. Thom had known Elena was pregnant before any of them. He carried the pureblooded Gadye penchant for healing and Sight, which of course made him a very useful chamberlain. He allowed himself exactly one breath of wonder: A baby girl . . . a daughter. Dark hair and Elena's eyes, with a rosy glow to her brown skin . . . so tiny and helpless . . .

"Draken? About Galbrait?"

His hand had strayed to Seaborn's hilt. "I don't know that he can stop them. I only know it is his duty to try. For all our sakes." The troops, when attacking a foreign country, surely wouldn't disobey their Prince if he stood right in front of them with an army of Akrasians at his back, would they?

"He isn't the only one who needs a duty, Khel Szi." Aarinnaie dropped into a perfect curtsey. "I hope you need your assassin soon. My knives have been idle too long."

"I will, Aarin. Remember what I told you before?"

"Find the Priest and the commanders and kill them."

He nodded. "Aye. Kill them all."

Her slender form descended the short flight of steps from the bow, all fluid, perilous grace. Draken cast a glance to the sky. And blinked. Khellian, faint as melting frost, lingered over the horizon, far away toward distant lands. Monoea, Felspirn, the Straits. Listening. Watching.

"A daughter, then?" he said softly to the god. Another female to rip his heart out when he lost her.

No. To protect. To love. A deep voice, so soft he barely heard it between the waves.

His back prickled. The gods did not speak, not in so many words. He was in a position to know. It could only be . . . *"Bruche?"*

Halmar glanced at him from where he lingered toward the rear of the prow deck. "Khel Szi?"

"Nothing, Halmar." Draken turned back to the sea, staring out, wishing to see land, to see Akrasia. Or a fleet of Monoean ships, at least. He listened hard, but heard no more words from the waves. The sea breeze swept over Draken's chest. He felt himself stiffen. The God of War was keeping a hawk eye on his swordbearer.

◆ ◆ ◆

Draken's dark cabin stank of sweat, fish, and piss. Galbrait curled on the bottom bunk, his face and knees toward the wall. He didn't move as Draken strode in and pushed the shutters open.

"Galbrait. The day is fine. Up."

"Why didn't they kill me?" Galbrait asked softly.

"What? Who?" He thrust open the shutters on the other side. Sunlight and fresh sea spray flooded the cabin, sweeping out the stink.

Galbrait turned his head, though he didn't look right at Draken. "Why didn't the Ashen kill me? I keep thinking about it."

"They hadn't been ordered." He sighed. "Your kind does nothing without orders."

Galbrait rubbed his hand over his face. His chin was bristly, his golden hair lank and tangled. Draken indulged the idea of tossing him into the ocean for a bath, but poured them two cups of warm ale instead.

"They are nothing without their King." Draken sat on the bench to drink, the sea wind buffeting the back of his head from the unshuttered window. "Not to put too fine a point on it, but Monoea is basically leaderless at the moment. Enough people saw me take you. You practically waved them down, if you recall."

Galbrait lowered his gaze. "I was frightened. I'm sorry."

"Don't apologize. You did us all a favor. Rumors you're alive will persist, no matter what tales the Ashen tell. Even if they put some Landed puppet on the throne, there will always be doubt. That gives you an opportunity to come in later and take command as the rightful King."

"Don't pretend you have honor, or that this is about me. You just want to use me to stop the attack on Akrasia."

Draken snorted. "My honor died with my wife. I'm merely pointing out the benefits of this situation to *you*."

"Which are few, and fewer still with time and distance," Galbrait said.

"Agreed. But you are alive and not a puppet. So that's something." Draken leaned back and tipped his head against the sill, catching a glimpse of the bright sky beyond.

Who's arguing? You command and they follow, Khel Szi.

Draken held perfectly still but for a muscle quivering beneath his eye. *Bruche?*

Of course. A hesitation and the voice softened, barely emerging from the waves. *Come in . . . I would see you again.*

Draken blinked. In? Into the sea? It could be a trap, damn it. But it sounded like him, *felt* like him. His sword hand relaxed as if ready to let the spirit command his muscles, to fight and kill. It must be a deception, or a trick of his own mind.

Galbrait hauled himself up, bent over, elbows on knees. His voice cut into Draken's fixation with his spirit swordhand. "There's nothing left for me there."

Draken blinked at him. "At the moment, no. But your army is just ahead of you. Go to Akrasia and take control of it. Let your army annoint you King. Then you can go back."

The Prince stared at him. "How? They've got a commander. That Rinwar priest."

Galbrait had no idea about Aarinnaie and her knives. Draken allowed himself a small smile. "Leave that bit to me."

"I will. I will do that."

It seemed too easy. But he was weary of arguing and worrying. Draken got up. "Now come. You need a wash and fresh air. I expect you up and helping with duties at first light and to spend afternoons keeping your sword skills sharp for the rest of our journey."

The Prince followed him out to the deck, obedient, saying little, keeping his gaze downcast under the curious stares of the crew. Draken retreated to the prow again as they hauled up water from the sea for the Prince to wash. Draken watched him strip and splash himself, scrubbing his hair and body with the caustic soap and rinsing as he shivered on the deck. Osias approached him and they spoke, though Draken couldn't hear what they said. Setia climbed the rigging as if she'd been shipbound her entire life. He listened for Bruche, but the sea was silent.

Tyrolean nodded to Galbrait and came up the steps to the bow. "You got him up, Your Highness. Well done."

"He couldn't sleep in there for the entire journey. We have a fight ahead of us and we all need practice with the blade, me most of all." Galbrait would make a formidable sparring opponent. But he didn't meet Tyrolean's eyes.

"And if our blades fail us against the Monoeans?" Tyrolean asked quietly.

Draken's hands tightened on the rail, saying nothing. He had no answer— not one Tyrolean would approve, anyway.

CHAPTER TWENTY-NINE

Two nights later bells pealed through Draken's tired mind, brutalizing his sleep. He groaned, still with a shadowy Elena, her long hair soft under his hand, her voice making his heart ease. She turned her head to listen, her smile faltering at Setia's voice—

"Khel Szi?"

His eyelids fluttered and he peered upward. Setia bent over him, her dappled brow furrowed. "Your Highness, there is a ship chasing our course and gaining. Osias confirms it."

Draken rolled over with a grunt, stomach swimming with exhaustion. Elena's pendant thumped against his bare chest, hot from his grip.

Tyrolean's silhouette blocked the doorway, the twin swords sticking over his shoulders like Khellian's horns. Wavering lantern light made him appear otherworldly and eerie. But his voice sounded firm, real. "We think it's a Monoean ship."

The warning bell still rung so that he could hardly think. "Stop the blasted bell," he growled. "They'll have heard it all the way to Dragonstar by now."

Gods, his mind was muggy, though he'd had only one cup of ale before succumbing to sleep. His body felt battered, worn; his joints ached deep. Galbrait and Tyrolean had schooled him with the sword in the heat of the afternoon and every muscle bellowed a protest at the effects. He reached for Seaborn, wincing. Old injuries had tightened in his sleep. His knee protested a little less; he could expect it to give way when he least expected it.

"A galleon?" he asked, voice rough.

"Not so big as all that, but bigger than the *Bane*. It's not close enough yet to make out its colors."

"How is the light?" He pushed past Tyrolean, tightening his belt around his trousers, forgoing boots and shirt. Abruptly Brînian coastal clothing made sense. If he was forced into the water at any point, the last thing he'd want was boots on. Of course, if he *was* forced into the water, boots would be the least of his problems.

Tyrolean didn't answer because soon enough Draken was striding over the deck, looking over the skies and light for himself. Only three moons yet, low on the horizon where Khellian had lingered the day before. Soon the sky would brighten, revealing all. He turned and stared into the darkness ahead. The ship was ghostly in the night, just barely catching a glint of the moonlight. Slowly his eyes adjusted and its masts and rigging formed jagged, stair-stepped peaks, sails billowing. Surely the *Bane* was their target. His ship abruptly felt very small. He glanced back at the peculiar moonglow, ghostly across the soft waves. Khellian had failed to appear for his Chosen's latest fight, he noted dryly, but Korde waited to see if he could ferry any dead to his high mountaintops this night.

He rubbed his hand over his chest and around the back of his neck, trying to wake up. The chill night air would do the rest.

"Eerie, that. Like an omen." He could detect the slight shudder in Aarinnaie's voice as she pressed against his arm.

"Aarin, you should go below."

"You need me. You need every hand when they attack."

"She's right." Galbrait had been hidden in the moonshadow of a mast and eased forward. "And hiding won't help if they board us."

Draken had given up worrying about the rearguard of the Monoean fleet after so many nights without seeing any sign of it, curse him to Eidola. He'd assumed they thought they were too powerful to attack. But . . . "They don't risk attack from the rear. They never have done." It was one of the tactics that made the Monoean Navy so good. So damned hard to beat.

"They must've sailed out of our sight-line and back round," Joran said. His forehead creased. That meant a quick sailing ship, surely faster than the *Bane*.

"Aye, and they knew they could outsail us before they left Sister Bay. They had plenty of time to look us over," Draken said. He cursed in two languages and stared at the ship. Then he turned to find every eye of the crew upon him as if he'd ever commanded a ship at battle before. He drew a breath and scoured his mind for what he did know. "They'll give chase, wear us down. We will end up fighting them. I think we must stand and fight here."

Galbrait scowled, his fingers twitching but not straying to his sword hilt.

"They may well attack in effort to try to 'rescue' Galbrait, if they know he's aboard," Aarinnaie pointed out, her emphasis making no secret of her disdain for the Monoeans. Draken wondered if she was falling for Galbrait. He'd been through a romantic entanglement of hers before and certainly had no time for it now.

"It's a thought," Tyrolean said.

Draken frowned and glanced back at the trailing ship. Seven bloody Eyes, it seemed even bigger. The night was quiet, but there was a faint glow on deck. Fires, ready for arrows and hurling balls.

"Stoke the fires, cock the ballistae, set the casts," he said.

Captain Joran nodded and passed the order. "And the harpaxes, Khel Szi?"

Draken shook his head slowly. A boarding could go both ways and they would be outnumbered. "Set them but do not fire until I order, no matter how close they get. We might use harpaxes to damage their hull if need."

"Aye, Khel Szi."

His sailors had already removed the oiled canvas covers and stowed them out of the way. Fires flared on the bow deck and behind the helm as sailors blew air through bellows into the metal troughs, stoking up the coals kept hot there. Ballistae creaked as men wound them to full tension. Casts were loaded with hurling balls. Sailors started hauling buckets of seawater to soak the decks; archers strung bows and strapped down heavy quivers at the rail. Draken noticed with no small pride their bows were stiff despite the salt air; every Brînian bowman worth his ale had an oscher bow from the humid Moonling woods of Khein, wood well-suited to harsh, damp conditions. Still, they were so few . . .

"Won't all that just make them attack?" Galbrait asked, nodding his chin to the firetroughs, which were surely visible to the Monoean ship.

"They aren't chasing us down to share an ale," Draken said. "Keep under cover. I don't need you taken out by an arrow."

"I can shoot," Galbrait said, lip curled.

"I'm aware."

Halmar approached Draken. "You should arm now, Khel Szi. I will fetch your harness."

Draken scowled at the approaching ship. The air was fair quiet, calm for these seas. Still it came quickly, cutting through the waves.

"I've no wish to drown in my armor." Besides, it would make him easy for the Monoeans to pick out among his bare-chested crew, especially if any of the enemy had a lens. And with three moons—no *four*, damn the gods—rising and shedding more cold white light with every breath, a lens might just be of some use.

He'd left his lens at Brîn—too valuable to bring along to his death. And there'd been a less fine one in his kit when he was a bowrank commander. Maybe it was kept in his mother's wardrobe . . . maybe even his bow had been tucked in the back. He missed that more. The realization startled him. This was his first battle at sea without a bow in his hand.

"Konnan."

The szi nêre stepped closer, his dark, dappled brow clear, his gaze steady. For an ex-slave abused by his former master he was solid as an anchor caught in a sea floor crevice. "Khel Szi?"

"Find me a bow, will you?"

Halmar's pierced brow raised, but Konnan simply inclined his head. "Aye, Khel Szi." He disappeared below. Draken was willing to wager there'd be a spare bow or three; some few sailors had been killed during his scuffle with Ghotze.

Sailors grunted as they locked the first of the harpaxes into firing position. Longer than a man was tall and banded in iron, the thick wooden bolts would take precious moments and manpower for the enemy to cut through—moments Draken had no intention of giving the Monoeans. Every breath counted, outnumbered as they were. But he still wasn't certain the harpaxes were needed. They numbered twenty-five. The enemy schooner must carry ten decades or a dozen, at least. It had to be a long-range battle if they had any hope at bringing the other ship down.

"Shall we fire, Khel Szi?" Joran had appeared at his elbow without his realizing.

It was tempting. Oiled hurling balls rested in leather slings. Sailors, even the galley lad, held smoldering bunts at the ready, and the bowmen had stretched and warmed their arms and shoulders. But the enemy ship was still far enough out that the odds of hitting the deck or sails were slim.

"Hold yet," he said.

"Wise," Tyrolean said. "This could be a protracted battle."

"Or a fair short one," Draken said quietly and strode to Brimlud for a few words. "They're bigger than us. We might have to swing round and ram them to take them down."

"That would take *us* down. Even with her metal-clad keel, I'd rather not."

He met Brimlud's eyes and spoke slowly. "If it comes to it, your duty is to make certain our sinking ship drags those Seven-cursed Ashen down with us."

Brimlud squinted at him, eyes almost disappearing amid the wrinkles. "I understand, Khel Szi. I'll do my best."

"Good man." Draken slapped Brimlud on the shoulder. He was proud of how nimble the *Bane* was; he hoped that pride wasn't misplaced. He really hoped they didn't have to use that agility to bring her down.

Konnan returned with the bow and two big, heavy quivers meant for sailors holding position, not for someone who was running all over the deck or climbing rigging. Draken did a quick estimate. Forty arrows. Ten quivers per man. Five thousand arrows, maybe six. "I'll position on the aft deck; put the arrows there. Akhanar?"

Joran turned, shoulders squared. "Khel Szi."

"The best bowmen on this crew, who are they?"

"Tolon and Hoka are best. The Mance." His gaze flicked up to Draken's face. "And you."

Draken frowned but didn't deny it. "How do you know?"

"I went ashore in Sevenfel and made inquiries, Khel Szi." His gaze was unwavering, unapologetic.

"And you're not asking for more coin?"

"You are Khel Szi. You will make it right between us. Or after this night it won't matter."

Ah. All pretense was dropping away. It made for a strange relief.

"Fair enough." He raised his voice so all could hear him. "They might have as many as one hundred souls onboard. We can't engage in a full-on battle with that ship, and we certainly can't board her. Heavy artillery, and aim for the sails to slow her down." He cast another glance at the moons. "Joran. Let the enemy give chase."

Orders rang out. The ship listed to swordside as it shifted position a bit. Their sails luffed and fell, then billowed with wind as they caught the stream filling the enemy sails.

Tyrolean frowned. "You said something about ramming them?"

Draken took a sharp breath, suppressing the almost insurmountable desire to ask Tyrolean how many sea battles he'd been in. "They out-weapon us, outsize us, outnumber us. Their ship is better; their sailing is better. If it comes to it we can ram them, lay in with the harpaxes, and disable them enough to take them down with us. We'll have done the best we can for Akrasia and Brîn, which by Korde isn't nearly enough." He paused and added, quieter, "We're likely going down, Ty. But by the gods, so are they."

Tyrolean drew in a sharp breath through parted lips. But the momentary shock passed and his back straightened. "I'll fetch a bow as well."

"Tyrolean, wait."

The Captain turned back, lined eyes narrowed.

"We have advantages. Fair winds to reduce their speed. Brimlud at the helm." A humorless smile twitched his lips. "And me."

Tyrolean stared at him. Gave a crisp nod. "Aye, Your Highness."

Tyrolean's nod shoved a little confidence through his fear. He might be a poor battle commander, but he was all these men had. "Aarinnaie and Galbrait, hold back. Let them capture you if it comes to it. You're worth more than any of us alive."

Aarinnaie opened her mouth to protest but Draken gave a sharp shake of his head and raised his voice enough the other sailors could hear him. "Take positions. Keep low until I call to fire. And then let Khellian's wrath fall on them."

The aft deck had little protection, and most of the room was taken by the ballistae. The men kept low now that the ballistae were cocked.

"Tolon and Hoka, to me." The bowmen gazed up at him from the steps of the quarterdeck. "You two climb. I'll watch from deck. Save your arrows until the Ashen are close enough to make real shots. When they're close enough, and make no mistake, they will be, we need you to pick off their bowrank commanders and specialists. Hit the large artillery first. Anyone in red is an officer. If you see a glint, aim for it. That'll be a lens in the hands of their akhanar or a bowrank commander."

They gave crisp nods and hurried to the masts.

"I'll be here, by you." Osias climbed onto deck. The moonlight gleamed on his silver skin and hair.

"Osias—"

"I've my bow." The Mance produced it from beneath his cloak, which wasn't long enough to conceal the longbow but always seemed to manage it anyway. "And I can better glamour you if I'm close."

A little glamour might buy Draken time. But the use of magic got him thinking. "Setia?"

"Here, Khel Szi." She climbed the short flight, a bucket in her hand.

"Can you use the Abeyance out here?"

She twisted her head to look at the waves, and then the enemy ship. "I think not. There is no magic for me to draw on in the sea. The ground is too far below us and there are no living plants within my reach. I am sorry."

"It's all right. We'll make do." But the idea of using magic still niggled at him, a fleeting thought quickly overcome by the approaching ship.

"I'll be drawing fire," he told the sailor manning the harpax next to him. "Down on deck until you're called. If I'm hit get the arrow out of me as quickly as possible. If I'm killed the timing falls to you. Your duty will be to use the harpaxes to join the ships, destroy their hull, and take them down with us."

He watched his face as he absorbed this. Before the sailor could reply, chainshot peppered the sea behind them. Draken cursed and lifted a hand to Joran to give permission to fire. Orders chattered through the sailors, fires flared, casts creaked, the salty, metallic scent of oiled flamed, and hurling balls streaked across the sky.

Draken turned and nocked and sighted an arrow, getting the feel of the bow, noting the stiff cobalt feathers. The bow felt familiar; the sword an odd weight. Konnan had left two quivers resting against the ballista. Eighty arrows. He had no idea how long his shoulder would hold to draw, nor if he'd run through his arrows before he was hit. He was out of practice and his cover was poor.

A sailor lit the bolts on the ballistae and ducked out of the way. The ballistae strained and shot, soaring clear of the ship. Draken grimaced. They had to do better than that. But he nodded to the sailors. "Again."

More of *Bane*'s hurling balls flamed across the sky. One bounced into a mainsheet on the enemy ship. Flames licked it, glaring against the night despite the moons, but it went out. The enemy answered with more chain-shot. One shredded a skysail. The pieces flapped uselessly. At least there were no flaming—

One of their hurling balls struck the deck, crashing and bouncing over the edge to sizzle into the sea. Another smashed into a sail and rolled down to wedge between a firetrough and the mizzen mast. Sparks flew and scattered. Setia rushed with a bucket of water and dumped it on the flaming ball, then jumped back as the water sizzled and spat back at her.

He tightened his jaw at his aching knee, strained by his position, and squinted into the darkness, willing his vision to clear as the moons rose. The nearing schooner loomed, though it moved glacially slow. Joran was holding their own speed for a final burst. The acrid scent of his own terror-laced sweat rose as he drew string to cheek. His shoulder ached deep, but he gritted his teeth and ignored it.

Past the voices of the crew, the *thrup* of the sails overhead, the ever-shifting waves, the near silent hiss of arrows, he heard the far off creak of a winch. Damn. Ballistae on the other ship, and casts. A flaming ball whizzed through the air. Overshot—it sizzled into the sea.

He squinted. Saw the flare as they lit another ball. A man-shaped shadow backed away from it, highlighted by his bunt. Draken drew and sighted, but with the movement of both ships and the distance, it was an impossible shot. He let it fly and it joined the flock of other arrows whistling by. Another volley, and so on, each bow nocked with two arrows for maximum coverage. Winches cranked and snapped as they released. Arrows peppered the sea and the hull and aft deck. Draken climbed up to the aft deck and glanced back at Brimlud. He was mostly protected on the lower quarterdeck, but Draken wished he had more cover. He wished his ruddy Brînian crew weren't so foolhardy and conceited that they wouldn't wear armor.

Gods forsake them, the Ashen were closing on them. Draken fought his rising blood, trying to keep calm as he watched for more shadows around the angled shapes of their artillery. He could pick out more moving people and artilery on the moon-side. The glow in their firetroughs resolved into flames as they drew on. He let his focus change. Damn. He needed to find bloodstone uniforms. When it was time, he could fair kill them by single shots.

A lower topsail on the *Bane* ripped and caught flame, flaring. Acrid smoke choked Draken's lungs. Several sailors coughed. Draken grabbed up a wet, filthy rag and tied it over his face. It smelled of salt and dirt and fish, but cut the impact of the smoke on his lungs. Someone shouted, another sailor answered. Hoka, perhaps. From the fighting top he could climb down to the bucket of water being winched up the mast. Hurling balls splashed all around both ships.

In the meantime Draken let more arrows fly, straining despite muscle memory. Behind, someone screamed and thudded hard against the deck. He grimly kept picking out bodies and shooting. He didn't know if he was hitting anything. Both the enemy and the *Bane* shifted over the waves, ruining most of his shots. He hit enough, alongside Osias, Tolon, Hoka, and the others, to keep the Monoeans ducking for cover.

A white light spread over the moonside of the enemy ship, revealing people and artillery in sharp relief against the glow of firetroughs. A little closer and they'd be easier to pick off.

More flaming arrows tore into the *Bane's* sails and clattered to the deck as the Monoean bowmen tried to shoot his people down and catch the ship. Setia, the galley lad, and another sailor raced about with water, drowning sparks. Two others worked lines with harsh grunts. Between the *thup-thup-thup* of Draken's bow and the whistling, metallic clatter as chainshot caught on sails, railings, and wood: another scream, a moment of deadly silence, a clattering thud that seemed to bubble up from belowdecks, and a splash. Damn.

The noise aboardship raised to a din; more arrows arced into the *Bane*, coming in sheets like hard, killing rain. An arrow sliced Draken's arm and the deck under his feet trembled as it healed. With a grunt he refocused his mind and his aim. Caught a glimpse of moonlight on crimson on the opposite deck. The world slowed, crawled. The *Bane* and the enemy ship both crested a wave at the same time. Draken drew to his cheek, breathed in a draught of sweat-stink air, and loosed. The officer fell.

He blinked, realized he could see the other ship far too well. Chainshot and balls and shafts hurtled into the *Bane*. He could feel and smell the flaming heat off their sails. The enemy was closing in now, too close. They would ram the *Bane*. No. Too soon. He bellowed, *"Brimlud! About!"*

The helmsman was already on it. The *Bane* listed steeply enough Draken had to grab the harpax cord to not slide across the deck. His eyes never left the enemy ship. Its name was emblazoned on the side in great script: *Kingsblood.*

"Man harpaxes!" Just in case. Arrows flew from Osias's bow, and his long hair streamed back like a banner. Draken rose up and lifted his bow, uncaring and uncovered, and nocked. A head peaked up over a ballista on the other ship;

Draken's arrow thudded through it with a spray of black. Someone on the other ship screamed. They were close enough to shout to one another. Arrows bristled from the *Kingsblood's* hull and railing and decks. His men had fought well. He gripped the ballista line, waiting for the scrape of hull against hull, for the Bane's hull to smash irreparably against the other ship. The moment he felt it, he'd give the order to shoot the great bolts into the *Kingsblood*.

But Brimlud cranked the *Bane* round so hard she shuddered and creaked in protest. Draken cursed, snatched up arrows from the quiver, and sent another Monoean archer screaming to his death. Two more took his place as the dead bowman slammed back into a fire trough. Sparks and kindling burst upward, drawing Draken's eye and blinding him to the battle.

Good shot, but a sword is a real weapon.

Bruche again? Draken shook his head. The world felt as if it wavered.

Galbrait, terrorized and shaky, cut through Draken's momentary fugue. *"The King is on board. Stop firing!"*

Draken turned his head. His curse didn't reach his lips. There wasn't time.

Something choked Galbrait's words like an axe hewing kindling. Aarinnaie had tackled him, dragging him down to the decking. He rolled and twisted away from her, leapt to his feet. They were nearly gone by the *Kingsblood*. The *Bane* was sound. Draken heard the winding creak of a great harpax, the thud of a great bolt. The *Bane* shuddered. Draken shouted to his men to stop; their hull wasn't breached, this would only ensure boarding. The fool Prince kept shouting at the other ship: *"Stop! The King is—!"* But an arrow skipped off a boom and changed course for Galbrait's head, donning him with a crimson mask of blood and drowning the last of his words.

CHAPTER THIRTY

Draken's lungs forgot to suck in air, but his hands didn't forget to nock an arrow. The muscle memory felt like an ancient command. Both ships jerked and twisted on the water, both listing and straining against the bolts that bound them. An archer on the *Kingsblood* fighting top fell screaming to the *Bane's* deck, hit the rail, and was lost to the sea. Two bowmen at the enemy rail died moments later, stuck with arrows. The ships were parting, sea and wind dragging them. A thud jarred through Draken's knees. Another. Wood creaked and groaned as it split. Harpax bolts from the damned *Kingsblood.* He scrambled to the side and clung to the wire holding the ballista in place, staying low, cursing. Sailors on both ships were too busy hanging on to the spinning ships to keep firing.

The ships were six strides apart, rotations gradually slowing, the *Kingsblood* reeling them in. He got his balance but hands caught his arm as he was drawing back again. Small but strong. He turned his head, the bow still taut.

Aarinnaie winced. "They're going to board us."

"Galbrait?" He struggled to look past her. The only thing left of the Prince was a bloody smear on the deck.

"Alive. Sliced his head. A lot of blood."

Her gaze slid around him and she released a slow breath. He realized he could hear her plainly. The hurling balls had stopped; the arrows ceased. He followed her gaze. Arrows encircled him like a small forest. He blinked up at Osias. "Glamour isn't just camouflage, is it?"

An unusual deadpan tone from Osias: "No use keeping secrets around you."

Ropes and wood creaked and heavy chains clunked. The *Bane* twitched under Draken's boots.

"They're laying bridges," Aarinnaie said.

Draken rose. The two ships were bound precariously by two harpax bolts, held at an odd angle. Dozens of men marked with ash were gathering on the near side of the *Kingsblood*, preparing to board them. Their captain had ordered them to stop firing, obviously. It was all very orderly and gave Draken a glimmer of something to work with.

One of his sailors was in the rigging cutting through the *Bane's* burning main topsail while another took cover behind the main mast and cranked up a bucket of water. Tyrolean stood panting and bleeding on the deck; an arrow had nicked his arm. Two sailors sprawled on the deck, surrounded by splatters of blood. One of them was Hoka. Down in the hold, someone's screams turned to moans and choked to a stop.

"Halmar, wrap Galbrait in chains and take him to the far side of the ship. Be quick about it. On my order, drop him over."

Halmar didn't stop to nod, just strode to pick up Galbrait. The Prince was limp in his brawny arms, out cold from the knock in the head. He carried him off to the far side of the ship and was hopefully hidden from the *Kingsblood* by the big mast. A clink of chain told Draken his orders were being obeyed.

A man in crimson uniform made bulky by armor, his helm under his arm, strode to the rail of the *Kingsblood*. Draken blinked at him. He was Ashen all right, marked across the forehead and twined moons embroidered into the fabric over his chest. And he knew the man. Scoured his memory for the name. Chaessar.

"Who is your Captain?" Chaessar asked.

Joran started forward, but Draken stepped over the arrows and leapt down the steps to the quarterdeck and down to the main. "I am in command of this ship."

Several bows creaked on the *Kingsblood* as archers took aim.

"Hold." Chaessar's gaze raked over Draken. "And you are?"

"Brînian merchants." A test to see if Chaessar really didn't know.

"You trespass."

"Fools all, one cannot trespass on open sea!" Aarinnaie's body was tight, low, her fingers gripping knives. Chaessar was within throwing range for her, but a dozen arrows would take her out before he hit the deck. Draken wrapped his free hand around her wrist.

"It is claimed for Moonminster Temple of Monoea," Chaessar said. "The gods own all, and shall recover what is stolen from them."

Draken frowned at that bit of audacious nonsense, but didn't argue. "I would seek terms, my lord. We mean you no harm and fought only in self-defense."

"Why would I treat with you? We have bested you soundly. You are my prisoner, mine to keep or dump into the sea. Lower aim, set fresh bolts. Cut them loose and sink that ship."

Bows strained on the *Bane*; Draken held up a hand to stop them firing. He sighed, bent, laid down his bow. His back and shoulders ached, tightening after so much exertion. He drew Seaborn. It glowed faintly, just enough to show it was more than just the moons' reflection. Chaessar stared hard at it and everyone on both ships stilled.

"That very well may be," Draken said, "but I am chosen by the gods. To touch me and mine means you are challenging the Seven Eyes. They are watching now, Chaessar. And truth, they do not fair tolerate disobedience." He'd learned that the hard way.

Chaessar stared unblinking at him. Or the sword. Draken couldn't tell which. Something crossed his face: a slight, cruel smile close on the heels of his disbelief. "You are Prince at Brîn."

"I am many things, Chaessar. What I am *not* is your prisoner."

"Yet. Bring him and Prince Galbrait."

"I don't know what use Galbrait will be," Draken said. "He is soon to die, thanks to your bows."

"His body will suffice."

This set him back a step. Maybe he should have anticipated it. Draken pretended to consider. "I'll willingly bring him over to your ship if you agree to terms."

Chaessar shook his head. "Or I simply take him."

"Halmar, toss Galbrait overboard."

"No!" Chaessar scowled, his lip upturned.

Draken very carefully did not smile. "Hold, Halmar."

"I assume these *terms* involve my letting your ship go."

Draken nodded. "Aye. In exchange for me and the Prince."

"They will only chase us and engage again."

"They're under strict orders to change course from yours in the event of terms," Draken lied.

Chaessar's lips pulled down into a caricature of a frown. Here, then, was the crux of it. Invoking the gods had worked but Draken had no illusions on how long that would last. A few well-placed arrows would solve Chaessar's problem with a minimum of fuss. The question Draken had was: why hadn't he exercised that option? Maybe he really did think Draken was some rightful King. He wasn't being terribly kind about it though; maybe he didn't think Draken should be King but couldn't disagree with his superiors.

Chaessar nodded. "Bring the Prince. You have your terms."

Draken blinked in surprise as the Ashen captain turned to give orders, not waiting for a reply.

"That's odd," Aarinnaie muttered.

"He's lying," Tyrolean said.

"No. He wants me alive. That priest Rinwar wants me alive," Draken said grimly. But not every Ashen was privy to that knowledge, that was for certain. He sensed every single one of the Monoean arrows trained on his back. "Halmar. Bring Galbrait. I'll carry him over."

Halmar gave a crisp nod. "Aye, Khel Szi."

"You said you'd protect him," Tyrolean said.

"I said I'd protect you all. Galbrait and I are our only bargaining stones."

Tyrolean nodded, but his eyes narrowed, flicked to Draken's sword. "You have a plan."

"Keep Aarinnaie safe for me."

Tyrolean shook his head. "There's no chance of your winning against him. Just by the look of the Captain's blade . . ." He gave Draken a level look and said without conceit, "Let me stand in your stead."

"Listen to him, Draken. You cannot do this," Aarinnaie said.

Draken sighed and looked at Osias.

The Mance narrowed his eyes, studied Draken, and nodded. "This he must do alone." The soft finality in his tone silenced them all.

Blood caked the side of Galbrait's head. Draken knelt by him as Halmar undid the chains and probed it. Still seeping blood. It needed sewing badly. Galbrait was pale as death and unconscious. Setia stood near him, a bloody rag in her hands. She'd only managed to push the blood around a bit.

He knew his sister believed their whole world had come down to this, to these men on this ship. But he couldn't forsake Brîn. He couldn't forsake Elena. He had to fight for her the only way he knew how. Once he had killed her. Her dying had saved them all. Now it was his turn.

"Be well, Szirin . . . my assassin." He leaned down to kiss her cheek and murmur in her ear, "Remember what I told you about the Priest."

Aarinnaie blinked and swallowed. Nodded.

"Good." He stroked a stray curl from her cheek and turned away, his throat tight.

Once when Draken had been a young bowman, they'd been boarded by pirates. He had thought they were dead for certain. But his Captain had concealed a blade and waited for the best opportunity to use it, killing the pirate captain. It had been a fair close thing.

This would be closer.

A few scrapes, grunts, and thuds and the bridge was set, latching onto the *Bane's* railing. Joran and his mate went to secure it onto the *Bane* at Draken's nod. Draken carried the limp Prince across, knowing the moment their feet hit the deck of the *Kingsblood* their lives were forfeit. He could only hope to save his sister, his friends, and his crew.

Chaessar watched him come aboard. Draken felt abruptly naked in his bare chest and feet with no paint. He wished he at least had the gruesome visage Aarinnaie had painted for him to meet Aissyth.

"Your Prince, Captain," he said. He knelt to lay Galbrait on the deck. The blood was slowing. He lolled against the deck, limp and unconscious.

"My King." Chaessar's eyes narrowed. His gaze flicked from Elena's pendant up to Draken's face. "Gods, I didn't believe it when I heard. You're the King's bastard cousin."

"I don't claim the King, nor does he claim me. I am Khel Szi of Brîn." He drew Seaborn and bolted forward to slash at Chaessar. He managed to get a strike, but his feet were wrong, misplaced, and he realized his mistake instantly. Chaessar whipped his sword from its sheath and blocked his next attempt. The Ashen cheered.

"Enough! Desist!" On an upswing, Chaessar's blade came perilously close to Draken's arm, feeling as if it sheared off the hairs. "Don't make me harm you."

"I'm going to make you kill me." Gods, he didn't even have a bracer on. Small wounds would heal. He had borne the pain. "Or die trying." Before he lost his chance, his footing, and his nerve, he again drove his sword at Chaessar.

Chaessar blocked with an odd twist to his arm and, shoving Draken's sword out of the way with his bracer, he struck. Blood spurted hot over Draken's chest, thick and fast. He grunted at the sharp, deep pain and felt the pinpricks surround the wound. The blood would hide the healing. He snarled and brought his sword around, clumsily because the prickly sensation of the wound closing was distracting.

A slight shudder passed through the ship and the wood groaned softly, as if the gods had given it a light shake. Draken leapt forward again, trying for a lowline strike. Chaessar blocked again. The swords clanged. Seaborn's moon-wrought notched Chaessar's steel. He used Chaessar's momentary surprise to slip under his guard. Seaborn skipped across Chaessar's belly, slicing through fabric and flesh. Chaessar hissed; it sounded more annoyance than pain. The crimson uniform hid the blood—Draken doubted there was much. But it did the trick. Chaessar forgot he wanted Draken alive. It was all Draken could do to block his first strike; the second sliced deep across his bare chest, cutting sinew and muscle. The cut in Draken's chest seared with pain as blood hit the sea air. Agony made Draken stagger back. Chaessar followed and Draken shoved past the pain to score a hit on Chaessar's arm. Not enough to stop the captain, but enough to make Draken seem worthy. Enough to make Chaessar work for it.

Beyond Chaessar, Khellian had finally risen to see what the fuss was about. His cold white light caught on Seaborn's blade, flashing in Draken's eyes. Chaessar took advantage of Draken's hesitation. He pressed in hard. Their swords locked and he shoved Draken back. Draken was bigger than Chaessar by half a head but weakened by pain and his sword was shorter. The shove came out of the bright light glaring in his eyes, catching him off guard. His bad leg went back as the ship rumbled under their feet again. His knee locked. The motion twitched Draken neatly to the deck. He landed on his weak shoulder and a low cry escaped his lips as he rolled to his back. The joint had slid out of place and back in, as it was prone to do. The ship rumbled again. A loud *crack* cut through worried murmurs of the crew. Draken heard a female voice shout; Aarinnaie, not an Ashen.

Chaessar blocked Khellian's light, looming over Draken in silent, sharp relief. The tip of his sword pricked the skin over Draken's heart. "Bind him and take him below."

Draken growled and shoved up as hard as he could against the blade. Cold metal sliced through his flesh, slid between and through bone. He summoned his flagging will and shoved harder, gasping in agony as his heart tried to pump around the unforgiving steel. The stilling of his blood *hurt*, every vein lit with hot flame. It overtook every cut and the deep ache in his dislocated shoulder. Draken drew in air but the labor of it proved too much to try again. Chaessar cursed and yanked his blade back. Draken got the vague impression of a cacophony of voices and boots.

The Eyes glowered down at him. Draken felt a sudden surge of terror—not of Chaessar or the Ashen or even death, but of the realization he had lost his way. Using their will against them yet again.

The tingling sharpened, pinpricks inside his skin, converging on his chest, searing the wound closed from the inside out: organs, muscles, skin knitting. It felt as if someone worked inside the wound with blades and a hot poker. His body arched, head flung back hard against the wooden deck under his back.

Screams and shouts invaded his fugue. Jarring cracks shuddered through the ship and the galleon under his back tilted precariously. Water splashed, sounding like high tide crashing on shore. His body slipped, moved. The prickling intensified to burning. His free hand scrabbled weakly at the deck and he groaned, drawing on the last of his scant air. His other hand gripped Seaborn tightly. This was what he wanted, what he needed. But he kept sliding, headfirst. His misshapen, dislocated shoulder caught on the rope rail. He released his grip on Seaborn in the shock of pain. The jarring on the taxed joint overtook the agony of healing. It started to retreat, to fade back to tingles.

The ship shuddered and cracked again. A swell carried it on a sickening ride, up and then down. More screams. He slipped again, the rope tugged on his shoulder again and ripped a scream from his throat. And then he was falling, tumbling end-over into the sea.

He hit on his side and the force of it shoved him to his back. His shoulder lurched back into place. He tried to scream again but his mouth and lungs filled with water. The sword spun away beneath the waves. Unable to move and worn from the healing, he let the depths drag him down. Blessed icy numbness started to overtake him. He thought he could still see the glow of the Eyes, liquid and moving through the waves.

Something bumped him . . . a fish? A man? He didn't know. He opened his eyes again to darkness, feeling only the slow drag of the sea all over his skin.

Quiet. Peace.

Not bloody again.

Draken's eyes strained without his meaning to. *Bruche?*

Korde's balls, I never knew someone who wanted to die worse than you. Too damned bad. The gods see fit to keep you alive yet. Cold invaded his body, icier than the sea. Bruche scolded on: *You should know by now the gods make your will their own. I'd have some peace if you'd quit trying resisting it.*

His body started to move without direction from his mind, arms and legs churning the water. Behind it, he felt paralyzed and exhausted. His head turned, his eyes turned. He saw a man waver nearby, highlighted by moonglow. It caught on pale blond hair but faded as the man drifted down. Beyond, a great, dark, sinking shadow. His body swam deeper, toward the blond glow.

You did your job well, but you're not finished yet. The gods would have you save him.

Who?

Galbrait, you bloody fool. Bruche's voice was hard but not uncaring. Draken's body kept swimming toward the drifting man. Bruche . . . Bruche was making him swim. He blinked; the water stung his eyes. He could feel more of himself as Bruche settled into his bone and muscle, as familiar as his own bed and coverlet.

His lungs started to burn. *And you?* he asked to distract himself. *Why are you along for this jaunt?*

The gods' will is mine as well.

He swam faster, joining Bruche's efforts and pushing past them. Reached out, grabbed Galbrait's limp, cold arm. The Prince didn't respond. He'd been hurt, and then dumped in the ocean, surely he was dead? But they started to swim upward anyway.

Clever, that. With the sword and the healing. Good to see you haven't lost your touch.

Just swim, Bruche. His chest seized on the last of the air; it was all he could do not to open his mouth and suck in water. His newly healed heart seemed to twist in his chest.

They emerged a few heartbeats later, Draken gulping air. He pulled Galbrait up into a secure embrace so he could hold his head above water, though the Prince was still and limp. He coughed up water until his throat stung. At last he mastered himself and looked around wildly. Wreckage and survivors scattered the waves. Men and women shouted, climbed on floating bits of wood. Half of the *Kingsblood* had tilted to its side and was sinking, the edges of sails, top-most mast, and rail still above the waves, but not for long. The other half was . . . gone. The *Bane* had freed herself and eased away, though her sails hung ragged and limp. The Brînian sailors were at the rail, staring out over the wreckage, shouting down to survivors. Draken rode a swell, wondering if Galbrait could possibly be alive, if his men were shouting taunts or offering aid.

He started swimming awkwardly that way. It was slow going with one arm, though Bruche kicked his legs rhythmically. The Monoean survivors were too busy scrabbling for their own lives to pay them mind and even with bright Zozia and powerful Khellian lighting the scene, Draken was certain his dark hair and skin made him a mere shadow against the black sea.

Draken paused to rest and spotted Aarinnaie, picking her out only by the silhouette of her mass of curls flying loose around her head. She called his name, voice high-pitched and frantic, cutting through the shouts of the clamor of frantic Monoeans.

"I'm here." His voice was too low, rough from swallowed water and exhaustion. He coughed again, tasting salt-tinged bile, and cleared his throat. "Aarinnaie! I'm here."

She turned toward him, scanned the seas. She made to climb the rail and jump but someone else pulled her back. Her screams of protest pierced the night, momentarily quieting the din of the survivors in the water. The silvery shape of Osias appeared, pointed. Halmar edged to the rail and then dove over in a perfect arc, splitting the wood-strewn waves with barely a splash.

Halmar emerged moments later near Draken, looked for him, and swam his way.

"Take the Prince." Draken shoved the limp body to Halmar. "Get him aboard."

"I came for you, Khel Szi," Halmar said, though he slipped a strong arm around Galbrait's chest. The Prince's head lolled to one side, eyes rolled back.

"I can swim."

Halmar nodded and turned to swim back.

Without thought, without words, Bruche's presence filled Draken's body again. He drew in a great draught of air and dove deep. All noise cut off but for Bruche's voice.

It's on some ship wreckage, sinking slow. I saw the glow, sensed the bloody thing. Bruche sounded oddly reverent.

Draken had barely dared to hope. He swam with the spirit's strength behind him, cutting the water, deeper and deeper until he approached the shadow of the ship-half that had sunk. Lungs burning he stared hard into the moonlit gloom underwater. Blinked. There. A faint glow coming from *below*. It lit a drifting body.

He pushed harder, lungs screaming as he released some air. As a sailor he was no stranger to ocean swimming, but he'd never been this deep. His swimming slowed, his mind thick and sluggish. Thoughts moved with the current, gentler down here under the waves. Back to his seafaring days, back in the navy . . . he'd had a friend, a second-mate called Waen. They'd gambled and whored together as young men, before Lesle, when Draken realized his uniform would attract women, if not the most chaste or noble . . .

Draken!

He blinked as his hand reached out for the pale light. His thumb found the loose leather on the grip and he relaxed into Bruche's control.

CHAPTER THIRTY-ONE

He lay on deck coughing up seawater, all his weight on his bad shoulder. It ached. His lungs and throat stung. His fingers gripped the familiar loose leather wrapping.

Be easy, mate.

He couldn't think to answer, couldn't think past the notion that Bruche was still with him. He was soaking wet and freezing.

The spirit drew back from Draken's consciousness, giving him a little space. Draken blinked up at a drenched long tunic clinging to a narrow leg. He tried to say Aarinnaie's name, but it only brought another round of coughing. His hand gripped Seaborn as coughing wracked his body. It went on for some time.

"Be easy. You had a rough go but you're fair safe now." Osias, his hand on Draken's back. It was the only warm thing Draken could feel.

Reality snuck back into his mind. He lay in a cold puddle on the cold deck of the *Bane*, night air seeping into his wet skin. He shivered and tried to push up, still coughing a little. Tyrolean caught his arm and helped him to sit.

"How did you do that?" Aarinnaie said. "You were unconscious. Half-drowned. How did you keep hold of your sword?"

"I can't believe you found it," Tyrolean said.

Draken could only shake his head and cough out, "Galbrait—alive?"

A beat. "Aye," Tyrolean said. "Halmar sewed him up. Says the cold water slowed the blood flow. They got the water from his lungs. He's still unconscious."

And may not be right again. Brace yourself, friend. You know what drowning can do.

He did. He'd seen a sailor drowned and brought back to the living. Unable to speak, to feed himself, helpless as a babe. What would he do with Galbrait if it came to that?

Throw him to Ma'Vanni. It's a better peace than life as a simpleton.

The spirit took command of Draken's arm and slid the blade into the soaked sheath still strapped to his leg. Draken drew in a careful breath and eased it from his throat. No coughing. He started to climb to his feet; Aarinnaie took one arm and Tyrolean the other. He shrugged them off and limped to the rail to look over. He only almost stumbled once, but he gripped the rail tightly. Osias joined him there, glowing silently. But he gave Draken a nod.

"Halmar's spitting mad," Aarinnaie mentioned. "He said you said you'd follow him when you gave him Galbrait."

"Had to get the godsdamned sword. How many Monoeans are left?"

"Less than half," Tyrolean answered.

A violent shiver ran through Draken. "You've just been watching them drown?"

"They attacked us," Aarinnaie said indignantly.

Truth, they had. "Call out orders. Drop lines over the side. Pull in as many as you can."

"We can't feed them all, much less control them. They'll take the ship and—"

Draken gave Aarinniae a flat look.

"I'll, um. Fetch you a cloak," Aarinnaie said with abrupt docility Draken didn't trust, and turned away.

"Aye, Your Highness," Tyrolean said, faint amusement tugging at the corners of his lips. He turned toward Joran.

Draken stared down at two men clinging to a makeshift raft of ship's hull. Their bodies were in the water and they glanced up at the *Bane* but said nothing. The shouts had ceased. The Monoeans had given up.

And you're about to be their savior, Bruche said. *Well done.*

I'm short fighting men. And Galbrait needs his people about him.

You'll make them swear to him, then?

That's the idea, but you know what they say about best laid plans. The first of the ropes were dropping over.

◆ ◆ ◆

Forty-seven. It was a number Draken wouldn't soon forget. The rescued Monoeans sat in ordered rows on the deck, a few obstinately rebellious fellows chained but most subdued by a few arrows trained on them and threats of being tossed back overboard. The sea sharks had come, turning the water around the ship into a roiling frenzy. Since most of the sailors left in the water were mere floating bodies, screams were few. The scent of brine and blood rose around the ship though, and Draken didn't want to wait around for the bigger monsters that made distracted sea sharks their prey. He gave Joran the order to set sail. They needed to get moving again, though it would take some careful maneuvering through the big chunks of debris, some of which were big and jagged enough to punch a hole through the *Bane's* hull if they met at top speed. The ship was hindered by lack of sails anyway. They'd get to clear water and make repairs.

The Ashen watched him charily as the healer bound his arm to his chest to immobilize his bad shoulder. It made Draken feel off-center. That, and getting used to having Bruche again.

Along with the soldiers, the Brînians had plucked a half-dozen casks from the sea as well. It was something of a Monoean superstition to leave some barrels half-full for just this sort of experience; it still wasn't anything like enough water for everyone aboard.

As Joran gave the orders, Tyrolean picked his way through the Monoeans crowding the small deck and ducked lines as the crew drew sails. "Galbrait is awake, Your Highness."

Draken heaved a sigh. It shifted his shoulder enough to deepen the dull ache. *Ah now, it won't be so bad. The lad idolizes you.*

Draken suppressed a snort and nodded to Tyrolean. He cast a glance out over the mostly light heads of the Ashen . . . *Captives? Soldiers?* Bruche asked. Draken didn't know, and he knew less what to do with them. "See they are given water and a little to eat."

"Bound to run out of provisions, Khel Szi," Joran said.

"We're not so far off the Zozian Coast and we can feed and water fair well at Khein," Draken said. "Third rations until then. Do *you* think the water will hold out?"

"Only just," Joran answered, shaking his head *no.*

Ah. No point in panicking the crew. Clever lad.

"See that it does."

"And if it doesn't, Khel Szi?"

"We're not throwing anyone overboard, if that's what you're asking."

Joran cast a worried glance to the lightening sky, which was turning brilliant blue. A steady wind buffeted the *Bane.* A good sailing day. But the *Bane's* crew had sour expressions, which deepened whenever they looked at the Ashen.

Sparing enemies thus isn't done. Brînians don't trust it.

"Pray Agria for rain and a stiff wind toward Akrasia then. We'll get this over with as soon as possible," Draken said.

He turned toward the back, edging his way through the prisoners to get to his cabin. Ashen leaned in to make way for him, and eyes followed him.

More than one face was reddening under the rising sun, though the wind was fair cool enough. The sails cast a little shade but room would need to be made for some of them in the hull. Sunsick would sweep through them, especially on thin water rations.

The cabin smelled of blood and salt. Tyrolean halted at the doorway as Draken stepped through. Aarinnaie leaned her hip against the table, arms crossed over her chest.

Galbrait opened his eyes. "Your Highness." He didn't struggle to move, just lay still. His voice was breathy and weak, but even enough. "Apparently I owe you my life."

"I only pulled you from the sea," Draken said. "Your life you owe to the healers and to the gods."

A slight quirk of a humorless smile. "They wouldn't have had their chance at me if not for you pulling me out."

Draken assented with a nod, but he wondered. After all, the gods had given him back Bruche. "Aarin, would you take Tyrolean and see to the provisions. I don't trust our crew to do the figuring fairly."

She cast another glance at Galbrait, but obediently went. Draken waited until they'd shut the door behind them to ease down onto the bench from the table. His knee hadn't benefited from his dunking, and his back and chest had stiffened from having his arm bound to his chest.

"We pulled nearly fifty of your men from the sea," he said.

Galbrait shifted on the bed, wincing as he made to sit up against the cushion stained in his blood. The sea had left his hair knotted and his injury had left his skin pale. "They won't want me."

"You must at least try," Draken said. "Speak to them when the wind and lack of water have worn them a bit, when the shock of it all falls away. They'll realize they need you."

"Monoea does not want me."

He suppressed a sigh at the melodrama and reminded himself Galbrait had barely seen twenty Tradeseasons. Still, that shouting about there being a king on board niggled at him. Who had he meant? Himself or Draken?

"You can't take the rebels' opinion as your own," Draken said. "Your mercy will indebt these men to you. They might well be enough to sway the rest of the army in your favor."

"In *your* favor, you mean."

A fair point.

Draken mentally shoved the spirit back. "I've never made a pretense that keeping war from Akrasia was my first concern. That serves Monoea, as well."

Galbrait's brows drew together as he considered this. "I'll see them," he said at last.

"When you can walk well," Draken said. "They need you strong."

Another hesitation, and then a grudging nod.

Bruche heaved a sigh that achieved Draken's lips. *Best you could hope for.*

◆ ◆ ◆

A sevennight later, they'd made all the repairs they could and had continued limping along on their course, having given up all prayer of catching the rest of the fleet. A few of the Monoeans had made themselves useful: hauling lines and raising sails, mending rope. There was no sunsalve aboard a Brînian ship so several Ashen were soon so burned they required the cover of below, and far more than their share of water. The rest did their best to stay out of the way, helping only when they were bid, talking amongst themselves, and watching the Brînians with narrowed eyes. Doubtless they all thought themselves prisoners of war and Draken did nothing to dissuade that. He spoke to none of them, but he heard his name in their conversations. Some few had placed him as Aissyth's bastard mixbreed cousin and made no secret of their contempt.

For Draken's part, he took his turn at guard and spent time in the aft cabin muttering over maps of Akrasia with Tyrolean and Bruche, working out where the Monoeans would land, which town they'd attack first, and how to best stop them. He also had ordered the prisoners given less water than the first day. Bruche thought it best to keep them weak and half-sick and Draken agreed.

Galbrait relieved Draken's worries; he emerged from the cabin the next morning with his back straight. A line of stitches marred his head, bruising spilling out from the wound like mud stirred from the bottom of a clean stream. His torq with the skystones glinted in the morning sun. He'd scrubbed his hair and body clean. Despite his lack of fine clothes, he looked every inch a Prince.

Or King.

Draken held back while Galbrait waited quietly to get their attention. They noticed him, in small groups at first, and edged his way. A couple bowed their heads to him but stopped when they saw no one else did.

"You know who I am. You might know I am the last of my line. Our country is in revolution and they killed the rest of my family, tried to kill me." Galbrait paused. "You were on your way to an unauthorized attack. Do any of you know where your orders came from?" A rough silence, broken only by a couple of coughs. Several heads dipped, not out of respect but to avoid the Prince's gaze.

Do you think they know? Draken asked Bruche.

I think they won't tell, the spirit replied.

"It matters not. I have the blood of kings running through me, and though I wanted none of you, here you are."

"It's why there's a rebellion, that arrogance," someone called from the back of the group. "That and your father's."

"My lord father is dead," Galbrait said, "and it was a rebel sword that did it."

"Tam's right," another called. "Arrogance!"

"Silence." It was a low shout but it carried through the crowd and rigging noises and the roll of the waves. Draken had a deal of practice at being heard at sea. Heads jerked toward him.

"Whatever it is, it is done," Draken said. "Kneel."

They stared at him, incredulous to a man.

"Kneel or I shall throw you over myself. You all swore to his father once, my cousin. He is dead, and Galbrait is his heir. *Kneel.*"

They stared some more and then the early ones who'd dipped their chins to Galbrait dropped to their knees. Faces red, muttering, the rest slowly followed suit. Galbrait waited, staring down at them, silent. At last he looked at Draken. Bruche groaned. The lad looked as if had no idea what to do or say next. But he spoke.

"I own you by blood and birthright. Do you swear yourselves freely to my service as well?"

There was a mumble of agreement. Draken studied the faces to make sure they were all at least pretending to pledge to Galbrait. His fingers twitched, anxious to find an example of what happened to those who disobey. But they all asquiesed.

"Our people have carried war to Akrasia's shores. They have attacked the Prince of Brîn in these efforts, nearly killed him, and me. Despite this, my cousin has twice drawn me from rebel swords and Ma'Vanni's embrace." Galbrait turned to Draken and knelt, moving slowly and stiffly. "I pledge myself to Prince Draken, who gave me new life. I am no King, nor Prince. Not any longer. I am a soldier, if he'll have me."

Silence. The Ashen stared at him in shock. Then a rumble of anxious dismay rose up from them.

Draken stared down at the bright head before him. Even the waves seemed to go quiet in the wake of this news. His body tightened. He didn't want this, another slave to the whims of the gods. *Damned bloody fool.*

Draken, use him. He just swore to you. You can use him to stop this war on Akrasia.

How? He's just given up all claim to the throne.

He can't disavow his own blood anymore than you could. When the time comes, I have a hunch his loyalty will be very valuable.

Gods curse him, Bruche was probably right.

Draken laid Seaborn on Galbrait's shoulder, hating himself as he said the words, "Rise and welcome to my service, Galbrait of House Khel."

CHAPTER THIRTY-TWO

Anchoring at Khein was rough, hardly the fair bright waters and peaceful skies of his exile landing. Draken glanced up at the grey skies and a couple of drips snuck past the hood of his oiled cloak. He rubbed at his nose with the back of his hand. "It was raining when I left, too. If I didn't know better, I'd say the gods are displeased with my being here."

Or with that trick you pulled on the Monoeans. Hardly keeping with their intent of your new gifted ability of healing.

"Not every weather event hinges on your decisions, Khel Szi." Osias shook his head. "That was Korde displeased with me."

At least the moons weren't blood red. "I'm the one who cut your fetter, remember?"

Osias chuckled low. "I know you resent the gods' favor, Draken. But it is far worse to be out of it than in."

"Tell that to Bruche, who isn't getting his 'well-deserved rest,' as he likes to put it."

It is well deserved. What it isn't, is happening.

Osias gave him a slight grin as if he'd heard the swordhand speak. He'd relaxed more the closer they got to Akrasia. Never mind that they were still a whole country away from Eidola. But then, perhaps he wouldn't be going back there.

"Do we really need to go ashore tonight?" Aarinnaie huddled under her own cloak.

"They're starving and dehydrated. We need to get everyone off the ship and onto land. There will be provisions enough at Khein for all." He glanced back at the Monoean soldiers sitting in rows in the stinging rain. This was the third day of it. The Monoeans, weakened from their dumping into the sea, harsh sun, and days without proper food and water, were already getting sick. He wished for Thom, who could manage them with barely a blink of his one eye.

263

"Who will guard them while we go?" Galbrait asked. "What if they take over the ship and run? We should bring them."

Draken regarded the young Prince. What had he been doing in the Norvern Wildes for all these years? Not learning to care for his people, that was certain. Did he not recognise how poorly they were?

"Most of them are too weak to walk over to the rail to take a piss," he said dryly. "I think Joran and the ship are safe enough from mutiny."

"We have greater concerns, Your Highness. Khein is a well-known stronghold. If the Ashen fleet came this way—and it's likely they did or at least dropped some soldiers here—it could be under siege," Tyrolean said.

"Or worse," Aarinnaie added, as if it needed to be said.

Osias stared out at the dark shore. The forest sprung from the ground like a living shadow, leaves and branches wavering in the rain and breeze. "Ashen might fill those woods. We wouldn't see them until they were upon us."

Or Moonlings, eh? Bruche said.

And their Abeyance, Draken answered.

Even they wouldn't dare use it against you.

Draken wasn't so sure about that. He hadn't forgotten Parne, nor the reports of animals killed along the border. Things here could have gotten very much worse in his absence.

That thought didn't make the trip from ship to shore any easier. Draken and Tyrolean fought the sea with their skiff oars until Draken's shoulders ached. Bruche had to numb his bad one with cold to carry him through. Sickening swells pitched and rolled the narrow skiff. Everyone was tense and wet by the time Tyrolean jumped out to haul it to shore. They gathered under the thick tree canopy to talk.

"I can find us the road, but Draken is right. We need him to get into the gates of the fortress." Osias looked all around, walked a circle around the little party, his head up, listening. Rain pattered the ocean. He gleamed in the dark, his silver hair slick and shiny.

Setia had her arms wrapped around herself, holding her cloak tight about her, but her nostrils flared as she sniffed the air. All Draken smelled was damp, but he felt a trepidation he thought he'd left behind in Monoea. "Let me guess. You sense Moonlings."

Osias nodded, still staring all around. "Just watching. For now."

Draken wished for horses a short while later as the thick, wet foliage clung to his cloak. As they made their way through the woods the rain eased and a bit of moonlight broke through the clouds, revealing their strained, dirty faces. Every now and then a big leaf overhead would dump a load of water onto some unsuspecting head. Draken finally drew Seaborn with a growl and started hacking away at the foliage. The rain eased, leaving soupy humidity in its wake. Draken sweated fiercely, but kept on. The physicality of cutting his way through the woods kept him from bolting up to the main road to Auwaer to seek out Elena. But first bloody things first.

Ooo. Techy.

Do you even feel the rain, Bruche?

No. But I also do not taste your wine nor feel the soft thighs of your Queen.

Draken considered this. *And yet you know when I am injured.*

Aye, when it lasted more than a few breaths. Your balance alters. And there is the screaming . . .

Very funny.

I'm not being—

A waft of something drifted by. *Sh! What is this?*

Draken stopped hacking to listen. Everyone around him stopped as well. There was a change in the atmosphere of the woods. He strained to take it in with all his senses. "Do I smell smoke?" he whispered.

Setia lifted her head to sniff the air, nostrils flared. "Aye, smoldering in the wet."

Aarinnaie looked around, her eyes wide. "It's too quiet."

"No animal sounds," Galbrait said.

That's what he was doing in the Norvern Wildes. Communing with animals.

Draken ignored Bruche. Doubtless his station in the Wildes had made Galbrait a decent tracker.

"There weren't any before. That's one of the ways we know Moonlings are near." The Abeyance had no sound. Maybe Moonlings carried it with them wherever they went. Intriguing thought, but it didn't answer their immediate questions about what was causing everyone's unease. A lifetime of living in danger had taught him those instincts were rarely wrong, and he was surrounded by people who were skilled at detecting and eliminating threat.

He looked at Osias and tipped his head.

Osias moved soundlessly to one side, disappearing into the forest. Setia went the other direction.

Galbrait bounced on his heels. His voice was low. "I can scout, Your Highness. I spent ten years tracking in woods."

It had been a long sevennight, Galbrait moping and unsure, spending much of it resting. The scar across his head was a sharp, red line punctuated by black thread. That he felt good enough to offer . . . "Go. Do not tarry, nor engage anyone you see."

"Yes, Your Highness." He slipped off ahead, fleet and silent as Setia.

"You didn't let me go," Aarinnaie said, her arms crossed.

"He can manage to look without killing whatever he finds," Draken retorted.

They walked on for a time, until Galbrait returned to them, shaking his head. "No people. But there's a road, I think." As he gestured, a body thrust itself through the brush. It crumpled onto the ground between Draken and Galbrait, leaking blood from several gashes. Everyone but Aarinnaie and Draken grunted in alarm. The lined, bloodshot eyes stared. Bloody spittle stained his lips.

Draken drew his blade and scanned the woods. Nothing. Galbrait stared down at the dead man, his lips parted. Tyrolean, Halmar and Konnan encircled them, swords out, eyes on the forest.

An Akrasian who didn't die well. Pity. Bruche didn't have one shred of sympathy in his tone.

There's no such bloody thing as dying well. Draken nearly jumped out of his skin as Osias reappeared. He nodded to Tyrolean and frowned at the dead man. The moon tattoo distorted as his brow furrowed. "Recently dead."

"Very recently." And they had made enough noise that this man's killer had to know they were there. He glanced at Osias. Draken had met his first bane in these woods. It had tried to force him to kill himself. What if this poor sod was the same, only the bane had succeeded?

Osias met Draken's eyes and shook his head. "He didn't do this to himself," Osias said. "Nor did a bane make him."

Setia knelt by him. "He's still warm."

Draken shifted closer to study the dead man under the bright moonlight filtered through broad, dripping leaves. Runoff splashed onto the man's face. Draken tugged at his neckline, pulled up his bloody shirt, checked the man's belt. He shook his head. He didn't recognize him. If he was part of a Khein cohort, he wore no mark of rank. "Civilian."

"Maybe a Moonling killed him," Aarinnaie whispered.

"No. I don't think so." Moonlings had the Abeyance. No need to waste strikes other than the killing sort. He lifted a limp hand. There were slashes down the back of the forearm. "Defensive cuts. The man was in a fight."

Aye, but what are the odds he drops right into the middle of our group? This is a message.

But what could such a message mean? He studied the man anew. Dug through his pockets again, his vest . . . he pulled out a flat envelope of leather. He had to tug a bit and the corner tore. It had been sewn into the man's vest, stitched to keep it in place.

"That's a messenger packet," Tyrolean said.

"I thought the dead man *is* the message." Draken turned it over in his hands.

"A foe would have already slit our throats," Aarinnaie said.

"But a friend would just talk to us, aye?" He opened the leather packet, which took some doing because it was folded into an intricate locking pattern. He couldn't do it without tearing a perforated piece of the leather.

"It's so they know it's been looked at. It can't be opened without tearing." Draken looked up at Tyrolean, who shrugged. "Aye, well. I designed it."

A slight grin slipped through as Draken pulled the parchment free. It was in Akrasian, and the few words he did know was no help. He handed it over to Tyrolean, who frowned as he read. "It's in code, but it amounts to news of a siege at Khein." He looked up. "Your fortress is under attack, Your Highness. You've lost over a hundred servii."

He eased a breath. A hundred wasn't so devastating to the thousands who held the fortress. Demoralizing though.

"Where was the message headed?" Galbrait asked.

Draken looked at him in surprise.

See Draken? There's hope for the lad yet.

"To Auwaer, I expect," Tyrolean said.

"Long hike, that," Draken said. "His are boots and clothes for walking, not riding. Besides, the Queen and her First Captain might still be at Brîn."

"We've been gone some sevennight. Long enough for her to move."

The thought slammed through him: If she lost the baby, moving wouldn't hurt her.

Be easy. You do not know the cause, or if she isn't still at the Citadel. The baby may be born and well. No use guessing.

Bruche was right. *I had missed you, but not for being the voice of reason.*

I have my moments.

"All right. First we had better see what the siege looks like at the fortress. We still have the Monoeans to feed and water." Maybe the village was still sound . . . likely not, if it were overrun with Ashen.

"Soldiers who will likely turn back to their masters once they see who has the upper hand," Galbrait said. He rubbed his hand over his face.

"You're their commander. They will follow you if you order them." Draken spoke with a confidence he didn't feel. He rose and directed Aarinnaie and Tyrolean to get as close as they could to the fortress to find out the condition of the siege. Osias offered to find Setia and take her on a quick scout for Moonlings. They could reconverge at the skiff.

"Galbrait, with me," Draken said.

"Where are we going?" Galbrait said.

"To see how far the siege extends and count the enemy. Quietly now."

Draken led him out and around from where he knew the fortress to be. He hadn't actually ever seen it; he'd been redirected by a couple of Escorts the last time he'd been this way—his arrival in Akrasia—and he hadn't been back since. But he'd studied the maps and there was nothing for it but to lead as if he knew what he was doing. They moved along the road but kept to the trees in near silence, thank whatever gods might have taken them in their favor. They weren't noticed by an Ashen scout walking ahead. His grey armor made gentle clinks and made him appear ghostlike in the moon-dappled woods. Draken raised a hand and Galbrait had the good sense to fall still.

It's only one. Kill him. Cold started to fill Draken's sword arm.

Hold. They'll know if he doesn't come back.

They might not, if they are so many. Perhaps he's the lad who killed our runner.

I don't think so. The Ashen was just a scout. *And someone will surely miss him.*

And, if they were stealthy enough, they could follow him. He let the scout get well ahead. Galbrait gave him a look but Draken ignored it. After a bit he glanced back. Galbrait ghosted through the wet woods nearly as well as Aarinnaie. The damp quieted their movements but perhaps the Norvern Wildes had trained Galbrait up even better than Draken thought.

The Ashen led them near to the direction Draken had been taking, though they went closer to the fortress than he'd planned. He heard the rumble of voices, but they were low, at-ease sounds, not the voices of people in pitched battle. He relaxed slightly. He hadn't known what he was coming upon.

I get the sense Ashen like to fight during the daylight hours.

Maybe. When Draken had fought at sea for the Monoeans, they'd been mostly about defense, which meant battles came whenever enemies brought them. The skulking Black Guard had worked at night, but most of their operations had been covert, the squads small.

The rain had stopped fully. The forest had been cleared a good distance from the fortress walls, baring a shock of night sky overhead. The clouds were bright grey, with white halos where the moonlight tried to penetrate it. The scout strode on, heedless of his followers, but Draken crouched in the shadows, feeling Galbrait take a knee by him. There was less need to be quiet here; the soldiers were busy amongst themselves.

The walls of the fortress were uneven and craggy, as if it had been erected quickly on the backs of slaves who cared only to avoid their next whipping. Convenient for climbing, though defensive crenellations and great pots on hinged levers spoke to some level of defense. He'd been briefed, but it was last season when everything about being a Prince was new and overwhelming.

The only impression he recalled was a lack of funding. It wasn't the most important fortress in the realm. Not until now.

Tents filled the open space at the foot of the walls, what appeared to be hundreds of them, curving in a wide swath and disappearing around the far side of the fortress. Fires burned amid them all. Draken's stomach churned. He couldn't remember how long it had been since he'd had a full meal.

Focus.

Draken scowled at Bruche's admonition but did as he was bid.

They certainly had settled into their siege. Soldiers grouped around some fires, cleaning armor and weapons or cooking and eating. They spoke and laughed. Others burned low, unattended. Many of the flaps on the tents were closed. Their nonchalance surprised him. But there seemed some other lacking quality. He couldn't put his finger on it.

He stared out at one fire a few tents over. The soldiers sat very still, hunched over. His eyes narrowed.

That's a grim lot.

But why? The closer group was chuckling over some joke or another, and others chatted while they supped. Draken had never sat siege before, but he'd heard tales. An awful lot of waiting. All in all it was a more peaceful type of battle, and it didn't match what he knew of Monoean military tactics at all, which tended to be more about rushing in and banging on the enemy until someone died.

There were decent, only slightly inaccurate maps of Akrasia in the maproom at the royal palace at Ashwyc. Even Draken had known upon landing here in exile that while Khein was a large post, it certainly was not the largest. The biggest concentration of soldiers were in and around the cities: Auwaer, Reschan, Brîn, Septonshir in the lake region, and the chilly Hoarfrost Sea trading cities of Algir and Rhineguard. Khein amounted to Draken's personal force, the soldiers that answered to the Night Lord directly. It was not a disregardable force at five thousand, but hardly the largest. The twenty thousand or so soldiers near Auwaer could wipe out the Monoean force, which he'd given the generous count of seven thousand, given the information culled from his rescued Ashen. That didn't count the unknown number of forces who had arrived before the attack at Seakeep, nor any forces since. He had a bad feeling, since the fleet of twenty ships had sailed from Sister Bay so efficiently, that they were on the heels of more.

They stared and watched for a long time. Draken studied the walls of his fortress, watching the dark shadows of servii appear in the crenels. Occasionally moonlight glinted off the shining points of spears or arrowheads. He still felt something was quite wrong with the scene, something he'd missed. At last he signaled a retreat to Galbrait and they melted back into the soft woods.

"If they'd kept quiet when they landed, made a quick march through these Moonling Woods, and headed straight for Auwaer, they might be there by now with Khein likely not the wiser," Draken said.

Galbrait twitched a glance back the way they'd come. "How many soldiers are in that fortress?"

He stared at the Prince for a moment, trying to gauge what to tell him. He reminded himself Galbrait had sworn to him. Grim as the lad had gotten, he seemed solid. "Five thousand. They do run regular patrols but with careful planning . . ."

"So . . . if they could pass by unnoticed, it's a waste of troops really."

"Right. And even if Khein did learn about it, they were shackled with me out of the country."

Galbrait furrowed his brow. "Why?"

"They answer to me. They only move on my command. They are sworn to me, their Night Lord first, before all else. They could send a message, but they can't fight without my orders."

I'll bet the Ashen don't know that.

If Galbrait's expression was any way to judge, the old spirithand was right.

"It's a way to balance power," Draken said. "Should rebels take command of the army, for instance, there are still five thousand servii outside their command. Not a huge force, but enough to shelter and protect the Queen, if need."

"Is that what happened before? We heard rumors of civil war here. Even as far as the Wildes."

Draken looked away. Not times he liked to revisit. "Khein helped put the pieces back together and stem further fighting, aye. That's all."

He ignored Galbrait's curious look. The lad could ask Queen Elena about it for all Draken cared; he just didn't want to go there again. He went too often in his dreams as it was. "None of which answers our questions. Why are they here? Much less with so many . . . troops . . ."

He stared into the moon-dappled shadows of the woods, voice fading as he thought hard. That one fire with the hunched soldiers kept nagging at him. He couldn't see it well enough, too far a distance. But what was wrong with them? Had they been dressed down for insubordination? In his experience disobedience was punished severely and immediately. Monoean soldiers were definitely not left to sulk.

Bruche agreed. *They were fair still. It was difficult to see so far, but none of them moved, did they?*

No. Which would be odd, but I think... His mind whirred with the implication and locked on one fact. The whole camp had been far too quiet for so many tents and soldiers. *They aren't real.* "Did you count the enemy, Galbrait?"

"What I could see, Your Highness, but—"

"And how many do you estimate we saw?"

Galbrait blinked rapidly. "Three hundred by my count. But with the tents and the fires—"

"Aye. All those buttoned up tents and unattended fires." That unmoving group. Not grim or under reprimand. But *false.*

Galbrait's eyes widened. His hand went to the torq at his throat as if it were a noose. "You think it's a ruse."

"Three hundred soldiers, which I think is a high estimate, but they were made to look like many more. I'd guess they're holding that siege with a hundred or less."

"To keep them from attacking the main army."

"Aye, and to handicap me."

"But how would they know? I didn't know Khein was your fortress, and I'm Prince."

Draken didn't snap back that he was a damned Prince too, nor that there was much Galbrait didn't know. It took a great deal of willpower.

Don't bother trying to impress me. I've been wanting to hit him for a sevennight now.

Draken grunted and cast a wary glare around at the trees and shadows. "Our friends the Moonlings must have told them."

Galbrait shook his head. "What? Why? I thought Moonlings hated people."

"Moonlings *are* people."

"Other people, I mean."

"I've a bad feeling they were already friendly with the Ashen. I didn't think of it before, but when I refused to go to Queen Elena on behalf of their enslaved, they threatened me with this very thing. Slaughter. Civil war."

Galbrait's face tightened. "What now?"

"There is nothing standing between them and my servii inside Khein but us. Soon it may be that we're the only thing standing between them and the Queen. If that happens, Akrasia falls."

"Isn't that what . . . the Monoean rebels want? To take Akrasia."

"They have no idea what Akrasia is, what dangers lurk here. They may try to take Akrasia, but they will never hold her." It was becoming increasingly clearer. "We save my people, we save yours. Come."

"Back to the ship?"

He wanted to find a way into the fortress, *his* fortress. He wanted to warn his servii that they could march out, wipe their feet on the Ashen at their gate, and rally them to the real fight. The last thing he wanted to do was walk all the way back to the ship.

"It'll be tough getting inside there." Bruche tugged his lips into a feral grin. "For that, we'll need a ghost. Let's go catch us one, shall we?"

CHAPTER THIRTY-THREE

Instead, the Ghost found them. Aarinnaie and Tyrolean caught them up before they could reach the skiff.

"Ashen on shore," Tyrolean reported. "Fair curious about your ship."

Draken was glad he'd ordered the banners drawn and the name covered with a tarp. "Won't take long for them to work out it's mine."

"If they bring a ship round into the Bay, we're trapped," Aarinnaie said.

"Then we must hurry." He explained what they'd worked out about the siege. "We need inside the fortress straightaway."

"Surely your servii will realize the truth of it," Tyrolean said.

"We don't have time to wait them out." He looked at Aarinnaie. "Can you get inside?"

She scowled. "Without getting an arrow through the eye? I don't see how. They'll think I'm a spy or some nonsense."

It's a point. Tempers are bound to be tight inside. And despite your best efforts, there's still little love lost between Brinians and Akrasians.

"They've seen you before, Aarin."

"Yeah, when I was done up like a sundry Akrasian. Who in there would recognize me now?" She tossed her thick braid over her shoulder and pursed her lips in a frown. Truth, days at sea had darkened her skin to a deep, rich brown.

Draken met Aarinnaie's gaze. "I'll have to go then."

◆ ◆ ◆

I don't like it.

Draken shook his head. *Is that how you encouraged Grandfather once his plans were already in play?*

Bruche's deep chuckle filled Draken's chest. He had to clamp down on his jaw to keep it from escaping his lips because he hid too close to the Ashen

273

siege to make noise. The uneven walls loomed up just beyond the miniature mountain range of tents, a shadow against the black night of the godless time before dawn. The fires burned like bright little grounded moons though. The fortress had standing orders to defend itself, but Draken was certain they were ignorant of the truth of the Ashen numbers or they would have crushed them by now and be standing in neat rows awaiting his inspection and orders.

He drew a breath and flexed his fingers, trying to keep his body loose. He had a bow slung over his back in case he needed it, and his sword. It wasn't time yet. At least, he didn't think so.

It just seems like waiting is the hardest bit. Climbing that wall will be much tougher.

The craggy walls would be easy to climb . . . for Aarinnaie. For him and his constantly aching shoulder and bad knee, it would be no small trick. *You're full of helpful wisdom tonight, Bruche. Keep it up and I might arrange to die again.*

A groan. *We've had quite enough of that.*

He kept his eyes on the wall. They narrowed. Was it happening? A light grey . . . *mist* was the only word he could think of . . . slithered over the blackness. He wrinkled his nose against a stench even before he caught a whiff. Mance magic often smelled of dead things and freshly inhabited graves. But maybe this was simple glamour . . . no, the silvery mist took the vague shape of a person and blackened. For a few breaths he had to fight down terror. What if it didn't work? What if that bane bound to Osias's will got free?

His body drew in a long, deep breath. Bruche did it again, for him. No words, just calming air filling his lungs. He nodded and let his shoulders ease and his fists uncurl.

Be ready.

Obviously. But the inane chatter showed how nervous Bruche was. It did little to soothe Draken's nerves. He did his best not to tighten back up. But his hand strayed to the knife in one of his wrist guards, a blade that might soon part flesh.

A flash near the edge of the woods, and a shout.

Answering shouts from within the camp, and boots against the ground.

Something else to his swordhand flared. More shouts. Damp, heavy smoke coated his airways, concealing the scent of death. Thanks to the rain, they didn't have to worry about the entire Moonling Woods going up. But the Moonlings residing here wouldn't be best pleased, nonetheless. Draken's throat screamed to cough as he breathed in smoke; he swallowed and steeled himself against it, still holding. Not time to move yet. Even with so few Monoeans and the cover of godless darkness, his movement could be detected. He knew he had to wait, but the wall beckoned . . . almost a voice. He rose but didn't step forward, bouncing on the balls of his feet, head swiveling between the Ashen nearest him and his friends' distraction on his swordhand.

Floating torches appeared between the trees, bobbing as if carried by something alive. As if *real*.

Nice touch. Bruche snorted. *Banes don't need light to see.*

But the Ashen do.

Several Ashen—he heard them, didn't see them—swept toward the distraction. He wondered if they would catch up any of his friends. There'd been fair little time to plan. But if anyone could pull off enough glamour to fool a paranoid company of Monoeans it was Osias. He just hoped Setia could do her part or this would never work.

He stared at the walls. The bane grew, limbs ribboning against the stone until it looked like a shadowy spider.

And then the world held its breath.

When he had been so anxious to get on with it before, now he paused. "What if it's not only Setia able to manage this? What if the Moonlings are involved?"

His voice sounded hollow and flat against the Abeyance.

Then your friends are dead and all is lost. But that's hardly stopped you before, has it?

Before he had been confined within his own world. Even Monoea felt relatively safe compared to this echoless, lifeless place. The Abeyance was as still as an underground temple crypt. Draken had a disconcerting apathy in this grey otherworld, no air brushing his skin, no quiet rustling or voices, no scent of fires, while also feeling distinctly vulnerable.

He stepped out and ran toward the fortress wall, fleet enough in the filmy nothingness that shrouded the ground to his knees. But he had to consciously force his legs to keep a quick pace. His heart thudded, the only sound piercing the roaring silence. It was like standing on the edge of a cliff; the more he tried not to think about falling the more his mind couldn't resist contemplating the risk.

He reached the wall and put his hands up, pausing the briefest of moments before he started climbing, stone rough under his fingers as he expected, but the same temperature as his skin, neither cold nor warm. Bruche hovered within his mind and body, a quiet chill prepared to aid him if need.

Draken hesitated again when he reached the bane. It clung to the stone two body lengths up, caught like the rest of the living world between moments or between worlds, whichever the Abeyance was. He hadn't been sure the Abeyance would have an effect on the dead, and he doubted it would last long enough. But he couldn't wait out his fear because Setia wasn't experienced and didn't have enough of the right magical blood to hold the Abeyance for long. She only had her limited sundry Moonling instinct to go on. Maybe Osias's magic bolstered hers; Draken had no idea. At any rate, he had to hurry. He started to climb.

The temperature changed as he entered the filmy bane clinging to the stone wall, and the residue of grave-stench and faint damp slicked his skin. *That* the Abeyance could not shield him from. He threw one hand and then the other up the wall, muscles straining with each reach, eager to escape the dead thing. His shoulder spiked with pain and his chest started heaving at the effort. He had been too long on meager ship provisions, too long at rest—

His boot missed a narrow ledge of stone and slipped back over it. His fingers clutched at their handholds and his toes curled in their boots. His bad knee banged against the stone and he gasped. He was just about to grumble to Bruche about the gods' magic failing to heal his old injuries— unhelpful but somewhat satisfying—when the death stench strengthened in his lungs.

His arms strained and he pulled up where he could catch the foothold again. An aching chill, not entirely unlike Bruche, snagged on the bone in his leg. He grimaced as the idea of just letting go slammed through his mind. It seemed so easy . . . it made sense. Why was he even trying anyway? His own servii would more likely shoot him down off the wall than let him climb over.

Bruche locked his fingers on the stone, stilled his body. *At ease, my friend. It's just the bane. You know how to resist them.*

A low rumble, the shifting of bodies and low voices, rose from the ground. The bane corded tight around his leg. He tried to pull up, kick it free, but he couldn't do that without risking tumbling back down the wall . . . *Damn!* A sinking feeling crept through him, more insidious this time. It wrapped a noose around his heart. Draken gasped, but ice filled his lungs. *Just let go.* The voice sounded like Bruche. Curious. Why would he say that just as he forced Draken's fingers to cling to the stone?

A cry went up from below and an arrow sparked against the stone next to his arm, then another, overhead. A bit of mortar crumbled down onto his head.

"CLIMB." Much more forceful this time, and not Bruche. Osias . . . damn, he'd done it again. Draken's body started climbing. The Voice rumbled through him again, wordlessly urging him on. He moved faster, cursing inwardly at his taxed muscles and injuries. More loose stone and mortar rained down on his straining arms. The bane strained to keep hold of him, pulling on Draken's leg. Bruche kicked hard and tightened Draken's grip on the wall. Draken

grimaced; it *hurt*. The bane released him, slithering from his heart and lungs and limbs. Draken could breathe again.

Osias's magical Voice had forced Bruche to move and maybe diverted the arrows, but it certainly had blown his cover. Every Moonling, bane, and Akrasian within a morning's walk knew a Mance was in their midst. Even the Ashen had heard it. Those in the fortress would know as well, and be forewarned of the bane. They might just think it had possession of the man climbing their wall. He sped up, rubbing his fingers raw on each handhold, his healing scratches sending tiny cracks through the stone.

He looked down between his boots to see several Ashen trying to climb after him. The first reached the baneshadow, paused, and tumbled back within the span of a breath. A smarter Ashen started climbing well to one side but the bane fingered out its limbs and caught him. The Ashen was partially concealed within the baneshadow for a few breaths only to emerge, legs and arms pumping futilely against the air, as the ground sucked him back down.

Bruche said something but Draken paid no attention as he stared down in morbid fascination.

Another arrow glanced off Seaborn's scabbard on his back, thudding against his armor and urging him to resume climbing. A direct shot could pierce the thick, boiled leather molded to his back. *Where's Osias's glamour? Their bloody aim is getting better.* Smoke drifted up to his lungs and shouts to his ears. He dared a glance over his shoulder. A tent was aflame. He squinted through the dark, searching for stealthy shadows amid the siege camp. Galbrait, Aarinnaie, and Tyrolean were supposed to be stealing among the tents causing as much havoc as possible. Nothing but darkness broken by a few small spots of fire. The damned moons had all gone to bed.

He heard a shout from above, and the squeal of straining rope. Osias and Aarinnaie had carefully chosen his line of ascent in order to avoid any pots of oil slick or the direct aim of arrows. He had to get close enough to let his servii know he was here to help.

Harsh voices filtered down: "Got a climber."

"Gimme a breath. I've got him." The creak of a bow.

"Damn you, I'm a friendly!" Draken shouted up, his voice hoarse with Bruche's influence on his movements and the strain of climbing.

He made it up two more stones. Arrows pinged the wall around him and another thumped his bracer. He growled softly. Osias was supposed to glamour him enough to keep arrows from hitting him. Maybe he'd gotten too far from him. He lost his grip with that arm and it swung down to his side; fortunately he had good toeholds. His arm hurt like a poker had pierced his wrist, a hot rush of blood cut through Bruche's cold, and bigger cracks sent chunks of grey rock tumbling down the wall as it healed. But something was wrong . . . he glanced down and his stomach turned. The feathered shaft still stuck from his arm. This time the flesh had knit around the arrow. He cursed. Below another Monoean tumbled off the wall. The screams continued as he hit the ground.

From above, a mystified voice: "It's a Brînian, sir."

"Hit by an arrow. Might not be one of theirs."

Draken breathlessly cursed their stupidity. Since when had Monoeans and Brinians ever been friendly on any battlefield? His lungs strained for air as he reached the top. If they chose to shove him back over, he doubted he could manage to cling to the stone. But hands actually reached forward and pulled him over the side. He moaned, the most he could manage, as their grip wrenched the arrow within his healed wrist. They tumbled him over the side of the battlement and four Akrasian servii, dirty and stinking without a stripe of rank among them, crouched around him as a flock of arrows sailed overhead. His sword was an uncomfortable lump against his back and one of theirs was an even more uncomfortable pressure at this throat.

"Why are you here, pirate?" He spat the slur.

Draken shifted his good arm. The servii's blade tightened. He couldn't help saying: "I'm no pirate." But he added in a forced conciliatory tone, "Just show-ing you something, friend." He reached up slowly and tugged on the chain around his neck. The pendant was wedged beneath his armor. One of the servii reached out and tugged, hard. Draken cursed inwardly, hoping she didn't break it. But he didn't speak as it came free.

The servii stared, then the pendant thumped down to his armored chest as if it had burned her. "Your Highness!" Hands reached to help him to a sit. He shrugged free of them and eased back against the wall. His shoulder and knee hurt and the arrow stung in the newformed flesh. He reached over and snapped it between his thumb and two fingers, winced, and then swore aloud as he started undoing the bracer. "Seven bloody gods."

"Be easy, Your Highness. I'm a medic," one of the servii said. Her hands were gentle as he pushed his fingers aside and worked the laces. Underneath the arrow tip poked through the paler skin on the inside of his wrist. Blood streamed from it though the skin had closed cleanly around the arrow. The servii blinked at it.

"Push it through," Draken said.

Her gaze flitted to his.

"Do it." He gritted his teeth.

She shoved on the broken end as quick as she could, but a breathy cry still escaped Draken's lips as the arrow widened the hole in his skin into a broad gash and then came through with a rush of blood. Draken tried to breathe through the pain but his head whirled. The stone beneath him rumbled as the flesh knit.

He opened his eyes to three pairs of widened, lined eyes of the servii. "Aye. I can heal myself. But that's not why I'm here. Take me down to your comhanar." He realized he was using Brinish but the one who'd held the blade on him must have understood because she rose and offered him a hand up. She was tall and stronger than she looked for her rather narrow frame, her eyes outlined in thick, graceful curves. "This way, Your Highness."

He followed her to the ground on a wide staircase with a rusted railing. Fresh pits for bodies smoked in the bailey. He paused. "What's this? From a fight during the seige?" How long had they been holding siege anyway?

"Scouts," she said shortly, also in Brinish. "The Comhanar can explain better than I."

Alongside the cloying smoke the reek of rubbish and human waste rose as they strode to the inner wall. A metal-strapped wooden door hung open under the arched gateway leading into the inner fortress, so security didn't seem too formal an arrangement, even under siege. However, passwords were apparently required and Draken's servii guide didn't know them. Odd thing, passwords at an inner gate that wasn't even locked.

To guard against banes gaining admittance.

That must have been it, because they had been a longtime threat in the Moonling woods. There was a consultation with the guard at the gate, who stared hard at Draken.

Draken shifted from foot to foot, thinking of his friends, his sister, out there at the mercy of a few hundred furious Monoeans. Inside the walls he couldn't hear a thing. He glanced at the sky, just lightening with earliest dawn. No moons remained; it was as if they were playing the old game of Blind-See, in which children pretended not to see the other do the most outrageous things until they couldn't pretend any longer.

The guard pushed past the servii who had brought him down. "The Queen's token. May I see it?"

Courteous, but not subservient in the least. The other guards were watching closely from behind, hands resting on weapons. Draken shoved down his anxious impatience and pulled the pendant from around his neck. He didn't like handing it over to some guard without even a stripe on his tabard. But the servii guard met his gaze steadily.

After a slight hesitation, Draken held it out. "How long have they kept you in siege?"

"Two sevennight."

His brows raised. *Two?* That meant they had arrived well before Draken had left Monoea. It confirmed that more troops had arrived in his absence, but not how many. He had half a dozen other questions ready to spring from his tongue, but he'd just have to ask them of the commander again. Maybe he should just draw his sword but this lot was too jumpy. Even so, they hadn't disarmed him, so he needed to respect that decision in kind by not drawing. Besides, knowing Seaborn, it would just do its ordinary-nicked-up-sword routine right when he needed it to be magical.

The guard held the pendant up. It spun, catching the torchlight, the Queen's image blurring with the headless snake on the back. Draken felt lighter without it, and not in a good way. The pendant and its expensive, thick chain was handed off and disappeared into the darker inner fortress.

After waiting several moments with no return of his necklace, Draken couldn't hold back any longer. "You know, I'm actually rather in a hurry here. I have people outside."

"There are a lot of people outside," the servii guard said.

Not nearly as many as you might think. But that was something to take up with the comhanar.

Apparently the pendant was evidence enough that Draken might actually be inside the fort that the Comhanar herself came down to see. She wore armor, her lined eyes had deep circles under them, and tight lines splayed out from her mouth. Grey tinged her black hair. She held the pendant in one hand and stared up at Draken, who had at least a head of height on her. Then she took a knee. "Your Highness. It's an honor. And a surprise."

"Rise. Your name escapes my memory." He should know, but it had been long days and nights at sea and battle.

She got to her feet, nimble despite the grey tinging her black hair. "Commander Geffen Bodlean, Your Highness."

"How do you know it's me, Commander?"

"I saw you once at court, before we knew who you were, before I was commander at Khein." A slight smile flickered across her face and he wondered if her commission here had been a demotion.

Paranoid, are we?

Just realistic.

Some in Akrasia thought him some sort of savior sent by the gods, but he knew he had plenty of enemies, too, as well as suffering from the rampant prejudice between the races. The rare Akrasian would readily accept a position under a Brînian, Prince or no. The rare Akrasian would accept a position under a commander of any other race.

"You look a little different, but not so much off your father that I wouldn't recognize a Prince of Brîn. How may I help you, Prince Draken?"

"I'm here to help you, actually. Is there somewhere we can talk?"

She gave a crisp nod and held out the pendant to him. "And get you a bite to eat. You look like you could use it." She guided him under the archway and through a courtyard sizeable enough to graze horses in. A few muddy mounts were loose and nosing puddles and sparse grasses. At the entrance to the main building, a rough stone monolith, its size belied by the walls outside, Draken bent to remove his boots out of habit.

She stopped and shook her head. "It's not necessary."

Mud tracked the entry hall and the corridor already. He straightened and followed her. "Has it been raining much?"

"For bloody days. But I can't complain. We need the water with the siege. Here we are."

A fire burned in the hearth of a monastical, small room. A few fat-burning torches stank in their brackets. A broad table sat in the middle, surrounded by a haphazard collection of chairs, and a couple of auxilory pieces of furniture rested against the far, windowless wall. Maps covered the surface of one end of the table and the other had what must be her personal array of weapons: a naked sword and two knives, a fine Mance-style longbow and a heavy quiver of arrows. Several muddy boots had rested under the table lately.

Draken frowned. "You disarmed to meet me?"

She gave a small bow before crossing to a sideboard. "Only proper. Drink? We've wine. Not very good, but there you are."

"Thank you." He took the cup and sipped. She was right. It was tangy and sour on the tongue as if it had gone off. But he was thirsty so he drank.

Besides, it's your fortress. It's your wine.

Indeed it was. He looked around again at the dingy room. "I think I've neglected you here too long."

She shrugged, though he barely made out the gesture under her full armor, molded metal plates over leather. It had been a nice suit once, but now the firelight picked out every ding and scrape in the dulled metal. It had been a long time since it had seen oil or paint. "It's been ten Sohalias since the last Night Lord died and Khein has always been an afterthought."

"At the moment, you are not, though." Down to business, then. "Do you realize there are far fewer Ashen outside these walls than they would have you think?"

She frowned. It was a few breaths before she answered. Draken passed the time finishing his goblet of awful wine.

"We knew they had too many tents for the numbers of troops we actually saw, but we sent a scout out a sevennight ago and there's been no word back from him nor from Auwaer."

"Yes. That. We found him dead of several knife wounds. Recent. He apparently didn't get very far."

Geffen cursed better than a Dragonstar pirate. "Tann was my Lieutenant Seneschal's brother. Say nothing for now, if you please, Your Highness."

"Of course. I don't know who killed him, but . . ." Should he tell her all of it? The Moonlings' anger with him? His trip to Monoea, the battle on the sea, and his prisoners? The Monoeans' plans to put him on their throne? She waited, her brow falling in the wake of his silence. No. Not all. "Someone dumped him on us. We believe . . . my friend Lord Mance Osias believes, they may have magicked themselves away. I think it only could be Moonlings. Are you friendly with any?"

Geffen frowned. "None in particular. Why?"

"I've reason to believe the Moonlings are interested in me and my . . . friends. But not in the way of helping us, if you take my meaning." He still didn't trust the room, even as enclosed as it was. Perhaps because the Palace at Sevenfel had so many secret passages and hidden doors.

"Is there anything I can do to help, Your Highness?"

"Not and live to tell the tale. No. Your duty is to put an end to this siege and accompany me to Auwaer. We can't kill all the Ashen outside, though. We need prisoners to interrogate." Suddenly he felt weary. It had been a long night on his feet and a hard climb up the wall. He pulled out a chair and eased into it, reckoning he need not ask permission in his own fortress. "We estimate there are only two hundred holding you siege—"

"*Two hundred?*"

He gave her a grim nod. "Aye. They were clever about it. I reckon they started with more troops and gradually slipped off. I assume they've gone to attack Auwaer but I can't know for certain until we interrogate them. Do you know where the Queen is at the moment?"

"We received word just before the siege that she'd relocated to Auwaer. I thought it . . . odd." This she delivered in a direct tone and met his eyes steadily despite her hesitation. Judgement on her betters' activities could be a dangerous thing, Draken knew. *I fair like her*, Bruche said. Draken silently agreed as Geffen continued. "Rumor had it she meant to finish the pregnancy in Brîn."

"For once the rumors speak true. There is no word on the child, then." He did his best to not stumble over the word, but something in her manner had his hackles up, as if she had bad news to deliver.

But she shook her head. "No word, Your Highness."

He looked down at the table. A diagram of the fortress lay on top of the maps. "Here. And here." He pointed. "These are the primary gatherings of the Ashen. The rest of the tents and fires are blinds. There might be a few troops keeping them up, but they tend to gather close, as people do. I think the leadership is lax."

She walked over and leaned both her hands on the table, gazing where he pointed. "It makes sense. If we're just a stopgap, then they'd send their best people with the army. How many ships? How many troops?"

"We heard tale of twenty ships. Maybe three hundred soldiers on each galleons. That would be crowded, though, unless they've built bigger ones since—" *Draken. Watch yourself.* "Since I last studied them." Heat flared on the back of his neck. He resisted rubbing it. How long could he keep the secret of his Monoean heritage? Was it even worth doing? He'd managed to escape Monoea, he'd *chosen* Brîn and Akrasia, and he was sick and tired of feeling as if there were always an arrow on his back.

"We took out their rearguard. Captured fifty Monoean souls. They're still sitting on my shipdeck slowly starving. And I've got Prince Galbrait."

Geffen pushed a strand of hair out of her face. "I'm not familiar with the royal family. He's a son?"

"The youngest. The King and Queen are dead. It's our belief the other Princes are dead."

Her eyes widened. "So you've got the new Monoean King hostage?"

"No. He's loyal to me." He looked down at the map. "Long story. I suggest we gather our people and strike as soon as possible. I don't want to risk my friends any longer. My sister is out there, as well."

"Another long story?"

He gave a weary nod. "You could say that."

CHAPTER THIRTY-FOUR

Word of Draken's presence spread through the fortress at an impressive rate. By the time he'd had a quick bite to eat and scrubbed his face and hands, over half his servii and all the officers had weaponed up and stood in neat rows in the muddy outer bailey awaiting his orders. The cold grey of dawn shadowed their dirty faces and as he walked among them, he smelled their deficit of hygiene odd among usually fastidious Akrasians. Sparing water for a protracted siege, no doubt.

Despite his lack of attention, they were armed and armored well. More than a few had grey at their temples and brows, but that didn't bother him. It took years to become proficient with the sword, and these servii would probably be very good indeed.

Besides, pointing it out would be the flames calling the fire hot, wouldn't it, old man?
Draken just shook his head.

Ranks of longbowmen—tall males, all—stood in separate rows, heavy quivers on their backs. At his inquiry, one of them handed over a longbow for inspection. He drew it, ignoring the strain on his shoulder, and found the weight sufficient. "An eye at two hundred, Your Highness, and a heart at four hundred," the bowman told him with no little pride. "It's what we've got to match to be a Kheinian."

Impressed, Draken gave a crisp nod and returned the bow to its owner.

Geffen and he had worked out a basic plan of attack, the most important being find whatever superiors were there and make sure they were taken alive. He gave them free reign with the rest. He didn't like the thought of the bloodbath—a thousand verses two hundred would make for a complete rout, but he couldn't deny his soldiers their due after two sevennight of siege. "You are Akrasian, and you answer to me. Give every Monoean a clean, honorable death. No raping. No torture. All supplies and foodstuffs belong to the fortress. Personal weapons and effects are free for the taking."

A few faces creased into scowls but none spoke out so he could hear. Draken ignored them. Of course they wanted revenge after their siege, but Draken didn't think it had been all that bad. Two sevennight of lean rations and water didn't compare to what his shipmates had gone through at sea. "And another thing. I've friends out there; a Mance and his companion, a Monoean Prince, Akrasian Envoy First Captain Tyrolean, and my own sister, Aarinnaie Szirin. They provided the distraction for me to climb the wall. See they are found and made comfortable within."

"I'll assign an officer and a few servii to see to their protection and needs," Geffen said. "Shall we go up to watch from the wall, Your Highness?"

He'd rather be in the thick of it, actually. Watching his new soldiers massacre his old countrymen from a distance was a sickening enough thought. Sending men into a battle in which he took no active part was far worse. But he nodded, not wanting to shock his own troops. He had a bad feeling he'd need their trust later. He glanced up at the sky. They'd best move quickly before rain made it all more difficult.

"Move out." He waved an arm as he'd seen Tyrolean do to troops on the field once and followed Geffen to the battlements. Draken couldn't help but lean out and look for the bane. No threatening shadow that he could see. Geffen murmured a warning and he backed up. No one shot at him from the camp, though. Maybe they were used to people on the walls, and with his cloak hood up and shadowing his face against the grim morning light, his race wasn't obvious.

Below the siege camp seemed in chaos. A few fires burned at the periphery between the woods and the tents, but most of the cooking fires had guttered out. From up here, the thick sea of tents and early morning movements did make them look like far more than their numbers. The ground around the fortress was churned mud from the night's rain. Some few Ashen slipped as they strode between tents.

Nearby on the battlements, archers arrayed themselves over the gates. Each longbow nocked two arrows for the initial volley. Clever, that. Though likely few would kill the enemy, it was a quick and relatively inexpensive way to create confusion from overhead.

Geffen was still studying the Monoeans. "This is what they look like every morning."

Draken sighed. "Aye, Comhanar. But they are far fewer than they appear."

She glanced at him and he repeated himself in Akrasian.

The first battle would be at the gates. *And the trickiest. Always difficult to fight in a bottleneck, no matter the odds.* Draken nodded at Bruche's assessment. It was heavily guarded by easily a third of the Ashen.

The first thick volley of arrows rained down from the battlements. Upon the field commander's word—too quiet to reach the Monoeans outside as they ducked for cover—the gates swung open. It took the Monoeans a breath to react, and by that time a second hailstorm of arrows fell. The first servii rushed out, swords at the ready. Draken found himself falling into distanced analysis. How would the Ashen and their seaxes hold up against the longswords of well-trained servii? He doubted the Ashen would have time to assemble a proper phalanx, though it was their best chance against footsoldiers.

Unfortunately, it seemed the Ashen were on top alert. Still jittery from Osias's diversion, apparently. The phalanx came together in a matter of breaths, shields raised over the dead, injured, and able in a rapid motion absurdly impressive from above. Draken's fingers curled against the rough stone of the crenel he peered through and his shoulders tightened.

The gates slammed outward, some mechanism or magic moving them quickly enough to knock a few close, foolhardy Ashen off their feet. A narrow stream of servii followed. One last storm of arrows peppered the shielded phalanx, then on command, the bowmen held their fire. *Here is where we will see their skill,* Bruche said. Draken endured a short battle with the spirit over which direction they'd look; he exerted enough will to shift his gaze to the edge of the woods where he expected his friends to be.

Daylight, thin and watery with rain, had yet to infiltrate the shadows under the thick canopy. He realized up here he could see quite well the top of the forest, But all was quiet in the woods. No shadows of his friends emerging, no silvery Osias or quick-moving Setia or ghostly Aarinnaie.

They'll come when it's safe, Khel Szi.

But Draken could feel the old warrior's worry. He supposed Tyrolean might manage to hold Aarinnaie back for a little bit, but she would struggle to get to the battle. She would suffer the same anxiety he did, standing on the sidelines. It must run in the damned family, but it had been longer since she'd drawn blood and the passion to kill ran far deeper in her.

The battle was over by the time morning turned to full day, though his archers on the battlements kept nocked arrows pointed through the crenels and slits in the wall. Draken and Geffen climbed down the fog-slicked stairs from the battlements to the ground, moving slow to mind their steps, and walked through the gates. Inside the fortress, dampness trapped within the grim stone walls beaded on every surface and made the bay horses, grazing unconcerned in the inner bailey, appear shiny and black. Only a few low voices broke the oppressive quiet of the camp, mostly servii organizing the few living Ashen.

It was still eerie, walking among so many tents. He could just see over the tops, catch sight of the helms of his servii as they went about the business of making certain the siege had died to a man. A few grunts and a few wet thuds filtered through the peaked layers of waxed canvas. Other than that it was very quiet.

"Khel Szi." Halmar strode between the tents toward him. Draken was actually relieved to see the big szi nêre. He would have exchanged grips, but Halmar wouldn't touch him except in dire need. "Where are the others?"

"Gathered at the fortress gate, Khel Szi. Except for the Szirin."

Draken suppressed a sigh. Why couldn't Aarinnaie follow orders just *once*?

"She went into the battle, in the camp. She went after an archer aiming for you."

Sounded like her. "She'll turn up when she's fair ready, Halmar. You know how she is. Meantime, I've got officers to question."

Halmar bowed his head and followed Draken through the mud-churned camp to two Ashen on their knees, hands tied behind their back with ropes looped through to their ankles.

He studied them closely: two men. Despite their hard faces, they were quite young and he didn't know them. He wondered if they knew him. From the chains hanging off their shoulders, they ranked high enough to have some idea of the overall strategy.

It doesn't matter.

Bruche was right. "Too often of late Monoeans come to my shores with weapons bared and I must rout and interrogate you. I tire of it and my time is short. So, to business. This is your part in some Ashen plan, to hold my fortress siege until . . ." he arched a brow. "When, exactly?"

"We did it for two sevennight," one of them said. He wore a red scarf around his throat, a wife's or mother's momento, or perhaps it was some casual mark of status among Monoean landed forces that Draken didn't know. He walked to the man, let the crimson fabric slide through his fingers, then gathered it in his fist and pulled upward, making the Ashen stretch to keep from choking.

"I know how bloody long you've been here," Draken growled. "I want to know how long you're meant to stay. And where the rest of the army was headed."

The man in his grip gagged and choked.

The other officer stared, his odd green eyes fixed on the Monoean's reddening face. "Let him go. There is no rest of the army—"

Tyrolean's boot thumped into his back and he sprawled on his face in the mud since he couldn't catch himself. He started to turn over; Tyrolean pressed down on his back with his boot, pinning him down. He turned his head, sputtering mud and curses.

Draken didn't release the scarf. "I followed twenty warships here from Sister Bay, and you've been here longer than they have. Of course there is an army. And you're going to tell me where it's headed." He jerked on the scarf and then dropped it. The man fell forward gulping air. "Take them into the fortress. Separate them. We'll find out who gets to live."

◆ ◆ ◆

A short while later he emerged from the second cell, cursing and bloody. Neither would reveal the Ashen's plan, and neither died cleanly.

You saw enough torture in Grym's cells to know it rarely gets results.

You didn't think to point it out before I got into all that?

You wouldn't have listened. And it was your only option. But one thing is clear. They aren't Ashen—not real believers. I think they would have been more . . . compliant to your wishes. You being practically a demi-god and all.

Draken snorted at that, then frowned. *Do you think they are mercenaries?*

No. I think they were simply not privy to Ashen grand plans and were taught well to resist torture.

Draken sighed and rubbed the back of his neck. He was sore, exhausted, and stank of blood. Again.

Tyrolean shifted from one foot to the other, his fingers gripping the knife hilts laced onto his belt. Draken realized he must have been oddly silent longer than convention or habit during his internal conversation with Bruche. "Aye, Tyrolean?"

"They must have marched to Auwaer, Your Highness."

"Aye, they must have done, but—"

Galbrait strode up, oddly alone. Draken frowned at him. "Where are Osias and Setia?"

"Tracking." His tone was short; he was out of breath. "I just came back to fetch you. Aarinnaie is gone. Captured."

Draken's heart slowed to a glacial pace. "The Moonlings?"

"No. Monoeans. A few broke away from camp during the attack. Setia saw them and ran after them. It's the strangest thing. I think she and Osias can talk . . . somehow . . ." he tapped his head. "Osias let Setia go but went after her when she didn't come back straightaway."

"Do you know where they are?" Tyrolean asked.

"On the move. Likely trying to find a good place to hole up."

"Damn her and Seven damn them." He rubbed his eyes with his forefinger and thumb, trying to think of what to do next. It might need to be handled carefully; he just didn't know enough.

"They won't hurt her. She is a useful hostage." Geffen studied Draken closely. "You aren't like your father, willing to throw away a wife or daughter or sister for political gain."

That last remark sparked his curiosity but he set it aside for now. "Aarin makes an even better hostage for the Moonlings than for the Ashen, and now Monoeans are traipsing about through Moonling woods with her."

Galbrait shook his head. "My people aren't defenseless, Your Highness."

Geffen gave Galbrait a look but added evenly, "The Ashen won't give her up easily to even Moonlings, not men who would use her to buy their lives."

"They very well could be defenseless against the Moonlings. There is much you don't know, Comhanar." Draken sighed and gave her a brief description of the Abeyance and its recent uses.

Geffen stared past them all, thinking. "Why haven't they used it yet, then?"

"Perhaps they were waiting to see how the siege played out," Halmar said.

Or for another reason. Draken had the disconcerting feeling of Bruche sifting through his memories. It felt like scrolls rustling in his mind. *That border guard who mentioned the attack. Was the attack on the Brinian side or Akrasian side?*

I don't know. I'd have to have him pinpoint it on a map. Why?

We need to map these attacks to be certain. But so far, it seems none have been in the Moonling Woods.

To be fair, there weren't all that many other races living in the Woods outside Khein. A few small freeholds, the village, the fortress. The Moonlings kept no holding but instead preferred to rove. "I'm not even sure why they call it Moonling Woods."

Geffen gave him a look, which told him he *should* know. "It was the last sizeable holding when the Gadye took power. None have ever really managed to take the Woods, not entirely."

Except for this bloody great fortress. Bruche turned Draken's head and gazed up at the imposing stone walls.

"Aye, that," Geffen said. "Even so, the village has never thrived. Most of the shops have closed and most freeholders only manage to last a generation or so. The wood takes back its own, it's said."

Draken shook his head. There might be some tidbit of useful information flitting just out of his reach, but he didn't have time to chase it down. "At any rate, we need to find her, and soon."

A panting servii, his boots and legs splattered with blood, came jogging up. "Just this way, Captain." Tyrolean and Galbrait strode behind him. Galbrait wore a length of fabric around his neck, concealing the torq.

Draken pushed past Geffen to greet them. "How did Aarin get captured?"

Tyrolean's quick gaze took in their little party. He gave Geffen a nod as if he knew her. Perhaps he did. His armor was grey with dirt and mud caked his boots. "She separated from us. Insisted on scouting, Your Highness."

"She was anxious once you disappeared into the fortress," Galbrait added. His face was pale and his knees and hands grimy, his tangle of hair bound back from his face. "Couldn't sit still."

Draken didn't ask if Tyrolean had tried to argue with her or if she'd joined in the battle. For now he'd keep her prowess at killing secret. He finally looked at the servii, who dipped his chin.

"You take command, Tyrolean. I need to find my sister."

Geffen drew a breath as if preparing to say something Draken wouldn't like. "Your Highness." Aye, definitely something he wouldn't like. "Khein servii know these woods, they know all the places they might hide. They can't have gotten far. Let me send out a few hundred to canvass the woods while you start for Auwaer."

Draken stiffened, his expression hardening.

Still trying to rescue every female who strays from your sight, eh?

Shut it, Bruche.

Geffen's attention dropped to his chest region, a gesture he first thought of as submissive but soon realized meant she was examining the pendant hanging against his armor.

"All respect, Your Highness, but your first responsibity *is* to the Queen." Tyrolean, quiet, firm, had no compunction against speaking his mind. "We must make haste to Auwaer."

Trust Tyrolean to see the tapestry for the threads. But at the moment all he could think of was Aarinnaie. "Even in a siege, Auwaer will keep. I'm going after my sister."

◆ ◆ ◆

Two mornings later, Draken kept his temper in check even when they started talking to him incessantly about stopping the search for Aarinnaie, but only just.

"Has it occurred she can take care of herself?" Tyrolean said. "Perhaps she's acting as a spy."

Draken had little doubt of that. He kept his horse moving.

"Or perhaps she's at Auwaer, thinking that's where you are."

Or perhaps she's dead from spite.

"We haven't even found Osias yet." He could fair feel their frustrated scowls at his back. "Besides, I can't leave her here to her own devices. The woods might never recover."

They all ignored his feeble joke. Galbrait urged his horse closer. "Your Highness, wouldn't they have come forward yet if they were going to? Perhaps the Captain is right. Perhaps it's time to see to Auwaer and the Queen."

For two men in love with the Szirin, odd they both want you to leave her.

Bruche and Draken had been having the same internal discussion for two days and nights. Next would come the argument that perhaps there was something to what they were saying. Draken declined to climb on the cart this time. "I need Aarin. Her wit. Her council." *Her silent knives.*

Rustling ahead. He slowed his horse and held up his hand. The mail over his arm clinked softly. He thought he saw a low shape flit between trees. A bane . . . ? *No. It would be on you before you saw it.*

Another flicker, closer, and then something tiny eased from the trees to stand before him. A fierce Moonling, eyes darting and wild, body still as a shadow.

Draken stared as his heart lurched, hard, in his chest. Sweat prickled his back and palms.

The Moonling bowed and straightened, lifting his chin. "Khel Szi."

Tyrolean drew a blade, and one of the bows from his Kheinian company creaked. Draken lifted his hand. "Hold." If they were surrounded—likely—a first strike would only be an excuse to massacre them.

No one moved for long breaths. The Moonling looked young enough, no silver in his dark curls, no lines around his dark, round eyes. The strips of his skirt were short in the male style, just below the knee. Better for making one's way through the undergrowth of the wood, at any rate. His chest was bare. Every dapple on his skin was etched and scarred with sigils, the Seven in their various phases and temple runes. Someone had spent a deal of time slicing up his skin with a fair sharp blade. Draken frowned. He hadn't seen that before.

Pale ribbons on his spear hung clean and limp against the wood. *Not bloodied yet.*

No. And it won't be. The scar sigils mean he's a priest. Sworn to peace.

"Well?" Draken said, lifting his chin. "I assume you're either here to make friends or make terms. Which is it?"

"Neither. I am Lowild of the Oscher Clan." His first flinch, very slight, but Draken was watching for it. "I come to help you. Indeed, I've done already. But I intend to continue."

Draken's eyes narrowed. "Why?"

"To stop war between our peoples."

"Isn't that treason, rather?" Tyrolean urged his horse up a step. "At least against your own kind?"

I'm not sure a priest can commit treason.

Lowild lifted his chin. "Is it treason when one seeks peace for one's kind and kingdom?"

Draken turned this over in his mind. Bruche remained quiet but to slide his hand to the blade at his belt. "That depends. What is the right way to make peace? And who gets to decide?"

"In this case, you, Khel Szi." Another bow, shallower this time, but a gesture of unmistakeable respect. "I've heard tavern tales of your own search for peace."

"That was a long time ago." It seemed it, anyway. Draken pried his hand free of the blade hilt and swung down from his horse. "And my time is too short to dance around whatever it is you've got to say."

"You search for your sister."

Remarkably well-informed, this one.

"Among other things."

"Please walk with me."

Without waiting for an answer, Lowild turned and started walking, using his spear as a walking stick, moving slowly. His head bowed as if in thought. When they got out of direct earshot of Draken's party, save Halmar who followed in close silence, Lowild said, "I gave you the scout."

"The scout . . . ?" What in the Seven was he talking about?

Drae, he means the dead one.

"I wondered if it was a Moonling who delivered it so neatly," Draken said, ignorning Bruche's snort. "But why? Being dead, he wasn't of much use to us."

"He wasn't dead a short while before your arrival."

"I realize that. The blood was fresh."

"Meaning one of you killed him."

Draken gave him a sharp look. "That's a serious accusation—"

"It is truth, Khel Szi. One of yours killed him. They must have done. I just don't know who." Lowild hesitated, then stopped walking to look up at Draken. Draken fought the urge to take a knee so they would be eye level. Actually, he wasn't sure they would be eye level even then. Lowild was one of the smaller Moonlings he'd ever seen.

"How can you be certain it was one of us if you don't know who?"

"It was no Moonling spear that cut him so."

Draken nodded. He'd already decided that for himself.

"And no one else walked these woods but yourselves and the foreigners. They carry those long knives—"

"Seaxes."

Lowild repeated the word as if tasting it on his tongue. His accent made quick work of mangling it. "They would not cause wounds like that."

"No. It was a dagger that did it, clearly."

Moonlings know their woods. They know everything that goes on. They talk to the ruddy trees for all I know. But if he says no one else was in the woods to kill that man, I'm inclined to believe.

And that was good enough for Draken. Unfortunately. "Thank you for telling me."

His armor felt very heavy of a sudden, the cloak dragging at his shoulders. He glanced back at the others. Tyrolean kept watching him. Halmar and Konnan, as well. Galbrait spoke lowly with Setia and Osias. And Aarinnaie . . . missing.

"Traitors abound, it seems, Khel Szi," Lowild said.

"Why are you telling me this?"

"I told you. To keep you from war."

"Your people could win a war against us." He hesitated and then took a chance. "The Abeyance is a formidable weapon. I've been warned it will be wielded against me."

Lowild's dappled brow creased. "Why?"

"Coersion to free the Moonling slaves."

A soft snort. "Ideology is a crueler slavemaster than any Akrasian. But some of my people do not see things that way. They see only help against enemies and a reverence for magic the Akrasians do not have."

Hmm. Oddly wise for one so young.

That was a diversion of thought Draken didn't need at the moment. He was still trying to work out whether he could trust Lowild, or if he even wanted to. He dragged his meandering twin minds back to the conversation at hand. "You mean the Ashen."

A solemn nod.

"Lowild. Are you alone in this . . . action to help me?"

Lowild kept walking as if he hadn't heard the question. "Another thing."

Draken sighed. There was more?

"I know where your sister is. Come. I will take you."

CHAPTER THIRTY-FIVE

They walked a dirt trail that Draken would call an animal water path, except it didn't lead to water. Instead the land swept upward in the woods, a hill ringed with nearly bare ground encircling a few great trees on top. To Draken it looked like a Norvern Wilde burial mound, but one thing the Akrasian myriad of peoples had in common was burial at sea. There were deadpaths all over the country, and for a fee sundry deadmongers would cart a family's deceased to coastal temples built for the purpose. One job sundry could do to spare themselves slavery, though they only made a pittance hauling the dead.

Quit thinking about the dead. She's fine. She's Aarinnaie, Mance-trained crown assassin.

Bruche had a point.

Besides, she's probably annoyed them enough with her incessant talking they all ran away screaming.

Don't enjoy yourself too much, Draken said grimly. *If something happens to her this war will escalate quickly.*

Draken. The old warrior took on a patronizing tone. *It already is escalated. Thousands of Ashen are trying to get to the Gods through you. You have to protect the Seven.*

Draken snorted. He had to protect the gods? What about their protecting him? *I think the Gods can fair take care of themselves.*

They drew up and gazed up at the hill Lowild led them to. It was broad and the height of two horses stacked. Atop it was a sizeable, mortared cairn. Moss had stained the stones dull green and rippled in shredded strips over the rounded structure. Perhaps it was a waystation for a deadtrail, or an old guard hut. Two Monoeans stood guard, arrows on the string, by a doorway framed in thick logs. The cairn was too high to see inside but a faint light flickered. No voices from within. A thin ribbon of smoke snaked out the top. Halmar and

Konnan started to edge in front of Draken. He sighed and pushed ahead of them. "Who is in charge? I want to speak to them about my royal sister, Szirin of Brîn."

He spoke in a clear, firm tone, hoping Aarinnaie would hear him and his presence might ease her fears. If she ever had such a thing.

One of the guards stiffened. He glanced behind himself. None in Draken's immediate party moved but more Khein servii were surrounding the hill, hooves and boots rustling in the undergrowth like a low, eerie wind.

An Ashen ducked out of the doorway, nearly knocking his shoulder on the low lintel as he straightened. Grime and worse stained his dull grey armor, which he probably hadn't been out of in days. Their rank odor filtered through the distance.

"You are?" Draken asked. If the Ashen didn't know who he was then this might end badly and quickly.

"Captain Brace. Your Highness." He bowed, then turned his head to eye the Kheinian servii surrounding his little hill.

The hypocrisy of courtesy grated on Draken. With difficulty he kept his voice even. "Aarinnaie. Is she well?"

"Well enough."

Draken eased a breath from his tight chest. He had no reason not to believe Brace. It was easily discoverable enough, and their lives were forfeit without Aarinnaie's, surrounded as they were. "Obviously I want her back. What do you want in exchange?"

"You, of course."

Draken didn't roll his eyes, but he did stretch his neck and straighten his shoulders. "Not going to happen. I won't be your pawn in your war against the gods."

"Ours is a war *for* the gods."

"Oh, had a nice chat with them, did you? They've taken the Ashen on as their army?"

Brace lifted his chin. "The scrolls say—"

"Hang the bloody scrolls! The scrolls don't say to take my sister, do they?"

"The scrolls said the godsworn must be brought to heel."

"Even if that were true, and if the godsworn is me, the Seven and I have history of disagreeing. At any rate, we've got you surrounded. Outnumbered by dozens. If you bring her out I'll turn you over unharmed to your army." Which meant little since he intended on routing said army.

"May the will of the Seven become the will of all."

Draken sighed. "How are we supposed to negotiate when you spout off idioms every other sentence?"

More to the point, how are you to resist killing him just out of irritation, Draken? Bruche moved his hand to his sword hilt.

"Negotiate this." A low feminine growl as Aarinnaie emerged from the cairn and darted up to Captain Brace from behind. Not a breath later, blood was spouting from his throat. Brace gaped at Draken and made wet choking noises before he was spun toward one of the Ashen guards with bows. An arrow aimed for Aarinnaie sank deep into Brace's body. Bowstrings thrummed from behind Draken and the two Ashen archers fell, one screaming. Aarinnaie shoved Brace, now dead, away from her and silenced the screaming with a flash of her blade.

The Kheinian soldiers sat in silence. Draken could taste their shock on the air.

"Never send an army to do a Princess's work," Draken said. "Is there a reason you're just now killing them and escaping, Szirin?"

"First time they've left me alone to give me a chance to get out of my bonds. Used a rigger knot."

Draken snorted. Any self-respecting sailor could slip that knot with a couple of tugs. "Just these three?"

Aarinnaie nodded and started to climb down. She was filthy, her clothes were torn and stained, and leaves and grasses stuck in her many braids. He wrinkled his nose as she drew near: waste and smoke odors thick enough to gag a Reschanian pelt trader surrounded her in an invisible fog. She was also one of the most beautiful sights Draken had ever seen. He offered her his hand.

She grabbed it, stepped up on a root, and swung a leg over the rump of his horse. Her arms encircled his waist, tighter than just to steady herself. Her cheek rested a moment against his armored shoulder before she loosened her grip. Draken bid a few of his soldiers to clean up the dead and extinguish the fire in the cairn before wheeling his horse back for the fortress. At some point during the scuffle, Lowild had disappeared. Damned Moonlings, but he had helped them find Aarinnaie, so Draken couldn't complain too much.

"Are you all right?" he asked lowly

"They didn't harm me, Drae."

"Learn anything besides their philosophy?"

"Aye. It's as we thought. They're holding Auwaer. They seem confident Elena is there."

He cursed softly and urged his horse a little ahead. He stared straight between his horse's ears. "And the child?"

She rested her chin on his shoulder again. "No. They might not be privy. Or they don't care."

Or the child was dead.

You're mistaking cynicism for intelligence again.

Draken ignored his swordhand. "We must go to Auwaer."

"May I have a bath first?"

He snorted. "Or don't and hold yourself as a weapon. You could eviscerate the whole Ashen army with your reek."

Galbrait rode up near them. He waited to speak until Draken gave him a nod. His eyes were wide as they rested on her, his cheeks pale. "That was very well done, Aarinnaie. I am glad to see you whole."

She met him with silence for a long moment. "I am sorry for your countrymen. It couldn't be helped."

"I'm sorry as well." Galbrait fell back to ride next to Tyrolean.

The land outside the Khein Fortress wall was largely cleared, tents in folded stacks to be removed into the fortress, foodstuffs—not a great deal of that—and unclaimed weapons in untidy, pointy heaps. Servii moved items into the fortress in a steady line and others tended the fires to burn the dead. Draken had suggested carting them to the sea—it wasn't so far off. But Geffen had argued that since they'd had to burn their own dead from the start of the siege, it was only fair the Ashen burn too. Draken relented, though he privately wondered if he'd just set loose several hundred banes. Osias was still unavailable for advice on that front.

Aarinnaie hissed a breath when she saw the fires and lack of prisoners. "You killed them all."

He was surprised at her reaction. "You think I am incapable of killing?"

"No, brother. I just thought you had no taste for it."

"I've little taste for the gods, either. Some things are inescapable."

Draken delivered her to the inner bailey and waited for Galbrait and Tyrolean to dismount and come forward. "Aarin has learned the Ashen believed Elena is at Auwaer, and there is definitely a siege there."

"You don't think it could be a trap?" Tyrolean said, his gaze following Aarinnaie as she trudged through the gate between the bemused guards and disappeared up the steps into the fortress. "They might have baited her with false information."

"And died for the pleasure?" He started for the same gate Aarinnaie had taken, but took the stairs up to the maproom. He opened the door to the windowless chamber and went to throw himself into a chair by the table.

"Some Moonminster faithful believe martyrdom is a way to embrace inevitable death," Tyrolean said. "I saw it during a Gadye uprising at Reschan."

"All death is inevitable. Martyrdom makes it valuable."

Galbrait stared at him. Draken ignored him and leaned forward, tugged a map idly toward him, eyed it, then shoved it away. "Hang the strategy or tactics, then, if it's about people who will die for their cause."

"We can give all of them that." Tyrolean sat by him and laid his arm on the table. Grime stained his usually fastidious hands and his fitted leather trousers were hairy from sitting a horse so much in the previous few days.

"Like we did with Aarinnaie's attackers. Like we did here at Khein." Like he had strangled the two officers when they wouldn't talk. Draken toyed with the edge of another map scroll, curling it and then flattening it with his fingertips. His fingers were relatively clean at the moment. Gods knew it meant little enough.

"What if they're right?" Galbrait said. "What if you are the emissary to the gods?"

"Fools all! It doesn't matter. The Ashen are on our land, an invading army. My Queen is held siege. We are going to free her. If you would revoke your loyalty to me, now is the time, Galbrait."

Galbrait's lips parted as if he might speak again, then his brows dropped. Draken watched him until he dropped his chin and murmured, "Your Highness."

Draken kept staring at him until Bruche murmured, *I'm not certain I like what you're thinking.*

Draken averted his gaze, shifted it to the Auwaer map that meant nothing to his strategy. *We can use him. You know we can. He doesn't have to die for it.*

You already used him once. You would do it again?

An entire country for the life of one Prince? No match.

Ah, but Draken. He is not the Prince they want.

But Galbrait was the one they were going to get. "We need to make our plan to roust these Ashen from our shores and protect the Queen."

◆ ◆ ◆

Their first order of business was to collect and feed the Ashen from the *Bane*. He sent his soldiers straightaway to do so, reckoning to give them two days' rest while they saw to arming and preparing the Kheinians. It was a short march to Auwaer and he wanted his soldiers ready to fight.

"We need scouts, too," he told Geffen, leaning on his hands over the maps table. "Three of your best. Horse and arm them well. I won't have them waylaid this time. I think they can take this route, here. Should be off the beaten track enough to keep them from getting caught." It had worked well enough for him when he had first arrived in Akrasia, an exile with nothing but rags on his back.

"Of course, my lord." Geffen had taken to calling him lord. Draken didn't mind; it was a title more suited to soldiers. *Highness* made him think of some fop in rustling satins carrying a pretty, unnotched sword.

"Your Highness, the Lord Mance is here to see you." The messenger dipped a knee to Draken.

He almost sputtered. "It's about bloody time. Show him in."

Osias glided through the door, silvery as a moon glowing in a newly darkened sky. The windowless room was dim and a little smokey from torches and the fire. Draken tightened. Something about Osias this day set his teeth on edge. Ugliness rippled across him as if someone had tossed a pebble into the pond of his beauty. To look so serene when Draken had killed Monoeans, fretted and worried over Elena, run round the woods searching out his sister, and then jumped into planning a major attack . . . "Thank you for the honor of your presence, Lord Mance."

Osias kept his tranquil smile but behind him, Setia winced. "We went to Auwaer."

Geffen glanced from the Mance to Draken. "I will see to the scouts. Pardon." She slipped out quietly.

It wasn't necessary; she would be leading the army to Auwaer and would need to know the lay of the land. But Osias's demeanor felt more careful than calm, and Setia's gaze flitted around the room as if it were prison with no escape.

Draken's throat tightened. *Easy, mate.* "And?"

Osias moved closer to him. "Things are not so well there. May I?" He gestured to a chair. Draken nodded and they both sat. Setia went to pour cups of wine for the three of them. Osias drank most of his before speaking. "We were right. The bulk of the army went to Auwaer. Some thousands strong. The city is surrounded but the Palisade holds."

"And Elena?"

"A Moonling called Lowild was there." It wasn't quite a question.

"Aye, we've met."

"He told me it is thought she is inside the city."

"Lowild moves quickly." It almost proved the Moonling priest used the Abeyance, at least for travel. Draken sank into a chair and rubbed a hand over his face. "The city won't last long. There's only that tributary off the Eros watering it. Not so difficult to dam up."

"They've got a fair jump on it already." Setia reached for the pitcher of wine again.

Draken held out his cup but Osias waved her off. "Lowild and I destroyed the dam but it won't take a day or two to rebuild."

Draken narrowed his eyes. "I'm a little battleshy of Moonling magic, Osias. Do you trust Lowild?"

A slight smile. "Do not fear him."

Not exactly an answer. Typical.

"We left him there to watch things in our absence," Setia said, her dappled brow wrinkled.

Draken forced himself to relax a little. He nodded to Setia. "It's not so much the Palisade falling I fear. I expect it to hold fair. It's the water. They can't last long inside, even with city and family cisterns. A sevennight at best."

"It's worse than all that," Osias said. He glanced at Setia. Breath barely raised her chest, as in an animal waiting on prey.

"Magic, I assume," Draken said dryly.

"Ma'Vanni controls the undersea, as you well know. But Korde controls freshwaters."

Draken's brow fell. "So when I fought Truls, and killed him, you raised the Eros using Korde's help."

"Help is a . . . *direct* term. It was more bending his will, as I am allowed. Mance have some control over freshwater through our bond with Korde."

Draken dropped his gaze to the Mance's arm. "And now that bond is broken."

Osias sighed. "His will is no longer mine. But his strength is still imbued in all my spirithands, as it is in Bruche. It is through them I was able to raise the tributary to destroy the dam. But it is not the people needing water that worries me. That tributary must reach the Palisade, Your Highness, or the city will fall. Freshwater fuels the magic which holds the Palisade in place."

Draken let that sink in. "*Thousands* of Ashen, you say?"

"This we knew, Draken."

He persisted. "More than five thousand?"

"More than twenty thousand."

Draken stared. Dozens of ships must have left Monoea before his arrival then. How had the King not known? And even more curious . . . "How are they feeding so many?"

"Remember the reports of herd slaughters along the old border? It seems the carcasses did not go to waste. Your theory was correct, I think. The Moonlings killed the animals. The farmers, trying to salvage their livelihoods, prepared as much of the meat as they could. Buyers appeared immediately."

"What buyers?"

"Our own people. Of all races. Too varied to pin down any central supplier."

"And sometimes it was simply stolen," Setia added.

Draken slumped against his elbow where it rested on the arm of his chair. "They've used our own resourcefulness against us."

"With a deal of help from our own peoples, aye. Which is odd. I doubt even the lowest Reschanian trader would take coin from a Monoean, not when we're under invasion."

It was a day's march for his measly fortress servii. The road was not broad and the woods thick with prickly undergrowth. He had a bad feeling they'd meet resistance from Moonlings, as well, since they'd obviously aided the Monoeans. And what could five thousand servii do against twenty thousand men?

"You must make terms," Osias said as if Draken had asked the question aloud.

He lifted his gaze to the Mance's face. His beauty was back, glowing faintly in the torchlight. Outside the sky had turned off bright and blue, the wind fair. His servii were preparing hard for the march, for the fight. For him. For the Queen.

"I have only one thing they want," Draken said.

And you've no idea if you're enough to pacify them.

"Aye." The Mance's voice was soft. "But you will have to do."

CHAPTER THIRTY-SIX

Once he decided to give the Ashen what they wanted, Draken fell into the rhythm of acceptance. He had no illusions it would work out so well for Akrasia. His only hope was to steal enough power as their new King to protect Elena. A bargain for their Prince and men returned, or in exchange for the gods' will. He brought only two cohorts of servii with him back to the *Bane* and the Monoeans he'd left behind. Commander Geffen led the rest to temple ruins near Auwaer, well uprange of the siege. He compulsively kept his hand on Seaborn and drew it several times in the day that followed. The sword was quiet.

Tough not to consider that silence disapproval.

It was one of these times he wished he'd left the sword at the bottom of the bloody ocean. Perhaps himself, as well.

You didn't bring yourself back up; I did. I should think you'd be grateful.

He ignored Bruche, preferring instead to concentrate on the hypnotic way his horse's ears framed bits of the passing forest. Gradually the oppressive woods thinned into wide trees with the strong roots to bear a constant onslaught of sea winds, and the brambly undergrowth gave way to scrubby beach grasses. They emerged onto the rocky sand, the horses picking their way over the stones. Draken lifted his gaze from the narrow view between his horse's ears to the sprawling bay and ocean.

The *Bane* was beached, listing irreparably to her swordside.

Fools all, bloody Monoeans.

Draken reined up, his body falling still and cold. His horse pawed at a rock under its hoof.

Low tide lapped the *Bane's* stern and bared her underside. Varieties of spiny, sucker creatures clung to the glossy saltmoss slicking the hull. Some had dropped off and were trying in vain to make their way back across the rocks to the sea; others died where they hung. The beaching and subsequent sheer listing had broken the innovative deep slice of keel that kept the light schooner so stable for a ship of its size and weight. Jagged, splintery chunks stuck up from the rocks.

Draken swung down and strode toward the lower rail. The hull had been chopped with an axe. Lines hung in a haphazard, wind-tossed tangle, sails sagged like the bellies of old peace-time kings. Despite the soft waves of low tide, the gentle wind tugging at the limp sails, and the thump of knotted ropes against the deck and masts, a tomblike silence hung over the wreckage.

Don't be so maudlin. It's just because you're used to seeing so many men aboard her.

And that she had died here on the beach, the wind whispering through her boards like breath rattling in diseased lungs.

Blood smeared the deck in a wide swath. Draken suppressed a wince. It reminded him sharply of the slave ship. He felt the spirithand rustle through his memories. *Look again. It's the same mark, I'll wager.*

He grasped a rope and climbed up, his szi nêre protesting from the beach as they strode closer.

"Your Highness? Perhaps it's best to say aground."

Draken ignored Tyrolean as he caught at the lopsided, broken rail and maneuvered himself up onto the steeply sloping deck. The mark of moons, smeared across the deck like on the *Sea Swallow*. He climbed past it, grabbing winches and ropes, and hauled himself on his belly to peer into the hold. Insects buzzed in a thick swarm and the reek of death was stronger here. A few bodies sprawled, tossed during the beaching like ugly, rancid dolls. Empty eye sockets stared into the distance. Joran hadn't gotten to be Akhanar for very long. His head was nearly severed. Blood had pooled in the corner by one of the water troughs where he sprawled.

Draken had seen enough. He climbed back down, sickness clawing at his gut. "The Monoeans killed the crew and escaped. If they got hold of the map inside the captain's cabin, they can find Auwaer easily enough."

"They're weak and thirsty."

He shook his head. "The crew has been dead a few nights." Insects had made steady progress on the soft facial skin and eyes. "I imagine the Monoeans are fed and watered well enough to travel."

But where were the servii he'd sent to keep watch over them?

"We'd best get after them then," Tyrolean said.

Galbrait shook his head. "They are less than fifty. Nothing to your five thousand."

Aarinnaie snorted. "They know too much. And they swore to you and Draken, and then deserted. Makes them traitors, doesn't it?"

Osias and Setia pushed ahead and disappeared into the trees, ready to track their errant shipmates. Within the morning Setia returned to report they'd found the trail. She led Draken and his party a bit astray of their course to Auwaer, and she hurried them. Their nimble horses made quick work of closing the distance to the Ashen; still, it was just getting on dark when they met up. The Ashen staggered in a ragged line down a deadpath, shoulders sloping and gait uneven as a seapede missing three legs. Most stumbled to a stop when they realized they were caught. One ran. Draken yanked an arrow from his quiver and it whistled through the woods. Despite cutting through a low hanging branch of leaves, it caught the runner in the back. He fell and didn't move again.

One of the Ashen turned on Draken, shoving through the foiliage. "Why'd you kill him? He did nothing wrong."

Draken stared down at him, then up and down the row of exhausted men. It struck him suddenly. Maybe it was the bare chests and shorn hair lined up like that. They were *all* men. "You didn't think to strip my crew to better clothe and arm a few of yourselves before you killed them?"

Sullen silence.

Osias rode near and spoke lowly. "I made a count, Khel Szi. They number forty-four."

"Fools all, they're three short."

"Perhaps they died trying to overcome the crew," Galbrait said.

"Perhaps they ran ahead, clothed and armed well." Draken spoke loudly enough for the raggety line of men to hear him. He watched them carefully. A couple shifted on their feet. Most eyes were lowered. One, more lad than man, met his gaze steadily.

The first to die. A grim whisper in the hollow of his chest.

Draken's breath felt shallow. He glanced back at the servii. Laid his hand on his swordhilt and jerked his chin.

A few of the Ashen twitched to life, scattering in the trees, as Draken's servii descended on them with bared blades and bows. Many fell to their knees and pleaded for mercy, which his szi nêre gave them with quick deaths. The ones who fought back found their limbs hacked off before their throats were cut. Draken's eyes stung, as if blinking or tears could shut out the reek of death or the screams of the dying. He kept his gaze on the dying though, except when he glanced at Galbrait to see that he was watching. The lad needed toughening. Tears rolled down his cheeks.

Aarinnaie sniffed and rode a short distance away, likely irritated Draken had not allowed her to participate in the killing. But this was an ugly duty, no honor or finesse in it. Simple killing, cutting down these soldiers who had betrayed them and now stood between Draken and his Queen. Assassin or not, this was not the kind of killing Draken wanted staining Aarinniae's hands.

He backed his horse toward her, still watching the death.

"I'm a better fighter than these servii," Aarinnaie said, her tone tight.

"Truth, you are."

Her eyes narrowed. "I'm a better fighter than *you*."

Ouch. Bit below the belt, isn't it?

This has more to do with her need for blood than my abilities.

A deep chuckle that rumbled Draken's chest. *Or lack thereof.*

"This is amusing to you, is it?" Aarinnaie lifted a hand to her cheek to wipe away a curl. Her hand trembled. "Fine. I'll see you at Auwaer. Perhaps I'll be of some use there!" She wheeled her horse and started off into the underbrush and deeper trees.

Curse you, Bruche! "Aarin!" He chased after her and headed her off with his bigger horse. He reached out and caught her rein. "That was Bruche. He is very apologetic for his lack of respect."

Bruche snorted.

"No tantrums, Szirin, not just now. We can ill afford it."

She snarled. "It's not a tantrum. I am not a child. Stop treating me like one."

"You're barely old enough to marry, Szirin, and I am twice your age. You think I do not recall what it was to have less than twenty Sohalias of life?" He didn't let go.

"I'm fair old enough to kill."

"Aye. And yet you are also Szirin."

"A title. It means nothing.

"It means everything to me. I rely on you utterly."

She blinked. "You don't. You have Elena. Tyrolean. The Mance . . . even Setia is more valuable to you than I."

Was this a jealous fit? He had no idea and no time to address it. "How would it look to my servii to see you kill this day, these people? To our nêre, sworn to shed their blood before ours? These Monoeans are not worthy of your blades. They are brambles over our path, and we must hack through them to be on our way. Akrasians already believe you and I are uncouth heathens. But you are a Princess. It's time you behaved accordingly. It's time you honor our house and Elena's."

Aarinnie tugged on the rein. Her horse snorted and tossed its head. Draken reluctantly let go. "Do not run. You say you are no child, so don't behave like one. This is certainly no child's game. My Queen and the heir to the Akrasian throne are at stake."

She looked down at her hands, tight on the rein.

He eased his tone, lowered his voice so not even a nearby Mance could hear. She could read lips well enough. "You had blood a day ago. Your captors. Those were worthy kills."

"*Worthy kills do not sate me,*" she whispered.

His chest tightened. He reached out again, this time to touch her shoulder. "I know. We will find a way out of this, Aarin. I will help you. Come back with me now and let us shift our attention to Auwaer. Doubtless there will be killing enough to suit even you."

She held for a moment, and then nodded, not meeting his gaze.

He rode back to the others, giving her some time to compose herself.

"Is she all right?" Tyrolean asked.

"Aye. She'll be all right."

But he wondered. Aarinnaie had endured long training under the Mance King in killing, made intimate with death as Korde himself at such a young age, now perhaps they were seeing the steep cost of such ability. How long would they be able to hide this from Galbrait? From Tyrolean? From the whole damned kingdom? How long could Aarinnaie even live with her deep urge to kill? He had seen no guilt or regret in her, only disregard for her victims. Once dead, they no longer ceased to be. She was his sister, and he loved her. But hers was a hunger he could ill afford to feed.

Except you are at war and have great need for killing.

Osias watched him, his body quiet but eyes swirling sickeningly purple.

Not like this. Not his little sister. *Curse Truls who inflicted Aarinnaie with Korde's compulsion,* Draken replied. *And curse the gods for sparing her no mercy.*

CHAPTER THIRTY-SEVEN

Aarinnaie remained sullen and quiet as they rode. Her eyes constantly roved the woods and her hand rested on the hilt of her sword. Setia rode near her, as did Konnan, who Aarinnie doubtless resented. Osias ranged ahead, occasionally flashing silver through the trees.

Galbrait was as dirty as the unwashed servii, shadowed by grime. His forehead had taken on a permanent crease between his eyes. He wore oft-repaired, sturdy mail topped with a battered leather breast plate, kilt, and perfunctory metal reinforced leg and arm protection from Khein. It looked incongruous against the golden torq gleaming around his throat at the collar of his hauberk.

Tyrolean rode close to Draken. "Looks as if the Prince has settled in all right."

"I wish he'd spend more time watching the woods than Aarin."

"He needs duties, regular work to perform."

"Things have been too hectic for duty rosters, if you haven't noticed."

Tyrolean went on as if he hadn't spoken. "He could be your personal aide perhaps. Keeping him close would give you the opportunity to teach him. He would learn about tactics, about managing loyalties, running an army, how to be a good King."

Draken snorted. "As if I know about any of those things."

"You know how to rely on the expertise of others. That is a far more valuable skill than all those put together."

Draken lowered his voice. "He likely won't get the chance to be King."

"And yet, he is. By virtue of his birth."

"Aye, and it may be the death of him yet." Even if he turned himself into the Ashen it was doubtful they would let Galbrait live. He hadn't decided what to do about that yet. Send him away? And yet . . . Galbrait's "virtue of birth" kept him from it. If it took the Prince's death to secure the safety of Akrasia and Elena, so be it.

"Tell me about the temple ruins, Ty. Have you been?" Draken asked.

He nodded. "They are close to the Eros. Legend says those who lay their heads to sleep inside the pillars will never wake. Indeed fog hangs over it and moss and damp creep into every crevice."

Draken raised his brows. "And that's where Geffen chose to gather?"

"Kheinians are a practical lot," Tyrolean said. "I daresay most of them doubt the existence of the gods at all."

Draken snorted at that. "Sounds like a place the Ashen would be interested in."

Osias' grin stretched his lips into part grimace, part smile. "The temple ruins are also highly defendable, Khel Szi."

Draken found himself matching the grin. "Right. Warn them of our arrival, then, if you would."

Osias gestured to Setia and they rode off together.

Giving orders to a former King, are we? With nary a please nor thank you.

Draken purposely misunderstood. *I need to get a look at this siege before we settle into the ruins. See what we're up against.*

He gathered his troops in close and raised his voice. "Wait here. I, with Tyrolean—" Aarinnaie was staring hard at him. "—and my sister are going to *observe* the siege." The emphasis was for Aarinnaie's benefit. "You wait here for the Lord Mance and we will reconvene at the temple ruins before daylight."

Not taking the lad?

Truth, Galbrait watched him closely with brows drawn. Draken thought for a moment. Every instinct told him to send the Prince on with the servii and szi nêre, who were scowling at him for not being included on his personal mission. But Galbrait was too valuable to risk on an operation like this. Getting so close to the siege was one thing; bringing a Prince the Ashen wanted was another. But out of some sense of false hope or other delusion, he knew it was a chance for Galbrait to learn: about what his people were capable of, about Auwaer and the Palisade, which was better seen than explained, and how no decision a leader made was simple or right.

He nodded to Galbrait. "You come, too."

They stripped their armor to cut any noise it would make, which made his szi nêre grit their teeth more, and wore only their under armor padding with a tunic over, tight breeches and boots. They packed their armor onto their saddles, gave the leads to servii, and strapped on swords.

"Feels fair odd. Like training," Draken said to Tyrolean.

"I'm surprised you remember. That must've been a long time ago for you," Aarinnaie said sweetly.

Bruche guffawed, Galbrait blinked rapidly at her, and Tyrolean didn't bother hiding his grin.

"Not as long ago as you might think." Draken's belt strap cracked like a whip as he buckled Seaborn at his side. He lashed a thick quiver to his back and carried a fine bow from the Khein Fortress armory, well-suited in weight. "And there is still time to send you with Halmar. Do not tempt me."

She rolled her eyes but fell quiet.

After leaving a few messages to pass on to Geffen, they headed off toward Auwaer. Tyrolean took the lead, his stride steady and confident.

"Do you know the whole of Akrasia?" Galbrait asked him, hurrying to his side. Tyrolean spoke lowly to Galbrait about his career as they walked. Galbrait seemed properly impressed.

"Do we need to keep on the chatter?" Draken finally said, though their voices were quite low. That made them fall quiet.

You're in a foul mood.

Draken scowled. What was there to be happy about? His Queen was surrounded and even the gods considered her, once again, a sacrifice rather than a key. He wondered that they had not told him to let them ruin Auwaer. The Moonling priest had laid out a suspicion of betrayal that he couldn't shake. His sister had Korde's addiction to killing and death, and his only option to salvage any parcel of this situation was to allow thousands of religious maniacs to turn him into a puppet king.

"We're getting closer. Let me scout ahead," Aarinnaie said.

Draken considered and relented with a nod. "No killing."

"I don't plan on getting so close—not so they will know, I mean." A flash of teeth, more grimace than grin, and she ran ahead before Draken could growl a reply. She was so fleet and silent, she barely rustled the leaves or undergrowth.

Tyrolean stared after her. "Maybe she's part Moonling."

"Keep moving. I want to see this tributary and the whole siege before third moon."

◆ ◆ ◆

By first moon Draken was wondering if Aarinnaie had simply run away for good. There was no sign of her, not so much as a bootprint or a snapped twig. The men had to slow to make their way as soundlessly as possible. The low rumble of many voices and *crack crack crack,* as if something were striking something else, drifted from ahead. It made Draken more cautious than usual, and even Bruche kept his swordhand numbed, ready to fight. Firelight flickered through the trees at a distance and well above the ground. They slowed further, maddeningly so, but necessary to hide their presence.

A shadow passed before them; Draken held up a closed fist to stop their progress. Everyone froze behind him.

A sentry, striding along, not bothering to hide his presence. Draken recalled the first time he'd seen Auwaer. A cohort of Escorts had waylaid him. He wondered if that was a regular patrol outside the Palisade. He wondered if they were dead.

They moved on until he could make out the men scurrying about, the snaking small river which hardly seemed enough to water a whole city no matter how many cisterns. Galbrait drew a sharp breath next to him and Draken laid a steadying hand on his arm. The Prince had seen the Palisade.

The wall of black magic, appearing as a void, as if the world dropped off into nothingness, tugged at Draken. He resisted the odd pull at the same time he felt his blood rise. The magic was in him, through him, after all. It wasn't just the sword. On one level he'd known it must have insinuated itself inside his very bones if he was able to heal himself of the most grievous of wounds. But to feel this great work of Mance magic pull on the magic within him as if it were a tether was another thing altogether.

"Inside *that* is a *city?*" Galbrait breathed, breaking the immediate hold the magic had on Draken. Noise rushed in: splashing, voices, the work on the dam.

"Aye." Now that they were this close, Draken realized that despite the sentries, most of the Ashen were busy working at damming up the tributary, and it was noisy work, so they didn't have to be as careful as he thought. "It's Mance-made, and similar to the wall that imprisons the banes at Eidola. It'll drive a man mad to cross it without permission. That kind of magic is the most powerful sort, the sort that mucks with the mind."

The land sloped gently downward to the tributary. Most of the trees were set apart and small, as if the woods had been thinned around the river either by magic, fire, or axe. The workers bore no weapons he could see. No tents stretched around the blackness. It was simply men felling trees, dragging them whole toward the water and submerging them as they built a wall to dam it up. Water already was building up behind the dam, breaking the narrow banks, though the logs had yet to breach the surface. The tributary must have cut deep into the little valley indeed, betraying how much water actually flowed off the Eros into Auwaer. More than he'd imagined.

Osias is right. A day, maybe two, before they manage to cut off the water for good.

And then Auwaer had a sevennight at most if the cisterns were filled. The Palisade could surely hold, but the people inside were at risk. How long before they attempted escape?

They crept through the woods as the moons climbed the sky, peeking at the army surrounding Auwaer and the Queen. A small city of tents crammed in pockets where the woods relented. Lanterns gave the oiled canvas an ethereal glow. There was no subterfuge around their numbers here. Every fire was manned by at least three soldiers, some bedded down in cloaks on the ground. The soft rumble of voices, swords on straps, and the snap of burning logs marked each encampment. The smells of cooking food, oiled leather and fabrics, and shallow-buried waste gave the Ashen soldiers just the right invasive feel. They went on and on and on through the woods. Draken had no doubt Osias' count was correct.

They retreated a safe distance for a rest and drink. Draken lowered his head and looked at his hands. Dirty. Scarred. Fair strong. His fingers curved slightly toward the thumbs from a lifetime of pulling ship lines. The skin was thick and scarred from the bowstring despite shooting gloves. The hands of a seaman and a bowman. A man who worked and killed with his hands rather than with royal decree.

"I always used to fight my way out of battles. Until I came here to Akrasia."

"You've done a fair bit of fighting, Khel Szi," Aarinnaie said.

"Perhaps not this time." He gave her a humorless smile at the thought of a life-time of balancing politics, sycophants, and hypocrits all under the guise of heresy.

Bruche's amusement rumbled in Draken's chest. *Heresy? And here I thought you hated the gods.*

I do. They're still fair superior to the Ashen.

"Something I thought of while you're brooding, brother, is letting our natural habitat do some of the work for us."

He lifted his head only to be met by her wicked grin.

She added. "They are spread out, these thirty thousand heretics, are they not?"

"I'm listening."

"Even an army of soldiers dies one man at a time."

He snorted. "That sounds like something Truls would say."

She dropped her eyes, making him wish he'd not spoken. The Mance King Truls had trained her. It wasn't something she talked about, ever.

"Guerilla attacks and ambushes. That is what we have come to?" Tyrolean shook his head.

"It's honorable to strike from the light, Captain. But it's far healthier to strike from the shadows." Draken rose. "Come. We've another siege to destroy."

CHAPTER THIRTY-EIGHT

Sunlight shone harsh and hot on dirty, strained faces and grimy tunics. Draken had bathed in the cold Eros and dressed in loose trousers again, his sword at his hip, his chest and feet bare in the way of his people. His servii from Khein stared but truth, he felt more comfortable now in his Brînian garb. Besides, it was too bloody hot for tunics and quilted armor padding and leather breeches and boots. Elena's pendant and chain still stuck to the sweat on Draken's neck and chest.

Geffen stroked her chin as she examined the map of siege encampments on the slab of stone that served as a rough council table. It was actually an overturned altar. The remains of Khellian lay nearby, face weathered smooth of righteous anger, horns broken to nubs. The ends lay like amputated fingers in the soft moss and tiny-leaved groundcover that carpeted the ruins. Draken nudged one with his bare foot as Geffen concentrated.

"Divided into cohorts, it might be doable. The thing is to cut communication. The main encampment with Priest Rinwar is here, we think." Her finger left a smudge on the map. "We take out them and the camps on either side early. That leaves them with no primary command."

"We don't know how they're organized, nor that they haven't placed other commanders in other camps." They wouldn't be so stupid as to put all the chained lords of rank in one camp, would they?

Geffen looked up at Draken. "You're right. We don't. But we have to make some assumptions here. I'd rather not die by indecision."

"I'd rather not die at all." Tyrolean pushed off the broken pillar he was leaning against and strode a couple of steps to the overturned altar. He, too, had braved the icy waters of the Eros to bathe. His hair was pulled into a neat tail and he wore tidy Escort greens over his armor. A sheen of sweat glimmered on his pale skin. The little group quieted at his voice. Even Aarinnaie looked up from cleaning her nails with her dagger.

"I have killed, Your Highess," Tyrolean continued. "I have seen war. This you know. Fair more than I ever thought I would. I have done as I was ordered, always. I will follow orders tonight, if you insist. But I cannot condone this. Attacking with only the light of the Seven Eyes to guide us is sacrilege."

Draken crossed his arms over his chest as everyone's gaze shifted to him. He lowered his head in thought. "I know, Ty." He had thought to recuse him from the action because he knew him well enough to guess his disapproval. "I don't like it any better than you do."

"I should think not. Even though the Ashen are going about this poorly, they are right about you."

"That I should be *King*? You know I wouldn't have that."

Osias had attended without a word, though he chose to incessantly pace round the temple, examining it close enough to memorize patterns in the moss. Now he, too, stepped forward. "But the gods chose you, Draken."

"I didn't choose them. I didn't choose their bloody sword, their magicks, nor the Brînian throne. I did choose Elena, though. I will see her and our . . . child freed."

No one reacted to the break in his voice. No one blinked. Tyrolean's face hardened to stone and Draken knew he had lost him, maybe for good this time. Geffen waited to take orders, feigning close attention to the rough map. Aarinnaie went back to her nails, sliced a finger. Blood dripped to the moss and her lips moved in a silent curse. Galbrait stood with his hands clasped before him, torq gleaming as if he were waiting in the gilded Great Hall for his father-King to speak. Draken had seen the pose before and thought how far they had fallen from Sevenfel to a court of war in the moss and temple ruins. Osias had spoken and retreated.

"You swore your oath to her in your time, Tyrolean," Draken said quietly.

Tyrolean's perfectly shaped lips quirked, a rare, brief asymmetry to his features. "I could not save her once."

"No amount of honor could save her from me. And she bears saving again, Captain. Her attackers are no more honorable than I was."

His lined eyes wouldn't meet Draken's. But he bowed his head in a nod.

Draken dragged his attention to Galbrait. "You stay here."

"Your Highness, but—"

Draken led him a little apart from the others, laid his hand on his shoulder, and gentled his tone. The young Prince deserved that much. "I would not have you kill your countrymen, Galbrait."

"Your countrymen as well," Galbrait said sullenly.

"Not any longer."

◆ ◆ ◆

War Night, old seamen had called it when Khellian was alone and full. Tonight the battle god hung pale, full, and heavy in the sky as Elena's pregnant belly, and his glow picked out every color better than daylight. The air was still hot and sultry, running down Draken's bare back. Draken stared up at the Eye and pressed the horn sign against his chest, his lips, his brow. But he was just going through the motions as Tyrolean led them in prayers before the attack. His mind was on his Queen. Had she birthed yet? Was there an infant with a tight cap of Draken's curls drawing breath through Elena's finely drawn lips? His jaw tightened. He had no way of knowing and he had to get through thirty-thousand Ashen to find out.

Draken still hadn't decided if he should kill the Priest Rinwar or not as he crept up toward the encampment. He could be a valuable prisoner, and if things went wrong, he'd be needed to convince them to accept Draken as their King. Smaller tents and guards encircled a grand, fringed tent, tasseled to signify the rank of commanders and aides within.

Makes them convenient to find, Bruche said.

Too convenient. He didn't trust it.

You'd like a little blood of your own, eh?

It would be better for us if he's dead. But I am still torn. Perhaps we can learn from him.

Bruche rumbled his disagreement. *I think we know all we need.*

Questioning Rinwar had been Draken's reason for dismissing their arguments that he and Aarinnaie participate in the attack. Besides, she was fair desperate for blood and Draken wasn't sure what she'd do if she didn't get it. The affliction seemed to worsen by the day.

He shoved the thought from his head. Aarinnaie was ready to follow the darkness that compelled her to kill. This night they could make good use of it. He'd worry about other nights later.

The forest was quiet around the Palisade, always had been, though the encampment was set between sight and safety, well back from the blackness. The magic repelled ordinary people, seeping nightmarish visions and terror into their psyches. Truth, Draken didn't know how the Ashen managed to stay this close for the sevennight they'd been here.

Back several paces where Draken had concealed himself in the woods with his servii and Aarinnaie, he had some small hope the Ashen would fail to realize the significance of the bird's whistle signal from the servii at his elbow—at least until after it *was* significant.

He nodded without looking back at the servii. He heard the slightest rustle of fabric, the soft chime of chainmail shifting over her arm as she brought fingers to lips.

Low-low-high. Low-low-high. Low-low-high.

Around them servii rose like spectres, swift and silent in waves of one hundred. They took out the patrolling guards first, most of whom managed to gape and yelp an alarm at the same time. Ashen in various stages of armor kits and undress rushed through tent-flaps, but servii slashed their way through the oiled canvas with one strike and killed with the second. Draken rushed forward with the second wave, all pretense of silence gone. His throat filled with guttural noises as he raced toward the fringed tent. Servii were already there, tugging a man out by the arms. He bled from a few places but was alive enough to protest noisily.

Draken pushed between servii busy with killing. His sister emerged from a tent splashed with blood made sharply crimson by Khellian's bright light. Her lips were drawn back from her teeth, knives in each hand. He dragged his attention from her as she disappeared into another tent, telling himself he was buying her time . . .

"So you're Rinwar."

The Ashen Priest dragged his greyed head up to look at Draken. He was Rinwar all right; same fleshy cheeks and lips. His narrow chest heaved. He was naked and had been recently . . . preoccupied . . . if the state of his organ was any indication. Behind him, in his tent, the theory was confirmed as a woman's scream was cut short with a wet thud. The scent of blood rose sickeningly up. Draken schooled his face against reacting to the wanton killing.

Rinwar fell to his knees. The fight went out of him. "Your Majesty. You came."

This time Draken couldn't keep the muscle in his clenched jaw from twitching. The Palisade tugged at him, making the world tilt. Bruche breathed cold through him, bolstering his muscles. *Easy, lad.*

Draken cleared his throat. "I assume you're in charge of this siege—"

A sharp, familiar battlecry made Draken turn. A swarm of sword-wielding Monoeans rushed into the clearing. The first of his servii hit the ground, her head rolling aside without a sound. All around him the camp erupted. Servii screamed orders and warnings. Swords clashed. Fresh blood splattered canvas peaks. The undulating warcries of the Ashen rose up from the trees.

Ice scoured Draken's muscles and he started to fight it, but then he realized: Bruche. His weight had shifted. The swordhand had drawn his sword without his realizing.

He killed an Ashen coming at him and then shifted toward Rinwar, who had come abruptly to life and had struggled free of the remaining servii holding his arm. He snatched the servii's sword and swung at him; the servii ducked and spun behind him in an acrobatic feat Draken could barely take in. The servii caught Rinwar around the chest and arms. Draken advanced with a growl, sword extended. He'd had enough of this. He should have killed the Landed priest when he first saw him. Without a leader, perhaps the Ashen movement would fail.

The edge of a blade stung the side of Draken's throat. "Halt now."

Draken kept moving despite the peril, but Bruche obeyed. Draken's chilled legs stumbled to a stop and his sword arm fell. So did his heart, right into his stomach. "Galbrait."

"Put down the sword."

Set aside Seaborn? But Galbrait's blade was still cold against his throat. He sighed and let his sword fall. It stuck into the ground at an inglorious angle. Galbrait grunted, "The rest of them."

Draken pulled the daggers from his belt and wrists and tossed them away, too. He spat, the blade nicking his throat. "I was warned of a betrayer. And here you swore to me."

"I am sworn to you. I'm saving your life just now."

Tyrolean was led up, arms bound behind his back, the Ashen holding one of his own swords against his throat. A shudder went through Draken, looking at him.

"Aarin?" he husked out.

Tyrolean shook his head and was shoved off in another direction. He was obviously being treated as a hostage; the Ashen were methodically killing the rest of his servii. The air filled with curses and screams cut short by blades. At least the blasted war cries had faded. Draken could only hope their encampment at the temple ruins was undiscovered as of yet. He had brought five hundred servii to this attack. With any luck some escaped to warn the rest of his troops before Galbrait warned the Ashen where they were.

He lowered his gaze to the boot-stomped dirt. The noises faded around him as he retreated into a calm resolution.

Someone came up behind Draken, pushed him to his knees. He dropped with a grunt. His bad knee was stiff and sore, like a dagger poked up into his thigh. Galbrait unbuckled his bracers, and tied his hands back with a scratchy rope that was too tight. It dug into the skin of his wrists.

The Priest Rinwar strode forward and yanked Seaborn from the dirt, then turned and went into his tasseled tent. Galbrait removed the blade from

Draken's throat. Two Ashen hauled him up and shoved him in the direction the Priest had gone.

Blood had been spilled inside the opulent tent, but the body had been removed. Rinwar's woman, he supposed, gone like she'd never been. A servant rolled up the bloody rug and hauled it outside.

Rinwar splashed his face in a thin, fine bowl of water—*Odd how the bowl made it through the battle intact when the woman did not*, Bruche remarked— and he dropped into a chair gilded with moons in their various phases. He didn't look at Draken, nor Galbrait. He propped an elbow on the armrest, his chin on the heel of his hand, and brooded.

Draken's jaw itched where a muscle spasmed. "If you're waiting for attack, you'll wait a long time. I'm not as worthy a hostage as you might think. Not to anyone outside Auwaer anyway."

Brilliant. Next beg them to kill you.

Rinwar waved an impatient hand and signaled a servant to bring him a drink. "I'm interested in a fantastic tale my men told me. Not only were you killed aboard their ship after an ill-trained attack on the captain, the ship broke up afterward. They reported the cracks emanated from your body where it lay on the deck—quite dead, I reiterate. And the ship broke up, sinking all of you to the bottom of the sea."

Draken growled low. "Except for the fifty Monoeans I saved."

"Which is the most interesting part of the tale, isn't it? You suffered certain death by both devastating stab wound and drowning, and yet, you lived to save them. And now, here you are."

"Your point?"

"The gods showed me the way." Rinwar drank his wine, set his cup down, and rose. "Just as they are now."

Another grunt. "What way?"

Rinwar nodded to Galbrait, who tightened his grip on Draken's arms. He tried to struggle free but the young Prince's long fingers were too strong.

Rinwar picked up Seaborn, held it this way and that to examine the blade. It was sound, fine, if basic. The sword had never had any pretenses at being a pretty thing. Draken struggled harder.

"I had thought you were to be King. But I ask myself, now that I've a whole kingdom of magic, what need do I have of you?"

Rinwar stepped closer. He raised Seaborn to the level of his hip and pressed the tip against Draken's chest. It stung. "Of course I can think of one thing you can do for me."

Draken fell still, teeth gritted. He would not bow to this religious lunatic. "Are you offering terms?"

"Of a sort."

"What would you have me do, Rinwar?"

"You're doing it," Galbrait said.

The lord's expression didn't change as he leaned against the sword. The sting oddly disappeared, fading as Seaborn sank into Draken's chest. Horribly familiar, powerful agony started deep as his heart struggled to pump blood around the foreign metal. A bubbly cough forced itself up Draken's throat. Rinwar pressed the sword deeper. Then he released it, leaving it in place. Blood splattered the expanse of metal still sticking outside Draken's chest. The world narrowed to those droplets. Draken gasped, tried to speak, as his body crumpled. Bruche shouted something but his words were incomprehensible echoes.

CHAPTER THIRTY-NINE

Rent flesh knitting, sinews and muscle and bone trying to reform into a beating heart, breathing lungs.

Draken blinked. His dry mouth gaped. Cruelly tight fingers had him by the arms. His heels dragged behind, scraping along the dirt and sticks and leaves. A blur passed above, the black of a night sky pierced by rays of moonlight. They glinted on the sword still sticking from his chest, glimpsed through his lower lashes.

Draken. The swordhand's voice was uncommonly gentle.

"What?" He forced the word between cracked lips, more cough than speech. Mostly to see if he could.

Be easy, my friend. I will bring you to Ma'Vanni.

Friend. Ah. There were no titles in death. That was a relief, then.

Whoever was dragging him tightened their grip with a sharp grunt. A hand reached out to twitch the sword in his chest, enough to yank his healing flesh apart again. Draken gasped a guttural cry, cut short as blackness tightened on him. No relief of unconsciousness but the Palisade, pulling him more surely than his two bearers, whose steps faltered the closer they got. His head sagged back. Nothingness swallowed his view ahead, the ground dying into it like sand into the sea.

It wavered before him, toward him. His eyes stared and his mind stretched until they ached. His fingers splayed, as if he could catch a bit of the black and pull himself inside.

The ground twitched toward him and he fell. No, they dropped him. Boots shifted back from him, thumping up through the ground into his torn body. He groaned and twisted his head to look. The Palisade wavered before him, swallowing ever more ground. Was it growing? No, reaching for him. He groaned and dragged himself onto his side. One arm stretched out to grip the ground. It bumped into the sword in his chest. He gasped, coughed, nearly succumbing to the oblivion lingering at the edges of pain. His arm continued on its path, fingers digging for purchase in the dirt. He managed to tug himself forward. A bit more—

Draken, no!

Draken got the sense Bruche couldn't pull him from the Palisade into Ma'Vanni's watery embrace. But no amount of ethereal cold and power could stop Draken's compulsion to take refuge inside that silent swath of darkness. Claws of magic hooked into bone and muscle, strengthening the arm dragging his flaccid body forward.

The Palisade reached out to embrace him, slinking over his arm like the shadow of the bane on the Khein fortress wall. The hooks in his bones tightened and he fell limp with relief as he tumbled into the Palisade's crevice of unrelenting oblivion.

The pain didn't release its hold on him, though he was vaguely aware the darkness felt like the perfect bath against his skin. But it didn't last. A glimmer split the Palisade from far away. It drew nearer, a flame or a small stripe of moonlight. Draken stared, straining his eyes until they ached in their sockets. Nearer still, and the pale flame took on a glimmering shape.

A Brînian szi nêre with locks thick as brush weeds about his shoulders, ornamented with chains and trinkets. A chain of rank hung diagonal against his bare chest in the fashion of Halmar, flat against his chest and disappearing under one brawny arm at the elbow. Crimson tattooed snakes swirled over his arms. He looked familiar . . . perhaps Draken had seen a painting somewhere, a mural . . . His high brow and flat cheeks creased with concern.

All he could do was gape up at the szi nêre as he spoke. "Draken. I'm getting you out of here."

"Bruche?" There was no air behind the words, just a grunt from the throat.

Bruche knelt over him, laid his hand on his shoulder and gripped Seaborn. "Apologies, Khel Szi. This will hurt." He gave Draken a savage grin but his wide-set eyes locked on Draken's, holding his attention as firmly as the hand on his shoulder. He pulled. Seaborn lit as it withdrew. Bruche pressed the grip into Draken's hand, closing his fingers around it.

Draken screamed as his heart and lungs healed. The Palisade spun, if Bruche was any marker because he swirled around Draken, into him—

A *crack!* split the blackness. The cold from the ground seeped up into Draken's muscles. The earth shifted and rumbled beneath his back, rocks pushing up against his back and head. Ahken Khel was the only thing that felt stable, and he gripped it as the sky expanded over him.

Up, Prince.

Draken grunted and sat up. His chest pulled where Seaborn had cut him but otherwise he was healing as usual. Rays of moonlight pierced his eyes and he squinted. Realized. The magical wall had shattered, tumbling into misshapen blocks of emptiness. Beyond the broken, leaning towers of Palisade, grey stone buildings shook and cracked, stones tumbling to the white graveled roads. They crunched the white gravel and dust rose up, shimmering under Khellian's light like shades of the dead. Screaming Akrasians burst from their homes. Most had weapons.

Draken turned his head and looked back at the woods. Narrow, deep cracks raidiated from him. Beyond his calm pocket, trees shuddered and fell, screaming in some secret language of destruction. Smooth earth burst into dusty clods as roots tore through the ground. Some Ashen were flung violently; others lay trapped or had fallen, tangled in tents and branches, fighting to get free of their own trampling kind. Others rushed through the rubble, climbing the broken nothingness of the Palisade and leaping to the attack, war cries echoing against the devastation. Akrasians erupted into fighting.

Cracks emanated from Draken's outstretched legs. He sighed and pushed to his feet. Stared at the people running *at* the destruction instead of from it. Fools all, it was the perfect scene of senseless courage.

And some of them must die.

"Not in the light this time," Draken muttered. Not from the light Tyrolean envisioned when he mentioned the proverb. Not even the light of the bloody moons. Khellian still glowed stoically, but even he was slipping down toward the trees.

It reminded him. He had work to do. People to find.

Draken ran hard, surprised he could run at all, for the Bastion.

CHAPTER FORTY

*N*o. *You must defend the city. Your soldiers need you. And you swore to keep Elena safe. That will be easier if the Akrasians and your troops can manage to drive off the Ashen.*

Who is the Prince here? You or me? But Draken's boots skidded to a stop on the white stone roadway, kicking up pale dust. All around him, Escorts, servii, nobles, and commoners rushed to the fight, some with gardening tools as weapons, or staffs ripped from brooms. A blacksmith and his apprentice wielded unfinished swords. Draken recognized an apprentice he'd met during his stay there. He'd been released from his duties in the bowels of the Bastion then. A promising future for the lad, if he survived the night.

I daresay they can do some proper damage with those, Bruche said.

He turned back, gripping his sword, ready to strike, his stride churning up the distance to the remains of the Palisade. He told himself Elena could wait a little longer. She'd be safe for now in the Bastion with its walls, errings, and Escorts to protect her.

He pushed his will in front of his swordhand—the killing had gotten Bruche riled—and kept moving through the rubble. His hand involuntarily edged toward a jagged chunk of Palisade, but Bruche jerked it back. *By the Seven, that could be addicting.*

Like Aarinnaie.

Lets hope she's indulging her addiction, eh? Bruche chuckled, but not in good humor.

Ashen slashed and stabbed their way into the city. The warcries were rising up, a grating killing song. Pockets of fighting had broken out. This first line of defense wasn't much, mostly civilians in bedclothes. Draken wondered where in Khellian's name the hundreds of Escorts residing in the city must be.

Defending the water, perhaps. Or at the Bastion.

They could only hope.

Draken searched the confusion for a familiar face, armor, anything. Nothing. He cursed and fought his way through an Ashen who was too young to wear such a vicious grin on his bloodsplattered face, much less have it fall slack in death. He couldn't have been much older than Galbrait and his light armor was no match for Seaborn. He gaped at Draken as he died on his sword. Draken let him down gently, his hand under the lad's arm, and stepped over him. He barely smelled the blood anymore, but his sword was slicked with it, and it had splattered onto his sword arm. His stomach churned but he shoved forward, pushing past a couple of overeager Akrasians risking their lives by studying pieces of the Palisade rather than fighting. They had the rounded bellies and colorful clothes of affluent shopkeepers.

Ahead he saw six Akrasians fighting—they might have been from Reavan's old honor guard since they were all female and bore the fine black leather armor and green cloaks of upper-rank Escorts. They were outnumbered by four. Draken rushed to their aid. But more came, and more. Draken couldn't find a rhythm to his strikes and had to let Bruche take over again. He slipped into the battle-trance to let Bruche do as he must without interference. His balance improved, his strikes smoothed into efficiency. From the distance of his retreat inside himself, Draken noted the warcries had died, at least nearby. Everything sounded a bit hollow. At last they killed the last of the Ashen in the immediate vicinity. Bruche herded all the Escorts toward the cover of trees.

One of them whirled on Draken, her lips drawn back in a snarl. "We had that. You should have—" Her gaze stalled at Elena's pendant. She blinked rapidly and dipped her chin. "Night Lord."

"Your Highness," another corrected, leaning on her sword to catch her breath.

"'My lord' is sufficient," Draken said, knowing they had to call him something and wanting to be as close to one of them as possible. "Who is your commander?"

More blinking. "Dead, my lord," the first said.

Draken frowned. "How? The Monoeans killed him? How many have they killed?"

"Several are dead, but not from attack. There is sickness in Auwaer."

"The water," the second added. "They poisoned the water. Even the errings have died."

"How are you alive?"

There was some shifting on feet, as if they felt guilty for surviving. "We realized after the others and drink wine only, and a little from the cisterns. They're nearly empty now."

Draken eased a breath from his tight chest. He'd known Auwaer wasn't likely to emerge from the siege undamaged, but this—

He looked back through the trees at the ring of crumbled Palisade. Ashen had disappeared into the city, leaving a trail of dead in their wake. One of the shopkeepers was gutted and bleeding on the white gravel. The other was gone. Ran, likely. Wise man. "How many Escorts in the city?"

"Five hundred, give or take. Maybe five thousand in the vicinity. They'll be entering riverside by now."

What was taking so godsforsaken long? "The Escorts and servii outside the wall didn't attack the Ashen? Nor did you attack from within. Why not?"

"Orders, my lord. From the Bastion itself. We were to wait. Bide our time. Then the sickness, and the Palisade . . ." She swallowed and stared at the broken pieces, seeming gaps in the world where even Khellian's fading light could not enter.

"We were ripe for the fight," the second said. "Doubtless all Akrasians were. But the Queen . . ." her voice faded.

Not like Auwaer slept through your breaking up the Palisade.

Draken snorted. *Warning them of impending attack was the the only advantage to my nearly dying. Again.*

"My troops from Khein are at the temple ruins. Did you see any Monoeans go that way?" Damned Galbrait knew all that. It would be a simple betrayal to guide Ashen there. Simpler perhaps than what he'd done to Draken.

Heads shook no all around. That made sense. They'd been stuck inside and then consumed with the fight these past hours. "All right. I have to go there."

"You can't go alone. Where are your guards?"

He sighed. "I was captured and . . . it's a long story." He glanced back to the city. Where he could see was all empty but he thought he saw wraithlike smoke filtering up through the night. He sniffed. Definitely smoke. "I don't have time to explain." He started away.

"Your Highness! Let us accompany you!"

"No. Back to the city with you. To the Bastion. Protect the Queen. I'll return for her when I'm able."

"But—"

"That's an order, Escort." He ran off through the trees.

◆ ◆ ◆

Things were quiet at the temple ruins, if tense. Draken accepted a cup of wine from Geffen and gulped it down. She stared at him. "What happened? My lord."

He drew a breath, and a few more, so he could speak without panting. He handed her the cup back for a refill. "Galbrait betrayed me. He is Ashen, has been all along."

She stared, his cup forgotten in her hand. "What did he do?"

It would be all over Akrasia in a matter of a few Sevennight: the Prince who couldn't be killed. "He and the Priest killed me. Or rather, they tried. I have a bit of a healing, er, magic. It tends to shake things up, quite literally. They stuck me with my own sword and tossed me into the Palisade. The earthquake broke the wall."

Her brows climbed further, if possible. "That was *you?*"

"Heard about it, did you?" He went to fetch the wine from the page himself. She looked a Moonling half. The girl shrank back and flushed hotly, making the pale dapples stand out more against her reddened skin.

"I had scouts in the trees, Geffen said. "They came back and reported the Palisade had broken. I didn't believe it and sent new scouts to confirm. They haven't come back."

They were probably dead. He took his cup back and poured. "We need to rally. We must attack now. The entire city is a battleground."

Look at you. You've become quite the bloodlord. Calm under fire and all that.

No point in rushing off without all my arrows nocked.

Geffen spoke to her servant and sent her scuttling off toward the collection of mean little horsemarshals' and company captains' tents crammed in between broken pillars. In typical calvalry fashion, the horses had roomier, cleaner lodging than their riders, staked among the trees with grooms to serve them.

His commander showed him a good map of Auwaer while they waited on the horsemarshals and captains to gather. The city was a lopsided heptagon encircling a city center with a market and play houses, parks and the black Bastion rising from the pale grey stone like a blocky shadow. It was on a hill.

"What do you know about the Bastion?"

Geffen shrugged. "I've been to court a few times."

"Any idea if there are escape tunnels under the hill and moat?"

"Wasn't offered the grand tour. I never served at the Bastion proper."

"Why not?"

"I believe I was too old to suit the King. I was definitely too married."

He raised his brows at the implication. "Are you still?"

"He's a drogher driver in the upper Eros." She paused. "In the grasslands."

"I know where Upper Eros is," he said.

"He's also Gadye," she added. "We had special dispensation from priests at Reschan."

He very carefully did not snort even though Reschanian priests were probably the least likely to have inroads with the gods about approving mixed marriages.

Horsemarshals and commanders were starting to file in, crowding the little space, some climbing up on the broken pillars and chunks of upheaved earth to see and hear him. He raised his voice and explained about the Palisade. No need for detail; rumor and taletellers would cover that. "Time is crucial. Look for Tyrolean. I think Galbrait might keep him close as personal insurance. Galbrait won't know the city, nor where to hide. But Tyrolean will, and it's likely he'll do what he can to make himself easy to find. I'll reward two hundred rare to whoever brings me Galbrait; a thousand if he is brought to me alive."

"The Princess? Is she found?" someone else asked.

"Aarinnaie disappeared in the fighting. Keep an eye out but don't go out of your way to search. She can handle herself." A vast understatement. He couldn't put a reward on her rescue because she'd like as fight it. Better if few knew what she was really capable of.

"And the Lord Mance?" Geffen asked.

Draken rubbed his chin. He felt grains of dirt caught in the bristles. His arms and bracers had an unnatural greyish hue, dust from the wreckage his healing had caused. "I have to believe Osias and Setia can look after themselves as well. Commander, divide and assign the troops as you see fit."

He started to make his way through the captains and marshals. They made a jagged path for him to escape through. Most eyed him silently. A few saluted or dipped their chins.

"What will be your position, my lord?"

"My place is with the Queen."

"You need guards."

His guards were captured or dead. "I'll travel quicker on my own."

"My lord—"

He turned. "I'd like to someday find a commander who does not question my decisions. Do you think one possibly exists in this godsforsaken country?"

Geffen, to her credit, replied primly. "I wish you well, my lord, and godspeed to the Queen's side."

Bruche chuckled. *Fair awkward, that.*

Draken lifted his chin and fixed her and the hardened officers with a long stare. "When you've rousted and killed the last of these Ashen, come find me at the Bastion."

CHAPTER FORTY-ONE

The moons had fled into the horizon and Auwaer huddled under shadows. Running figures appeared bent, as if to make smaller targets. Only fires interrupted them; torches wavering as they were carried, some few wooden structures alight by arson, smithy fires burning untended. More than a few stone structures had flames sprouting from the windows. As well, fires burned in Draken's injured knee, his heaving chest, and his bad shoulder. War cries echoed from far and near, swelling and rippling down alleyways and bounding against the stone. The air trembled with them.

Few people threatened Draken as he jogged lopsidedly through the streets with his sword drawn, shirtless, armorless. Truth, he regretted his earlier trip to the temple ruins and his rest there. Even so, his steps were staggered.

'You can rest when you're dead,' the old saying goes. I'm here to tell you not to believe all the adages you hear. Bruche sounded annoyed, and well he should. Draken was restraining him as best he could. The swordhand was nervous, wary of the battlegrounds splayed out between buildings. Draken had the feeling if he let Bruche go, he'd fight his way into battle rage.

Be easy, Draken retorted, equally annoyed. Every sound made Bruche startle or turn his head, which made him lose his balance.

On his first visit to the city, Draken had spent the better part of a sevennight traversing Auwaer street-by-street, alley-by-alley, questioning its cloistered inhabitants about an attempt on Queen Elena's life. He'd judged them prejudiced, arrogant, and soft. Whatever collective faults marred them, this night they proved not to be the latter. It seemed the whole city had turned out to defend itself. The roads were slick with blood and gore. Bodies sprawled everywhere. The stink of death clung to his lungs, tainting each breath. Draken passed enough dead in the street to remind him of the massacre at Parne. By far most of them were Akrasian, lined eyes staring with horror into the face of Korde. The thought brought him up short. He ducked in an alleyway and pressed his back against a door inset into a thick stone wall. What if Moonlings were at work here? What if they could use the Abeyance to break the Bastion?

Then you had best bloody well go stop them.

He shook himself and started off again. Smoke and dust and the reek of blood made breathing difficult. He had to make his way around several clusters of fighting. He looked down one street and saw a large group of Ashen moving house to house, splitting off into doorways to search residences. A couple of them dragged a family out into the street, highlighted by torches. One of the Ashen shouted something. Draken wasn't sure if they saw him, but he darted off, heart twisting at being unable to help. He had to trust that his servii were entering the city and following orders.

Greater good and all that, Bruche said.

Draken resisted saying something derogatory about the greater good. Bruche chuckled anyway.

As he neared the white road leading to the Bastion gates, he was forced to slow. Dead scattered the gravel, some of the bodies small. Bile burned in Draken's throat and the last traces of Bruche's good humor died. Moreover, a mass of terrified Akrasians were trying to force their way into the palace. Escorts held them back from higher ground with a row of shields. Archers lined the battlements. So far bows were strung but no arrows were flying. Perhaps orders from Elena. But the crowd was in the way of Draken getting inside.

The Bastion was two squares centered on two courtyards, elegant in its simplicity. Seemingly impenetrable black walls loomed over the people gathered at its gates.

If he had a line and grappling hook, he'd trust the errings were dead as the Escort had claimed, swim the moat, and climb in a window, bad knee be damned. But a mean metal fence surrounded the moat and he had nothing but this blasted sword. He glared at it and lowered it to his side as he walked up to the crowd. Most of them were aged, or mothers and children.

He gently pushed along, using his height and breadth to move between them. He also smelled of battle: sweat, blood, metal. A little boy looked up at him. His eyes went round as Sohalia moons and he mouthed *"Pirate"* as he backed away toward the knees of an adult behind him, maybe a grandfather. The man turned with a scowl. "Fools all, watch where—" His gaze flicked over Draken and landed on the chain and pendant hanging around Draken's neck. It was stuck in the blood coating his chest from the healed wound.

"My lord," he said, eyes wide.

"I need to get to the Bastion. I've word for the Queen." Close enough to the truth.

"Here now, who are you, Brînian?" said another man. "They aren't letting any of us in. What makes you think they'll let one of your lot in?"

Bruche breathed cold warning through Draken's sword arm. *Princes have enemies.* Even in Brîn he had plenty who hated him, who would just as soon slip a blade between his ribs instead of pay him any honor and respect. Not that he couldn't heal himself, but that would create a whole host of other problems.

He couldn't say who he was. They might blame him for this attack; for not being here. They might blame Elena and take it out on him. He started to edge back.

Someone shouted down the darkened street, and then the warcries of the Ashen rose up. The crowd pressed up against him from behind and the low hum of voices sharpened. Draken twisted and maneuvered so he could look back over the heads of the people behind him. Torches glinted on the red crescent moons on their tabbards. Draken's jaw tightened. A couple of well-placed arrows would smear the moons in to bloodstains. He tried harder to push back through, toward the enemy. There was no room, though. The people made a living, terrified wall. Between the enemy, the sheer walls of the Bastion, and the moat, they were trapped.

The unmistakeable swoosh of many arrows overhead cut through the mob's voices and hammered down on the Ashen troops. War cries broke into screams as arrows hit. Akrasian heavy longbows, designed for a standing attack, shot thick shafts that could take on leather, chainmail, and fishscale.

But the Ashen were still coming, crowding the mob at the Bastion gate.

These Akrasians weren't armed, weren't fighters. The only one in this crowd with a sword was Draken.

"Make way," he shouted, pushing more firmly. His heart tore at going the opposite direction from Elena, and he knew without discussing it with Bruche that he had little to no chance against the Ashen still standing. But a strange fierceness filled him.

He met the first Ashen and cut him down in two strikes. Seaborn slashed through the gap between the high-necked hauberk and helm. Blood gouted, obscuring the twined crescent design on the dead man's tabard. Draken didn't wait to watch him fall but took two strides toward the next. His sword clanged on the metal-strapped bracer, but the man's seax was no match for Seaborn in pitched battle. Two more Ashen ran at him. An arrow took one, and then more arrows hailed down around them. He'd been protected from arrows on the

Bane by Osias's glamour. He had no idea if that was happening now. He didn't have time to look for it. Three Ashen came at him. One occupied his sword arm while the other darted in to stab him. The seax stuck into his arm. Agony radiated through him, but Bruche rushed cold to the arm, numbing it while fighting off the other Ashen. The ground rumbled beneath his feet and Draken concentrated on staying upright as Bruche cut down the attacker and swung wide, catching the one who stabbed him against the helm. It wasn't a kill shot but the man fell from the impact, probably unconscious.

Bruche switched Seaborn to the injured arm, ripped the seax from the wound, and rushed into the Ashen who still survived the arrows. There was no time to take a count, Draken was caught deep within battle fury, his awareness pushed aside as Bruche took total control and fought. He was vaguely aware of wounds, of lancing pain in several parts of his body, of his chest desperate for air. Ashen surrounded him. He heard snatches of war cries.

And then a roar, vicious and hard, surrounded them. The ground shook and gravel sprayed as warhorses circled them. Something flashed in the fallen torchlight and the man fighting Draken fell with a spray of blood. Then they all were falling. Draken could taste blood in every breath. Bruche pulled back a little. Draken swayed as his balance altered and he gaped up at the horse. The rider dipped his chin. The armor looked oddly loose over what Draken realized was a slighter form than most and pulled off his helm.

Braids tumbled out. "It seems I'm constantly saving your arse, brothermine." Aarinnaie had a cut across one cheek that would probably scar. Her tone softened. "We've been looking everywhere. I could kill Geffen for letting you go off on your own. Truth, you're a bloody fool."

Bruche retreated more fully, leaving Draken's head whirling. The ground trembled under Draken's feet and his head swam toward making sense of it. At first he thought it was the horses moving but he realized several gashes and a couple of stab wounds were healing. He steadied himself against the horse, who tossed his mane and stomped at the rumbling vibrations from the ground. People shouted in fear and huddled low. Some spilled out from the Bastion bridge. Nothing life threatening though, because the ground didn't crack open.

He should be asking questions and fought to think of one.

Where is Geffen? Where does the fighting stand?

He repeated Bruche's suggestions out loud.

"I'm here, my lord." Geffen pushed her horse forward, her voice muffled behind her helm. "I believe the term is 'mopping up.' The city seems to have fought off the Ashen. Most escaped, a few are captive, many are dead."

"Elena," he said hoarsely, turning back toward the Bastion.

The crowd of Akrasians were staring their way, caught within the shadow of the tall black wall. Above, archers still lined the battlements. The early sun lit on the vicious row of drawn arrows.

"I don't know. They seem jumpy. Might want to get out of range," Aarinnaie said.

Shouts and then the great gates nudged open. "Make way! Make way for Draken, Night Lord and Prince of Brîn." Harsh voices, loud, and female. The Akrasians shuffled forward, spilling back out on to the road. Escorts swung the gates open and filed out in two quickly-assembled rows. They lined the bridge, putting themselves between the people and making an aisle for Draken to walk through. Several of them were the company of Escorts he'd met at the edge of the city. They broke protocol and dipped their chins to him as he walked between them, his gory sword still dangling from his hand, stinking of sweat, sticky all over with blood. He needed a piss and a hot bath. It took him some time to hobble the distance. His knee was probably swollen again.

Inside the Bastion walls, the noise of the city fell away. His healing damage to the city and the Palisade hadn't touched the magic here, then. It was quiet, though. Too quiet.

The fountain had ceased. From the water shortage, likely. He swung his head around drunkenly to stare at the black walls, the shadowed balconies and walk-ways, and stopped at a small contingent of Escorts and courtiers. He blinked as he limped their way. "Tyrolean."

A ghost of a smile. His friend walked forward, hand outstretched. They exchanged grips; then Tyrolean slung an arm around his neck and pulled him forward into an embrace. "Your Highness. It is good to see you alive."

The motion made Draken stumble on his bad knee. Tyrolean held him around the shoulders to steady him.

"I thought Galbrait had you. How did you get into the Bastion?"

"I stole a grappling hook and rope and climbed the wall."

"You learned from Aarinnaie then."

"Aye." He set Draken back but kept hold of his shoulder. The lined eyes lifted to meet his, lips set in a firm line. Bruche tightened within him. "Galbrait released me in order to give you a message."

"Which is?"

"He will return to Monoea but not take the throne. He said to tell you, 'There are no more kings and the gods will make us pay.' He said that would be of some significance to you."

Draken hissed a breath.

"Are you all right, Your Highness?"

"It's just something from Monoean legend. Tough to shake off the old stories. Where is Elena?"

Silence.

"Well?"

"She and your daughter—" Tyrolean's hand tightened on Draken's shoulder. "—went to hide in the mountains with the Moonlings. Ilumat took her."

His other hand pressed a small scroll into Draken's. The seal was broken.

CHAPTER FORTY-TWO

The healers fussed over Draken for two days. The third morning saw him ensconsed on a comfortable couch in Elena's quarters, the offending leg up on a cushion. They'd taken the wrap off and the swelling had gone down, but the healers insisted it yet be propped, especially since he intended on riding for the mountains tomorrow. Bossy sorts, Elena's healers. He itched to move but there was business yet in the city and no one to tend it but Draken. He tapped Elena's scroll, which sketched her plans to her top officers, against his knee.

The room was warm, comfortable. Strings of colorful beads cast stippled shadows across Aarinnaie's and Tyrolean's faces. Osias, though, looked as if the shine had come off him in the previous days. Setia kept close to him, watching the others restlessly. Draken thought he knew a little how she felt. He had a distracting hollow place in his chest, nerves buzzing from inactivity. He wondered how Elena fared. If she realized now the mistake she'd made or if the Moonlings held her under the subterfuge of protection.

And . . . a daughter. He had a daughter. Though perhaps he didn't anymore. She could be dead. *Small thing to kill an infant . . .* Bruche made a warning noise low in Draken's throat. Draken had to keep shoving his mind from gruesome speculation to the topics at hand.

Aarinnaie wore a plain ensemble: a loose tunic over Brînian-style trousers and barefoot. The fabric was black and the long sleeves undoubtedly hid her throwing knives. Draken fingered one of his own but didn't take it out of the sheath. Bruche had insisted he go back to wearing bracers with knives at all times. *Even well-loved Princes have enemies.*

Indeed. Lesson learned.

Aarin tossed her long braids over her shoulder. Someone had redone them, again binding up most of the loose strands. The slaves cast her odd looks as they served wine. They had to chase Tyrolean as he paced around the room to get him to take a cup.

"The city will rebuild, after a fashion, but there was more damage than I originally thought," Aarinnaie said. "Some of the buildings burned from the inside, making the stone walls unstable. There have already been collapses. Additionally, gangs of bandits are here from the upper woods. Sundry peddlers have filled the market."

Osias leaned forward, elbows on his knees. Not his customary stature. The past two days he and Setia had passed in the city, speaking to priests and citizens. "As well, swindlers dress as priests and try to steal 'donations' for victims."

"They're not very successful," Setia added.

Draken sipped the wine. It was cold and fruity. It slid down his throat and soured in his stomach. "No one is much interested in religion at the moment. Anyone killed?"

He meant from more than just collapsing buildings.

Aarinnaie shrugged. "Not today."

The day was young. "Ty? What word?"

The Captain still hadn't sat down, but roamed the room, his horned swords on his back, knives bristling at his wrists and belt, hand resting on the hilt of another broadsword after the fashion of Seaborn. He wore the striped green tabard, fishscale, and cloak of an Escort officer. There were few trinkets to pick up and he touched nothing, mostly examining the stone floor. Draken couldn't tell if he was listening or lost in his own thoughts, but he looked at Draken quick enough when he said his name.

"The Lord Marshal is dead, Your Highness." This time there was no hesitation and his gaze was steady on Draken's face. If he hadn't known how to properly deliver bad news two days ago, he had learned since. Plenty of practice.

Draken smoothed his face into blank regard. "What happened?"

"They were apparently on their way from Brîn and were attacked on this side of Reschan."

Truth, she had been at Brîn when Draken had left for Monoea. He couldn't fathom that she'd stayed, nor that Elena had left Brîn and traveled without her. On the one hand, he had learned Elena had left double-blinds to conceal her movements all over Akrasia. On the other he couldn't fathom that she had actually traveled largely alone to Skyhaven in the mountains.

"They killed every stripe in the company, left most of the servii to report what happened. They limped in this morning and sent messengers to the Bastion. The company was most of the upper officers, but for the city barons and a few third and fourth ranks."

Even Aarinnaie didn't move or speak, recognizing what a blow this was.

"I suppose it was too much to ask that the Ashen have actually given up."

"It wasn't the Ashen that did it." He glanced at Aarinnaie.

She hissed a breath. "Khissons."

"The rebel faction you were tracking back in Brîn?" Draken cursed, then cleared his throat. "Any sign of the Ashen generals? That Priest, Rinwar. Galbrait?"

A round of shaking heads. They had vanished during the night of chaos in Auwaer. Draken knew he'd be running across them again. He rubbed his chin, eyed Tyrolean.

"Apparently we're in need of a new Lord Marshal. I think it's time you take a turn, aye, Tyrolean?"

Tyrolean's lips parted, probably in protest. Draken just looked at him. At last Tyrolean blinked and bowed his head. "As you say, Your Highness. I still plan on traveling with you."

"As you say," Draken echoed him with a dry smile. It actually was appropriate. He very well might be riding to war.

Aarinnaie sighed. "I can't talk you out of this?"

"The same as I can't talk you out of going with me."

◆ ◆ ◆

For a sevennight of hard riding, Draken watched the trees pass, thickening in trunk and foliage, encroaching on a road that narrowed to a dirt lane and finally to a path. The ground was flat; the only relief in a hard slog. A full cohort of ten servii walked ahead, slashing back foliage to allow the horses through. Three more cohorts of full rank Escorts, Draken, Aarinnaie, Osias, Setia, and Tyrolean, plus Halmar made their group nearly one hundred.

"By the map, it would be quicker to cut to the grasslands and ride hard along the woods rather than stay in the trees," Draken had said.

Osias shook his head. "Too dangerous. We'd need three times as many servii. Bandit bands and horselords are fearless and defensive now that the country is in upheaval. Apparently some Ashen escaped that way and killed the wrong people."

Draken had forbidden wagons to accompany them on the advice of Tyrolean, who had been born in the Skymarke Lake region and told him real roads were impossible to maintain and traverse. Without much supplies, every third day they had to stop to hunt hares and small foul to feed themselves. While Draken's battered knee relished the time off his horse and his body craved rest, his mind went dangerous places when idle. By the ninth day when the earth started to drop into the valleys containing Skymarke Lake and her river, he was nearly mad with impatience.

The trees relented abruptly at the edge of a valley. The path widened, switching back across the hill leading down to Skymarke Lake. The water spread out before them, glittering in the midday sun. Little structures encircled it, docks stretching out onto the calm waters. Fishing boats dotted the surface, marring the perfect reflection of the mountains and clouds in its azure depths. He didn't need a glass to see across to the Agrian Range, a collection of rolling mountains easing ever higher into the sky. He could fair see the tops of each one, hard edges softened by trees. These mountains didn't make him feel anxious like the mistclad, stony Eidolas. Instead a gentle breeze, fresh scents of woods and water, and the soft lap of the lake on the shores soothed his anxiety.

Bruche moved his hand to Seaborn's hilt. A slight humming vibration resonated up his arm. *Magic here. The air is thick with it.*

Draken turned his head one way and then the other. The narrow lake was long enough it curved away out of sight at either end. How would they ever cross it? "Are we at the center of the lake?"

"No, Highness. We are at the upper end, fair close to where it spills into River Skymarke. Not half a day to Skyhaven," Tyrolean added.

Draken nodded and watched as Halmar and three Escorts started down the path first, then pushed on to follow. His knee ached, his thighs chafed from being too long out of, and then abruptly too long *in*, the saddle. With all the damage and healing his body had gone through in the past several sevennight, he wondered yet again why his old injuries remained.

The gods remind you you're getting old, my friend.

Draken snorted. *Too old for this business, to be certain.*

The business of saving the crown, who also happen to be your family, belongs to you alone. Age is your smallest barrier.

Aye, it seems to be the way of it. Too many duties seemed to belong to him, only. This was one he couldn't resent. His family—he hadn't let himself think of Elena and the child in those terms until this moment—was held captive by people who took them for their own gain. The old resentment rose. He had told Oklai he intended on freeing her people. He did intend on freeing all the slaves. But she had to know it would take time. He thought of thousands of sundry slaves, turned out of their homes or demanding wages. The economy and social structure of Akrasia would collapse. Though there were parts of slavery of which he highly disapproved, he couldn't deny what would follow might be fair worse.

Tyrolean was right. The switchbacks into the lake valley were packed dirt and easy and quick for horses' hooves, but were impassible for wagons. Setia had scouted ahead on her sturdy pony and waited for them lakeside, gazing at the water and moutains beyond. Osias smoked his pipe next to her, letting his horse graze and have a drink. At lake level, the path widened enough to accommodate three wagons side by side and their group was able to ease into organized cohorts rather than the vulnerable single file they'd endured in the woods. Everyone let their horses get a drink and went on. The servii fell behind and voices rose in cheerful, easy chatter.

Draken frowned. *A relaxed lot, aren't they?*

The magic eases their worries.

I wonder that it's not a purposeful defense on the part of the Moonlings. He halted his horse and raised a hand. They slowly halted too, and turned their horses to him to listen. It took several breaths for the servii to catch up.

"We are about to enter the erring's lair. You all know what I am about here. You all have sworn to die before seeing the Queen and Princess remain captive." He stared around at them all. Eyes, lined and otherwise, met his steadily. He drew his sword. The blade flashed—whether by trick of magic or sunlight, Draken didn't know. But some few hands sought weapons and backs straightened. When he urged his horse onward they fell into proper rows. The servii hurried along behind to keep pace with the horses. Almost at once a scout ranging ahead returned to say he'd seen Moonlings in the woods up ahead. A full war party awaited them with spears.

Draken gave a grim nod. He had expected nothing less.

◆ ◆ ◆

Draken pushed to the front of the servii and his szi nêre, ignoring the frowns of Tyrolean and Halmar. "I have come to see the Queen."

They stared, and then one stepped forward, his slashed skirts rippling about his knees. His spear ribbons had been colorful once, but now had faded to dull greens, blues, and the rarest red. The sharp end of the sweat-darkened wood was stained black a third of the way up with old blood.

"I am instructed to accompany you, Khel Szi." His gaze didn't waver off Draken's face. "We have known for some days of your arrival. You will enter alone, though you may keep your weapons. Her residence is a short walk. Queen Oklai will greet you and take you to her."

It was the best he could hope for. He swung down, keeping his face turned toward the horse so his wince when his bad knee took his weight wouldn't be readily evident to the Moonlings.

"Drae." Aarinnaie dismounted and strode forward to catch his sleeve.

There was nothing to say. He leaned down and kissed her brow, then pulled his arm away. He looked at Setia and Osias. They both gave him slight nods. Then he turned and walked toward the Moonlings, his soldiers and friends silent behind him.

They had to cross the river by bridge. The other side was treed, though not as thickly as the Moonling woods. The path was dry, packed dirt with log steps to accommodate the slope. Even so, occasionally his knee twinged deeply and threatened to give out. He grabbed at a sapling once. It supported his weight enough to get his balance and then snapped in his hand.

Gradually, log buildings with intricate thatched roofs appeared amid the trees. He paused to study one. It was a war scene, sophisticated and horrible, with actual spears woven in to depict the killing of large men by smaller Moonlings. Some of the thatch was dyed red for blood. Another paid homage to the gods with a Sohalian night sky, bleached golden moons hanging amid a dyed blue sky.

Oklai met him on the path, studied him with her face set, and led him to an open air pavilion. Inside refreshments and wine were set out on a glossy wooden table low enough Draken had to kneel to reach anything on it comfortably. She gestured. "You must be thirsty."

"I drank from the lake. Where is the Queen?"

"With the babe."

He eased a breath from his chest. That didn't mean she yet lived. "Take me to Elena."

"Why would I grant you this favor?"

"Because I come in good faith, leaving my soldiers behind. Because I rousted Akrasia's ememies and will hunt them to the shores. Because I hold at least a thousand of your people and even now my servii range over Akrasia and Brîn, ordering that every single Moonling be safely interred until our Queen is free and our peoples are allies once again." He let a cruel smile play on his lips. "As you asked, they are slaves no more."

"Small difference, slave to prisoner," she hissed. Her guards shifted. Fingers tightened on spears.

His eyes narrowed. "As the Queen is a prisoner. Take me to her."

"You intend on taking her home?"

"I intend on seeing how well she and the child fare, and then you and I will decide what to do."

Bruche remained silent, locked down, not so much as a thought trickling into Draken's consciousness. They'd gotten a hunch that the Moonlings might be able to hear their communication, or sense his will, or something. Draken could feel his presence, always, and right now Bruche's will was coiled tight. If . . . when . . . he burst forth it would be a dangerous time to be near Draken.

"And what reassurance do you give me in exchange for this visit?"

"I have given it. We have not attacked." Yet. He held his temper in check, though more than anything he wanted to draw his sword and cut the supercilious smile from her face.

His words did it well enough. The smile dissipated like smoke from a guttered candle. "This way."

She turned and led him up a path that wove between trees. Her guards encircled them, keeping off the path and grips tight on spears. Draken did his best to pay them no mind.

There was another pavilion, closed on two sides by woven twigs and shaded beneath the thatched roof. The air was warm and filled with quiet woodland sounds. Leaves rustling. Birdsong. Somewhere off in the woods someone laughed softly. And then a gentle, breathy coo, much closer.

Draken's heart tumbled in his chest.

The Moonlings stopped. Oklai gestured to the building. "You may have some time. If you fight us, you will die. These are my conditions."

"I have no intention of fighting you, only to take my family home."

"That will take more talk. Freeing my people. Great reparations."

Indeed it would, since the Moonlings were traitors. "Then why are you allowing me to come at all?"

"Seeing them may persuade you in our negotiations."

Bruche coiled tighter. Draken walked forward. His eyes took a moment to adjust. But he recognized Elena's gasp well enough, her voice curving around his name, breathlessly.

She took shape from where she stood in the corner, her arms up, cradling their child. Her figure was slim, willowy once again, her gown draping over the slight swelling in her middle betraying where their child had been so recently.

"Draken." Breathless.

He strode forward and caught her gently, pulling them both to his chest, carefully in order to not crush the babe. She laid her head against his arm, the baby cooed again, and he drew a breath into his tight throat.

"Are you all right?"

"I'm recovered. It was not a difficult birth."

Birth . . . "The child."

"Your daughter, Draken."

He set her back to look at the babe. Black whisps of hair edged out from beneath the blanket. A tiny hand crept from beneath her blanket as her blue eyes locked on Draken's. Her lips parted and she made that noise again. It struck him deeper in the heart than any sword.

"Our daughter is well. Fair strong." Elena's eyes brimmed but no tears spilled. Draken laid his hand on her shoulder, his fingers sliding up to curl around the back of her neck. She shuddered under his touch.

He tore his gaze from the baby's to hers. Pressed a kiss to her lips, to her brow.

"I didn't believe you were here," Elena said. "I thought it a trick. Oklai says she won't allow us to leave."

"Us . . . and me?"

"She says you may come and go as you wish. But not me. Not the baby. Please, you must find a way."

"You fear they will kill you."

"No. Her. They take her from me and bring her only to feed. I'm sorry. You tried to warn me. You tried to tell me they were against us. But when the Monoeans attacked I didn't know what to do. I shouldn't have run, but she is so young. Not two sevennight old. I couldn't find a wet nurse, nor anyone I trusted to take her away. When Oklai offered her protection here, I thought . . . I thought . . ." The words choked to a stop. "I have failed our people."

"No. Auwaer is freed. It wasn't all on you, Elena. It never was. You've never let me help you enough." His fingers tightened on her shoulder.

"I am Queen."

They didn't have time for this. "I'm not leaving you here."

"You must." She glanced beyond him, then tipped her head down to look at their child. "Hold her."

Draken dropped his hand from her shoulder and took his daughter. She settled lightly against his chest. Her eyes, a moment ago staring so intently, closed. She sighed and pursed her lips.

"Now take her away," Elena whispered.

Draken blinked at Elena. "You said they won't let me."

"They will soon have worse things to worry about than a Princess babe." Her face fell into the hard planes of a Queen with a distasteful duty. "Back away now. Take her."

He obeyed without thinking. Bruche had filled him, not hard and fervent as he expected, still contained. But there. Dangerous.

Elena lifted her delicate hand between them, forefinger pressed to thumb. A small flame flickered there. Draken blinked at the spark of Mance-fire. "Elena—"

Elena turned and touched her hand to the woven wall. It only took a moment for flame to come to life there. Then she threw flames up from her hand, to the roof. She didn't look at him, just watched as the thatch and the wall caught. More fire lit on her fingers. "Go. Run."

He stared. She'd been lighting candles, once she lit Osias's pipe in jest. He'd thought that was the extent of the magic inherited from Truls when his death brought her back to life.

Her voice was tight. "I am not asking, Night Lord."

Bruche called out a single name: *Osias.* He tried to get Draken to step back.

Draken stared, resisting Bruche's pull. "No! Elena. Come!"

Behind him, Moonlings cried out. Elena threw more fire at the wall and at the other open side as Moonlings appeared. Cries of warning turned into screams of pain. One Moonling wrapped her arms over her flaming head, stumbling off into the woods. Embers from the roof drifted to the dirt floor. Choking smoke clogged Draken's throat. Elena screamed at Draken, something inarticulate, and threw more fire at another wall. The thatch crackled with sharp heat.

It finally registered, what she was doing. He wanted to call to her again but she had commanded him. And the baby would not last long in here. She opened her eyes and gasped out a tiny cry. He realized an ember had landed on her forehead. He swept it away with his thumb, drew his sword, and turned to face attack. Behind him Moonlings screamed as fire leapt to the trees overhead. A spear came his way and he knocked it away with his sword. Moonlings rushed him, eyes wild. He cursed and cut two of them down. Others passed him to get to her, but thick smoke clogged the pavilion and obscured his view. He couldn't see if Elena was in there any longer, with the flames and the heat. Choking heat roiled toward him and flames crackled overhead. He coughed and backed a single step, cradling the baby tighter. She cried, muffled, against his chest.

More insistent: *OSIAS.*

Aye, they come.

Draken turned his head at Osias's voice, but he wasn't there. Instead, a spirit . . . eyes black holes into nothing, mouth gaping, smelling like grave dirt and burned flesh, swept through the trees toward the Moonlings. One threw a spear but it passed through the spirit and tumbled off into the trees. The Moonling let out a raucous, terrified cry and sprinted away, quick as prey. All around spirits were appearing, misty among the trees, soundless but wavering toward Moonlings, arms outstretched. They created a ring of space around the flames and pavilion.

Gods, are they banes?

"Draken, run! Save her!" Elena stepped out from under the pavilion and threw fire at a tree. It quickly spread to another. She cast him a fleeting look and ran away, deeper into the woods, pausing only slightly as she passed through a spirit.

Draken's body pulled him down the path, the log steps. His boots beat a tattoo on the ground: *The path was short. The path was short.* He could be with his soldiers in no time, protected—

The flames stopped, held. Frozen. The world went dead and silent. Draken slowed. His daughter whimpered. No . . . *No.* Elena should have known . . . would have known about the Abeyance if he had just bloody told her. Now her effort was for naught.

I think this is your Abeyance. Not theirs. But you know Setia can't hold it for long. Keep moving, Draken. Use what small time you have.

He drew a breath. "Elena." The word fell flat on the empty air.

Lost. Or not. I do not know. You must keep moving, Draken. She gave you this chance. She gave her *this chance. She is your Queen and she has commanded you.*

Draken looked back. The flames held like great witchlights against the shadowy trees. He couldn't see the little pavilion anymore. A nearby structure was mid-collapse. It was all he could do not to go back. He had saved Elena once with the Abeyance. But he couldn't see her. He couldn't see Elena anywhere.

Their daughter whimpered and squirmed, loud against the Abeyance. The flames flickered and went still again. And Draken ran.

CHAPTER FORTY-THREE

Four sevennight later, Draken held his daughter as he stood on the Bastion battlements and stared out at dawn spreading over the broken city, as was his habit every morning. Even cluttered with people, it felt empty of life somehow.

Aarinnaie leaned her elbows on the flat stone. A cocky servii waved up at her from the street. Trash fluttered in corners like the servii's hand.

She gave a wry grin and waved back.

Auwaer was no longer the pristine capital it had been. It would never be again. Dirtier. Definitely more crowded. Elena would be shocked.

"A lifetime alone for a few nights of pleasure," he murmured. "It is the Monoean way."

But you're no longer Monoean.

I don't know what I am, or what I am not. He looked down at his daughter. "I should take you to Brîn."

"The baby needs a name first, don't you think, before she starts traveling the kingdom?"

"Not without Elena."

They'd had this argument before. This time Aarinnaie relented. "Elena will come when she pleases. In the meantime your daughter needs a name. She is a Princess."

"And Szirin."

"Aye. One without a *name*."

Draken studied her face, her round cheeks. The baby cooed up at him, pursed her little lips. *Are you trying to kiss me, my love?* "She rather favors my mother."

Aarinnaie gave a noisy sigh. "And *her* name was?"

A beat. "Sikyra."

Aarinnaie was silent. Below a tinker-merchant shouted his wares. His wagon wheels squeaked and the baby turned her head toward the sound, face crinkled in concentration. Draken examined the lines around her eyes, already darkening with the series of tattoos to outline them. Big eyes, she had, and plumpening cheeks. Her wrists looked as if someone had tied cords around them.

"It fair suits her." Aarinnaie took the baby from him and cradled her. The baby giggled. Aarinnaie could always get the baby to giggle, more than even the wet nurse. "Kyra for short."

"Aye, then. Kyra for short."

"You should go down. Tyrolean is waiting," Aarinnaie said. "He's determined to make a swordsman of you yet."

I don't know why, when I have you back.

A low chuckle from Bruche. *Maybe he knows how much it amuses me.*

Draken pressed his hands against the cool stone of the battlements and stared back toward the Agrian Range that he could not see.

"Khel Szi?" Aarinnaie said it in a silly voice and Kyra giggled again.

He nodded. "I'm going, I'm going." He touched her arm and the top of his baby's head, and strode for the guard tower steps.

Elena was alive. She had to be. She would come to him as surely as war.

But not this day.

This day, his daughter had a name, and she was laughing.

grace

ACKNOWLEDGMENTS

This book has traveled a long road and, fitting, since Draken travels so much in it. There was a time when, like Draken, I feared it was lost. But because of a lot of hardworking industry folks, *Emissary* found the way again.

My editors, Jason Katzman, Jeremy Lassen, Cory Allyn, and the whole Night Shade team, you make my books better and my least favorite parts of writing fun. Your care and dedication are so evident. It's a pleasure working with you. John Stanko, too, has once again captured Draken and his story in the amazing cover and William McAusland has done the same with the maps that grace the front pages.

My agent, Sara Megibow, you put astounding effort into seeing this book through. I couldn't ask for anyone better at my back.

Mom, Al, Jo, Emily, Jennifer, Natalie, Mara, Madissyn, Jordan, Julie, Kelly, Kevin, Karen, LaRoux, Sandi, Jim, Jimmy, Tiffany, Hunter, Kolby, KK, and Tiff, see this big book? It's why I don't get to see you enough.

Readers, you are my favorite people ever. I love hanging out with you online and at cons. I hope I meet lots more of you in the coming years.

I got some particular help from Marcus Harris and Marc MacYoung on the armoring, care, and feeding of fictional warriors, David Hughes on the writing, and quite a few of the Writers in the Storm folks on story and logistics. All my other many friends, online and RL, industry and muggle, you know who you are. I'm so lucky to have you.

Carlin, I love you. You know all the rest.

Alex, yeah, Draken gets beat up a few times in this one, too. Thanks for being my favorite reader anyway.

Gracie, this one is for you. Thanks for drawing an amazing dragon to go in my (your) book.